DEAD MAN'S
TRAIL

DEAD MAN'S
TRAIL

A Carson Stone Western

NATE
MORGAN

PINNACLE BOOKS
KENSINGTON PUBLISHING CORP.

www.kensingtonbooks.com

PINNACLE BOOKS are published by

Kensington Publishing Corp.
119 West 40th Street
New York, NY 10018

First Printing: December 2022
ISBN-13: 978-0-7860-4941-7
ISBN-13: 978-0-7860-4942-4 (eBook)

10 9 8 7 6 5 4 3 2 1

Printed in the United States of America

PROLOGUE

They were all killers, and they filled the small office with their menace.

Not that Bill Cartwright was intimidated. He'd just turned fifty and had accomplished more in his years than ten ordinary men in ten lifetimes. He was formidable in a bigger and more lasting way than a simple assassin, a wealthy man by any measurement. If he wanted women, he had only to snap his fingers. If he wanted champagne from Paris, he could bathe in it. He made men and broke them every day as a matter of routine. If he wanted expensive things or exotic pleasures, he simply had to pay for them.

But what he wanted now was power, and that couldn't be bought; no, not quite. His money would help, of course. As with any such undertaking, money could solve a myriad of problems.

Thus the killers. The problem solvers.

And then Cartwright would be on the path to the power he craved. Idaho would be a state soon. It was coming. Even a blind man could see it. And when such things happened, certain men would rise—smart, crafty men who'd had the foresight to position themselves, who'd made themselves ready to seize such an opportunity.

Cartwright took a cigar from the humidor, clipped the

end, then lit it with a gold desk lighter big enough to choke a mule. He sat back, puffing, giving each of the killers the once-over, taking their measure.

The Mexican looked so obviously a killer, it was difficult to take him seriously. But he'd come highly recommended, a man both ruthless and cunning. He wore a black sombrero, crisscrossed bandoliers over a red shirt, and a black vest. He cradled a garish, gold-plated Winchester, intricately engraved with a thorny, twisting vine. His mustache looked as if a ferret had taken ownership of his face. Carlos Ruiz stood stoically, waiting for whatever Cartwright was about to say.

The Englishman was something different. Slender, shorter than average, mousy hair thinning and so blond as to be nearly white. Bland, watery eyes. He stood, timidly clutching a bowler hat to his chest. He didn't look like a killer. He looked like a man there to balance Cartwright's books. *Don't turn your back on the quiet ones*, Cartwright's mother had been fond of saying. The man's name was Nigel Evers.

The two brothers worked as a team. Larry and Barry Hanson were both cut from the same cloth, as one might imagine with brothers. Lean and hard and tall. They looked like any other cowboys in off the trail. The older one—Barry—wore his Peacemaker for a left-handed draw, and when he grinned, he showed off a gold front tooth. Larry had one cheek perpetually bulging with chewing tobacco. They'd do just about any dastardly thing for money, and their résumé included arson, armed robbery—of both train and stagecoach—cattle rustling, extortion, and murder of every variety.

Cartwright wasn't sure what to make of the fifth killer. The jury was still out on that one.

Well, time to get this meeting started. Cartwright puffed his cigar and said, "You don't know me."

The killers said nothing to this peculiar statement. They knew more was coming.

"I want to look you in the eye, let you know that this is serious business," Cartwright said. "And I expect results. I get the results I want, and you'll all be well-rewarded. If I don't get the results I want, then I'll be unhappy. They say misery loves company, so if I'm unhappy, I can promise you'll be unhappy with me. You take my meaning?"

The killers offered a sort of vague, group shrug in return. They were hard types and wouldn't intimidate easily. He wouldn't want them if they did.

Cartwright blew out a fresh stream of blue-gray cigar smoke. "Yeah, I think we understand one another. But I reiterate: You don't know me. You fail or get caught, I'm not to be mentioned. You get drunk and my name falls out of your mouth, I'll bury you so deep, them laborers will be digging you up in their flower gardens. You keep your mouths shut or I'll see they get shut permanently."

Not even the shrug this time. These individuals weren't accustomed to being spoken to in such a way. Cartwright didn't give a damn. It had to be said.

"The man who initially contacted each of you is named Doyle," Cartwright reminded them. "You need something or you have a question, see Doyle. When it's time to be paid, see Doyle. As soon as you walk out the door, forget my face."

"Why bother to meet with us at all, then?" The question had come from Larry. He was either stupider or braver than the others. Not that it mattered.

Cartwright took a long draw on the cigar, letting Larry's question hang in the air. Larry shifted from one foot to the other, glancing at his brother, then back at Cartwright.

Cartwright exhaled smoke, then said, "Because I'm the boss, and what I say goes. And if you've never seen me, I'm just an abstract concept, some ghost issuing commands from the ether. But I'm not a ghost. I'm reality. And reality sinks in."

Another pregnant pause. None of the killers had anything to say to that.

Cartwright stood and yanked a cord dangling over his head. From somewhere, the sound of a muffled bell reached them, and a moment later, an efficient little man in a striped suit and slicked-back hair entered the room with five sheets of paper. He handed one sheet to each of the killers.

"Mr. Doyle has presented each of you with an identical list," Cartwright said. "There are forty-three names on the list, the location where they can be found, and a dollar amount to be paid for their corpses. Your mission is simple. Kill. Any questions?"

They shook their heads, mumbling there were none.

"I suggest you check in with our Mr. Doyle every few days," Cartwright said. "There's always a chance I'll be adding names to the list. Now go. Do your jobs."

The killers began to file out of the room.

"Not you." Cartwright pointed a finger at the fifth killer. "I want to talk to you."

She paused, one eyebrow arching into a question. "Oh?"

Cartwright smiled in a way he knew to be charming. "Just for a moment. Indulge me."

The woman considered a moment and then nodded her consent.

The other killers left, Doyle following and shutting the door behind him.

The woman had a good shape and a pretty face and sly eyes. Her skin was clear and very white. Lips a glistening red. Glossy, black hair pulled into a tight bun at the nape of her neck. A flat-crowned, black bolero hat perched at a jaunty angle atop her head. She wore a red jacket, cropped just above her waist with black lapels, a white blouse underneath. Tan pants tucked into high, black boots. Altogether, a tidy, eye-catching package.

"And what can I do for you, Mr. Cartwright?" she asked.

"I just wanted a chance to exchange pleasantries," he said. "Perhaps get to know each other a little better."

"I thought the point of your speech earlier is that I *don't* know you."

Cartwright chuckled. "Fair enough. But you're not like those other hired killers. That's obvious."

"You mean you're not sure if a woman is up to the job?" She reached into her jacket and came out with a long, thin cigarillo. She stuck it into her mouth and leaned forward. "Do you mind?"

Cartwright lit her cigarillo with the desk lighter. She puffed. The smoke hung in the air between them, cloying and sweet. "What do they call you?"

"Kate."

"Just Kate?"

"Like you, I often find it useful to be forgettable. Last names have a way of sticking to people."

"May I offer you a drink?" Cartwright moved toward a sideboard with a collection of bottles and decanters. "There's a rather good sherry."

"When I've crossed forty-three names off this list, I'll have my fill of champagne," Kate said. "For now, some of that coffin varnish will do me just fine."

"As you like." Cartwright filled a shot glass with whisky and handed it to her.

She tossed it back in one go, then wiped her lips with the back of a slender hand. She handed the glass back, nodding at the bottle. "I'll sip this one."

Cartwright refilled her glass and poured himself a sherry. They sipped, reconsidering each other.

"I've known enough women to know that murder can

certainly be in a woman's heart, so I don't doubt you've the will for it," Cartwright said. "As for being up to the job . . . well, that's what I'm hoping to determine. Frankly, I notice you don't even carry a gun."

"Well, they're so awfully heavy." She batted her eyes comically. "And I'm just a frail little girl."

"You're having some fun with me."

"A little. Have faith, Mr. Cartwright. Pistols aren't the only way to kill. Now, I must take my leave, if you don't mind. There's work to do." Kate offered her hand, palm down, expecting a gentlemanly kiss on her knuckles.

Cartwright grinned. He was all too happy to oblige. He reached for her hand.

Kate flipped it over quickly and, as if by magic, a gleaming derringer appeared in her tight fist, the double barrels pointed at his chest. Cartwright felt a stab of panic, his heartbeat thudding rapidly. He took a moment, composed himself, and forced a smile.

"I mean, I do *have* a gun," Kate said. "More than one, in fact. But if all you wanted were guns, you could buy them by the wagonload. What I offer is far more valuable." She tapped the side of her head. "A certain kind of know-how."

"I believe you've made your point."

Kate lowered the derringer. "Sincere apologies if that startled you. I just wanted you to know you're getting your money's worth."

Cartwright was tempted to be cross with her. He let it pass and let his intrigue intensify instead. "There's more to you than meets the eye, Kate. I think I'd like to find out more. Over dinner?"

Her smile brightened the room. "I guess a gal's gotta eat."

CHAPTER 1

Carson Stone looked down the Spencer rifle's barrel at the shabby camp below. He huddled in his heavy wool coat under the low-hanging branches of an evergreen. Only September and already the nights were cold, the mornings slow to warm, a white mist creeping across the forest floor.

He fought off a shiver. *Idaho sure ain't Texas*.

He panned left to right with the rifle, looking for signs of life among the circle of tents. Last night's coals in the cookfire still smoked. A picket line stretched between two skinny ponderosa pines, three horses tethered there. It wasn't the worst spot for a camp if a fella was looking to hide himself. Ten miles deep into the Payette Forest, up in the rocky foothills about thirty-five hundred feet. It wasn't a place anyone would have happened upon by accident, an area at the top of a hill but surrounded on all sides by rock walls, like the indention of a thumb smashed into the top of a mashed potato mound.

They'd never have found the place if not for the Indian, a rangy Bannock on the run from Howard after the surrender. He'd given them detailed directions for a dollar. How the Indian had come to have the information Carson didn't know, but he'd perfectly described the huge Bavarian, and there was no doubt it was the man they were after.

Carson glanced to his left to check Tate's progress.

Colby Tate worked his way down the narrow crevice between two boulders. He'd be out of sight for a moment when he circled below Carson, but he wasn't worried about Tate. The bounty hunter could take care of himself. Carson's job was to cover him if anyone tried to hit Tate from his blind side.

How do I let Tate talk me into these things?

But Carson knew the answer. Money. Carson had ideas and plans, and very few of them came for free. He'd wintered as a cattle hand on a ranch in Colorado. When the spring thaw had rolled around, Tate had returned and said he needed help with a job. They'd tracked four cattle rustlers, brought them in alive and, after splitting the reward with Tate, Carson had made as much in three days as he had working the ranch all winter.

So, when Tate had taken off after a notorious murderer and robber, Carson tagged along. Half of a five-hundred-dollar reward was nothing to sneeze at. They'd chased the outlaw as far as Cheyenne, and the job had gone bloody. Carson had remembered why he'd wanted no part of bounty hunting, had sworn he was finished with it, but then the next job had gone smoother, and so had the one after that, and pretty soon both men looked up and found they'd stumbled into Boise.

That was where the local sheriff had told them about the Bavarian.

Tate disappeared from view, and Carson slowly swung the Spencer back the other way, eyes peeled for movement.

As Carson had already observed, it was a good place for a camp: hidden, sheltered from the wind, the only drawback being what Carson was doing right now. Shooting down into the sunken area made the place a killing ground. He could pick off ten of them before they even knew what was happening.

Of course, he'd have to spot them first.

And he doubted there were ten of them. Reports varied, saying the Bavarian rode with a few men or a dozen, depending on who was telling the tale and how much whisky they'd had, but Carson figured three horses meant three men.

On the other hand, there were four tents.

So who the hell could say?

Carson could see Tate below him now, one of his twin Colt Peacemakers in his hand as he crouched halfway behind a boulder, with a good view of the tents.

"I'd like to address the gentleman in the tents if I may," Tate shouted. "I know it's a bit early in the morning for unpleasant surprises, so if you'd please give me your full attention, we can get through this with as little bloodshed as possible. Your complete cooperation is absolutely crucial to your continued good health."

Carson grinned. Colby Tate sure must love the feel of words flying out of his mouth because he never chose to say things fast and simple.

"I strongly suggest throwing your guns out first," Tate continued. "Followed slowly by your person. It goes without saying that having your hands up and not making any moves that could be interpreted as hostile will serve to facilitate a smooth conclusion to this whole affair."

Nothing. Somewhere in the distance, a bald eagle screeched.

"Indicating that you've heard my instructions and are hastening to comply would now be a good idea," Tate called.

A moment later, "Just who in the hell are you?"

Carson couldn't be sure which tent the voice came from.

"A fair question. My name is Tate and I'm a bounty hunter. My colleagues and I mean to collect the two-hundred-and-fifty-dollar reward currently being offered for Hans Mueller. This actually brings me to my next point. There's no paper that I know of on anyone else here. If Mueller gives himself up without a fuss, we'll leave without troubling the rest of you. I think that's a very generous offer and I'd like to hear your opinion."

A moment passed. "Opinion?" asked the same voice.

"Yes," Tate said. "I'd like you to weigh in on my proposal. I don't detect a German accent, so I take it you're not Mueller, but rather one of his compatriots."

"I ain't Mueller," the voice confirmed.

"Just so. I imagine it would save you and your other friends a good deal of stress if Mueller would give himself up without a lot of tedious shooting."

"You go to hell, bounty hunter," shouted a different voice.

Carson swung the Spencer to aim it at a tent two over from the first voice. He had a better fix on them now.

"These men are my friends. They won't give me up without a fight." Thick accent. The words sounded like *Zese men are my vrends. Zey von't giff me up vithout a fight.*

"Now hold on just a minute, Hans," the first voice said. "Let's be smart about this."

"I quite agree," Tate said. "Listen to your friend, Hans."

"Just do what the man says, Hans," the first voice said. "You'll take him peaceable like and he gets a fair trial, right, mister?"

"As long as everyone cooperates," Tate said.

"You hear that, Hans? Just play along with the fella."

"You go straight to hell, Ralph McNally," Hans shouted. "This could be a trick. You want I should get shot?"

"I'll shoot you my own damn self," Meriweather shouted

back. "I know what tent you're in. No sense all of us getting taken. Now get out there with your damn hands up."

Grumbling, then cursing in German, and then, "Fine, okay. I'm coming. But you don't shoot, yes?"

"I don't shoot, yes," confirmed Tate.

Movement in the corner of Carson's eye drew attention. He swung the Spencer to the far-right side of the clearing, where a man emerged from between two boulders. The man was tall and stooped and stork thin, with buckteeth and a battered hat pushed back on his head. He was pulling up his pants as he walked, and Carson figured the man had been off doing his business.

Stork Man suddenly understood what was going on and ducked back against one of the boulders, eyes going wide as he hurriedly buckled his belt. Carson assessed the situation. Tate faced the tents and couldn't see the newcomer unless he happened to turn his head. Carson could shout a warning, but that would give away his position.

The Bavarian emerged from his tent. Hans Mueller was a beefy man, with a glistening bald head, clean-shaven pink cheeks. He wore a big Colt Dragoon on his left hip. He raised his hands and looked nervous. "No shooting, remember!"

"Unbuckle that belt and let it drop," Tate told him.

The Bavarian hesitated.

Carson took aim at Stork Man. He didn't want to shoot if he didn't have to. Tate had told the truth when he said they were only interested in Mueller. *Just walk away, friend. Better for all concerned.*

Hans moved his hands slowly toward his gun belt.

Stork Man drew his six-shooter.

Don't do it. Don't do it. Don't—

Stork Man took aim.

The Spencer bucked in Carson's hands, and Stork Man

spun away, blood trailing from a hole above his left temple, six-gun flying and clattering along the rocky ground.

Tate's head came around to see what was happening, and that was when the Bavarian drew.

But Tate was fast and fanned his Colt three times. The blasts made a neat triangle of wet red dots across Mueller's chest. The beefy man stumbled back into his tent and fell over, smashing it flat.

A shotgun blast shook the world, and Tate dove behind his boulder. It had come from Ralph Meriweather's tent, and another blast immediately followed, buckshot scorching Tate's boulder.

Carson emptied the Spencer into the tent, levering one cartridge in after another.

Silence. Smoke hung in the air.

"You okay?" Carson called.

"Unscathed," Tate said. "What are you doing?"

"Reloading the Spencer. Want to take a look?"

"Do you think you got him?"

"No idea."

"You alive in there, Meriweather?" Tate called. "My partner's going to open up again in ten seconds if you don't say something. We've got ammunition to spare."

Ten seconds went by and they heard nothing from Meriweather.

"You don't really want me to shoot up that tent again, do you?"

"Never mind," Tate said. "Cover me. I'll take a look."

Meriweather had a hole in his head and a very surprised look on his face.

CHAPTER 2

They draped the bodies over the dead men's horses.

"You never know," Tate said. "There might be paper on the others. Anyway, it's bad form to leave corpses lying about. We'll let the law sort out the details. We'll get something for the guns and horses anyway."

A noncommittal grunt from Carson.

"Now don't do that," Tate said.

"Do what?"

"You're in one of your moods," Tate said. "You always get sullen when there's shooting. It was necessary, you know. That gentleman coming back from relieving himself would have had me if you hadn't nailed him first."

"Necessary doesn't mean I like it."

"Well, I'm not especially fond of bloodshed either." A shrug from Tate. "It's simply part of the business."

"Well, that's why it's not the business for me," Carson said for maybe the hundredth time. "Soon as I get the money I need, that's it."

"So you've told me."

They led the horses down a narrow path to where they'd left their own mounts about a thousand feet below. Carson's was a big black gelding named Jet, and he gave the animal a stroke down the nose before climbing into the saddle.

They found the southern trail and rode out of the Payette at an easy pace.

"How much do you need, actually?" Tate asked. "To start your own ranch."

Carson thought about it. "I don't really know, to be honest. As much as I can get. Breeding cattle. Lumber for a house, barn, corral, about a hundred other things, I guess. And the land, of course."

"What land?" Tate asked. "We've been from Arkansas to Idaho. You haven't picked a place."

Carson grinned. "I haven't *seen* all the places."

"Aha." Tate wagged a finger. "I don't think you're a settle-down-in-one-place sort of man, old sport. I think you have the wanderlust. A desire to see the world."

"Might be something to that," Carson admitted. "But I still don't want to shoot people for a living."

"Well, like it or not, I'm glad you happen to be good at it," Tate said. "Saved my bacon more than once. You've a keen eye with that Spencer."

Carson made an indifferent noise in his throat. "It shoots fine, I guess. I preferred my Winchester. Before it got thrown into a river."

Tate frowned. "Oh, that's right. *She* did that, didn't she?"

Carson nodded.

The *she* Tate referred to was a hellacious redhead who'd tried to murder them both at different times. She'd been a bounty hunter like Tate. Now she was a fugitive. Tate had a superstition about saying her name out loud, something about summoning demons.

"Buy a new Winchester," Tate suggested. "You can afford it."

"The Spencer shoots fine," Carson said. "I'm saving my money."

"Buy some land here in Idaho. It's pretty country."

Carson shook his head. "Tell me how pretty you think it is in January."

"How much money do you really need for this ranch?" Tate asked.

"A dollar and a quarter an acre. Or free, if I homestead," Carson said. "But that's five years staying on the land and doing something with it."

"I can't think of anywhere I've been that I'd want to stay five years. I suppose people do it—settle down with a family and so on. I just can't see it for myself."

Carson said nothing but admitted similar thoughts to himself. What If he got to the end of five years and discovered he'd chosen wrong? He only had one life to live and didn't relish a five-year mistake. A ranch had seemed obvious. Carson knew the work, was good at it, and liked being outdoors. He'd considered other choices. He loved a good saloon but running one would be a nonstop headache. Drunks and men getting too rough with the gals who worked the saloon, shootings over poker games gone bad. Half the trouble Carson had ever gotten into had started in saloons.

A store clerk, a farmer, join the army? Carson had to do something with his life, anything but shoot men and collect money for it.

They left the Payette and angled toward Boise. The road was empty and quiet.

Tate squinted up at the sun, then looked back at Carson. "I don't suppose we'll make Boise tonight."

Carson shook his head. "Nope."

"What do you think, then?" Tate asked. "Porter Bend?"

Carson nodded. "Yep."

They made the bend with a little less than an hour's daylight left. The bend was formed where Porter Creek took a sharp turn left to feed the Payette River. The creek was just big enough to justify a small, wooden bridge, although the water wouldn't get high again until spring thaw. There was also a crossroads, the road they were on continuing south into Boise. The crossroad went one way to the northeast into the Salmon-Challis, the other way due west. On the far side of the trading post was a small landing for traffic on the Payette.

The trading post itself had been burned to the ground by the Bannock at the start of the war back in June. Carson had been told it had once been a thriving establishment, a long, low dry goods store that doubled as a hash house, a corral of fresh horses for the stagecoach, and a blacksmith's shop.

Carson had just finished building a fire and putting on a pot of coffee when he heard voices and horses. He looked up and saw the column approach in two lines. Twenty bluecoats, dusty from the road. They came from the western road and then crossed the bridge. A line of five unmounted Indians brought up the rear, tethered to a long rope, hands tied in front of them. Two more cavalrymen rode a buckboard behind the Indians. It pulled a huge, multibarreled gun mounted like a cannon. Carson had never seen a Gatling gun, but from what he'd heard, he couldn't be looking at anything else.

The two men at the head of the column broke off and trotted toward Carson.

"Hello, the campfire," called the officer as he rode forward.

Carson waved. "Welcome."

The two riders reined in their horses as they entered the circle of campfire light. They dismounted, and Carson looked them over. The first cavalryman was short but broad, black muttonchops down the sides of a beefy face, three sergeant stripes on one sleeve. The man with the major's insignia on his shoulder was only a little taller, trim and neat, a brown mustache and dark eyes, a bland brown but keen and searching.

The major glanced to one side, where the horses were tethered to a picket line. Close by were three lumps under blankets, clearly dead bodies. "Don't suppose I'd be doing my job if I didn't ask about them."

Tate stood and doffed his hat. "Colby Tate, Major. Licensed in Texas to hunt bounties. The unfortunate souls under the blankets are Hans Mueller and his so-called friends. There's paper on him in Boise. The local sheriff put us onto this job, and I'm sure you can check with him if you're passing through."

"You have anything to show me that can verify any of this?" the major asked.

Tate produced a packet of papers wrapped in leather and handed them over to the major, who shuffled through them, giving each page a cursory look. He nodded and handed them back. "Seems in order." He turned to Carson. "What about you?"

Carson touched the brim of his hat. "Carson Stone, sir. Don't have no papers. I just sort of help him."

"Okay, then." The major stuck his nose in the air and sniffed pointedly. "Coffee smells good."

Carson took the hint. "If you can come up with a cup, there's plenty to share."

The major went into a saddlebag and came out with a cup. "Sergeant, get the men set up, will you?"

"Yessir." The sergeant snapped off a salute, then went away to bark an order at the troopers.

The major handed the empty cup to Carson, and Carson handed it back full.

"Name's Grady. George Grady," the major told them. "Obliged for the hospitality."

Carson watched the other troopers ride past as the three

men exchanged bland pleasantries. The Indians were herded together, and two troopers were set to watch over them, pacing idly, Springfield carbines resting lazily on their shoulders.

"Where you taking those Bannock?" Carson asked.

"Fort Hall," Grady said. "Then I'm shed of 'em. Bunch of strays running all over the place, causing minor trouble since the surrender. One of my lieutenants has the other platoon chasing a few halfway to the Snake River. I told him good luck with it. Been too long since I slept in a real bed, so I'm heading back."

"You don't worry about splitting your forces?" Tate asked. "I mean, ever since the Little Bighorn . . ."

Grady chuckled. "No fight left in this particular group of Indian. Bessie made sure of that." He nodded toward the Gatling gun, the barrels glinting metallic in the firelight. "She tore 'em up pretty bad at Fox Valley. We drag her around where everyone can see. It's a good reminder."

They traded news they'd heard from around the region. The troopers strung a picket line and tethered their horses. The Bannock prisoners were each given a plate of cold beans. Carson refilled the tin cups with fresh coffee.

"Thanks again." Grady sipped coffee. "A shame the damn redskins burned the trading post. Coffee's good, but a shot of whisky wouldn't hurt it none."

"A good spot for a trading post. I bet the owner did good business," Carson said. "Surprised he hasn't started rebuilding yet."

"Don't think he's going to," Grady said. "I heard he sold the land and headed west. Don't know who bought it or why. Maybe a new trading post."

"You'd think the new owner would get building, then," Carson suggested. "Before the snows come."

"You'd think," Grady agreed.

Carson cast a glance just as one of the Indians turned his face toward the firelight, and Carson felt a jolt of recognition. It was the Bannock who'd sold them the location to Mueller's camp. The Indian had seemed tired and defeated at the time, and Carson was surprised to see him among the other prisoners.

Grady finished his coffee and wiped his mouth on his sleeve. "Thanks again for the coffee. Guess I'd better check on the men. You two travel safe in the morning."

Carson nudged Tate after the major left. "See those Indians?"

"What about them?" Tate said without looking up.

"I think that's Laughing Otter," Carson said.

"Who?" Tate looked now, the name ringing a bell.

"The Bannock who helped us find Mueller."

Tate grunted, considering. "Seems the old boy has landed himself in a bit of hot soup. I wonder what he did."

"I wonder, too," Carson said. "He told us he was headed deep into the mountains to get away from all the trouble."

"Trouble found him anyway."

"I'm going to talk to him," Carson said.

"What good will that do?"

"None at all, I'm guessing, but I'm curious."

Carson walked toward the circle of Indians sitting on the ground.

Halfway there, one of the troopers stepped in front of him. "Help you with something?"

"I know that Bannock," Carson told the trooper. "His name is Laughing Otter."

"And?"

Carson shrugged. "And nothing, I guess. Just wanted to talk to him a minute."

"What for?"

"Just curious how he ended up here. Don't worry, you'll still have your Indian when I'm done."

The trooper looked back at the Bannock, then at Carson again. "I guess it don't matter. Wait here."

The trooper separated Laughing Otter from the other Bannock and brought him to Carson. The trooper stepped away a few feet to give the two men a modicum of privacy.

"Friend Carson, I am surprised to see you." Laughing Otter's English was good, and again Carson wondered where he'd learned it.

Carson wouldn't go as far as to call Laughing Otter a friend, but he'd done business with the Indian and certainly wished him no harm. The Bannock seemed affable enough, and the dollar Carson had paid him to find Hans Mueller's hidden camp had been well spent.

"I think I'm more surprised to see you here," Carson told Laughing Otter. "Last I saw, you were headed north fast. How'd you get rounded up by these bluecoats?"

"Two days after I left you, I met with a number of my tribe who were also fleeing," Laughing Otter explained. "They convinced me to turn west for Oregon, where the bluecoats still hunt the Bannock, but not as much. They caught us in the open with many others of my people. Many were shot trying to run. Those here are all who survived."

Carson sighed. "Hard stuff."

"There are winners in war, and there are losers." Laughing Otter shrugged. "This time the Bannock are the losers, and with losing there are consequences."

Carson cast about, not sure what to say to that. His eyes landed on the blackened timber of the burned trading post. "Was that you?"

"Not me, but the Bannock, yes."

"I guess that's just part of war."

Laughing Otter seemed about to say something but hesitated.

Carson's eyes narrowed. "Something on your mind, Laughing Otter?"

"Burning the trading post was part of war, yes," the Indian said. "But also not."

"If you want me to understand, you'll have to do better than that," Carson said.

"A man approached a war party of the Bannock to strike a bargain. A white man. The war party was led by a brave named Eyes of Fire," Laughing Otter explained. "This white man wanted the trading post burned. He paid Eyes of Fire and his braves many cases of whisky for the deed. It was Eyes of Fire's task to make war on the white man anyway, so why not also get the whisky? So the trading post was burned, and the war was blamed."

Carson wasn't sure what to make of that.

"Okay, conversation's over, mister," the trooper said. "We got an early start in the morning, and these Indians need to bed down."

"Farewell, friend Carson," the Bannock said.

"Good luck, Laughing Otter." Carson offered his hand, and they shook.

When Carson went back to his own campfire, he found Tate already resting his head on his saddle, hat pulled down over his eyes.

"Satisfy your curiosity?" Tate asked.

Carson leaned back on his own saddle. "I think I've got more questions now than when I started."

He closed his eyes, and the fire died, and darkness and silence consumed the place that had once been a thriving trading post. Carson let slumber take him, and he snored lightly, a deep, restful sleep without dreams.

Shouting.

Carson blinked and tried to sit up. Disoriented. Had it been hours or minutes?

A gunshot brought him the rest of the way awake. He sprang to his feet, the Spencer rifle in his hands an eyeblink later. Tate was already standing, a Peacemaker filling each hand.

"What is it?" Carson asked.

"Haven't the foggiest," Tate replied. "Some commotion down by the river."

They headed for the river, the silhouettes of cavalrymen visible in the jerky light of swinging lanterns. More shouting, and then an eruption of Springfield rifles. Carson almost tripped over the body of a dead Bannock. He paused and saw two more bodies, checked quickly, but none were Laughing Otter.

A squad of cavalrymen were there in a flash, surrounding Carson and Tate. One lifted a lantern, and Carson flinched, squinting into the sudden light.

"Put up them shooters!" shouted one of them.

Tate holstered his pistols. "No trouble here, friend."

Carson held his rifle over his head. "We heard shots and just wanted to see what was happening."

Another trooper pushed his way into the lantern light. "That's him!" It was the soldier who'd been guarding the Bannock earlier. "That's the one who wanted to speak to the Indian."

CHAPTER 3

Their pistols were taken from them, and Carson and Tate were taken to Major Grady at gunpoint. The man sat next to his campfire, a hastily brewed cup of coffee in his hand. He didn't wear his coat, the sleeves of his shirt rolled up, his hair mussed. He was a man who'd clearly woken up annoyed, and his mood had gone south since.

"Major Grady," Carson began. "I can assure you we weren't doing anything—"

Grady held up a hand to forestall anything Carson might have said next, then turned to his sergeant. "Let's have it."

"They all ran at once," the sergeant reported. "I think the idea was they'd scatter, and then maybe some would make it."

"Did any make it?" Grady asked.

"Hard to say for sure," the sergeant said. "Three of 'em got it right away. Two made it to the river. Trooper Thorn's squad reported firing on them."

Grady stood and rubbed his temples. "Step forward and report, Thorn."

A gangly cavalryman with wide eyes stepped up and saluted. "We cut one down just as he reached the bank. The body went into the water, but I know we hit him. We opened up on the other one just as he dove into the river. Might have hit him . . . I think. Can't say for certain."

"Take your squad downriver and see if the bodies washed up," Grady told Thorn. "A mile or two, just to say we tried."

"Yessir!" Thorn saluted and left.

Grady turned back to his sergeant. "Detail some men to dig graves for the other three."

The sergeant saluted and turned away, already shouting orders as he went. The major's tired eyes went to Carson.

"I'm told you spoke to one of the Bannock," Grady said.

Carson nodded. "That's right."

"Who is he?"

"Name's Laughing Otter," Carson said. "He sold us some information. The whereabouts of the camp where we collected that bounty."

"And he didn't say anything about trying to escape?"

"Not a word."

"I'd like to believe you," Grady said. "Why did you want to talk to him? Is he a friend of yours?"

"I wouldn't go that far," Carson told the major. "Last I saw him, he was running for the hills. Didn't seem like he was going to be any trouble to anyone. I was just curious how he'd got himself captured."

"As a major, it's above my pay grade to decide which Bannock are trouble and which aren't. I've orders to round them up, so that's what I'm doing," Grady said. "I hope you understand that."

"I understand."

"What else did this Laughing Otter tell you?" Grady asked. "Anything about where he might go after escaping, any plans?"

Carson hesitated, wondering if he should mention what Laughing Otter had said about a white man paying whisky to a Bannock war party to burn down the trading post. No, he supposed not. It didn't have anything to do with the Indian's escape.

Grady gave Carson a piercing look. "You about to say something?"

"No, sir. Just running over the conversation in my head. Laughing Otter didn't say anything about escape, or plans, or anything like that." Carson could always tell the major later about the trading post if it turned out to be important.

"Okay, then," Grady said. "I had to ask."

The sergeant returned at that moment to report a squad of men were now working on the graves.

"Pass the word, Sergeant. We leave at first light, but not all together. I want you to take the bulk of the men and link up with Lieutenant Fitzpatrick to aid his continued efforts to round up stray Bannock. I'll take a squad to handle Bessie and ride into Boise with Mr. Stone and his friend." Grady's eyes flicked to Carson. "If you're amenable to that."

"The more the merrier," Carson said.

Grady nodded. "Good. If I can't bring my prisoners to Fort Hall as instructed, I can at least wire in an explanation. Mr. Stone, you may have to fill out some kind of statement. I may have lost my Indians, but I'll be damned if I'll take the heat for not at least filing a thorough report detailing why."

Grady dismissed everyone, and Carson and Tate were given back their guns before walking back to the glowing remains of their campfire.

"How long until daylight?" Tate asked.

"Not long enough to bother trying to sleep again," Carson said.

"I was afraid of that."

They made coffee and packed, and by the time the horses were saddled, the sun was humping up orange over the foothills in the east. The sergeant led his men back over the bridge and away along the road west. Major Grady reined in his horse next to Carson. "Boise awaits, gentlemen."

They fell into line and took the road south. They spoke off and on but mostly road in silence, the buckboard creaking and jostling behind them, dragging the Gatling gun. They rested the horses at midday, ate a simple lunch, and a few hours later trotted into Boise.

"Gentlemen, if you'd accompany me to the sheriff's office," Grady said. "As a courtesy, I'll tell him what's happened, and I'd like you to corroborate my report. The wire office is next door, so we can get something off to Fort Hall as well."

"Happy to cooperate, Major," Carson said.

"We need to see the sheriff anyway," Tate chimed in. "I'd like him to take these corpses off our hands."

The sheriff was a cool customer named Justin Bedford. He'd been a Confederate captain under Stonewall Jackson, had taken defeat in stride when Lee had called it quits at Appomattox, and had come west in search of a clean slate. Idaho was everything Mississippi wasn't, so he'd stuck. He was tall and broad-shouldered, hairline retreating faster than McClellan, and three days of salt-and-pepper stubble on his face. He had keen eyes and greeted his visitors with an easy smile.

"Didn't expect to see you boys back so soon," Bedford said to Carson and Tate. "Figured it would take you longer to dig Mueller out of the Payette."

"Never underestimate the value of an Indian guide, old boy," Tate said. "Allow me to present Major Grady of the US Cavalry."

"Justin Bedford." He shook hands with the major. "Always glad to meet one of our brave Indian fighters."

"I know I'm not obligated to report to civilian authority, but I'm the sort of man who likes to dot his i's and cross his t's." Grady briefly explained his mission and the killed—and possibly escaped—Bannock. "These two men can verify my story."

Bedford looked at Carson and Tate. "That's right?"

Carson told what he knew, none of it contradicting Grady's account.

"I can't add anything to that," Tate said. "Except to say none of those Bannock will be troubling your citizens again."

"Good enough," Bedford said. "Major Grady, I'll go with you next door and we'll wire Fort Hall together. You'll get it on the record, so don't worry, but honestly, I imagine if you simply told your colonel your prisoners were shot while escaping, it would be good enough."

"Well, you don't know my colonel." Grady chuckled. "But I've always been a careful man, and if I'm not able to follow orders, I'm damn well going to make it clear why."

"It would seem you have further business with Major Grady, Sheriff," Tate interjected. "If you could conclude with us before you go too far off on a tangent, I'd be obliged."

"I can give you a voucher for Mueller. They'll honor it at the bank," Bedford said. "Usually you have to go through a US Marshal to get paid, but this bounty was issued by territorial authorities. Just let me know if they give you any trouble over there. I don't know if there's paper on the other two men, but I'll check."

Bedford made out a voucher and a deputy took charge of the corpses.

"I'd like to get to the bank before it closes and get our money," Tate said.

Carson's eyes went to the saloon down the street.

Tate followed his gaze. "Ah. She's there?"

"I reckon. If not, she will be later."

"I'll attend to our banking and meet you there later, then. I could use a stiff drink."

"Same."

"Carson, old boy, you know I'd never meddle in a man's personal affairs," Tate began.

Carson smiled. "Go on, then."

"Is it right to get in so deep with a working girl?"

A shrug. "Might not be right, but it's a fairly pleasant way of being wrong."

CHAPTER 4

It was too early in the Three Kings for the piano player, so the only noise in the smoky saloon was the minor din of conversation, the clink of glasses, occasional laughter, and the rare clang of an old school bell, which had been installed at the end of the bar to announce when someone bought a round for the house. The late afternoon crowd grew steadily as the world eased into evening.

Carson Stone haunted a corner table. He'd always loved a good saloon, even though he'd never been sure exactly why. There was nearly always a card game or two, but Carson had never cared for cards. He drank but seldom got drunk. There was just something alive about a saloon, the variety of humanity shuffling in and out, the crowd re-inventing itself nightly, sometimes even hourly. Mostly he didn't think about why. Carson was three beers into his evening when he began to get anxious that Mary might not show.

Maybe Colby's right. Maybe I've put too much of myself into this thing with her.

It was all still new, and part of Carson admitted it was probably moving too fast. But it quickly became clear there was some spark between them. Mary wasn't just any other saloon gal and Carson wasn't just another customer. What any of that meant remained to be seen.

I've been here before and it didn't work out. Maybe this really is a mistake.

He'd fallen for a working girl named Annie in El Paso but had to leave her behind when he was on the run for a crime he didn't commit. By the time he cleared his name, it was too late. A rancher had made an honest woman of her. She was better off.

Was this some kind of pattern, that he fall for a certain kind of woman? What did that say about him? Maybe nothing. Maybe everything.

Carson sipped his beer.

Colby Tate pushed through the saloon's swinging doors and spotted him across the room. He snaked his way through the crowd and sat at Carson's table. He reached into his jacket, came out with a short stack of bills, and slid them across the table. "Your half. Not exactly a fortune, but another step closer to your ranch."

Carson folded the bills and shoved them in a pants pocket. "Thanks."

"Or maybe buy yourself a Winchester," Tate suggested. "Frankly, if you're going to be covering me, old boy, I'd feel more confident knowing you were perfectly happy with your rifle."

"I told you, the Spencer shoots fine," Carson said irritably.

Tate narrowed his eyes and then smiled slowly. "Mary hasn't shown herself yet, I take it."

"You take it correctly."

"Be patient. She works late, so she can't start so early."

The idea of her working late irritated him, but Carson reckoned Colby was right. He was impatient to come in so early, and if he kept drinking, his mood would sour, and then he'd likely not make a good impression. Carson was doing everything wrong. He might as well just go now and—

Carson turned his head to the stairway across the room, watching as the ladies descended in a line, slowly, milking their entrance. The chatter rose in the room, a smattering of applause and a few whistles. It was an irregular ritual. Some evenings they didn't bother, the gals filtering down one or two at a time to mingle with the cowboys. But a couple of nights a week, they made a parade out of it, seven or eight of them in all shapes and sizes, freshly powdered, easing down the stairs, waving and blowing kisses. On nights when the liquor was really flowing, it could get pretty rowdy.

Mary was the third one down, and seeing her did things to Carson's insides.

Tall and slender with butter-yellow hair. Features so fine they might have been carved from pure white marble, rose-petal lips red as an apple. She took each stair with grace, looking out over the crowd with secrets in her eyes and a promise in her smile. All the ladies were dressed similarly, various bright colors, clothing tight enough in some places to show off and loose enough in other places to fall open at strategic moments. Their appearance wasn't quite wanton, but they weren't quite dressed for Sunday church either.

The ladies hit the bottom of the stairs and filtered into the crowd. Mary exchanged smiles and salutations with a number of cowboys but was clearly headed for Carson's table.

Tate stood. "I'll give you two some privacy."

"It's okay. Stay and have a drink." But Carson couldn't quite make it sound sincere.

Tate laughed. "Later, maybe." He headed for the bar.

Mary arrived, leaned in, and kissed Carson on the cheek. She let her lips linger an extra second, and Carson felt a hot rush of blood to his face. She sat in the chair next to him, her hand finding his leg.

"You're back already?" she asked. "Did you catch your man?"

"Three of them." Carson refrained from saying they were all dead now.

"Well, glad I didn't have to wait to see you." She squeezed his leg, leaned forward, and whispered, "I'm off tomorrow."

Carson understood what that meant. She'd have time for him tomorrow but not now. Mary was popular and she probably had some clients lined up already. It was pointless to be upset about it. Carson knew what this was when he got into it, and the woman had to earn a living, after all.

With the money in my pocket, I could monopolize her all night. Hell, I could have her to myself the rest of the month.

But then, what about the next month? And the month after that?

"Sounds good," Carson said. "What do you want to do?"

She brightened. "Go riding, maybe. I can borrow a horse."

Carson nodded. "Okay, then."

Mary traced a slender finger down Carson's jawline. "I still have a few minutes. You want a drink?"

"Don't spend your money."

"Don't be silly. I'll tell the bartender to put it on my tab, but he won't." She stood. "A beer?"

"Something stronger. Whisky."

"Be right back."

He was making a mistake. Carson knew it. He didn't care. Even the smartest men were stupid about women.

Mary returned and handed him a shot glass. Carson took half in a gulp, enjoying the low-level burn down his throat.

Mary leaned in, kissed him on the lips this time, and pulled away slowly. "Tomorrow."

Carson smiled at her. "Tomorrow."

She drifted back into the crowd, but Carson didn't watch her go.

A minute later, Colby Tate plopped into the chair across from him. "Want some advice?"

Carson tossed back the rest of the whisky. "Nope."

"Probably for the best," Tate admitted. "I'm sort of rubbish at advice."

Carson laughed.

"You're empty," Tate observed. "Let me get you another."

"Why not?"

Tate left and returned a few moments later with two more shot glasses. Tate sipped. Carson sipped. They made a point of talking about nothing important. At one point Carson glanced around the room for Mary but didn't see her. He didn't look any more after that.

Carson stood. "My turn to buy." He went to the bar and flagged down a sweaty, harried man in an apron. Carson tried to picture how many more drinks would take him to bedtime but couldn't. "Better make it a bottle."

"Gimmee a second." The bartender scurried down to the other end of the bar.

One of the other saloon gals scooted up to the bar next to Carson and flashed him a smile. "Now I just know one of us other ladies will eventually steal you away from Mary. At least for one night?"

Carson smiled back at her. She was shorter than Mary and curvier, with rouge-red cheeks and a pile of hair, a copper red that had certainly come from a bottle. "Not tonight, Sue, but if I ever do, you'll be the one."

Sue tittered, and to Carson, it seemed genuine.

The bartender brought the bottle and Carson paid. He was about to rejoin Tate at the table when raised voices drew his attention.

Two men stood on either side of another working girl

several feet away. Carson didn't know her name, but he'd seen her before, a lanky brunette with big eyes. She was clearly the subject of the argument between the two men, both dusty cowboys who looked like they were just in off the trail.

Others in the saloon stepped back to give them room. It seldom paid to get in the way of another man's business, especially where a woman was concerned.

"I was talking to her, so shove off," said the beefy one.

"I already explained to you, mister." The other man had a lean, sharp look. Mean eyes. "I was talking to her earlier and went away a second to tell my pals I was going upstairs. Now back off."

The entire saloon felt the tension. The girl between the two men had withdrawn into herself, shrinking before the impending altercation. She was young, or she might have known how to handle them. Carson had seen this sort of thing before. At best, it ended with somebody getting a black eye. At worst, guns were drawn.

"You lined up any business yet?" Carson asked Sue.

She shook her head. "Just got here."

"Come on." Carson grabbed her by the wrist and pulled her along. She might have guessed what Carson was up to because she didn't resist.

Carson put his hand on the beefy man's shoulder in a friendly fashion. "You're in luck tonight, partner."

The big man spun, eyes narrowing and muscles tensing for trouble. "Who in the hell are you?"

Carson removed his hand. "Easy. I'm just a fella looking to do you a favor." He pulled Sue forward.

"The hell you say," Beefy barked.

"The best gal in here's been giving you the eye," Carson said. "And you didn't even notice. Figured I'd best introduce you to Sue."

The big man's eyes seemed to land on Sue for the first time, some of the hostility going out of him. "Well, I was . . . uh . . . I was just trying to talk to . . . uh . . . this other gal."

Carson leaned in and lowered his voice. "She's young and new. Inexperienced. Now Sue . . . well, Sue knows things, if you catch my meaning."

Beefy's eyes widened. "Oh?"

Sue stepped in, running a hand across the big man's wide chest. "Oh, I do like a *big* man. Would you like to keep me company, big man?"

Beefy blinked. "Well, I . . . I mean . . . uh . . . sure. Sounds like a mighty good idea to me."

Sue said something, and they both laughed.

But Carson didn't hear it. He was already on his way back to the bar to grab his bottle. The man with the brunette had also taken the opportunity to skedaddle. Sue would handle the situation from here and Carson could go back to his drinking.

Back at the table with Tate, another man stood waiting, in his midfifties, ruddy-cheeked, a bowler hat pushed back on his head and a string tie pulled loose. A half-empty beer mug in one hand. Whatever the man had been doing all day, he was obviously finished doing it and had come into the saloon to relax.

"I like the way you handled that, son," he said. "Could have been a big blowup, but everyone left happy."

"I took a chance." Carson shrugged. "This time it worked out."

Tate gestured to the man in the bowler. "Carson Stone, meet Meriweather Lemmings. The mayor of Boise."

That caught Carson's attention and he extended his hand. "Your honor."

They shook hands.

"None of that honor stuff, son," Lemmings said. "I'm

just here having a drink like everyone else. Listen, I'm a pretty good judge of character. That's how I got to be mayor. I think you've a good way with people. Boise could always use someone like you as a lawman. I've been talking to your friend here, and he says you can handle yourself."

"You already have a sheriff," Carson said. "From what I hear, Bedford's a good man."

"You trying to give away my job again, Mayor?" Bedford came up behind them and stood next to Lemmings. "So much for gratitude."

Lemmings chuckled. "Speak of the devil. No, your job's safe, Justin. But you know we're short on deputies. You tell me that yourself three times a week."

"How 'bout it?" the sheriff asked Carson.

"I appreciate the offer, but I don't think it's for me."

Lemmings frowned at Tate, who spread his hands and grinned. "Told you."

"Join us for a beer?" the mayor asked the sheriff.

"Actually, I came in looking for those two." Bedford gestured to Carson and Tate. "About that business we were talking about earlier."

Lemmings waved his hand and made an exasperated sound. "I'll leave it to you, then. I'm off duty." He nodded to Tate and Carson. "Gentlemen." Then wandered toward the bar.

"You fellas handled that Mueller job good," Bedford told them. "Sorry to say there was no paper on them other two, so no reward's coming, but they were known bad apples. Good riddance."

"That's something at least," Carson said.

"Anyway, I might have some more work for you if you're interested," Bedford said.

Tate shoved a chair away from the table with a boot. "Have a seat and tell us about it."

Bedford shook his head. "Not here. Too many ears. Follow me back to the jailhouse."

"We just got a bottle," Carson said.

"Bring it," the sheriff told him. "Hell, I could use a stiff one myself."

CHAPTER 5

They sat around the sheriff's desk, each holding a shot glass. The jailhouse was empty except for the three of them, so they had complete privacy. The quiet jailhouse was a change from the rowdy saloon.

Probably for the best, Carson thought. He'd been on his way to a colossal drunk, and that would have meant a throbbing headache tomorrow. He took it easier now, sipping his booze at an easy pace, enjoying the relaxed, numb feeling in his limbs, his head a little light, but not so much that he couldn't follow what Bedford was telling them.

"Let me ask you something," Bedford said. "Did you two search that camp after you bagged Mueller and his pals?"

"Yes," Tate admitted. "There wasn't much of value."

"That strike you as odd?"

Tate frowned. "I'm not sure I follow."

"What were them men wanted for?"

"Claim jumping," Tate said.

Bedford sat back in his chair, sipped whisky. "Right. Jumping claims. So think again. What did you find when searching the camp?"

A long pause. Tate looked at Carson. *What's he getting at?*

"Not what we found," Carson said finally. "What we didn't find."

"Go on," Bedford encouraged. "You're getting there."

"Gold. If they were jumping claims, they'd have gold."

"Oh, I see," Tate said. "Yes, I'll admit I hadn't thought of that. I hesitate to point this out, but isn't it possible we did find gold but decided not to mention it? A nice little bonus for us, eh?"

"Maybe," Bedford said. "But I don't figure it that way."

"Our honest faces?" Tate finished his whisky, then refilled the glass.

"It's always the ones who look honest I trust the least," Bedford said. "But, no, I've got other reasons."

The sheriff stood up from his desk and opened a gun cabinet behind him, revealing three Henry rifles and two shotguns, but the weapons weren't what he wanted to show them. There was a map of the Idaho territory tacked onto the inside of one of the cabinet doors. There were locations marked on the map, circled, running in a more or less straight line from Boise to a place called Nugget City, two days' ride north, nudging a little west.

"These circles mark all the places where a claim was jumped," Bedford said. "I don't think you stole any gold, Mr. Tate, because there weren't no gold to steal, at least not enough to bother with."

"I don't understand," Tate said. "I thought that was a big mining area."

"And ten years ago you'd have been right," the sheriff told him. "That whole area was hit first when the rush came. Nugget City is a gold town. Grew up almost overnight back in '61 or '62. Thousands of miners picked the area clean and there's not much to it now, just some old-timers here and there panning enough to keep themselves fed. There's still plenty of gold left in Idaho, but the vast majority of operations have moved east."

Bedford sighed, leaned against the wall, looking at the map like maybe this time there'd be answers there. "Gentlemen, you shot Hans Mueller and his pals dead, but the fact is there was nothing left in that area worth dying for."

"My experience is that criminal types are often not masterminds," Tate said. "Isn't it possible that Mueller was simply very bad at claim jumping?"

"It's possible," conceded Bedford. "But how long does it take a fella to wise up and realize he's not turning a buck?"

Carson pointed at the map. "Is there a road or something connecting up all those circles?"

"You've a keen eye, Mr. Stone," Bedford said. "You're wondering why all these claims are lined up like this south to north."

"I thought maybe they were on their way somewhere."

"Nope. There's no single road explaining why these were the claims they decided to jump." Bedford tapped the map to the left and right of the line of circles. "Plenty of claims east and west, but they didn't bother."

"Any idea why that might be?" Carson asked.

"I've got a notion it's not anything to do with gold at all," Bedford said. "But beyond that . . . well, hell. I don't know. Just seems like something strange is going on is all."

Carson asked, "Do you know the Porter Bend trading post?"

"Of course. Everybody does. It burned."

"Where's that on your map?"

Bedford tapped a spot north of Boise, between the third and fourth claim-jumping circles, right in line with all of them. "Why? You having notions of your own?"

Carson thought a moment, then shook his head. "Probably nothing."

"You said you might have a job for us," Tate reminded the sheriff.

"The mayor wasn't kidding when he said I was short of deputies," Bedford told them. "I can't spare anyone to look into this based on some vague hunch. To anyone looking in from the outside, it would just seem like claim jumping, and since you've put our claim jumper out of business, case closed. But I just *know* something else is going on. I'd like you two to look into it."

Carson and Tate exchanged looks.

"I know, I know," Bedford said. "You're not lawmen. Investigating this sort of thing isn't your business."

"A few Pinkertons might suit you better," Tate suggested.

"I reckon maybe you're right," Bedford said. "But we seem short of Pinkertons at the moment."

"Still," Carson said. "Not exactly our line of work."

Bedford sat at his desk and opened a drawer. He pulled out a wanted poster and set it on his desk, sliding it toward Carson and Tate, who leaned in to look at it. "This more your speed?"

Carson read the poster carefully.

CHESTER POTTS.
WANTED FOR MURDER AND HIGHWAY ROBBERY.

☛ Reward: 300 dollars. ☚

The illustration showed a hollow-cheeked man with beady eyes, a sparse mustache and beard. Sharp nose. He looked like a bad sort, but then again, nobody ever looked friendly on a wanted poster. Carson remembered when his own face had been on just such a one, the illustration exaggerating the shot-off part of one earlobe, his facial expression an unnatural scowl.

"I have it from a reliable source that old Chester was seen recently in Nugget City," Bedford said. "You've got to go past all them jumped claims anyway to get to him, so all I'm asking is that you keep your ears and eyes open and maybe ask a few questions along the way."

Tate looked at Carson. "What do you think?"

Carson sighed. "Can't hurt I guess, but we can't promise to find out anything."

"Do your best and I'll be obliged," Bedford said.

"First thing in the morning?" Tate asked.

Carson shook his head. "I've got some business tomorrow. Day after."

"It's kept this long, I guess it'll keep one more day," Bedford said. "Who knows? Maybe you'll get lucky and find out something useful."

Carson stood. "If there's nothing else, Sheriff . . ."

"There is one more thing, actually," Bedford said. "Hans Mueller had a brother. Taller, wider, meaner, and just as Bavarian."

Carson frowned. "I'm not going to like hearing this, am I?"

Bedford grinned. "Yeah. He'll be looking for you two. Just thought I'd warn you."

CHAPTER 6

They rode the wide-open lands just north of Boise.

Mary was comfortable in the saddle, leaning low as her borrowed mare galloped, the wind blowing her hair. There was a wild giddiness to the way she rode, grin wide, showing straight, white teeth. Glee in her eyes. It was almost as if she were free for the first time.

Maybe there was a certain freedom in simply riding a horse under a blue sky, Carson figured. For at least a few hours Mary had escaped the saloon world where she lived and worked. To Carson there was nothing better after a week or a month away, camping out in the cold and the rain, than a smoky saloon and a cold beer and the laughter and chatter of people relaxing.

It was different for Mary, of course. Her world was one far away from daylight and fresh air. She lived and worked in the nighttime world of tobacco smoke and stale beer, a world populated with sweaty, leering men, unshaven, unwashed, and whisky-breathed.

Mary raced to the top of the bluff and turned her horse to grin at Carson, who rode up a second later.

"You let me win," she said.

He returned the grin. "Not at all." *Maybe a little.*

"What a gorgeous day." She looked at the sky, then

back at Carson. "Thank you for taking me riding. I needed to get out."

He pulled his horse alongside hers. "Of course. I wanted to be with you. Just us. Away from all the noise."

Mary leaned over and grabbed a fistful of his shirt, pulling him toward her. She pressed her lips hard against him, the kiss going on and on. Carson felt himself flush.

She pulled away slowly, smiling. "When I thank a man, I mean it."

Carson groped for something to say. "Where'd you get the horse?"

"Mr. Dewey lent her to me."

Ray Dewey owned the Three Kings. Carson inferred, from the way the ladies talked, they could do a lot worse for a boss.

"Speaking of Mr. Dewey . . . well, there's some interesting news," Mary said.

"Oh?"

"He's looking to sell the Three Kings," Mary said. "Claims he's getting too old."

Carson felt a spark of hope. Maybe the notion of working for someone else would make her finally decide it was time for a change.

"So the other girls and I were talking, and . . . well, this might seem funny . . . but we've all been saving money. I think we can buy the Three Kings from him. Can you imagine that? Then we'd be *our own* bosses, working for ourselves."

Carson blinked at her. *What?*

Mary frowned. "You don't look excited."

Carson cleared his throat. "I've been thinking of making some changes, too. Putting down some roots instead of always chasing across the countryside."

Mary's face went blank. "That's part of your job, isn't it? You and Mr. Tate are a team."

"That's just for now," Carson said. "I've been helping Colby chase bounties for the money. I'm saving up. I'm figuring to get my own place, raise cattle. A place I can call my own." He looked at her pointedly. "A place a man could bring up a family."

The moment he said it, Carson knew he'd made a mistake.

Mary's eyes slowly widened. "I . . ."

"Never mind," Carson said. "I just wanted you to know what I was thinking. Just . . . I dunno . . . on the chance it matched up with anything you might be thinking."

"Carson, you're special," Mary began. "If you were like other men, I wouldn't even be here with you now. I wouldn't bother. But . . . I guess I'm not like other women either. I'm . . . well, I guess I'm fine with the way things are, fine with who I am. I thought you were fine with it, too."

"I'm fine with it. Really." But it wasn't true, he suddenly realized. And it never would be.

Carson forced a smile. "Let's not spoil our ride. If we circle back the long way, we can—"

He looked past her, stood in his stirrups to see better down the other side of the bluff.

"What is it?" Mary turned her horse and looked.

In the farmland below, a house burned, black smoke rising into the air. Men on horses. Two people ran from the house. The crack of pistol shots carried to the bluff.

"Stay here!" Carson spurred Jet and galloped toward the burning house.

He was vaguely aware Mary hadn't listened to him and was galloping right behind him.

As he moved closer, Carson could see what was happening. An old man lay on the ground bleeding, a young girl sobbing over him, a rifle in the dirt nearby. He'd obviously come out to face the marauders and it had cost him his life.

One of the men on horseback, a menacing figure in a black sombrero, pointed his pistol at the crying girl. He thumbed back the revolver's hammer.

Carson drew his Peacemaker and fired.

Their heads jerked around, the marauders seeing Carson riding down on them fast. They wheeled their horses and rode away at top speed. Carson reined in Jet near the old man and the girl. "Are you okay?"

She didn't look up, sobbing over the old man, fat tears falling.

"Mary, stay with her."

Carson didn't wait to see if Mary had heard him. He spurred Jet hard and took off after the marauders. They headed up a dirt road north. It occurred to Carson that he was one man chasing three. If they all turned around to face him, it might be a problem, but likely they thought the old man and the girl easy pickings and a stranger arriving had caught them off guard.

It didn't matter. Carson was angry. Three armed men against an old man and a girl. What was the sense of it? Robbery? Carson couldn't imagine what they could have gained from a simple farmer that was worth murder and arson.

The marauders turned off the road and headed for a stand of trees.

The one in the sombrero drew his revolver, twisted in the saddle, and fired. The shot whizzed past Carson's ear. He drew his Peacemaker and returned fire. White fluff exploded from the shoulder pad of the Mexican's jacket. A grazing shot, but enough to knock him off his balance.

The Mexican was tossed from the saddle as the marauders reached the trees. He landed hard but came up fast, a pistol in his hand. His two pals kept riding, the Mexican's riderless horse following after them.

The Mexican scrambled behind a tree.

Carson reined in Jet, dismounted, and scrambled behind another tree twenty feet away, shooing Jet out of the way. Now what? He'd chased after the men with no real notion of what he was going to do, acting on pure reflex.

"Gringo!" called the marauder from his hiding place. "Hey, gringo!"

Carson didn't answer. Waited.

"You poking your nose in where it don't belong, eh, amigo?" the bandito called. "I think that's a good way to get hurt. A good way to get dead."

Carson was only listening to keep track of where the guy was hiding. He needed to move so he could get an angle on him; otherwise, they'd be playing cat and mouse in the trees all day long. He spotted a fat-trunked tree that would provide good cover and give him a shot at the bandito, but it was pretty far. There was another tree at a halfway point. He took a deep breath, let it out slowly, readying himself to bolt.

Okay, when you go, go fast. One . . . two . . .

Carson sprang from his spot, running for all he was worth, arms pumping.

He reached the tree at the halfway point, just as a pistol shot split the air behind him. Bark flew up from the tree an inch from his head, just as he ducked around it. He counted to three again and ran. More gunshots whizzed through the branches over his head, and to Carson, it sounded like they were coming from a slightly different direction.

Damn. He's moving, too. But of course, why wouldn't he? The bandito wasn't just going to stand still and wait to be shot.

Carson reached the tree with the fat trunk and put his

back to it, panting hard, his right palm sweaty on the hilt of his Peacemaker. He'd made it to the spot he'd picked, but with the bandito on the move, too, Carson hadn't really accomplished anything. Again, he was wondering about his decision to ride after the marauders. If all three had decided to turn and face him, he'd be in an even worse jam than he was. Dumb luck the other two had kept going.

Luck always runs out. Next time, think before you do something stupid.

Carson glanced up. The limb over his head looked just thick enough to hold his weight. He reached and was able to barely brush his fingers against the bottom of it. He holstered the Peacemaker and jumped, grabbing the limb with two hands. He hauled himself up. The tree limb bent alarmingly but didn't break. The leaves were thick and green, not yet turning their fall colors. In six weeks he wouldn't have been able to hide this way. All the leaves would have fallen, the branches now bare. For now, there was enough thick, green cover to prevent the bandito from seeing what he was doing.

He shifted across to a sturdier branch and braced himself. Carson held his breath and listened, but the bandito wasn't talking anymore. He'd been trying to goad Carson, and when it didn't work, he probably figured out he was giving his position away and fell silent. Carson kept listening anyway, and soon heard what he was waiting for.

The crunch of boots on dry leaves and gravel, furtive at first, then faster. He glimpsed the Mexican coming through the foliage, crouched, six-gun in one fist. He came around the tree and stopped short when he saw Carson wasn't there.

Carson leaped from his perch.

The bandito looked up. His eyes shot wide, his mouth falling open to scream.

Carson hit hard and they both went down, the Mexican's

sombrero flying one way, Carson's hat the other. The bandito had the air knocked out of him but recovered quickly, and both of them rolled in the dust, pulling and gouging, each trying to gain an advantage. They rolled again, and Carson came out on top. He punched down, popping a good one across the bandito's jaw. It stunned him for a moment, and Carson took the opportunity to stagger to his feet and back up against the tree, chest heaving as he drew breath.

The bandito shook the bells from his head, got up to one knee, hand going to an empty holster. The man's pistol was twenty feet away in the dirt.

Carson pointed at him. "Just stay down, friend."

But the bandito's hand had gone to his boot, came out with a flash of steel.

Carson drew his Peacemaker and fired.

Blood splattered. The bandito's hands going to his chest as he grunted and fell back. He kicked once, then went still. Carson waited for a moment or two, but the other man didn't get up. He glanced to his left. A huge bowie knife stuck in the tree next to him.

Fast with a knife, Carson thought. *Just not on target.*

CHAPTER 7

Carson found Jet easily enough and then spent fifteen minutes chasing down the bandito's horse. He draped the dead Mexican over his own saddle, then mounted Jet and led the other horse back to the burning farmhouse. Black smoke rose into the air and must have been visible for miles.

When he got back, he found that Mary and the other girl had moved the old man closer to the barn and away from the searing heat of the fire. The girl sat with her head down, not moving, all cried out. The old man didn't move.

Carson dismounted twenty yards away as Mary approached.

"The old man's dead," Mary said. "Her grandfather."

Carson let a tired sigh leak out of him. "She have any kin close by? Is there someplace we can take her?"

"I don't know. I can ask."

"Do it. Be gentle with her."

Mary went back to the girl.

Carson inspected the bandito's horse and other possessions. There was a fine Winchester rifle in a leather saddle sheath, and he took it for himself. Call it the spoils of war. Anyway, the bandito wouldn't need it anymore. At Tate's goading, he'd been tempted to replace the Spencer with a new Winchester. Now he wouldn't have to. He hated that it was gold-plated with thorny etchings. Carson never fancied himself a show-off. Still, it was a top-quality Winchester.

He went through the dead man's pockets and found a folded piece of paper. He unfolded it and read.

A list of names. Numbers next to the names like dollar amounts. About ten names down the list, one of them had been crossed through.

He saw Mary returning, quickly refolded the paper, and stashed it in his shirt pocket.

"There's a cousin in town," Mary said.

"Okay, we'll take her." Carson looked toward the barn. "I'll see if there's a shovel. Ask her if there's a spot she likes to bury the old man. There's plenty of daylight left, so it's no trouble to . . ."

Carson trailed off when he saw the girl coming. She took slow, halting steps, and he wondered if she was in some kind of shock. She stopped within ten feet of the dead man draped across the horse and stood unblinking. Carson had a better look at her now. She was older than he'd thought at first, twenty or maybe a year or two more. A spray of freckles across the bridge of her nose, a heart-shaped face. Smudges around her red eyes from crying. Brown hair trending toward auburn in a tangled state of disarray.

In another time and place, Carson might have found her pretty in an uncomplicated sort of way. There was nothing to her like the glamour Mary and the other ladies at the Three Kings had, which was simultaneously not as good and a whole lot better. There was a gentleness to her, a sweetness, and Carson wished he'd met her at a church picnic, not here, not like this. At the moment she just seemed squashed and defeated.

"Is that the one?" she asked.

It took Carson a moment to realize she meant the man who'd shot her grandfather. "Yes. The other two got away."

She went tense all of a sudden, slender, pale hands making fists of themselves, her mouth hardening to a tight line. Carson expected her to strike the corpse, or spit on it, or scream at it, but in the next moment she went limp again, as if the effort for anger was beyond her.

"If there's a shovel in the barn, I can bury your grandfather. Then we can take you to town," Carson said. "Is there a particular place you'd like to lay him to rest?"

She sighed, and it took her a moment to find the energy to speak. "There's a tree."

There was a willow with low-hanging branches about forty yards behind the barn. It stood alone, the mountains spread out in the distance behind it. There were already two grave markers there. Carson dug a third grave and they laid the old man to rest in a horse blanket. They gave the girl a moment alone to say her own goodbyes.

Carson still didn't know her name.

He went back to the barn to hitch the family's single horse, a tired gelding, to an old but well-kept buckboard and brought it out of the barn. He tied Jet and the dead man's horse to the back of it, finishing just as Mary walked up to him.

"I'll take her back on this," Carson said. "I don't know if she's fit to ride or not. Do me a favor, would you? Ride ahead and tell the sheriff what's happened. Tell him I'm coming."

Mary's eyes shifted to the girl still standing under the willow. Hesitated.

"Is that okay?" Carson asked.

"Of course." Mary kissed him on the cheek. "I'll ask the sheriff to send somebody for her cousin."

She climbed onto her horse and left at a trot. Carson

watched her go until she was up over the bluff and gone. He looked back toward the willow. The girl hadn't moved. He sighed and walked back toward her, not hurrying. He didn't want to rush her, but he didn't want to linger.

Carson stood next to her, hands clasped in front of him, not speaking.

She looked up from the grave. "Just another minute."

"It's okay."

A few seconds later she turned away and Carson followed. They situated themselves on the buckboard and in the next minute were on their way.

"Who were the other two graves?" Carson asked.

"My parents."

"I'm sorry. What happened to them?"

"Is it okay if we don't talk?"

"Okay."

The buckboard ate up the miles slowly but surely, and the last of the daylight fled the world as they entered Boise, and Carson reined in the horse, pulling the wagon in front of the sheriff's office. Sheriff Bedford and Colby Tate both waited.

Bedford took off his hat, holding out his other hand to help the girl down from the buckboard. "Hello, Claire. I'm so sorry about Amos."

The girl's name was Claire, Carson noted. He realized he'd never thought to ask.

"Go on and wait in my office," Bedford told her. "I've sent a deputy for Sally Anne and Pastor Clarke."

That was the cousin, Carson supposed. Sally Anne.

Claire headed for the front door, paused, and looked back. "I didn't catch your name, mister."

"Carson Stone."

"Thank you for your help, Mr. Stone. I apologize if I was

rude. My folks both got the fever back in '73. We buried them a week apart."

"No apologizes needed, ma'am. I'm sorry about your folks. And about your grandpa."

She nodded, then turned slowly and went into the sheriff's office.

"Well, then." Tate circled behind the buckboard and took a look at the dead man. "Maybe we'll get lucky. If there's paper on the fellow, you might have earned yourself a few extra dollars."

"I didn't think of that," Carson said. "That's not why I did it."

"Perhaps not," Tate said. "Still, it would be a nice surprise."

"If we can find out who he is, I'll let you know," Bedford said. "Probably best if you tell me the whole thing from the beginning."

Carson related the story.

"Doesn't make sense," Bedford said. "Potato farmers. What would robbers even want from them?"

Carson thought about it, then plucked the folded sheet of paper from his pocket with two fingers. "What's Claire and Amos's last name?"

"Grainger."

Carson unfolded the paper. He found the name about halfway down. *Amos Grainger—50 dollars*. Carson's eyes came back up to the crossed-out name. *Casper Jansen*. Carson asked Bedford if he knew the name.

"Old Dutch Casper? Sure. Lives with an Indian woman along the Black River between here and Nugget City. He runs the ferry."

Carson handed the list to Bedford and explained how he'd come by it. "Casper Jansen's name is crossed out.

Maybe those three men visited him before they found Amos Grainger. Maybe Old Dutch Casper met the same fate."

Bedford shook his head. "Jesus wept. Is that what a man's life is worth? Fifty dollars? What did Amos Grainger ever do to anybody? Or Casper, for that matter. It's got to mean something."

"That map on the inside of your gun cabinet showing the jumped claims," Carson said. "Where's Jansen's ferry on that map?"

"I don't even have to look," Bedford said. "Yeah, it's right in line. You getting some kind of notion?"

"Couldn't even guess," Carson admitted. "I just don't believe in coincidences is all."

Bedford blew out a sigh and scratched a spot behind his ear. "You fellas still of a mind to go after that bounty on Chester Potts?"

"I intend to," Tate said, then looked at Carson.

A pause, then Carson nodded. "I reckon so."

"Then you've got to cross the river at some point anyway," Bedford said. "I'd consider it a personal favor if you looked in on Old Dutch."

"No trouble," Tate said. "If he's alive, we'll take the ferry. If he's not . . . well, then we'll know."

"First thing in the morning." *I'll see Mary tonight and say goodbye*, Carson thought.

"Obliged to you." Bedford's attention went back to the list of names. "I'll need to investigate this, talk to the mayor. Even the governor might need to hear . . . oh, hell."

"What's wrong?" Carson asked.

Bedford looked up. His face had gone grim. "My name's on this list."

CHAPTER 8

Bill Cartwright stood at his office window, looking out across the many acres of his huge ranch. A world out there for the taking. He was quite aware he had an inflated sense of himself, and just as confident that this view of who he was and his place in the world was perfectly justified. Truly powerful men knew how powerful they were and were even more acutely aware how much more powerful they could be if only they had the will to do what had to be done.

This morning's appointment was Cartwright's first opportunity of the day to demonstrate that he did, indeed, have the willpower to do what needed to be done.

A light knock at the door, which opened immediately. Doyle stepped in. "He's here."

"Show him in," Cartwright said. "And bring coffee."

"Yes, sir."

A second later Doyle ushered in another man, young, in his late twenties but with an air of authority. He wore an expensive gray suit. Well-trimmed mustache and sideburns. He took off his hat as he entered and offered his hand to Cartwright.

Cartwright shook it. "Thanks for meeting again, Edward."

Edward Vance was a railroad man. He'd never laid a rail

or driven a single spike and had no idea about the workings of a locomotive engine, but that wasn't the point. He helped make big decisions, and one of those big decisions could mean a fortune to Cartwright. He'd met the man by chance in a hotel lobby in Chicago, and over an extravagantly expensive bottle of brandy, Vance had explained his position with the railroad company and the work ahead of him. Cartwright had immediately realized the opportunity in front of him and, over the next few months, had cultivated his relationship with the railroad man. Most men had at least a spark of greed in them and Vance was no different.

"My pleasure, Mr. Cartwright," Vance said. "It's understandable you'd want a progress report."

"First make yourself comfortable." Cartwright gestured to the chair on the other side of his desk. "I took the liberty of ordering in some coffee."

As if on cue, Doyle entered the room with a silver tray, a large coffeepot, and three porcelain cups. He set the tray on the edge of the desk.

"Thanks, Doyle. I think we can help ourselves from here."

With a curt nod, Doyle left the room.

Cartwright looked at Vance. "Cream or sugar?"

"Black is fine."

"That's how I take it, too."

Cartwright filled two cups, handed one to Vance, and then eased himself into the plush chair on the other side of the desk. He closed his eyes and inhaled deeply. He'd developed a keen appreciation for fine things, including imported coffee.

Vance sipped his coffee and said, "So, the first thing you'll probably want to know is that we've narrowed the new line to one of two possible—"

Cartwright held up a hand to forestall Vance. "If you'll

indulge me, I'd like to wait. Another party will be joining us shortly."

Vance raised an eyebrow. "Oh?"

"It'll just be a minute." Cartwright sipped coffee.

Vance sipped, too.

The next minute she walked in. Kate closed the door behind her, sauntered across the room, and filled the remaining cup with coffee. She stirred in a single spoonful of sugar, pulled a chair around to the side of Cartwright's desk, and sat. She propped her boots up on the corner and said, "Sorry I'm late."

Vance raised an eyebrow. "I don't believe I've had the pleasure."

"That's Kate," Cartwright said. "She's my special assistant. With special skills."

"I see," Vance said stoically. "It's just that our business is somewhat . . . confidential."

"When you talk to Kate, you talk to me," Cartwright said. "Her eyes and ears are my eyes and ears. Certain minor obstacles have arisen to hinder our business venture. Kate's job is to remove those obstacles as quietly and as efficiently as possible. To that end, she needs to hear whatever you have to say."

Kate said nothing. A mischievous smile briefly quirked her lips before she took her next sip of coffee.

Cartwright smiled, too, but immediately erased it from his face. He didn't want Vance to think he wasn't taking the situation seriously. He'd meant what he'd said about Kate. They'd spent a pleasant evening together—a *very* pleasant evening—and Cartwright had observed she was a sharp, talented, intriguing woman. There was more to her than her ability to cross names off a list. The extent of her employment with Cartwright remained to be seen, but she was an asset, and he wanted her by his side.

Vance took a moment to digest what he'd heard, then

said, "Very well. I'll yield to your good judgment in this matter."

"You were about to say something about the new line," Cartwright prompted.

Vance nodded, sipping his own coffee. "For the sake of context, I'll back up a bit. To the south, a branch line has been completed right up to the Idaho Territory line. Where it goes from there is something that's currently being decided, and when we began the process, there were five or six choices. I'm the head man for the project, and they'll likely make a final decision almost exclusively on my recommendation. I've crisscrossed the region numerous times, evaluating the benefits of each option, and so far we've eliminated all but two."

Kate set her empty coffee cup on the desk. "Mr. Cartwright has told me some of this already. Obviously one choice benefits Mr. Cartwright more than the other. Why not skip right to that choice and get on with it?"

"The men I work for are not fools," Vance said. "One doesn't connect two coasts across a vast expanse without learning a thing or two. They would certainly notice if I weren't doing my due diligence. They might not suspect corruption, but they know incompetence when they see it. The best way to help Mr. Cartwright in his endeavors is simply to do my job. I've carefully and legitimately eliminated most of the other routes and nobody is suspicious about the way I've done it."

"The first route left to consider goes north and into Montana. And eventually into Canada, I would imagine," Cartwright speculated. "The final option is the one that benefits me, the route that goes through Boise, up past Nugget City, until it angles west toward Oregon and Washington."

"The coasts are a big draw for the western route," Vance said. "Ports and railways to move imported products are a natural marriage. So Union Pacific already have a good reason to decide in favor of that route. One more good reason would tip the balance in favor of our preference."

"And that reason would be?" Kate asked.

Vance grinned. "That we make it so easy for them, they'd be stupid to choose otherwise."

"That's where you come in," Cartwright told Kate. "You and the other . . . uh . . . independent builders. Yes, let's call them that."

Vance cleared his throat and shifted uncomfortably in his chair. "The less I know about your efforts in this area the better, but let me explain it like this. The railroad will either need to buy land or pay for rights-of-way. If we do this two or three times and then word gets out, the price goes up as we move farther down the line. Once they start laying track, they won't want to stop until the job is done." A shrug. "What I need to be able to do is tell them something to ease these concerns."

Cartwright laughed. "You came in here to give me a progress report, but what I think you really want is for *me* to give *you* a progress report." He turned to Kate. "Our dear Mr. Vance wants to be able to tell his bosses at the Union Pacific Railroad that they can secure all the rights-of-way they need between Boise and Nugget City in a single pen stroke."

"That's all?" Kate asked. "Boise to Nugget City?"

"It's enough," Vance said. "The territory beyond that is more sparsely populated, easier to secure, and there are numerous options going west. If we can give them Nugget City, they'll take it and figure out the rest later."

"Everything you said is being arranged even as we speak," Cartwright said.

"But when?"

Cartwright frowned. "As soon as possible."

Vance spread his hands, as if to say *sorry, but this can't be helped*. "My superiors are eager to bring this matter to a close so they can move forward. I can only stall them so long."

"How long?"

"A week. Ten days at most."

Cartwright's mouth tightened, the muscle in his jaw working. He'd anticipated that time was of the essence, which was why he'd taken the extreme measure of hiring the assassins, but he hadn't realized things were coming to a head quite so quickly. "It's being handled. The properties in question are . . . being acquired." Cartwright stood to indicate the meeting was at an end. "If there's nothing else . . ."

Vance shifted in his chair again. He didn't stand.

"Is there something more?"

"I've put in a good bit of effort on your behalf," Vance said. "At considerable risk to myself. I just want to make sure we're thinking alike in terms of . . . my compensation."

"Fifty thousand dollars. However . . ." Cartwright leaned forward, fixed Vance with an iron stare, ". . . not a penny until it's all signed and legal."

"I take it you have lawyers who can draw up the appropriate paperwork. It will facilitate matters if you do. Union Pacific's legal team are notoriously slow about such things."

"Fine. Fine," Cartwright said. "I'll have my people do it. It's not an issue."

Vance stood and buttoned his jacket. "In that case, I believe I've taken up enough of your time. I'll be in touch."

Vance gave Cartwright and Kate each a curt nod and then left the office.

Cartwright refilled his coffee cup, replaying the conversation with Vance in his mind, wondering if he'd missed anything.

"Fifty thousand is rather a lot of money," Kate said.

"I fully expect a return on my investment."

"You're paying him a lot more than you're paying us to do your killing for you," she said.

He laughed. There was the hint of a challenge in her voice, but if she expected him to be concerned, she didn't know him at all. "Simple supply and demand, my dear. Vance is the only one in a position to help me make this scheme work. Hired killers, on the other hand, are plentiful."

"Well." A mischievous smile worked across her face. "Now I feel cheap."

"I do wonder why you're not out there earning your keep."

"A lot of names on that list for fifty or a hundred dollars apiece," she said. "That's a lot of chasing around for petty cash."

"You've something else in mind?"

Kate took a piece of paper from her jacket pocket and unfolded it. The death list, the names of all the men Cartwright wanted killed. "You've got dollar amounts next to each name . . . except one."

"I was wondering if anyone would notice."

"Why?"

Cartwright grinned at her, not quite leering but close. "In the short time I've enjoyed your company, you've struck me as an intelligent woman. Let's put that intelligence to the test. You tell me why."

Kate steepled her hands under her chin. "I asked around. The man's a sheriff."

"You've done your homework. Go on."

"He doesn't own any property you want, does he?" Kate said.

"Not a single acre."

"Then he's a target because he's sheriff," Kate said. "My guess is that he's asking awkward questions."

"As smart as you are beautiful."

"Have any of your other killers tried for him yet?" she asked.

Cartwright turned to the door and shouted, "Doyle!"

The assistant scurried into the room a second later. "Sir?"

"A couple of our independent builders stopped by first thing this morning, yes?" Cartwright asked. "Those two brothers?"

"That's correct, sir," Doyle said. "They were looking for payment. Apparently, they'd attended to a couple of minor items on the to-do list you'd provided them. You'd told me you didn't want to be bothered with the details, so I paid them out of petty cash."

"Not our *special* item," Cartwright said. "Just minor ones."

"Very minor, sir."

"Thank you, Doyle. That'll be all."

Doyle nodded and left.

"Nobody's going to kill a lawman when they don't even know what it pays," Kate said. "My guess is you already figured that. You've been waiting for somebody like me to come along and mention it."

Cartwright grinned. "And why on Earth would I do that?"

"Because then you'll know who's smart and who's dumb," Kate said. "I'm smart."

"Oh? Tell me something smart, then."

"Are you attached to those two brothers?"

"Not especially."

"Give them to me," Kate said. "And I'll take care of the sheriff. Maybe."

"Maybe?"

"We haven't talked price," she said. "And my guess is that killing a lawman is going to draw unwanted attention. This isn't like shooting some farmer or hermit." She explained her plan.

Cartwright nodded as he listened to her explain. "That could work."

"Except you still haven't said how much."

"Five thousand dollars," he told her. "But I suppose you'll have to split it with the brothers."

"I won't be splitting it with anyone," she said. "Not if things go as planned."

Cartwright grinned. "You are a ruthless little thing, aren't you?"

She returned the grin. "I can't imagine you object."

"Of course not. It's one of your many endearing qualities, Kate." Cartwright opened his top desk drawer and took out a wanted poster, slid it across the desk toward her. "Or should I call you Lady Pain?"

The derringer fell from her sleeve and was in her hand in an eyeblink.

Cartwright was already across the desk, grabbing her wrist, overpowering her, pointing the little pistol at the ceiling. "That was a good trick . . . once."

Her eyes flared rage at him.

He laughed. "What do you think? That I want the reward?"

They both glanced at the wanted poster. One thousand dollars for Katherine "Kat" Payne, also known as "Lady Pain." For murder.

"What's a thousand dollars to a man like me?" Cartwright asked. "You're worth more to me than the money. A woman like you."

He pulled her to him and kissed her hard. Kat resisted, but only for a moment. Her arms went around him and she kissed back with equal ferocity.

CHAPTER 9

They rode out from Boise at sunrise, heading north. Carson had said his goodbyes to Mary the night before. She'd seemed a little cool to him, maybe put off that he was leaving again so soon, but she'd warmed eventually. He told her he'd be back soon but didn't really know if it was true.

Carson patted the list in his shirt pocket, making sure it was still there. Sheriff Bedford had made a copy for him.

"When you're a lawman, it just figures there's folks out there gunning for you," Bedford had said. "But it's another thing altogether to actually see it in writing."

Carson had admired the way Bedford had taken it all in stride. Carson would have been a lot more nervous about it. Maybe Bedford was worried and just wasn't letting it show. The sheriff made it clear he'd be looking over his shoulder a lot more often, but he couldn't just run away and hide in a hole. He was a lawman with a job to do.

And Carson and Tate had their own errands to attend to. The sun climbed higher in the sky, warming the day, although not fast enough for Carson's liking. God help him if he were still in Idaho come December or January.

Except Mary's here. Would she come with me someplace warmer? Is it worth freezing my backside off to stay here with her?

"A penny for your thoughts." Colby Tate pulled his horse alongside Carson's.

Carson forced a smile. "Is that all they're worth?"

Tate shrugged. "Well, a penny was worth quite a bit more when Sir Thomas More said it."

"Then I suppose I'd tell old Tom More I'm wondering what we've gotten ourselves mixed up in," Carson said. "If I was Sheriff Bedford, I'd be packing my bags."

Tate laughed.

"Don't see what's so funny."

"You, my friend, and all your talk of packing bags," Tate said. "Sound advice for anyone else, but you'd never take it."

"Oh?"

"You're the conscience of our little duo," Tate explained. "Don't get me wrong. I think I'm a decent sort of fellow, but I'm looking out for me. If Sheriff Bedford's problems start looking as if they're about to become *my* problems, I'm on the next train out. But that's not you, Carson. You'd stay and face whatever it was needed to be faced. You're too good for your own good."

"You're making me out like some kind of hero," Carson said. "I'm not."

"Of course you wouldn't think so," Tate replied. "That would spoil it."

Carson frowned and changed the subject. "If we pushed hard, we could probably get to Dutch Casper's place by nightfall, but I don't want to have to find the place in the dark. And I'd prefer not to wear down the horses." Jet had stamina and could ride hard for a long time, but better to save that strength for an emergency. "I say we stop early, have a proper supper, and then it'll be an easy ride in the morning."

"Sounds reasonable to me," Tate said.

Carson picked a good spot in a copse of trees atop a

modest rise within sight of the road. They built a fire and gathered lots of extra wood. Carson expected the temperature to dip. *Just don't snow. That's all I ask. No snow.*

Tate sat on his saddle, methodically cleaning his guns. Carson cooked a pot of beans with a chunk of bacon in them and made biscuits. They ate in companionable silence, forgoing coffee in favor of a few slugs of whisky from Tate's bottle. Then Carson cleaned his guns.

"I see you finally replaced your Winchester," Tate said. "A bit flashy."

"Took it off that bandito," Carson said. "Figured he didn't need it no more."

He looked it over. It was a good rifle, maybe even better than the one he'd lost last year. Too bad it looked so stupid.

Thinking about it took him back. He'd had a price on his head, and he and Tate had thrown in with a woman bounty hunter, a fiery redhead who had tried to kill him. He was embarrassed to admit to himself he'd been falling for her. Might as well fall for a rattlesnake. Not for the first time, Carson questioned his judgment with women, and that made him think of Mary.

And then he thought about Claire Grainger. He hadn't meant to. Her sweet face had popped into his head unbidden. Where was a man like Carson supposed to meet a woman like her? Carson chased after bounties with Tate, slept on the ground every night or in a different hotel, a different town. And then, when he did have some free time, he spent it holding down a chair in some dank saloon.

"You seem pensive," Tate said.

"Don't know what that means."

"Deep in thought about serious matters."

Carson blew out a sigh. "Guess I'm a bit pensive, then. Mostly just tired. Let's get some shut-eye. Tomorrow we'll see if Dutch Casper is alive or not."

Carson lay his head on his saddle and pulled his blanket up to his chin. He closed his eyes and was immediately drawn in to deep, dark sleep.

Morning came early and cold. They gulped bitter, black coffee and saddled up. After riding for an hour they left the road, angling east straight for the Black River. They only had Bedford's vague directions to guide them to Casper's ferry, so they let the gentle downward slope of the land take them on the path of least resistance. Soon enough they spotted wagon-wheel grooves here and there in the ground; not quite a road, but clearly others had traveled this way.

An hour later they spotted the river curving lazily below them.

"Smoke." Tate pointed west. "A chimney maybe, or a cookfire. Not too far."

"We'll go straight down to the river, then follow it toward the smoke," Carson suggested. "It'll either be the ferry crossing or somebody who can direct us."

They hit the river, turned west, and found it ten minutes later. Both the ferry and the landing had been hewn from local timber, rough and sturdy. Thick ropes stretched across to another landing on the far bank, a system to pull the ferry back and forth.

A small shack sat fifty yards up the bank. A small pen next to the shack with a half-dozen pigs. Smoke came from the chimney. They dismounted and walked their horses toward the shack, taking it slowly so as not to alarm anyone within.

They saw movement in the front window, and a moment later the front door creaked open. An old Indian woman emerged and walked toward them, taking small steps. She was small and dark-skinned, face deeply lined. Her hair hung in a long braid, jet black save for a single white streak that started a few inches above her left ear and went all the way back.

"Good morning, ma'am," Carson said. "My name's Stone. This is my partner, Tate. I take it you're Casper Jansen's wife."

The woman nodded, her mouth a tight line across her face.

"Sheriff Bedford down in Boise asked us to look in on him," Carson said. "Can you tell us where he is?"

She turned slowly, pointing through a stand of evergreens. "In the meadow."

The meadow on the other side of the trees wasn't a bad place for a grave, Carson thought. He could tell it was freshly dug, a rough, wooden cross marking Dutch Casper Jansen's final resting place.

Dutch Casper's widow was an Indian named Mary *White Dove*. Her English wasn't the best, but good enough to get the story. She'd been out checking traps when it happened. She returned to find the door of the shack standing open, her husband bleeding on the floor, two bullet holes in his chest. She had no idea why someone would murder him, and she hadn't seen who'd done it. She delivered her tale in a stoic, lifeless monotone.

Carson and Tate expressed their sympathies. Sally charged them each a nickel to ferry them across the Black River. The Indian woman worked the ropes with expertise and refused any offer of help.

Ten minutes later, Carson and Tate were again on their horses heading north.

"What do you think a ferry like that earns in a year?" Tate wondered.

"Couldn't say," Carson admitted. "Nickels add up, I reckon, but I'm guessing Jansen set up that ferry at the height of the boom, when there was a lot more traffic through the area."

"Gold miners on the way to Nugget City."

Carson nodded. "Yep. Right where we're headed now."

"Remind me who Bedford said we should talk to."

"Sheriff there's a man named Tad Rawlings. Bedford said be careful around him."

Tate frowned. "What's that supposed to mean?"

"Guess we're going to find out."

CHAPTER 10

There was still plenty of daylight left when they rode into Nugget City.

If Carson squinted just right, he thought he could see the town Nugget City used to be, a bustling place, the streets crowded with gold miners looking to strike it rich and streets lined with hotels, saloons, brothels, and merchants, all trying to get a piece of each miner's new wealth. The place looked tired now. A number of storefronts were boarded up, and people shuffled tiredly up and down the wooden sidewalks. The whole place looked like it could use a fresh coat of paint. An old-timer with a wild beard and the most battered hat Carson had ever seen led a mule past them on the way out of town as Carson and Tate headed in. The town had a defeated feel to it, and Carson wondered why the remaining citizens didn't call it a day and seek greener pastures. He said as much to Tate.

"A hard choice, I imagine," Tate said. "To build something from the ground up, to add calluses on top of calluses, sawing lumber and hammering nails. Then one day it's over. The dream is dead. Do you hang on and scratch out a living, a nickel at a time for a ferry ride? Or start over somewhere else with no guarantee it will work out there either? Daunting to consider."

Carson supposed that was right.

They found the sheriff's office at the far end of Main Street and the sheriff himself sitting on a chair out front, leaned back, boots up on a railing. He smoked a cigar the size of a giant redwood. A shiny tin star on his vest.

Carson climbed down from Jet. "Afternoon. You're Rawlings?"

"Who's asking?" he said around the cigar, smoke billowing like a belch from hell.

Tate dismounted and handed the sheriff a packet of papers, his credentials as a bounty hunter, along with the wanted poster for Chester Potts. "Sheriff Bedford down in Boise said it would be polite to check in with you." Tate introduced himself and Carson.

"Polite, huh?" Rawlings gave Tate's papers the once-over in no particular hurry, still puffing his cigar and leaning back in the chair. "So you boys want to come into Tad Rawlings's town and shoot people for money, is that it?"

"Unless Potts would prefer to come quietly."

"Uh-huh. And how often does that happen?'

"Sadly, not as often as it should," Tate admitted.

"I appreciate your paying me a polite visit." Rawlings stood. He was tall, a big belly and a barrel chest adding to an imposing presence. "If you know what's good for you, you'll go on being polite. I don't tolerate trouble in my town. Your business is Potts and that's all. Behave yourself and there's no need for us to have words again."

"I understand," Tate said. "I don't suppose you'd happen to know where Chester Potts is keeping himself these days."

"I do not." *Puff-puff.*

"We won't take any more of your time, then." Tate started to turn away.

"Just one more thing, Sheriff," Carson said.

Rawlings turned his scowl toward Carson.

"Somebody murdered Dutch Casper Jansen," Carson told the sheriff. "We stopped in on Sally White Dove on the way here."

Rawlings digested the information and said, "Sorry to hear that. Casper wasn't a bad fella. Next time I'm in the vicinity, I'll have to look in on Sally."

Carson frowned. "Man's been killed. Don't you want to send someone out to investigate?"

Rawlings took the cigar out of his mouth and leaned in to squint down at Carson with hard eyes. "I must be hearing things. You're not really telling Tad Rawlings how to go about law and order in his own town, are you?"

Carson returned the sheriff's gaze, unflinching.

Tate took Carson by the elbow. "Come on. There's a saloon down here with our names on it. You have a good afternoon, Sheriff."

They led their horses down the street, and Tate said, "My experience is that it seldom pays to annoy the local constabulary."

Carson sighed. "I reckon you're right. Still, the man should do his job."

"Let's just worry about doing ours." Tate nodded at the saloon ahead. "A shot of whisky and showing Chester's wanted poster to the barkeep is a good way to start. Two birds with one stone and all that."

Carson felt his irritation evaporate two seconds after he and Tate set foot in the saloon. There were only a few other patrons, scattered at tables here and there. No piano player tickling ivories at the battered upright in the corner. He didn't see any shady ladies working the room, but there were stairs along one side, and Carson imagined they'd come down later when the crowd got bigger. There was a whole lot of nothing going on, but the place had that saloon smell, that dim saloon interior, warmed slightly by lanterns hanging in a circular chandelier overhead. The place was called the Lucky Strike, and Carson figured every gold rush town probably had a saloon called something like that.

"Bar or table?" Carson asked.

"Let's start at the bar," Tate said. "I want to show off our wanted poster. The bartender in a place like this usually sees everyone who comes and goes."

They bellied up to the bar, and the bartender came down to meet them, a skeletal man with sunken cheeks and thinning red hair. "Pour you boys a drink?"

"A shot and a beer," Tate said.

Carson nodded. "Same."

The bartender returned with the drinks, and Tate set the wanted poster on the bar. "Have you seen this gentleman, perchance?"

The bartender glanced at the poster and shook his head. "Nope." He started to move away again.

"Can you take a closer look, please, and perhaps read the description?" Tate suggested. "The illustrations often don't do the subject justice. Also, these criminal types sometimes go under a different name."

The bartender frowned, an annoyed noise coming from deep in his throat, but he paused and took a closer look at the poster. "Sorry, friend."

"Well, thanks for your time anyway." Tate paid him for the whisky and beer.

Carson and Tate carried their drinks to a table in the far corner and plopped down.

Tate lifted his shot glass. "Man being reasonable must get drunk. The best of life is but intoxication." He tossed the hooch down his throat.

Carson drank his, too. "That more Shakespeare?"

"Lord Byron. I forget how the rest of it goes."

The beers they sipped more slowly. They sat without

talking, letting the shot of whisky find its way to all the right places, seeping into sore bones and soothing muscles. Carson was a young man and fit, but sleeping on the ground and so much time in the saddle took its toll. As a ranch hand, he'd worked hard all day, but somehow, flopping into a proper bed at the end of it made it okay.

Carson nursed his beer, and from the corner of his eye kept track of a man sitting at the far end of the bar for the simple reason that the man had been watching Carson and Tate with interest. A moment later, the man tossed back the rest of his drink, wiped his mouth on the back of his hand, stood, and came toward Carson's table.

"Company coming to say hello," Carson said in a low voice.

"Anyone I need to worry about?" Tate asked.

Carson figured probably not. The man wasn't wearing a gun—not openly anyway—and there was nothing in the fellow's demeanor to suggest hostility. His gray-striped suit was well-tailored and had once been expensive, but the closer the man came, the more Carson could see it was going a bit tattered. There was an empty space in the man's tiepin, which possibly had held a gem or a pearl once upon a time.

"Looks like a feller fallen on hard times," Carson said. "I don't think he wants trouble."

A moment later, the slicker stood at Carson's table, hat in hand. His mustache was so thin, it looked drawn on, his smile so wide, it threatened to crack the man's face in two.

"Gentlemen, if I'm not disturbing you, I'd like to take this opportunity to introduce myself," he said. "My name is Benson Cassidy."

He paused, clearly waiting for Carson and Tate to give their names, which they did.

"A pleasure to make both of your acquaintances," he said.

"From back East, unless my ears deceive me," Tate said. "Do I detect hints of Philadelphia in your accent, sir?"

"Well done, sir," Cassidy said. "And do I hear Boston?"

"Cambridge, to be specific."

Cassidy nodded. "Of course."

"What can we do for you, Mr. Cassidy?" Carson asked, eager to move past the where-ya-from part of the conversation.

"Actually, I thought we might discuss what *I* could do for *you*," Cassidy said.

Tate and Carson exchanged looks. Too many bad ideas started the same way.

"It's my understanding that you gentlemen are looking for someone," Cassidy said. "Although I hail from back East, I've made Nugget City my home for a number of years now. I have sharp eyes and keen ears and a memory like a steel trap. Would it be possible to cast my eyes upon the wanted poster you showed our friendly barkeep?"

Tate and Carson exchanged another look. Carson shrugged. *Can't hurt.*

Tate showed Cassidy the poster.

Cassidy wrinkled his nose, squinting as he read. "My goodness. Quite the scalawag, isn't he? This countenance does look familiar . . . vaguely."

"If you can remember where you might have seen him, it would help," Carson said. "We'd be grateful."

"How grateful?"

"Depends on how well you remember," Carson said.

"I see." Cassidy licked his lips nervously. "I feel certain I've seen this man around. For a small retainer, I can ferret out where this gentleman might—"

Carson held up a hand. Cassidy stopped talking.

"Mr. Cassidy, I don't mean to be rude, but I can save us

some time," Carson said. "There's no version of this where you leave this saloon with our money unless you've given us something for it first. If you think you can dig up some useful information, go dig it up and come back and we'll talk price."

Cassidy blinked. Then he turned to Tate.

"Don't look at me, old sport. I'm just the muscle," Tate said. "He's the brains."

Cassidy licked his lips again, his eyes bouncing between Carson and Tate. His cool demeanor returned a second later, and he smiled as if delighted by the opportunity. "I understand completely, gentlemen. Very prudent. I beg just a bit of patience. I feel with a bit of ingenuity, I can bring you something useful."

"Sounds good," Carson said. "We'll be around. Probably have another beer, then get rooms in one of the local hotels."

"Gentlemen, I look forward to doing business with you." Cassidy snugged his hat on his head and exited the Lucky Strike.

"Quite the character," Tate said. "Doesn't exactly inspire trust, does he?"

"I trust him as far as I can throw him." Carson stood. "Another beer?"

"Please."

Carson fetched two more mugs of beer, and the two men chatted another hour, mostly about how to go about snooping around for Chester Potts come morning. Carson said he didn't have much faith in Cassidy coming up with anything useful.

"Oh, I don't know," Tate said. "Those oily types always seem to find a way to keep their heads above water. He smells an easy dollar, I think."

"We'd better get hotel rooms before it gets too late," Carson suggested.

"Agreed."

Carson headed for the exit, Tate right behind him.

He pushed his way through the swinging doors into the waning light of the day. A blur and a grunt and Carson felt something slam into his face, the sharp smack of flesh on flesh. Stars exploded in front of his eyes, and the world spun. He felt his feet go out from under him and Carson hit the wooden sidewalk hard.

CHAPTER 11

The barber looked up at the man standing in his shop door. "Help you, sir?"

He was short and slight and held his bowler hat to his chest, shifting from one foot to the other, as if hesitant to trouble anyone. "Sorry. I don't have an appointment."

The barber chuckled. He was a genial, good-tempered fellow named Ezra Snopes, and the idea that anyone would need an appointment genuinely amused him. "Not at all, sir, not at all. Happy to serve you today. Please have a seat." He gestured to the barber's chair, an expensive piece of equipment he was absurdly proud of, brought all the way from Chicago. It was comfortable, reclined, and the height could be adjusted.

The newcomer eased into the chair, and Snopes turned him toward the mirror. "What can we do for you, sir? Hot towel treatment? A shave?"

"Just a haircut, please. I'm afraid it's gone a bit thin up there, but I'd like it off my ears and collar."

"Absolutely, sir. Nice and neat. We'll smarten you up in a jiffy. Lean forward and I'll take your jacket, if you don't mind. I can hang it up out of the way with your hat."

Snopes took the man's jacket. It was from a plain brown suit, nothing ostentatious, but the tailoring was good. He hung the jacket along with the bowler on pegs across the room. He draped the apron over the customer and tied it in the back, then picked up comb and scissors and went to work.

"Couldn't help but notice your accent, sir." Snopes combed the hair down over the man's left ear and began to trim. "You wouldn't be from England at all, would you?"

"I suppose I must stick out a bit," he said. "Yes, from London. I've been over here a few years, but I still sound like old Blighty."

"Idaho's a long way from London," Snopes said. "What brings you all this way, if you don't mind my asking?"

"I don't mind at all, but it's rather a long story. I could ask the same of you. How does a barber earn a living in a place this small and remote?"

The man had a point, Snopes thought. Ponderosa Crossing consisted of six buildings—soon to be seven—and a population of less than sixty people if the farmers in the surrounding area were included. Snopes had been heading for the Pacific Northwest six years ago when he'd passed through. At the time there'd only been a trading post and an old man ready to sell it. On a whim, Snopes had made the old man an offer. Snopes had been here ever since.

"I suppose you're right," Snopes said. "Folks around here would need to get haircuts nonstop if that's how I kept myself fed. But I rent out some rooms upstairs. Got some other things going, too."

"Oh? So you're an entrepreneur, then?" The man seemed interested.

"I suppose I am," Snopes said. "I've expanded the general store, put in a post office. Ponderosa Mercantile. That's my hotel going up down the street."

"Is it really?" The man twisted in the chair to look out the window, and Snopes had to yank back the scissors quickly to avoid snipping a piece of ear.

"We're exactly a day's ride out of Nugget City for anyone heading to Oregon or Washington," Snopes explained. "Figured a hotel was a good investment."

"Sounds like you own the whole town."

"Well, Luke Jessup runs the blacksmith and livery and Maggie Crenshaw runs the little restaurant down the road, but I own several hundred acres just west of town, so there's plenty of room to expand. Maybe I'll appoint myself mayor. Mayor Ezra Snopes has a nice ring to it."

Both men laughed.

"I commend you on your achievements," the man said. "Well done, my good man."

"You know how it is, sir. Right place at the right time. My dad was a barber and I learned the trade from him. I like to keep a hand in."

Snopes stepped back, examining his work. "There we go, sir. Very smart. Neat and presentable."

The man looked at himself in the mirror, turning his head one way and then the other. "Good job. Very nice."

"I appreciate that, sir. There's tonic as well. Good for the scalp. We have a variety of scents. A nice musk or vanilla is quite popular, although it strikes me as a might sweet."

"I'm not sure I'd enjoy either of those," the Englishman said. "Is there anything else?"

"Yes, sir, but I'll have to check." Ezra turned to the cabinet behind him. "There's a fresh sort of juniper thing. And lilac." He opened the cabinet and squinted at the bottles.

A few were half empty, most completely out. Had it really been so long since he'd sent for new inventory? Most of the stuff he used came from St. Louis. He supposed there was no hurry. Few of the men in Ponderosa Crossing were keen on anything too sweet or fancy. Perhaps Snopes would start catering to lady clients. It might be an opportunity to—

Snopes felt his hair grabbed from behind. His head was yanked back. He opened his mouth to yell—

—felt something cold against the flesh of his throat. It went hot as it was dragged from one side to the other. Sharp pain exploded across his throat.

He turned, opened his mouth to shout but tasted blood. The Englishman stood in front of him, face expressionless. He held a folding knife in one hand, blood dripping from the blade. Snopes reached for the man, mouth working but only choking sounds emerged from his lips. His head went light.

Darkness crowded Snopes's vision . . . closing in . . . darkness . . .

Nigel Evers watched the barber's eyelids go heavy and close. Ezra Snopes slumped to the floor. Evers considered the body for a moment.

That flutter of excitement. Evers stood a moment and enjoyed it, the sweet release of something that had been building ever since deciding on Snopes as his target.

He glanced over his shoulder, looked out the window. Nobody had seen him do it.

Evers wiped the blade on the smock Snopes had draped over him. Nice of the barber to provide some protection against the blood splatter. He closed the simple lock blade and slipped it into his pocket. Like every other man out west, Evers carried a gun, but it was astounding how often a simple, small blade could take care of a problem quickly and quietly. He kept it razor-sharp and handy at all times.

He untied the smock and draped it over Snopes's corpse. Evers stood a moment, looking down at the dead barber.

Seemed a shame. Snopes had struck him as a good fellow, a man who was making something of himself yet remained humble.

A kindred spirit perhaps. Evers felt he was making something of himself also. He'd been born in the Bethnal Green slums and knew even at an early age he'd need to get out if he intended to transform himself into something else. He realized he was marked, his every utterance reminding the listener that he was scum from the wrong part of London. He'd learned manners—truly *learned* them, rather than just aping his betters. He could pass for a gentleman and had on numerous occasions, but no matter how convincing his act, it would never be the truth.

So he'd come to America, where that sort of thing didn't matter as much and had migrated west where it had mattered even less.

And he was good at killing.

To most west of the Mississippi River, "good at killing" meant fast with a gun. Evers hadn't found that to be the case. Oh, it didn't hurt. Evers kept in practice with his six-shooter. He wasn't the fastest, but he was better than average. In any case, being fast was more useful than being slow, but that wasn't the key when it came to killing, not to Evers.

The *will* to do it. That was the key.

Even now, he felt bad for the kindred spirit who used to be a barber. He'd taken away everything the man had ever accomplished, anything he might be in the future. But Snopes's death fed something inside Evers. He let the feeling wash over him.

For a minute.

Then, like shutting off a spigot, it was over. The trick wasn't to deny emotions but to control them, like a boiler letting off just enough steam to prevent an explosion. In the next instant, the barber was simply a dead man. Evers was finished here. He took the list from his front pocket, unfolded it, and crossed through the name "Ezra Snopes" with a pencil. At three hundred dollars, Snopes was worth quite a bit more than most of the other names on the list, and Evers had supposed it was because it was such a long trek to Ponderosa Crossing. Now he suspected it had something to do with the amount of land the man owned. Something to ponder at a later time.

The Englishman took his jacket from the peg and shrugged into it. He paused to admire his haircut in the mirror before putting on his bowler. Snopes really had done a fine job.

Nigel Evers turned the sign in the front window from "Open" to "Closed," then stepped outside into the construction din of the town's new hotel.

CHAPTER 12

Carson looked up at the giant looming over him.

"Get up, little man." A thick, German accent. "Gunter will break your back with his bare hands!"

And he looks like he could do it, too, Carson thought. The man calling himself Gunter was at least six and a half feet tall. Huge shoulders, broad chest, thick legs, and a glistening bald head.

Colby Tate emerged from the Lucky Strike behind Carson. "Now let's behave ourselves, shall we? No more talk of back breaking and such."

Gunter went for his gun, but it never made it out of the holster.

Tate's six-shooter was in his hand almost faster than the eye could follow. He pointed it directly at Gunter's face. The click-click of the hammer thumbed back focused the big man's attention.

"Hitting a fellow without warning is unsportsmanlike," Tate said. "But shooting a man is just rude."

Carson stood, dusted himself off. "Let me guess. You're Hans Mueller's brother."

"Yes." Gunter slowly moved his hand off his gun. "The two of you murdered him."

"If your brother had come along quietly, he'd still be alive," Carson said. "Cooling his heels in a cell but alive."

"It doesn't matter. He was my brother. Gunter won't forget. Nowhere you can go and hide. Sleep with one eye open if you think it will help. It won't. When you let your guard down, when you least expect it, Gunter will be there."

The big Bavarian turned abruptly and walked away.

Carson stood, dusted himself off. "It's been an interesting day."

Tate was still watching Gunter walk away. "I despise people who refer to themselves in the third person."

"Yeah, well, Carson is hungry," Carson said. "Carson suggests we get dinner and then find a hotel."

"Please stop," Tate said. "I'm surprised he flattened you so easily. Didn't your father teach you those fighting tricks?"

Carson's father had been a Confederate spy and had done a lot of his fighting out of uniform, behind enemy lines and without weapons. He could hit a man in a certain place and make him drop, or twist his wrist in a certain fashion to make him give up his weapon, or knock him cold with a single blow. He'd passed a number of these tricks on to his son.

"The problem is that the tricks don't work so well if you have no idea you're about to be punched," Carson said.

They found a place serving big slabs of ham and huge baked potatoes dripping with butter and mustard greens. Tate asked for a wine list and the proprietor looked at Tate as if he'd asked for a kidney. Carson ate until his belly was tight.

The proprietor said there used to be five or six hotels in town at the height of the boom, but that Nugget City was now down to two. An inexpensive, straightforward place at the north end of town and an upscale place that nearly always had vacancies because of the relatively high prices. The cheap place was nearly always full.

They thanked the man for the meal, paid him, and walked outside.

"Shall we walk down to the cheap place and see if they have rooms?" Carson asked.

"Certainly not," Tate said. "Come now, old sport, I know you're saving for a ranch or some nonsense, but one must live life, after all, and there's more to it than privation."

"You've twisted my arm."

At first glance, the lobby of the Golden Duchess Hotel reflected the wealth associated with the heyday of Nugget City's gold boom. A closer look reflected something else: the decline in recent years and the town's dwindling population and ebbing prosperity. The plush furniture showed wear at the edges, curtains frayed, walls in need of paint, a bar constructed of some dark, rich wood desperately in need of a polish. The lobby was dimly lit, oil lamps turned low, like an aging beauty seeking to hide her age in the shadows.

But even an aging beauty could retain some semblance of poise and grace, and even in its current state, it was clear the Golden Duchess was an upscale establishment meant to cater to men of means.

An elderly gentleman at the front desk greeted them with subdued enthusiasm. He wore a green jacket with gold piping. "Rooms for you gentlemen? As it happens, we have vacancies at the moment."

Carson and Tate each took a room. The rates were higher than Carson was used to paying, but not quite as high as he would have imagined. They each signed the register and paid the man.

"Is there an evening service?" Tate glanced sideways at the long bar across the lobby.

"We have a selection of after-dinner drinks, including an

especially good cognac. There is also a wine list, although we've had trouble recently restocking the cellar."

"You have a wine cellar?"

"Alas, no, sir. My pardon. I was speaking figuratively. I must also confess that we're not able to offer anything from the kitchen at this time. Our chef left us several months ago and we've been unable to replace him."

"No worries," Carson said. "We ate. Are there baths?"

"Of course, sir. All the rooms at the Golden Duchess come with private baths."

"I'll need some hot water, then, if that can be arranged," Carson said.

"Of course, sir," the old man said. "I'll arrange it straightaway."

"And I suppose we'll be down for a night cap later," Tate said.

"Very good, sir. Shall I call the boy for your luggage?"

Carson slapped the saddlebags over his shoulder. "Got it. But we've got horses. Is there a stable?"

"Yes, sir. I shall summon Jackrabbit. Your animals will be well cared for."

"Jackrabbit?"

"Our groom, sir."

Carson frowned. "His mother named him Jackrabbit?"

"I doubt any mother would be so cruel. It's a nickname . . . although I must admit I never learned the man's given name. You'll know him when you see him, sir. He's a hunchback and wears a sombrero."

"Mexican fella?"

"No, sir. He's just fond of wearing the sombrero. Says it keeps the sun off. You'll need to get in front of him where he can see you to get his attention. He's stone deaf."

"Are you having some fun with me?" Carson asked. "I'm

handing my horse over to a deaf hunchback in a sombrero named Jackrabbit?"

The clerk looked chagrined. "I assure you, sir, your animal will be in good hands."

Carson held up his hands in surrender. "It's fine. I shouldn't be surprised at anything anymore."

"Welcome again to the Golden Duchess, and don't hesitate to let me know if there's anything at all I can do to make your stay more pleasant."

Carson and Tate adjourned to their separate rooms. Servants brought hot water and Carson's bath was filled. He washed off the road grime and sweat and horse stink. He dressed in his good pants and a clean shirt. Carson looked at himself in the mirror, remembering a time not long ago when he only owned a single pair of raggedy trousers. His life had changed a lot in the past year. He'd been a wanted outlaw.

Now he hunted outlaws.

Carson kept telling himself it wasn't the type of life he wanted, yet somehow there was always a reason to keep living it. Maybe it was the money. Maybe because he liked Tate's company.

Or maybe I can't think of what else I want to do with myself.

He told himself to forget it. He was thinking all the same thoughts around in a circle. Carson told himself to focus on getting Chester Potts. After that, he could ponder his aimless life.

He found Tate already in the lobby. The bounty hunter sat in an overstuffed, high-backed chair, a large glass of amber liquid on a small table next to him. He puffed his pipe, looked up as Carson approached, and gestured to another high-backed chair next to him.

"Join me in a cognac?" Tate blew out a long stream of gray smoke. "Carlton was right. It really is excellent."

The old man in the green jacket—whose name was apparently Carlton—arrived just as Carson's butt hit the seat. He carried a silver tray, a white linen napkin draped over one arm. "Something to drink, sir? The cognac would seem to have your friend's endorsement."

Carson shook his head. "It would be wasted on me. A shot of whisky."

Carlton disappeared in a flash but returned promptly with the whisky. "Please let me know at once should you need anything else."

"Obliged," Carson said.

They sat a moment in silence, drinking.

"How's your face feel?" Tate asked.

Carson prodded at his fat lip and winced. "Feels about how it looks. That Gunter fella's serious. We need to watch out for that one."

"Maybe we should go to the sheriff," Tate suggested.

"Rawlings?" Carson considered it. "I think if Gunter had his way, Rawlings would be delighted."

"I can't really disagree," Tate said. "I don't think we worked our way onto his good side. If he has a good side."

"So we've got two headaches," Carson said. "Finding Chester Potts and looking over our shoulders the whole time for Gunter Mueller."

"Well summed up, old sport."

"We can't control when or where Gunter will come at us." Carson said. "So we get after Potts and just be as alert for trouble as we can be."

Tate's head turned toward the hotel's front entrance. "Perhaps this is the break we've been waiting for."

Carson looked.

Benson Cassidy came toward them, a smug grin plastered

across his face. He sat in another of the high-backed chairs without being invited. "Enjoying your evening, gentlemen?"

Carson did his best to keep the disdain off his face. There was something about the oily opportunist that rubbed Carson the wrong way and he was just figuring out what it might be. "Hadn't expected to see you again so soon, Mr. Cassidy."

"It's a small town and I work fast," Cassidy said.

Tate puffed his pipe. "Out with it, then. What do you have for us?"

"Not so fast. You know how this works." Cassidy leaned forward, held out his hand. "You must first cross my palm with silver."

Carson leaned forward to match the other man's posture, met Cassidy's eyes with a hard gaze. They sat that way for a moment, Cassidy with his hand out for a bribe, Carson looking daggers back at the man.

Then Carson's hand flashed out faster than a rattlesnake strike. He latched onto Cassidy's wrist and twisted, wrenching the arm until the palm almost made a full circle, open to the ceiling again but this time from the wrong direction. Cassidy yelped in pain and came out of the chair, going to his knees.

"Stop! Stop! You'll break it!" Cassidy shouted.

"I'm just getting your attention," Carson said.

Tate raised an eyebrow, still puffing the pipe. "Carson, old sport, do you have something in mind or are you just in a bad mood?"

"Mr. Cassidy here likes to sell information," Carson said. "We give him the name Chester Potts and then he comes along and tells us where to find him. I'm sort of thinking we're not Cassidy's only customers. We gave him our names back at the Lucky Strike. What if we were just giving him something to sell?"

Tate tapped the stem of his pipe against his teeth, thinking. "Now that I think of it, Gunter did seem to know right where to find us at the Lucky Strike." His eyes narrowed at Cassidy. "I say, old sport, you didn't run off and sell us out to Gunter Mueller, did you?"

Cassidy shook his head. "No, of course not. I'd never—"

Carson twisted the arm. Cassidy grunted and stopped talking.

Carlton chose that moment to appear, eyes wide. "Gentlemen, please. This sort of behavior is unheard of in the Golden Duchess. I must protest."

"Get the sheriff," Cassidy bleated.

"Now, you'll do no such thing, Carlton," Tate said. "This is a friendly disagreement between gentlemen. We'll have it all sorted in a moment."

Carlton shifted nervously from one foot to the other but finally retreated to let the three men work out the situation for themselves.

"I should have ordered another cognac before he left," Tate lamented.

"Now listen close, Mr. Cassidy," Carson said. "I just need some honest answers, and then we can all be friendly again."

"I didn't sell you out to Mueller. I swear!"

Carson twisted and Cassidy winced.

"You ever broken a bone before?" Carson asked. "I don't mean a toe or a pinkie finger. I mean a big bone. You hear it before you feel it. This wet, sickening snap. And you feel odd. Sometimes there's pain first, sometimes nausea. Your body's been surprised that something terrible has happened. But don't worry. The pain comes eventually. And it's bad. And then forget using that arm for a couple of months. Hopefully it heals back right."

Carson twisted.

"Okay! Okay!" Cassidy pleaded. "Yes, I told him. I'd heard he was keeping an eye out for two strangers. Took a chance it was you two and it was. He didn't pay me much. I didn't know what he was going to do."

"You can see how we might take issue with what you've done," Carson said.

"I understand. I can see how it might seem like . . . a conflict of interest."

"Then you're going to tell us what you know about Potts, and we'll call it even," Carson said. "Nobody's crossing anyone's palm with nothing."

"Yes. Fine. Okay."

Carson let go of the man.

Cassidy lurched to his feet and plopped back down into the chair, flexing his wrist and then rubbing his shoulder. He showed no signs that he intended retaliation. Still, Carson kept his gun hand loose in case he needed to draw.

"A man matching Chester Potts's description has been seen in Darby's Mercantile a few times," Cassidy said. "Darby told me he'd never seen the man before a month ago. He's apparently taken over one of the old claims up October Gorge, except Darby says the man never buys any mining equipment. Just coffee and hooch and provisions."

"I'm glad you didn't pay him, Carson," Tate said. "Pretty thin stuff."

"Some old, out-of-the-way mining camp? Could be a man hiding out," Carson supposed. "Where is this place?"

"West of town." Cassidy gave them directions.

Then he stood, rubbing his shoulder again. "Well, if that square's us . . ."

"One more thing." Carson pulled something out of his pants pocket and held it up for Cassidy to see. It was a ten-dollar Liberty Head coin. "From now on, information flows one way. To us."

Cassidy reached for the coin.

"No, no." Carson put the Liberty Head back in his pocket. "Bring us something. Then we'll talk."

Cassidy stood, nodded to Carson and Tate in turn. "Gentlemen, it's been . . . interesting."

He turned and walked out without looking back.

Carlton was there a second later, towel over one arm, silver tray in hand, only his deep frown ruining his perfect servant's veneer.

Tate cleared his throat. "My apologies, Carlton. Obviously, an establishment of the Golden Duchess's repute would not normally tolerate disruptive fisticuffs." He dropped a heavy coin onto Carlton's tray.

"Ah. Yes." Carlton cleared his throat. "As you say, a dispute between gentlemen. Water under the bridge. More drinks?"

"Another cognac would be delightful," Tate said. "Thank you, Carlton."

Carton turned his attention to Carson. "And another whisky for the gentleman?"

"Make it a double."

CHAPTER 13

They didn't hurry the next morning. Eggs, bacon, biscuits, and black coffee. And then Carson and Tate found themselves on their horses heading west toward October Gorge.

"It's getting colder." Carson flipped his coat collar up over his neck.

"It's still September," Tate said. "You wouldn't last long in Massachusetts in January. I think you just like to complain."

"Maybe," Carson said. "Maybe I just miss Texas."

"It gets cold in Texas, too."

"Yeah, but later in the year," Carson said. "And in Texas."

Cassidy's direction took them along a river until they turned north into gentle hill country. The terrain grew rocky as they entered October Gorge. They followed a stream up until the land leveled out and they spotted the claim across a wide clearing, the stream running through the center. A sluice had been set up for a panning operation. A shack sat at the edge of the clearing with a dilapidated corral next to it. There were no animals in the corral and no smoke coming from the shack's chimney.

"Doesn't look promising, does it?" Tate said.

Carson couldn't disagree. As they approached, rusty picks and shovels leaning against the side of the shack added to the place's abandoned appearance. They tied their horses to a porch post and paused in front of the door.

"Perhaps we should knock," Tate suggested. "Might not be the right place."

"Cassidy's directions were clear enough. This is the place all right," Carson said. "Whether or not Cassidy was full of dung or not about Potts being here remains to be seen."

Carson glanced through the front window, then pushed the door open and entered, Tate right behind him.

The interior of the one-room shack told a different story than the exterior. The dust and cobwebs one might have expected from long abandonment were absent. Instead, fresh supplies lined the shelves across the far wall. A bunk with freshly rumpled bedding. A shabby table with a half-empty bottle of whisky.

Carson reached into the fireplace, hand over gray ashes. "Warm. A few hours. Yeah, somebody was here."

They searched the small shack but found little of interest.

"He'll be back," Carson said. "He left all his supplies. I say we take the horses somewhere out of sight where we can keep an eye on the place. We'll watch and wait."

"Sounds like a long, dull day in the making, but I suppose it's a sensible plan," Tate said.

They made to leave, and when Carson was framed in the open doorway, the crack of a rifle shot split the air. Wood splinters kicked up from the doorframe three inches from Carson's face.

He and Tate dove for the floor, and more shots tore through the shack, peppering the back wall and shattering the front window, glass raining over the two men. Carson kicked the shack door closed. Gunfire continued to pour into the shack.

"I think Chester Potts has friends," Tate said, arms over his head to fend off the glass shards.

"I count three rifles," Carson said. "I think."

"You think?"

"Could be two firing quick or four taking it easy." Carson shrugged. "Three, I think."

"Blast. You think they were waiting for us?"

Carson growled. "Should've broken Cassidy's damn arm."

The gunfire died away. Carson and Tate remained on the floor, not moving.

"Wish I hadn't left my Winchester on Jet," Carson whispered.

"You have to see them to shoot them," Tate said.

Carson sighed. "Best have a look, then."

He eased himself up to take a peek at the lower right corner of the window. Another barrage of lead tore through the shack, and Carson threw himself to the floor again.

"I saw smoke up and to the left," he said.

Tate checked the load on each of his six-shooters. "Now what?"

"They won't wait forever," Carson said. "Once it's clear we're not going to run out there, it won't take them long to figure out they can toss a lantern or some torches down and catch this place pretty easy. Then we'll have to decide between running out and getting shot or staying inside to burn."

Tate frowned. "I'm keen on choice number three."

"If you can think of one, I'm all ears."

Both men looked around the interior of the small shack, hoping for an idea. No back door and no other windows.

"Hold on." Carson crawled across the floor to the other side of the shack and examined the back wall near the narrow bunk. He prodded it with his fingers, a half-baked plan forming.

Half is better than nothing, I reckon.

"Which way is the wind blowing?"

"What's that matter?" Tate asked.

"Sort of in a hurry here, Colby."

Tate craned his neck to get a view through the window without exposing himself to rifle fire. "Okay, I'm looking at the tops of those trees. I'd say the wind's blowing west to east."

Carson gathered the bedding into the middle of the bunk. He grabbed a lantern off the table and went back to the bed, keeping low. He emptied the lantern oil onto the bedding. "You carry matches, right? To light that pipe of yours?"

Tate raised an eyebrow. "I thought a fire is what we *didn't* want."

"Listen. Here's what we're going to do," Carson explained. "The wood's thin and has rotted along the back wall. I think I can kick loose a few boards and make a big enough space to crawl out. I'll need you to toss some lead at those fellas while I do it."

"I'm not likely to hit much at this range with a revolver," Tate said. "Even if I can see them."

"Just keep their heads down," Carson said. "Mostly I want the shooting to cover the racket of me kicking the wall out."

"I still don't understand why you're lighting the bed on fire."

"The smoke will cover me," Carson said. "And Potts and his buddies will be distracted by the fire. I'll circle around and get the drop on them."

"And I'm still in the burning shack?"

"I'll admit this is where the plan gets tricky."

"I hate this plan," Tate said. "You haven't even finished telling me, but I already hate it."

"Light the bed and that back wall will go up. You stay as close to the front as possible," Carson explained. "You know the difference between a rifle shot and a pistol shot. When you hear my Peacemaker, that's your signal I got them. You run out the front door fast. Make sure to get the horses."

"There's one problem with your plan."

"I know you hate the damn plan, Colby, but we don't have time to think up nothing else."

"I don't mean my opinion. I mean an actual problem," Tate said. "I'm more proficient with six-guns than you are. If you were shooting the Winchester, it would be different. It should be me that goes out there."

Carson thought about it. "Damn."

"Sorry, old sport."

"I suppose you like the plan a lot better now."

Tate drew his six-guns. "Let's get on with it."

Carson positioned himself across the shack. "Start shooting!"

Tate rose up, both guns blazing out the front window. Carson began kicking the boards of the back wall. They splintered and cracked. The boards were even more rotten than he'd thought, and by the time Tate had emptied his guns and the men outside had returned fire, Carson had kicked a big enough hole to crawl through.

"Just give me a moment to reload," Tate said.

Carson drew his own pistol and crawled to the front of the shack.

Tate took out his matches, paused to look at Carson. "I'll go as fast as I can."

"Obliged," Carson said. "But wait for the smoke. That's your cover."

"Right."

Tate lit a match and dropped it on the bedding. It went up fast, and by the time Tate had crawled through the hole Carson had kicked open, the flames had leaped from the bunk to the back wall, climbing to the ceiling. Smoke filled the little shack. Carson's eyes watered, and the heat forced him back against the front door. He got as low as he could, gulping for good air, but soon he was coughing like mad. Tears streamed from the corners of his eyes, snot running down over his upper lip.

I can see why Colby hated this plan.

The heat threatened to overwhelm him. He listened for the shots but heard only Jet and Tate's horse whinnying, near panic.

I can't wait. I'll have to risk it. Maybe the smoke will cover me, but if I stay in here another second—

Pistol shots!

That was all Carson needed to hear. He shoved open the front door and stumbled out, smoke billowing around him. His eyes stung. Everything was a blur. The horses were going crazy. He untied Tate's horse and the animal bolted. Carson stroked Jet's nose. The horse calmed, but not by much, the flames sending jolts of panic through both man and animal.

Carson untied the horse and led him away until the heat no longer washed over them. He felt along the saddle and saddlebags until his hands came across his canteen. He opened it, tilted his head back, and splashed water on his face, rubbing his eyes. He filled his mouth, swirled it around, and spat, then drank deeply. He took off his hat. He was matted with sweat all over, hair flat, his shirt sticking to him under his jacket.

Carson blinked, turned to look at the shack. It was completely engulfed in flames. A column of black smoke spiraled into the air. He tied Jet to a tree branch, put his hat back on, and headed up the ridge at a slow trudge.

He came through a stand of trees and spotted Tate standing over three bodies, one of his pistols trained on a fourth man sitting and leaning against a tree trunk, both hands clutching his gut. Blood seeped between his fingers and his face had gone ashen.

Tate gestured at one of the dead men. "That's Potts there." He shook his gun at the man sitting against the tree. "Tell him what you told me."

"Please . . . so cold." He was a couple of years younger than Carson, had a bland, soft look about him. He grunted, holding his gut tighter. "Can I have some water maybe?"

"In a minute," Tate said. "Tell him."

"My buddies used to ride with Chester back in the day. They told me Chester had a thing lined up, a bank . . . a bank robbery." He paused to cough, his whole body shaking. "A bank down in Boise. We met up with Potts here, but then he told us we had to bushwhack some fellas who were after him. Guess that didn't work out so well." He laughed but immediately began coughing again.

"How did Potts know we were coming?" Carson asked.

"No idea. Maybe . . . maybe I could get that water now? Unless you got a sip of whisky."

"Hold on."

Carson went back down the ridge. There wasn't much left in his canteen, but the dying man was welcome to it. He reached Jet and took the canteen, then paused to watch the shack fall in on itself, the flames roaring and crackling, the heat uncomfortable even all the way across the clearing.

Carson climbed back up the ridge with the canteen, but the man was already dead.

CHAPTER 14

She'd been attracted to men who were handsome, playthings to pass the time. And she'd been attracted to powerful men for the simple reason that power itself was attractive. And she'd been attracted to rich men because of their money. That one didn't take many smarts.

Bill Cartwright was a mix of all three.

But one of the things Katherine Payne—Kat—found most attractive about Cartwright was his arrogant belief he had Kat tied around his little finger. He was a man used to getting his own way and he didn't see why it would be any different when it came to Kat, a fact that would make her ultimate victory all the more delicious when she used him to get what she wanted and then cast him aside like an empty whisky bottle.

Speaking of which . . .

Kat filled her shot glass, then sat back, putting her boots up on the table, watching the quiet streets of Boise through the front window of the Three Kings Saloon. It was early afternoon and the place was mostly empty. Kat drank.

And waited.

Eventually the two brothers wandered in. They stopped just inside the doorway when they saw Kat. The older one—Barry—looked right at her and shook his head.

Kat sighed. *Damn.*

Barry continued on to the bar, but the younger one came over to Kat's table and plopped down on one of the other chairs. Larry sighed extravagantly, like he was the most put-upon man in the world. He took off his hat and dropped it on the table.

"You sure they was supposed to meet us this morning?" Larry asked.

Kat nodded. "Yeah."

"Well, they didn't."

"So I see."

"We looked everywhere you said, even waited a while at that saloon across town in case there was a mix-up," Larry assured her. "Looks like they ain't showing."

Kat took her boots off the table and refilled her glass. "Looks like."

Barry came back from the bar and took the third chair. He set two empty shot glasses on the table and reached for the bottle.

Kat's eyes narrowed. "Hey."

Barry's hand froze halfway to the bottle.

"Ask first. Nicely."

Barry grinned, light glinting off his gold tooth. "Can my brother and me please have some of your whisky, *ma'am*?"

Kat smiled the kind of smile that didn't touch her eyes. "Of course. We're all friends here."

A snort came from Barry as he filled the glasses. He tossed his back, filled the glass again, and said, "I guess Larry told you. No sign of them fellas."

Kat put a disappointed look on her face. "I guess we'll have to call it off then."

"Naw, to hell with that," Larry said. "We can handle it our own selves, and that way we don't have to split it so many ways, right, Barry?"

The older brother nodded. "I reckon so."

Kat could have guessed it would be Larry who spoke up first. The kid was all big mouth. Barry wasn't as rash, but he smelled a better payday without the others involved.

"Maybe." Kat pretended to mull it over. "Might be better to wait."

Larry shook his head vehemently. "No, no, no. You as good with your rifle as you claim?"

"I can shoot."

"Okay, then. You pick a roof and cover us like you say. We hit the place early and get out fast. Boise don't have much trouble. Nobody will be expecting anyone to hit the bank. Not like we're in Dodge City."

Kat hesitated, as if she hadn't thought of all this already. "Okay. Let's do it. But remember what your mission is. You've got to shoot the bank manager." The bank manager was an officious little man named Curtis Everly. According to Cartwright, Everly used his position as bank manager to connect with homesteaders who decided they couldn't make a go of it, and he picked up the land for a song. He was very keen to buy, but not eager to sell, so he'd made the death list and was worth two hundred dollars dead.

The two brothers gave each other a look.

Kat's eyes went from one to the other. "Is there something else?"

"We'll gun the bank manager. That's easy," Larry said. "But me and Barry are the ones going into the bank. We'll be right there in the thick of things. Not safe on a roof far away like you."

Kat sat back in her chair and crossed her arms. "I think I see where this is going."

"An equal split of the bank take ain't right," Larry said. "We should get more."

Barry tossed back his whisky. "Dang right."

"What did you have in mind?" Kat asked.

"Forty percent for each of us," Larry said. "Twenty percent for you."

Kat's features hardened. It was playacting, pretending to be offended by the proposal. If the robbery went as anticipated, none of them would see a cent of that bank money, so she didn't give a tinker's damn what the split was. She blew out a tired sigh, as if she had no choice but to accept the raw deal. "Fine. Like you say. You're the ones sticking your necks out."

The brothers looked at each other and smiled, half glad for the increased share and half relieved Kat was going along with it.

"Bank opens at nine in the morning," Kat reminded them. "You know what to do. Any questions?"

No questions.

"In that case, I'll see you boys tomorrow." She stood and gestured at the two-thirds-empty whisky bottle. "Finish that off if you want."

Barry grabbed the bottle and filled his own glass, then his brother's. "Obliged."

Kat left the saloon and stood a moment with her thumbs in her belt, considering how to pass the rest of the afternoon and evening. She wouldn't mind another drink and she'd need to get some food, but the company of the Hanson brothers had worn thin. She'd find a different place to sit, and sip whisky, and ponder the wide world.

She headed down the sidewalk in no particular hurry, taking a good, long look at Boise and wondering what the town had to offer. There was a decent-looking café, but it was too early to eat. She might come back later. Kat had enjoyed just enough whisky to want some more. Maybe she'd find another saloon and sit quietly at a corner table. It wouldn't be the worst idea in the world to get to bed early. Tomorrow could get hectic and—

She turned abruptly, pretending to look at a dress in a shop window.

Kat's eyes slowly slid back to the street to see if she'd seen what she thought she saw. From her peripheral vision, Kat watched the man ride down the street, leading four horses, a corpse draped over each animal. Pedestrians paused to gawk.

The man was dressed in a nice gray suit, twin pistols on his hips. She let him get a little closer to be sure it was who she thought it was.

Colby Tate. Bounty hunter.

A little over a year ago, Kat and Colby Tate and a man named Carson Stone had all been mixed up together. The affair hadn't ended well for Kat; instead of making off with a fortune, she'd found herself on the run with a price on her head.

She no longer had her fiery red hair. She'd cut it short and dyed it black, but she still pulled her hat down low to hide her face. Having the bounty hunter recognize her now would ruin her plans in a big way. When she'd been a bounty hunter, the men she'd chased were wanted dead or alive, and Katherine Payne usually found that *dead* was less trouble. Now she found herself on the other end of it. She was wanted dead or alive, and Colby Tate was under no obligation to offer her the easy option.

Kat watched Tate dismount and go into the sheriff's office. It didn't take her long to put two and two together. There were plenty of times Kat had ridden up to a sheriff or marshal's office with dead men draped over a saddle.

He's collecting a bounty.

And in a flash of intuition, Kat knew who the dead men were. She'd never met Chester Potts, only knew him by reputation. He and his cohorts were simply convenient manpower for tomorrow's bank job.

I guess we know why they didn't show up now. Can't rob a bank if you're dead.

Her mind raced. Did Tate know she was in Boise? Was he coming after her next? Kat wondered if the men had talked before Tate had gunned them down. What did Tate know?

She turned and headed back the way she'd come. There was a general store up ahead. She'd purchase a bottle of whisky and go back to her room. She didn't intend to come out until the next morning. If Tate recognized her, it would spoil everything.

Maybe I'll get lucky. Maybe Tate will collect his bounty and ride on.

As far as Kat was concerned, she was overdue for some luck.

Sheriff Bedford signed the voucher and handed it to Tate. "That's for Potts. Take it to the bank down the street like last time. As far as I know, there's no paper on those other fellas. Sorry."

"I suppose we'll just call it a service to the community, then," Tate said. "Thanks again for quick payment. Usually I have to hunt down a federal marshal to get paid."

"The mayor has an understanding with the bank," Bedford explained. "They front us the money to pay fellas like you."

"I'm grateful," Tate said.

"Were you able to do me the favor I asked?"

Tate told Bedford how they'd found Sally White Dove at the ferry crossing, and how she'd shown them Dutch's grave.

"Damn." The sheriff shook his head. "I was afraid of

something like that. I've had my deputies getting word to other folks on that list, letting 'em know they need to watch out."

"How are you holding up?" Tate asked. "Your name's on that list, too."

"I haven't forgotten," Bedford said. "But I'm the sheriff here. I can't run away and hide when there are people counting on me."

"Never said you'd hide, old sport," Tate assured him. "But if my name was on a list like that, I'd be nervous, too."

"I'm sleeping with one eye open, if that's what you mean. Where's that partner of yours anyway?"

"Carson stayed in Nugget City," Tate said. "He's . . . looking into a few things."

"Glad to hear it. Buy you a drink when I get off duty?"

Tate considered it. A drink, a meal, and a soft hotel bed were tempting.

Tate sighed. "Sorry, Sheriff. There's a good bit of daylight left. If I push hard, I can get back to Nugget City tomorrow by dinnertime. If I know my good friend Carson, he's even now getting himself in some spot of trouble I'll need to get him out of."

CHAPTER 15

After gunning down Potts and his gang, Carson and Tate agreed taking the corpses back to Boise was a better bet than dealing with Nugget City's ill-tempered sheriff. Tad Rawlings gave Carson a bad feeling and steering clear of the man seemed best.

"Can you take those dead men to Boise on your own?" Carson had asked. "I want to look into something. Potts knew we were coming. I plan to have a word with Nugget City's local big mouth."

Tate hadn't liked it, but he took the bodies south to collect the bounty. Carson rode Jet back to Nugget City. Rawlings leaned in his chair outside the sheriff's office, apparently his customary perch. Carson rode past on the other side of the street, and the two men pretended not to see each other.

At the end of the street, Carson tied Jet's reins to the hitching post, then entered the saloon and scanned the place for the slicker Benson Cassidy. Carson felt tight and ready, eager to get his hands on the oily snitch. Cassidy tipping him off that there were bounty hunters on the way was the only thing that explained how Chester Potts had been ready for them.

Should have broken the sidewinder's arm. I'll shut his mouth for good this time.

Cassidy was nowhere to be seen, so Carson bellied up to the bar.

"Welcome back," the bartender said. "Whisky?"

Carson realized he was in a mood. If he started on a bottle of whisky, he wouldn't stop until it was empty. "Just a beer."

The bartender brought it. Carson took a big first gulp, then leaned against the bar. He took a deep breath and let it out slowly, feeling the tension drain from his neck and shoulders. He'd been keyed up and ready for violence all the way back from October Gorge. As much as Carson wanted to murder Benson Cassidy with his own hands, doing so would obviously do more harm than good. Rawlings had been clear about not wanting trouble in his town, and he'd probably relish the excuse to slam Carson into a jail cell.

But I can't let it pass. I'll need to do something to put the fear of God into Cassidy. The rotten snake almost got me killed.

Two beers later, Carson felt bone-tired. Cassidy could wait. He needed a meal and a bed. He'd finish one more beer, then get his room back at the Golden Duchess.

A well-dressed stranger appeared at the bar, and for a split second, Carson thought it might be Cassidy. But this man's suit was new and well-kept, unlike Cassidy's. The newcomer set his bowler hat on the bar next to him, then waved his hand to get the bartender's attention. "A moment of your time, my good man."

Some kind of accent. British, Carson figured.

The bartender stopped in front of the Brit. "Help you, sir?"

"I'm looking for a man named Rollo Kramer," the Brit said. "You don't happen to know him?"

"I do. Owns a stretch of land west of town," the bartender

said. "But I ain't seen him in here for a while. You just get into town?"

"Down from Ponderosa Crossing."

"Something to wash the dust from your throat?"

"An excellent suggestion," the Brit said. "Leave the bottle, if you please."

The bartender filled a shot glass and left the bottle as instructed.

"What's it like up there?" Carson asked.

The Brit turned, as if just realizing Carson existed. "Excuse me?"

"Beg pardon," Carson said. "You mentioned Ponderosa Crossing. I've only been in the territory a few months. Haven't made it that far north yet."

A thoughtful look crossed the Brit's face. "Not a large place, but tidy. They're building a hotel. I think if you went back in ten years, the place might be something. Sorry, I wasn't there long. I can't tell you more."

"That's fine." Carson offered his hand. "Carson Stone."

"Nigel Evers." He shook Carson's hand. "Can I offer you a shot of whisky?"

"Obliged, but no. Sticking to beer."

"As you like."

Carson drained the rest of his beer and set the mug on the bar. "Good talking with you. Safe travels."

"And to you, my good man."

Carson left the saloon and found a simple slop house and ordered a meal, pork roast with thick gravy and potatoes and carrots. He found himself still thinking about the genial Brit as he sopped up the last of the gravy on his plate with a biscuit. He wasn't sure why. Something nagged him about the man.

In his room at the Golden Duchess, he disrobed and

flopped into bed. Carson was bushed and should have fallen asleep instantly.

But he didn't.

He kept thinking about Nigel Evers. The man hadn't done anything wrong as far as Carson could tell. If anything, he had some pretty darn nice manners. Was it something the Brit had said, some small thing still tugging at Carson's mind? Carson replayed his encounter with the man. What had Evers wanted? He'd asked the bartender about a man— what was the name? Rollo Kramer.

Carson rolled out of bed, felt along the nightstand for the matches, struck one. It flared bright. He lit the kerosene lamp. He shuffled across the room and found his clothes thrown over the back of a chair and went through his pants pockets and then his shirt pocket until he found the folded piece of paper. He took it back to the light, opened it, and ran his finger down the list of names and dollar amounts. Just when he thought he was wasting his time, there it was, all the way at the bottom of the list.

Rollo Kramer—100 dollars

Carson woke up the next morning, his body rested but his mind occupied with both Nigel Evers and Benson Cassidy. He kept thinking about it over coffee, and finally decided Nigel Evers was none of his business. Rollo Kramer's name on a list could be nothing more than coincidence. There could be a hundred reasons why Evers wanted to talk to the man.

Cassidy was a different story. Carson had his own business with the snitch. That settled it. He put the Englishman out of his mind and focused on finding Cassidy.

Carson left the hotel the back way and stopped at the stables to check on Jet. The horse had been well fed and watered, and Carson saw that someone had brushed him down. Jackrabbit was on the job. One thing at least Carson wouldn't have to worry about.

He walked down the street, taking it easy, thumbs hooked into his belt. The people of Nugget City went about their business. Carson paused to look through the window of an empty store, a haberdashery, according to the sign. The business had gone under long ago.

What happens to a gold town when the gold runs out? Maybe they turn to farming. Or timber. Anything but just lie down and die.

But Carson didn't know. He kept walking, turned down a side street, and stopped again in front of a boardinghouse. A sign hung over the front door: "Rooms for rent."

Cassidy has to lay his head somewhere. Might as well start here. I haven't seen any other boardinghouses, and I doubt he can afford a room at the Golden Duchess.

He knocked on the front door.

A young girl wearing an apron opened the front door, wide-eyed, with an innocent face. Behind her, an even younger girl cleared a long table, perhaps cleaning up from the breakfast service. Both the girls had a similar look. Maybe sisters.

"Help you, sir?"

"Sorry to disturb your work, ma'am," Carson said. "But I'm looking for a man named Benson Cassidy and wondered if this is where he might live."

"Maisie and me just do cooking and cleaning," the girl said. "If you'd wait, I'll fetch the owner. She'd know about the tenants. Can you wait?"

"That's no problem." Carson stepped back again as the door closed.

It opened again ten seconds later, and a sturdy woman in her early fifties stood there and gave Carson a long, appraising look. She wore a deep burgundy dress buttoned all the way up. High collar. A drawn, hawkish face. Proper bordering on severe.

"I'm Doris Beckinridge, the owner." She held her hands clasped in front of her, back straight. "I'm told you have an inquiry about one of our residents."

"If he even is a resident," Carson said. "I'm looking for a man named Benson Cassidy. To be honest, I've no idea where the man hangs his hat, but I haven't seen any other boardinghouses, so I thought I'd take a chance."

"There used to be another boardinghouse, but John and Judy Bishop decided to call it quits two years ago. I heard they were giving Utah a try," Beckinridge explained. "This Benson Cassidy, he's a friend of yours?"

Carson rubbed the back of his neck, not quite sure how to answer. "We have some unfinished business. Wouldn't say he's a friend exactly."

Beckinridge's demeanor softened slightly. "Let me guess. Cassidy owes you some money. Never mind. None of my business. Yes, Cassidy used to live here, but it's been at least six weeks since he was asked to leave. His ability to pay the rent was . . . intermittent. Have you considered consulting Sheriff Rawlings? He might know Cassidy's whereabouts."

Carson shifted from one foot to the other. "I appreciate the advice, ma'am, but dealing with Rawlings doesn't sound too appealing. I won't trouble you with a dull story, but somehow I got on Rawlings's bad side. I doubt he'd go out of his way to help me."

Carson thought he saw what could almost be called a smile trying to break through the woman's severe expression.

"I didn't catch your name, young man."

"Carson Stone, ma'am."

"Well, Mr. Stone, you wouldn't be the first to get on the

sheriff's bad side. Frankly, if he has a good side, nobody's seen it."

Carson chuckled. "Well, I'm new in town, ma'am. Far be it from me to cast aspersions on the local law. I just want to find Cassidy while ruffling as few feathers as possible."

"I suggest you talk to Jefferson Gallo," Beckinridge said. "He runs Nugget City Mercantile. At last week's town council meeting, he was complaining rather loudly to anyone who'd listen that Cassidy had run up quite a tab at the store. Gallo said it probably served him right, extending credit to questionable characters."

"And Gallo knows where Cassidy is?"

"I wouldn't know," Beckinridge admitted. "But you're both looking for him. Perhaps you could share information."

Carson touched the brim of his hat. "Appreciate the advice, ma'am. Sorry to take up your time."

"Not at all. Good luck to you, Mr. Stone."

Carson headed back to Main Street and turned south. He remembered passing the mercantile on the way into town the first day. Maybe Gallo knew something about Cassidy's whereabouts and maybe he didn't, but Carson figured it couldn't hurt to ask.

Carson walked into Nugget City Mercantile and stood a moment, looking the place over. The shelves were sparsely stocked and there were no customers. A swarthy, fat man in an apron emerged from the back room carrying two big sacks of flour on each shoulder. He was a big man, and the sacks gave him little trouble. Blue-black stubble on his jaws, thick black hair.

"Help you, mister?"

"You'd be Gallo?"

"Indeed, I would."

"Doris Beckinridge said you might be able to help me,"

Carson said. "If I'm not disturbing you in the middle of something."

Gallo gestured to the empty store around him. "Not exactly swamped. What can I do you for?"

Carson introduced himself. "I'm looking for Benson Cassidy. I thought you might know where he's keeping himself."

"That deadbeat?" Gallo dropped the flour bags and scowled. "If I knew where he was keeping himself, I'd go there and kick him square in the ass."

Carson chuckled. "I'm guessing he's into you for a few dollars."

"Talked me into giving him credit." Gallo shook his head. "Last thing I sold him was a US Cavalry surplus tent of all things. Beckinridge told me she gave the man the boot from her boardinghouse the next day. Should have figured."

"But no idea where Cassidy is now?"

"Sorry," Gallo said. "Wish I could help you."

"Well, I figured there was no harm asking," Carson said. "Anyway, I can at least give you some business. Wrap me up two pounds of coffee?" Carson's supply for the road was getting low.

"Happy to. Might be the only business I do this morning." Gallo sighed. "Used to sell to the prospectors nonstop back in the day—picks, shovels, pans. Sure ain't like it used to be."

Gallo wrapped up the coffee and Carson paid.

Carson left the mercantile and was halfway down the block when he heard somebody calling his name. He turned and saw Gallo chasing after him.

"Everything okay?" Carson asked.

Gallo wiped sweat from his face. He wasn't a man accustomed to moving fast. "I feel like a damn fool, but I think I just put two and two together. It was your buying the coffee that reminded me. Skunk McEntire came in yesterday to buy coffee, said he was up along Koot Creek, fishing for trout."

"What kind of name is Skunk?" Carson asked. "Does he smell bad?"

Gallo laughed. "He's got black hair with a white streak straight up the middle. Tells people he was hit by lightning. I don't believe a word of it."

Carson didn't blame him.

"Anyway, he said he saw a fella camping," Gallo continued. "I don't know what kind of tent, didn't think to ask. But Skunk said the fella seemed a little out of his element, not dressed for camping. In a suit. No law says a man can't dress up to camp out, and there's no proof it was Cassidy . . ." A shrug.

"Maybe worth a look-see," Carson said. "How do I find Koot Creek?"

Gallo gave him directions.

"Thanks again, Mr. Gallo. If I find him, I'll let you know."

Carson took his coffee back to the hotel, stashed it in his room, and grabbed his Winchester. On the way back down, he told Carlton he'd be staying another night, and then he went out the back to the stable. He saddled Jet and headed north out of town.

He veered east as per Gallo's instructions. The land rose gently into foothills and then leveled off into high evergreen country. Koot Creek was wide and shallow. If he'd had a pole, Carson would have tried for a few trout himself. The morning had started cold, and it would be cold again when the sun set. But at the moment the weather was just about perfect for a lazy day of fishing, bright but mild; not the bitter winter that was on its way in the coming weeks, but far from an oppressive Texas summer.

That was the problem with just about any place on the

map, Carson supposed. Moments of perfection sometimes but take a place in its entirety year-round and there were always pluses and minuses. How was a man ever to settle on one place for the rest of his days? If Tate were here, he'd point out that Carson had taken quite a shine to the Golden Duchess—soft beds and clean sheets. Wasn't Carson supposed to be squirreling away his money for a ranch? He'd told Tate as much, but already the Carson Stone who'd said such things seemed like a different person.

Maybe I keep trying to be the person I think I'm supposed to be instead of being the person I am.

Carson wondered if that even made sense and laughed at himself.

His good humor vanished when he remembered what he was supposed to be doing. His white-hot anger at Benson Cassidy had ebbed. But there was still a healthy annoyance that needed to be satisfied. The man needed to answer for his big mouth.

He turned upstream and rode for over an hour. He smelled the campfire before he saw it.

Carson dismounted and looped Jet's reins around the low branch of a skinny ponderosa pine. He looked upstream and saw the bank of the creek make a sharp bend out and then back. He decided to cut through the trees, walking as lightly and as quietly as possible. He came through the trees, pausing at the edge, and saw the camp next to the creek, a single tent and a cookfire with a cast-iron pot hanging from a tripod. He smelled something cooking but couldn't identify it.

Carson squatted next to the thick trunk of a tall pine and watched for a few minutes. He cocked his head and listened but heard only the babble of Koot Creek. Carson was about to give up his watch when the tent flap moved and a man emerged.

Benson Cassidy yawned and stretched. He wore the

same suit Carson had seen him in before but without the jacket, the sleeves rolled up. He approached the cookpot, bent, and stirred the contents with a stick.

Carson drew his Peacemaker and left the trees.

Cassidy turned and saw him coming. At first, Cassidy didn't seem to understand what was happening, but then his eyes shot wide and he turned to run.

"Don't!" Carson shouted. "I'll shoot, you weasel!"

Cassidy didn't listen.

"Damn it." Carson holstered his six-shooter and chased after him.

The chase didn't last long. Cassidy tripped over one of the lines tied to a tent stake and went sprawling. By the time he got to his feet, Carson was there. Carson punched Cassidy square in the nose. The rat staggered back, blood streaming from both nostrils. Cassidy turned and ran, splashing into Koot Creek.

Carson pursued, the fast-moving water splashing cold.

He caught up with Cassidy and shoved him from behind. Cassidy went down hard into the shallow water, came up spitting and coughing on his hands and knees. Carson stood over him, pushed his head back under the water. Cassidy struggled, but Carson held him down.

Carson counted to ten, then jerked Cassidy out of the water by his collar. More coughing and sputtering.

"Not completely pleased with you right now, Benson," Carson said. "Chester Potts and his pals were waiting for me in October Gorge."

"It wasn't me!" Cassidy insisted. "I didn't say a word to Potts."

Carson shoved him back under again. More struggling. This time Carson counted to twenty before hauling him back out.

Cassidy gulped for air. "I didn't tell Potts. It was Rawlings! I swear!"

Carson paused before dunking him again. "The sheriff?"

"He's the only one I told," Cassidy said. "I swear it!"

Carson sighed and pulled the man to his feet in the knee-deep water. "Finish this story on land. The water's freezing."

Cassidy stood as close to the small cookfire as he could get without burning himself, dripping and shivering. He'd lost the will to fight or flee and seemed resigned to take whatever Carson was ready to dish out, but Carson's urge to pummel the man had passed. He was far more concerned with what Cassidy had told him about Rawlings.

"He got word somehow I'd talked to you and your partner," Cassidy explained. "The sheriff demanded to know what I told you. So I told him I'd sent you to October Gorge looking for Potts."

Carson took off his hat, wiped a sleeve across his forehead. "How did he react when you told him?"

"He seemed thoughtful for a moment. Then he told me to keep a walk softly and not to talk to anyone about it. I was due to make a change in accommodations anyway."

"Yeah. I talked to Mrs. Beckinridge"

Cassidy looked sheepish, turned to stick his wet backside toward the fire.

Carson considered his next move. As sheriff, Rawlings had every right to keep track of what was going on in his town. It didn't mean he was up to no good, but Carson had never had a good feeling about the man and didn't trust him.

Carson cleared his throat. "Listen to me."

Cassidy turned around, his hands over the fire.

"I feel like I still want to break every bone in your body," Carson said. "But let's try something different."

Cassidy nodded eagerly. "That would suit me."

Carson fished into his pocket and came out with the

same ten-dollar coin he'd showed Cassidy before. "I'm not sure threats are motivating you properly." He handed Cassidy the coin. "You work for me now. I'm your boss."

Cassidy looked at the coin in his hand but made no move to put it away. He was clearly wary of some trick.

"I need to know what's going on, especially Rawlings's interest in all this," Carson said. "If the sheriff really tipped off Chester Potts we were coming, it might just be so Potts could cut out before we arrived. Or maybe he told Potts and his pals to set up an ambush. Either way, it's not what I expect from a lawman."

Cassidy slowly put the coin into his pocket, keeping a suspicious eye on Carson. "Now what?"

"Like I told you, you work for me now," Carson said. "Anything you think I need to know, you come tell me first. Especially if it concerns Rawlings. Or that big Bavarian who wants to push my face in. Or anything. From here on, if it turns out I'm the last guy to know something, then you're in trouble. I want to know beforehand for a change."

"I mean, the man's the sheriff," Cassidy said. "I had to answer his questions. I didn't know what he planned to do with the information."

"I hear you. But I'm just as dead if Potts had been a slightly better marksman. I'm not interested in good intentions. You get what I'm saying?"

Cassidy nodded. "You're the boss."

Carson forced a smile. "I think we might get along." He gestured to the tent. "This is where I'll find you?"

"I suppose. I doubt Doris Beckinridge is eager to have me back. Unless you'd like to front me the money for a room at the Golden Duchess."

"I would not. See you soon, Benson."

Carson made his way back through the trees, found Jet, and mounted. He headed back down to the valley at a slow walk, a jumble of thoughts knocking around inside his skull.

Cassidy could have been lying, of course. For all Carson knew, the man had told a dozen people about him and Tate. Word could have gotten back to Potts any number of ways. And yet Carson had a gut feeling Sheriff Rawlings was no good. Even Doris Beckinridge hadn't seemed fond of the man. If Rawlings was a rotten apple, how did it connect to Old Dutch's death and Bedford's concerns?

Or maybe it doesn't connect at all. Still, Rawlings hardly seemed surprised at all when I told him Dutch was dead. There's a bunch of bad stuff going on, and my gut's telling me it's all part of the same thing.

He needed Tate back. Carson had good instincts, but Tate was educated and had a knack for looking at things logically. They'd hunker down over a bottle of whisky and sort this out. He wanted his partner back for other reasons as well. He'd hate to have his guard down when that enormous Bavarian—

Carson's head came up quick, and it took him a second to realize what had caught his attention. To the average greenhorn, Indian bird calls sounded like the real thing. Men like Carson, who'd lived on the trail a few years, could tell the difference.

One call came from high up in the trees off to the left. The answering call came from the right.

Damn.

Carson kept Jet at a steady walk. Nice and easy. Could be the Indians were just giving him a look-see. Still, best to be ready. He leaned in the saddle and drew the Winchester from the long, leather sheath along Jet's right side. He set the rifle across his lap, ready for quick use.

More bird calls back and forth.

He rounded a bend, and a dozen of them blocked his

path, bows up and ready, arrows knocked. Others came from the woods on both sides of him. Carson considered spurring Jet on and making a run for it, but he'd be sprouting arrows before he made it twenty yards. He waited, hoping one of them would start a conversation.

One of the big bucks spoke to the others in his own tongue, then dragged a thumb across his throat.

So much for conversation. Carson lifted the Winchester and levered in a shell.

"Wait!" Another Indian emerged from the woods, rapidly speaking to the others.

Carson saw who it was and sighed relief. "Laughing Otter. Glad to see you."

CHAPTER 16

Kat watched the kids frolic from her second-floor hotel room window, a mixed group of boys and girls playing some form of tag. It was early, and Boise was just waking up. Kat might have slept in another half hour if the kids hadn't woken her. She took her saddlebags down to the stable behind the hotel and asked the stable hand to saddle her horse. She took her canteen—not the one for water but the other one—and slung it over her shoulder.

She crossed back through the hotel and out the front door, where she found the kids playing in the street. She caught a young boy's eye, maybe nine or ten years old, and waved him over. He was bucktoothed, dishwater hair in his eyes.

"Ma'am?"

"When does Sheriff Bedford usually get into his office?"

"'Bout eight or so, I reckon," the boy told her. "Not too much longer."

"Can you take him this message for me?" Kat handed him a sealed envelope. "It's important, but I can't wait around."

"Sure. I'll give it to him soon as he gets here."

"Don't forget. It's very important." She handed the boy a dime.

His eyes shot wide, as if he'd been handed the treasure of the pharaohs. "Thanks, lady!"

Kat winked at him, turned, and headed down the sidewalk. She needed to position herself on one of the roofs and get set up for a quick getaway.

She found the slop house where she'd had dinner the night before and entered. The place was doing a brisk business for breakfast and the smell of bacon tempted her to linger.

The same haggard woman who'd served her the night before approached, pushing loose strands of gray-brown hair out of her eyes. "Breakfast?"

"I wish I could." Kat handed her the canteen. "How much to fill this with coffee?"

"Hold on."

The woman waddled away with the canteen, returned sixty seconds later, and handed it to her. "You was in here last night, wasn't ya?"

"That's right. Had a good chicken dinner and a slice of apple pie."

"Okay, then. Take the coffee. We appreciate the business."

"That's kind," Kat said. "I'll remember it."

The woman waved it away and waddled toward a group of cowboys shouting for biscuits.

Kat left the slop house and took her coffee back to the stable. She tipped the young man for saddling the horse. According to her calculations, the sheriff should be getting her message soon, and then the Hanson brothers would take the bank when it opened at nine. She closed her eyes a moment, pictured the position of the sheriff's office in relation to the bank's location. She'd already figured this out the night before but wanted to double-check herself.

The results were the same. By her reckoning, the roof of the hotel would give her the best shot.

"Okay if I leave my horse tied up by the water trough

outside?" she asked the stable hand. "I just need to run a few errands before I leave town. Shouldn't take long."

"That's fine," he said. "She won't be in the way."

She waited until he wandered back into the stable, then took her Henry rifle from the saddle sheath and her field glasses from her saddlebag. She headed back into the hotel lobby. The clerk didn't even look up as she passed through. Kat headed up past the second and third floors, then out onto the roof.

She picked a spot near the front edge and knelt, setting the Henry aside and taking a quick swig of coffee from the canteen. Then she scanned the street with the field glasses, sweeping from the area just in front of the hotel up a half block to the sheriff's office. The kids were still playing their game, but Kat didn't see the bucktoothed boy. It would annoy her to no end if the boy simply ran off without—

There he was. Kat spotted the boy coming out of the sheriff's office, hands in his pockets. Sheriff Bedford was right behind him. He put a hand on the boy's shoulder, bent to look the kid in the eye and told him something. Kat could only imagine what.

The boy left at a run and caught up with the other children, shouting for their attention. He told them something, and two seconds later the children ran, all in one direction, not playing now but obviously clearing out. In a heartbeat there was no sign of them.

Kat jerked the field glasses back to the sheriff's office. Two other men had joined Bedford. Maybe deputies. They spoke, the sheriff pointing one way up the street and down the other. The deputies ran off to do . . . something.

Kat's note was apparently having the desired effect. The news that a gang—she'd made sure to use the word "gang"—was coming to rob the bank would naturally galvanize Bedford into action. She panned down the street with the field glasses and saw the Hanson brothers at the far end, walking their horses toward the bank.

Here we go. Now if everyone can just stay predictable...

Kat had an educated guess how this would go. Dumb crooks usually did what dumb crooks usually do. Lawmen were even more unoriginal. If Bedford went according to the playbook, he'd gather as many guns as he could and wait outside the bank, waiting to catch the perpetrators as they emerged. Then the usual speech—hands up or die bloody.

The bank wouldn't open for a few more minutes. Kat swigged coffee from the canteen and checked the Henry. She was ready to go.

One at a time, she saw a half dozen men enter the sheriff's office.

Kat levered a shell into the rifle's chamber and held it across her knee. Soon.

A few minutes later, the bank opened. Larry and Barry tied their horses to the hitching post out front and ambled inside. They hadn't been inside two seconds when Bedford and a mob of deputies poured out of the sheriff's office, each holding a rifle. Bedford arranged them in a line, ready to meet the robbers as they exited the bank.

Kat took a last gulp of coffee, then went to her belly, bringing the Henry to her shoulder. Her dad had taught her to shoot with a Henry years ago when the man had still been alive, before bandits had bushwhacked him on the road. Years later she'd been taught to use a Spencer by a man she thought she might fancy. Both man and Spencer were out of her life now, and Kat was glad to be shooting a Henry again.

She sighted along the barrel, taking dead aim at the side of Bedford's head an inch above his right ear.

I could do it right now. I could spread his brains all over the street.

But that would draw everyone's attention to the hotel roof.

She needed to wait until the gunplay started. Then, in the racket and confusion, nobody would notice a stray shot that came from elsewhere.

The Hanson brothers came out shooting.

Bedford and the deputies hadn't expected it. The plan had been for the robbers to be surprised, maybe throw down their guns in a panic to save their own skins.

Instead, they'd come out blasting. Two deputies went down immediately, clutching bloody chests, and a third felt his kneecap explode, blood spraying. He went down, screaming and screaming.

Bedford and the deputies returned fire. Smoke hung in the air, the once-quiet street a racket of rifle and pistol shots. Barry took a slug to the thigh, shouted pain, and went down, still firing.

Kat kept her gunsight on Bedford's head, exhaled slowly, and squeezed the trigger.

Just as a deputy stepped back into her line of fire.

He jerked when the slug tore through his neck, and he spun away, blood trailing through the air.

"Damn it!"

Kat levered in another shell and took aim again.

Bedford looked down at the deputy she'd just killed, then back up at the hotel roof. He spotted her, lifted a hand to point, and shouted a warning.

Kat fired.

Bedford took the lead square in the chest. He staggered back and dropped his gun, looking around as if seeking the answers to everything that had gone wrong in his life. He tried to walk, but his legs went out and he dropped.

That was all Kat needed to see.

She was vaguely aware of gunfire raking across Larry's chest. He stumbled back, tripping over his prone brother. Kat didn't see anymore. She was already on her way downstairs.

She made herself slow to a walk in the lobby so as not to draw attention. She needn't have worried. The front-desk clerk and a few of the other guests had crowded the front window to gawk at the spectacle out on the street. Kat heard the gunfire finally stop as she headed out back to her horse.

Kat mounted and rode away at an easy trot, taking back-streets. She paused once when she was out of town and looked back. No pursuit.

That was an easy five thousand dollars in her pocket and two competitors eliminated to boot. The Hanson brothers were too stupid to be anything but cannon fodder. She wondered if that was what Cartwright had in mind all along, hiring morons who'd stumble along the way and get themselves killed so he wouldn't have to pay them. Best to keep an eye on him.

Kat spurred her horse and went to collect her bounty.

CHAPTER 17

The rapid-fire patter of multiple gunshots woke Colby Tate out of a sound sleep. He sat bolt upright in bed, blinked. It took him a moment to remember where he was. The hotel room in Boise. He'd gotten into a card game at the Three Kings the night before. He'd more or less broken even by the end of the night, but he'd stayed up too late and drunk too much. He'd meant to head back to Nugget City yesterday like he'd told Bedford, but Tate's backside was saddle sore, and he didn't think Carson would grudge him a night of rest and relaxation.

Tate rolled out of bed, rubbing his eyes. A headache pounded.

He went to the window to see what the shooting was about but remembered he had a room at the back of the building. The window looked down at the narrow alley and the hotel's stable.

Tate went to the basin across the room, splashed cold water in his face. By the time he'd finished dressing, the gunfire had waned. He went to the window again.

The area out back of the hotel was still quiet except for a lone woman mounting her horse. Probably looking to ride away from the gunfire. Tate couldn't blame her.

She took off her hat and ran her fingers through her

short, dark hair, and Tate was afforded a better look at her face. A stab of recognition. It took him a moment. The long, red hair had been so striking, but it was gone now. But he knew the woman. There was no mistake.

Kat Payne! Lady Pain herself. What the hell is she doing here?

Kat spurred her horse and took off at a trot.

Tate turned from the window, grabbing his gun belt as he dashed from the room. He buckled it on as he flew down the stairs. Katherine Payne was a wanted woman with a price on her head. He needed to notify Bedford that he'd be going after her. It wasn't just about the money. A year ago the woman had tried to murder him and had nearly succeeded. Tate would gladly collect the bounty . . . but it was also personal.

In the lobby, people crowded the front windows. The gunfire had stopped, but apparently there was still plenty to see. Tate rushed past them out the front door.

Bodies lay bleeding in the street. Townspeople rushed to the scene to help the wounded. He stopped a man jogging toward him and asked, "What happened here?"

"Bandits robbed the bank. Bedford and his boys was waiting for 'em when they came out and then all hell broke loose. Damnedest thing I ever saw."

"Where's the sheriff now?"

"No idea. You'll have to excuse me, mister. I got to fetch Doc Parker right quick!"

Tate waded into the crowd. The mixed stink of blood and gunpowder hung in the air. He eventually did find Sheriff Bedford. The man's corpse lay at an awkward angle in the mud, a huge hole in his vest leaking blood into the dirt.

Tate took off his hat and shook his head. *Damn.*

* * *

Carson had dismounted and led Jet by the reins, following the Bannock Indians into the forest. Laughing Otter had spoken for him, and Carson no longer feared his imminent demise from a dozen arrows suddenly entering his body.

"Glad you were able to get away from the cavalry soldiers," Carson told the Indian. He'd been told the Bannock had caused a lot of trouble in the area, but Laughing Otter seemed the sort who just wanted to avoid trouble and get on with his life.

"The soldiers tried to shoot me," Laughing Otter said. "And the river tried to drown me. I went very far downstream, then traveled in the darkness, walking many miles in a roundabout way, avoiding the white man always."

They entered a clearing where there were more Bannock, cookfires, makeshift lean-tos of sticks and animal hide. A camp, but not anything permanent. There seemed to be mostly braves present, but there was a small number of women and children also.

"The bluecoat soldiers do not hunt for us in this area," Laughing Otter said. "At least not at this time. We continue to gather for another day, maybe two. Then we plan to travel north. We wish only to get away from the white man and live in peace. There is safety in numbers, so we are collecting as many as wish to go."

"Sounds like a reasonable plan." Carson guessed it was probably hopeless in the long run. There would be no place the Bannock could hide forever, but that was a problem for later. "Don't worry about me. I won't mention I saw you to anyone." These Indians were tired and just wanted to be left alone. He seriously doubted they'd be forming raiding parties and harming anyone.

"I've sent braves to warn all of our scouts that you are passing through," Laughing Otter explained. "You will be able to travel safely. Then, in a few days, it will no longer matter, for we will be gone."

"There's another man." Carson briefly explained about Benson Cassidy. "Maybe you can give him a pass, too? I'd appreciate it."

"You mean the ragged man camping along what the white man calls Koot Creek? This man is your friend?"

"I wouldn't say 'friend,'" Carson said. "But I have a use for the man."

"Then he shall have protection also," Laughing Otter assured him. "I will pass the word."

Carson scratched the stubble on his jaw, thoughtful. "You remember telling me about the brave and his band who burned the trading post? I forget the name, but you told me a white man had hired him to do it."

"I remember," Laughing Otter said. "Eyes of Fire. A courageous fighter, but often reckless."

"I don't suppose he's here? I wouldn't mind asking him a question or two."

"He is not among us," the Bannock said. "He died in the south, cornered by the bluecoats."

Carson shook his head and tsked. "A shame."

"But there is another," Laughing Otter explained. "Moon Dancer used to ride with Eyes of Fire. I can fetch him if you wish."

"I'd appreciate that," Carson said. "I just have a few questions. Hell, it might not even be anything important, but he might have useful information."

Carson stood and waited, warming next to one of the cookfires. None of the Bannock paid him any mind. Five minutes turned into ten, and then a half hour.

At last Laughing Otter returned with another Bannock, lean and short with hard eyes, a wolf pelt draped around his shoulders like a cloak. The Indian eyed Carson with curiosity.

"Moon Dancer does not speak the white man's tongue," Laughing Otter explained. "I will translate as best I can."

"Tell him I appreciate his time," Carson said. "I'm curious about the trading post he burned along the Payette River."

Laughing Eyes translated, and the two Bannock went back and forth for a moment.

"Moon Dancer asks if you knew the men who worked the trading post," Laughing Otter said. "He fears you have come to avenge them."

Carson shook his head. "Nothing like that. I got no wolf in that particular hunt. I'm just curious who ordered it and why."

Laughing Otter exchanged more words with Moon Dancer.

"Moon Dancer says Eyes of Fire did not trust the white man, so he took Moon Dancer with him to the meeting," Laughing Otter explained. "So Moon Dancer was there to witness the agreement. The white man was called by the name Foster McNeil. Moon Dancer says he does not know why the white man wanted this, but he does think this McNeil was not a chief, but simply spoke the words of his chief. They were ordered not to kill any of the white men at the trading post but only to burn the buildings. Moon Dancer apologizes, but he knows nothing more."

"Thank him for me," Carson said. "And thank you, Laughing Otter. I don't suppose I'll see you again."

"No, but I wish you luck, Friend Carson."

They clasped hands, and then Carson mounted Jet and left.

He turned back toward Koot Creek. He didn't bother with stealth this time. Carson rode Jet right up to Cassidy's small camp, where the man stood by the fire in nothing but his underwear. Cassidy had shoved a bunch of long sticks into the mud around the campfire. He'd hung his sopping clothes on the sticks to dry.

"You need a clothesline," Carson observed.

Cassidy shifted from one foot to the other, rubbed the back of his neck. "I didn't expect to see you again so soon."

Carson leaned forward in the saddle. "Tell me everything you know about Foster McNeil."

Cassidy looked confused for only a moment before perking up. "Happy to."

CHAPTER 18

On the way back to Nugget City, Carson pondered what Cassidy had told him about Foster McNeil. As a wheeler and dealer of information, Cassidy had finally been in his element and had been eager to be useful for a change.

McNeil was the Nugget City representative of a man named Bill Cartwright. Carson had never heard of Cartwright, but that just figured, since Cartwright was apparently some kind of big millionaire, and Carson didn't run in those circles. But Cartwright owned a building in Nugget City, and back when the boom town was at its boomiest, the building had housed the offices for Cartwright Stage Lines, Cartwright Mining, and Cartwright Lumber.

Travel to Nugget City had dwindled to a trickle, so the stage line had been discontinued. With nearly preternatural intuition, Cartwright had sold off his mining interests at top dollar just before everything went bust. Timing was everything, Carson reckoned. And when the population began to ebb, construction stopped, and so Cartwright Lumber had called it quits.

As far as Carson could tell, this Cartwright fellow was currently doing zero business in Nugget City but still saw fit to keep an office open and at least one employee on the payroll.

All of this was according to Cassidy, but the wily slicker seemed confident of his information. Foster McNeil remained in Nugget City to conduct Bill Cartwright's business.

The nature of the business remained to be seen.

As Carson rode into town at a slow walk, he was obliged to nudge Jet to one side as a buckboard came clattering up behind him. The driver whipped the horse as he galloped past, then jerked the reins, halting horse and buckboard right in front of the sheriff's office.

"Somebody fetch the doc!" shouted the driver. "Get the sheriff!"

People on the street gathered around to see what the commotion was about. Carson halted Jet to watch the scene unfold.

An old man, smartly dressed and carrying a black doctor's bag, elbowed his way through the crowd. "One side. I'm here."

The doctor went to the back of the buckboard, where there was a body with a blanket thrown over it. The doc pulled back the blanket, revealing a bald, middle-aged man. A black beard with streaks of white. Carson stood in the saddle to get a better look down into the back of the buckboard. The man had a red gash from one ear to the other across his throat. His skin was ashen.

"Not sure what you wanted me for," the doc said. "There's nothing I can do for him."

The buckboard driver shrugged. "Don't you have to pronounce him dead or something?"

"In due course," the doctor said. "Right now, it's the sheriff's business."

As if on cue, Rawlings lumbered out of his office, raking the crowd with his scowl. "What's going on here?"

"Rollo Kramer," the buckboard driver said. "I found the poor slob just like this in his barn."

Rawlings came down the steps in no particular hurry, then leaned in to look at Kramer's face. The sheriff shook his head and tsked. "That's a shame. He was about to propose marriage to the Widow Jenkins, wasn't he?"

A general murmur of ascent came from the crowd.

"Break it gently, whoever tells her," Rawlings said. "Now, let's go on and get about our business, people." He flipped the blanket back over Kramer's face.

The crowd dispersed, all of them murmuring about *poor Rollo*.

Carson lingered, turning over the name Rollo Kramer in his mind.

Rawlings squinted up at Carson on the back of his horse. "What the hell do you want, bounty hunter?"

"Just passing by and took an interest."

"Well, the show's over. Move along."

"Did you ever look in on Sally White Dove?"

The sheriff's scowl deepened. "Not that it's any of your damn business, but Sally's doing just fine. She sold the ferry and got a decent price for it, too, and now she's gone off to be with her people. So you can stop worrying about Sally White Dove."

"Sold?" Carson raised an eyebrow. "Who'd she sell it to?"

"Who'd she sell it to? Kiss my you-know-what that's who she sold it to. Now ride on."

"Sorry to take up your time, Sheriff." Carson clicked his tongue and Jet moved away at a walk.

Of course, he'd recognized the name Rollo Kramer right away. The polite Englishman had been looking for the man. Nigel Evers. There were too many strange things going on for Carson to believe in coincidences. Bad things.

Carson stopped into the saloon. The same bartender was on duty, and Carson asked if he'd seen the Englishman. The bartender remembered Evers but said he hadn't seen him. Carson thanked the bartender and left.

It had been Carson's intention to poke around Nugget City to see if he could dig up Foster McNeil. If he'd been in Boise, Carson would have gone to Sheriff Bedford and spilled the whole story. McNeil—and by extension Cartwright?—wanted that trading post burned. Why? Taking the story to Rawlings seemed a bad bet. Nugget City's sheriff didn't strike Carson as the sort to take the word of a Bannock Indian.

So forget McNeil for the moment. The mystery of Rollo Kramer's death and the Englishman's possible involvement took center stage in Carson's imagination. When he'd met Evers, the Englishman said he'd just come south from a place called Ponderosa Crossing.

Carson's curiosity took charge and he pointed Jet north. He wasn't sure what he'd find in Ponderosa Crossing, wasn't even sure what he was looking for. Probably he was wasting his time, but his mind was set. He set a quick pace.

The sky was wide and blue, the country raw and vast. He rode for hours, stopping periodically. It was Carson's understanding that Ponderosa Crossing was just about exactly a day's ride from Nugget City. He'd hoped a fast pace would make up for a late start, but the sun sank, and Carson estimated he was still a few miles from his destination.

He found a sheltered spot off the beaten path and set up camp. Soon he had a campfire going. He tended to Jet, cooked a simple meal, and made a pot of coffee. He sat quietly, listening to the fire crackle and the call of night birds— real birds this time, not Bannock signaling to one another.

Sitting alone with nothing but miles of wilderness in every direction reminded Carson of his unfortunate days as an outlaw. Often short of money and usually hiding from the law, he spent many nights camping away from the eyes and ears of civilization. Now, it was different. He never looked forward to sleeping on the ground, but the solitude came as a welcome relief. He put thoughts of murders and mysterious Englishmen out of his mind and let his thoughts drift elsewhere.

I wonder what Mary's doing right now.

Probably working the room at the Three Kings, he thought.

And then he found himself thinking about Claire Grainger. The poor woman had no family left except for a cousin. Carson hoped she was okay, and the more he tried to picture Mary's glamorous looks, the more Claire's sweet face floated in front of his mind's eye.

He decided to think about something else.

Hopefully Colby Tate had delivered the corpses to Bedford in Boise without incident. It occurred to Carson he'd left Nugget City sort of half-cocked. Tate would be riding into town looking for him, and if Carson had taken a minute to think about it, he would have left him a note at the Golden Duchess's front desk. But Tate wasn't stupid. He'd figure Carson was off on some errand and sit tight, probably enjoying his pipe in the lobby, drinking expensive port or something while reading a dusty old book of poetry.

Carson enjoyed the night a while longer, then finally curled up on the hard ground and slept.

He woke up with the dawn, rekindled last night's coals, and brewed a fresh pot of coffee. He fed and watered Jet, then saddled him and headed into Ponderosa Crossing. Nigel Evers had been right about the place. Small but tidy.

Carson's attention was drawn to a half-constructed building on the main street, and Carson recalled Evers mentioning there was a hotel under construction. He watched a husky, broad-chested man shouting orders at a handful of workers. The boss wore a tweed vest and a red tie pulled loose but no jacket, the sleeves of his shirt rolled up past thick forearms. He looked familiar.

A wide grin split Carson's face. He raised his voice to shout, "Good God, is that Hank Baily over there shooting his damn mouth off again?"

Baily turned abruptly, looking for the source of this harassment. Baily's eyes landed on Carson, and his scowl exploded into a big grin. "Carson!"

Baily ran forward just as Carson dismounted. The burly man swept Carson into a huge bear hug, and Carson was surprised to find that he didn't mind. He and Baily hadn't started off as friends, but now Carson was actually happy to see the big ox.

"Hot damn, it's my old pal, Carson Stone!" Baily announced to the world. "What in hell brings you out to a spec on the map like Ponderosa Crossing?"

Carson laughed. "Kind of a long story. I see you're still working in construction."

"Working? Hell, I'm the boss."

Carson raised an eyebrow, genuinely surprised. He'd grown mildly fond of Baily but had never considered him capable of being the boss of anything. "Sounds like you got your own long story to tell."

"Too long to tell with a dry throat," Baily said. "Let me get the boys squared away and then I'm pretty sure I can put my hands on a bottle."

Ponderosa Crossing didn't have a saloon, but such minor obstacles would never keep Hank Baily from a drink of whisky. He lay a plank across two sawhorses in the middle of what would have been the hotel lobby and pulled up two casks of nails to serve as barstools. He opened a new bottle of whisky and filled two tin cups, handing one to Carson. They toasted each other's health and tossed back the hooch.

Baily refilled the cups. "I got the rest of the day off and nothing to do. Might as well get drunk." He guzzled the whisky and refilled the cup again.

"Lots of daylight left and good weather," Carson said. "Why'd you send your crew home?"

Baily shook his head and muttered a couple of obscenities. "The whole project got called off. I had 'em put all the loose lumber somewhere dry in case we start up again, but then had to send all of them home. A damn shame. It was going to be a beautiful hotel."

Carson held up a hand. "Back up a minute. How is it you're running your own construction crew? When you were working construction back in Arkansas, you were the low man."

"Yeah, I guess I pretty much moved up," Baily said. "I've got you to thank for that."

"Me? I don't follow."

"You remember when I punched out Gordon McGraw in that saloon in Fort Smith?" Baily asked.

Carson remembered. In an effort to clear his name, Carson had been obliged to tangle with Big Bob McGraw and his gang, including McGraw's brother, Gordon. Carson had bested most of the gang, but Gordon had caught up to him in an attempt for one last shot at vengeance. He hadn't counted on Hank Baily. Baily had knocked Gordon cold and probably saved Carson's life.

"You told me there was a fat reward on Gordon McGraw," Baily said. "Well, it was true. After you took off, I waited around for the federal marshal. I got credit for capturing Gordon, and a few days later I got the reward money. I wasn't sure what was the best thing to do with all that cash. Turns out I made the best decision of my life."

"Oh? What did you do with the money?"

"Nothing."

"Nothing?"

"Nothing at first," Baily said. "I mean, let's face it. We both know my first instinct would have been to spend it on hooch and women and probably gamble it away. That was when I was trying to straighten out life. I wasn't smart enough to know what to do with the money, but I was smart enough to know I wasn't smart enough, if you get my meaning."

They paused while Baily refilled the cups. He sipped and smacked his lips.

"So anyway, I just put the money in the bank and left it there," Baily continued. "I didn't even take a little to celebrate. I put the money in the bank and forgot about it. Then, for the next eight months, I learned everything I could about construction, not just how to hammer a nail or fit a pipe, but how to organize schedules and work crews and all that."

Carson had to admit it. He was impressed. When he'd first met Hank Baily, the man was a directionless slob whose only ambitions were getting to the bottom of a whisky bottle and getting too familiar with the gals in the saloon.

"There was already muttering among the crew that my boss had hired too many men and might need to let some go," Baily said. "And I'd heard somebody on the edge of town needed a barn built. It wasn't a big job, but it was my chance to do something on my own. I took a chunk of the money from the bank and bought tools and materials. I picked a couple of guys from the crew to be my right-hand men. We built the barn and got paid. I was a boss. Honestly, it was sort of hard to believe at first. We worked our way west, taking on jobs and making money. A couple of weeks ago we were in Cheyenne. Big cattle baron wanted a huge house built and there weren't enough men left to build the stables for his horses. Me and my boys stepped in and got the job done. Then we heard about this hotel job and . . . well, here we are. Except now that job's been pushed back I'm not sure if I should take my boys down to Boise and look for a project there or keep heading west."

"Hank, I never thought I'd hear these words come out of my own mouth," Carson said. "But I'm proud of you." He laughed. "I maybe didn't say that right."

Baily laughed, too. "No, I get it. I surprised myself."

"So what happened?" Carson asked. "Why can't you finish the hotel?"

"The fella who commissioned the job . . . . well, it's actually kind of an awful story," Baily said. "He was found dead on the floor of the barbershop in a pool of his own blood."

"Somebody killed him while he was getting a haircut?"

"Naw, he was the barber," Baily said. "Poor peckerwood had his throat cut from ear to ear."

Throat cut? Just like Rollo Kramer. "Barbering must pay pretty well if he can afford to build a hotel."

"He was some kind of big man around here," Baily said. "Owned half these businesses and a bunch of land just outside of town."

"Land?"

Baily shrugged. "That's what I heard."

Carson's mind raced. Sally White Dove sold her ferry. Miners were being run off their claims. He tried to picture Sheriff Bedford's map. He'd need to see it again to be sure, but Carson was certain all of these events were connected. He was starting to think he should have stayed in Nugget City to find out more about Foster McNeil.

But I'm here now. Might as well get all the information I can.

He took the death list out of his shirt pocket.

Carson's eyes narrowed. "This barber fella. What was his name?"

CHAPTER 19

Colby Tate looked for Carson at the Golden Duchess and then again at the Lucky Strike Saloon with no luck. They'd agreed to meet back at Nugget City after Tate had delivered Potts and his comrades to Sheriff Bedford in Boise.

But Bedford was dead, and Tate had spotted that harpy Katherine Payne, and now Carson had disappeared and—

Now don't get in a panic, old sport, Tate told himself. *Carson hasn't* disappeared. *You simply don't know where he is*.

There could be a thousand explanations. Something had obviously tugged at Carson's curiosity and he was off investigating. Because of course he was.

Why can't he leave well enough alone? Tate had been happy to indulge Carson's curiosity and to do the Boise sheriff a good turn, but enough was enough. Bedford was dead, and whatever was going on in this territory was liable to get Tate dead, too. Time to tell Carson to say his good-byes and they could resume their slow but steady trek to California. He'd tell Carson . . .

Well, Carson would just have to understand.

Tate stood at the Lucky Strike's bar, sipped whisky, and wondered where his stubborn partner had gotten off to. Carson had the irritating quality of always insisting they do the right thing. Tate was as fond of "the right thing" as any man . . . it was just that Tate defined "the right thing" a bit more loosely than most. Getting involved with other people's problems was almost never profitable and almost always a pain in the backside.

He sighed and downed the shot of whisky.

The bartender floated over with the whisky bottle. "Another?"

"I suppose so."

The bartender filled the glass. "Your friend ever find that Englishman?"

Tate blinked. "Find who?"

"That other fella you were with last time you were here," the bartender said. "He's your partner, right? He was asking about some Englishman that breezed through here the other day. I assumed it was somebody you were both looking for. I guess not."

Tate asked the bartender questions, but the man didn't know anything more. Carson had been in the saloon recently, looking for some Englishman. Well, Carson must have his reasons. All Tate could do was wait for him to come back and explain himself.

Tate stayed a while, kept drinking whisky. He looked up an hour later and saw most of the bottle was empty.

I should probably put myself to bed while I can still walk. We'll see what tomorrow brings.

He left the Lucky Strike and ambled toward the Golden Duchess. The streets of Nugget City were deserted. Tate wondered how long a boomtown could go on after it was all boomed out. *Maybe they'll discover some new industry to give them a lift.*

Tate didn't dwell on it. Nugget City was hardly his concern. Tate's first order of business upon Carson's return would be to impress upon his friend in the most earnest terms possible that the Idaho Territory had officially lost its charm. They'd collected on Potts and attempted to help Sheriff Bedford, but Bedford was dead.

When sheriffs start dropping dead, it's a sure sign to pull up stakes and go.

He checked in with Carlton at the front desk of the Golden Duchess.

"Someone left a message for you, sir." Carlton handed Tate a small envelope.

Ah, this was it, then, Tate thought. Carson had left a note. He should have thought to check at the hotel in the first place. Carson wouldn't simply wander off without leaving word. Tate opened the envelope.

The message wasn't from Carson. It read:

Your partner Stone is in trouble. He got into trouble looking for the Englishman. I can't talk openly.
Meet me in back of the hotel stables as soon as you read this.

That just figured, Tate thought. Of course Carson got himself in some sort of fix without Tate around to keep him out of trouble. He headed out the hotel's back door into the dark alley. It was dead quiet, and Tate suddenly wondered if it wouldn't be better to wait until morning.

No, the note had instructed him to come right away. Tate could be walking into trouble, sure, but he could also handle himself. If Carson had gotten himself into this mess, Tate needed to know now, not in the morning. He let a hand rest on the hilt of one of his six-shooters and slowly circled the stable.

The corral out back was empty of horses and lit by a single lantern that hung from a post. The lantern swung in the cool breeze, making strange shadows on the ground. A long shadow grew up from behind him and—

Tate spun, drawing his six-shooters. The man coming up behind him lifted a shotgun. Tate fired twice. Red blotches bloomed across the man's chest. He saw two more coming from the shadows in his peripheral vision and fired as he dove behind a water trough. Bullets flew over his head, shots slamming into the trough, water splashing up. More shots cracked in the night.

Tate rose to one knee and blazed away with both hands, Peacemakers spiting fire as he cocked hammers with his thumbs, alternating between the two pistols, tossing lead with abandon at his two assailants. They hunched up and screamed as lead slapped into their flesh, both falling into the mud.

The crack of a pistol shot and the hot jolt of something slamming into Tate's right shoulder. The pistol flew from his hand and he fell back. Strangely, there was no pain, just a sick, shocked feeling. He knew the pain would come later. He struggled to a sitting position, another shot whizzing past his ear. He backed up until he hit a corral post,

And then he saw him, the big man emerging from the darkness, his bald head glistening in the lantern light. Gunter. Hans Mueller's brother out for revenge.

Tate lifted his other pistol and shot left-handed, but he was hurt, too full of whisky, fired too fast. The shot went wide. Gunter returned fire, the wood splintering on the post two inches above Tate's head.

Gunter lumbered forward, growling, and cocked his pistol again.

Tate fired.

He caught Gunter low on the hip. The big man grunted and stutter-stepped. Tate fired again, and the Bavarian's forehead exploded with blood and bone. Gunter jerked straight, mouth working but no words coming out. He stood there frozen for a moment and then slowly tipped forward and fell face-first into the trough, water splashing out on both sides. Gunter bobbed on the surface but otherwise didn't move.

Tate let his gun hand drop and blew out a sigh.

That was sloppy. I let that oaf and his friends catch me unaware. Not my finest moment.

His shoulder throbbed. Now that the excitement was over, the pain would come. It would get much worse before it got better. Tate felt light-headed. He wasn't bleeding too badly.

But he was definitely bleeding.

Another figure strolled out of the darkness. Tate tried to find the strength to lift his pistol again but stopped himself when he saw who it was. "Hello, Sheriff Rawlings. I hope you're having a pleasant evening. It's good you've happened along. I'd like to lodge a complaint against these men."

"Uh-huh." Rawlings sauntered past each corpse, thumbs hooked in his gun belt. He gave each man the eye, nodding to himself. He finally walked over to Tate, looked down at him with a sly smile on his face. "You're under arrest, you sniveling piece of dirt."

CHAPTER 20

Baily showed Carson the barbershop where the dead man was found, and then he introduced him to a few people around town. Carson asked questions. The folks of Ponderosa Crossing were friendly and wanted to be helpful, but no one had any useful information about the brutal murder. Everyone thought of Ezra Snopes as likable, not a man with enemies as far as anyone could tell. The barbershop hadn't even been robbed. It all seemed so senseless and random.

There was still plenty of daylight and Carson could see no reason to remain in Ponderosa Crossing. He bid farewell to Hank Baily, who gave him one of his trademark bone-crushing bear hugs. He hoped to see the man again sometime soon.

Carson rode until sundown. He made camp and passed another quiet night alone, all the same thoughts tumbling through his head again.

He rode into Nugget City late the next morning. The first thing that caught Carson's attention as he rode into town was Bessie parked outside the sheriff's office, her barrels gleaming in the sunlight. A few cavalry officers stood leaning against the buckboard to which the Gatling gun was attached. They smoked cigarettes and seemed in no hurry to do anything in particular.

Carson had no doubt he was looking at Major Grady's men, although Grady himself was nowhere in sight. He wondered briefly what had brought the US Cavalry to Nugget City. Possibly the town was on Grady's route, some routine visit. A few of the passing townsfolk paused to gawk at Bessie.

Carson had already seen the gun, so he bent his thoughts on what to do next. If he started for Boise now, he'd be spending another night on the ground, and anyway, he'd need to poke around first to see if Colby had arrived. He turned Jet toward the Golden Duchess. First, he'd get a room for the night and then he'd think about some lunch.

But he reined in his horse when he saw Grady come out of the sheriff's office, followed by Rawlings. The two men exchanged final words. And then Rawlings went back inside. Grady went to have words with his men.

Carson nudged Jet toward the cavalry troops. "Major Grady. Small world."

Grady squinted up at Carson. "Mr. Stone. I should have known you'd be nearby."

Carson wasn't sure what that meant but let it go. "What brings the US Cavalry to Nugget City?"

"The usual," Grady said. "We're still rounding up Bannock strays. We got word some had been sighted in the area, so here we are." Grady paused to look up and down the street. "Not much of a town, is it?"

"Nugget City's seen better times, I reckon," Carson agreed.

He considered telling Grady about the Bannock hiding in the forest near Koot Creek but decided against it. That particular group of Indians didn't want any trouble and were only looking to take themselves out of harm's way. Anyway, Laughing Otter had said they'd be moving on soon. They might not even be there anymore.

"Well, good luck to you, Major," Carson said. "There's

lots of Idaho out there. Plenty of places for Bannock to hide."

Grady pitched his voice low. "To tell the truth, we're not looking too hard for them. Oh sure, I'll arrest them and bring them in if I happen to stumble right over them, but other than that, I figure the boys can use a few nights R and R before we ride back. Anyway, you didn't hear none of that from me."

Carson smiled. "Hear what?"

Grady laughed. "Sorry about your partner, by the way. I hope the judge sees it his way."

Carson frowned. "Come again?"

"Your partner, Mr. Tate," Grady said. "My guess is it has to be some sort of misunderstanding. I'm sure the judge will get it all sorted."

Carson shook his head. "I have to admit you're catching me off guard, Major Grady. I really have no idea what you're talking about."

"Aw, hell. Sorry. I just assumed that was what you were doing here." The captain jerked a thumb over his shoulder back at the sheriff's office. "Colby Tate's in there right now, cooling his heels in one of Rawlings's cells. Seems he shot some fellas, and most sheriffs frown on that sort of thing."

Carson pushed back his hat and blew out a tired sigh. Grady's comment, *I should have known you'd be nearby,* made sense now. Damn. Of all the places to end up in a jail cell, why did it have to be in Sheriff Rawlings's town?

Just figures. I leave that tenderfoot Easterner alone for a few nights and he goes and gets himself arrested.

Carson dismounted and tied Jet to the hitching post in front of the sheriff's office. "I'm glad I ran into you, Major. Otherwise I might have ridden right on out of town never knowing Tate was in there. I sure as hell don't relish the thought of talking to Rawlings, but I guess I better see what this is all about."

"He can be a prickly pear, I suppose," Grady said. "I need to get my boys squared away. All I can do is say good luck." He offered his hand.

Carson shook it. "I'll take all the luck I can get. If you're around for a couple of days, maybe I'll stand you a drink at the Lucky Strike."

"I'll never turn down a free drink," Grady said. "Not on cavalry pay."

They said goodbye, and Carson found himself in front of the sheriff's door. He took a deep breath, let it out, then knocked.

"It's open," came the voice from the other side.

Carson entered.

Rawlings's expression twisted unpleasantly, as if he'd just smelled bad cheese. "Well, looky here. It's the other one. Figured you'd be along sooner or later."

Carson took off his hat. "I know you got my partner in here, Sheriff. I'm sure there's been some kind of mistake."

"Everybody who shoots somebody always says the same damn thing. 'Must be a mistake.' Well, you don't kill three men in my town without the law taking an interest. Or is law and order too inconvenient for you and your partner?"

Carson felt his face go hot but made himself keep a civil tongue. "We're all for law and order. Can I talk to him?"

"I guess it don't make no difference." Rawlings heaved himself out of his chair with a grunt. "Follow me."

Carson followed the sheriff around a corner and down a short hall. There were two jail cells and Tate was in the second. He got up from his narrow bunk when he saw Carson. His right arm was in a sling.

"I was wondering when you'd be along, old boy." Tate wiggled his bandaged arm. "Don't worry. Just a scratch."

"Looks like you got yourself scratched right into the clink," Carson observed. "How'd you let that happen?"

Tate's eyes flicked momentarily to Rawlings.

Carson cleared his throat. "Sheriff, could we have a minute?"

"Nope." Rawlings crossed his arms and leaned back against the wall. "Whatever you want to say, you can say in front of me."

Carson turned back to Tate and rolled his eyes.

"Our friend Gunter had another go at revenge," Tate explained. "He brought a couple of friends this time. I got lured into a bad situation. Shot the three of them—in *self-defense*—but took a slug in the process."

"The doc fixed him up good," Rawlings said. "He's being treated fair."

"Except he's behind bars," Carson said. "You heard the man. Self-defense."

"That's for a judge to decide."

"You know that Gunter fella was gunning for us," Carson said.

"And you can tell that to the judge." Rawlings shrugged. "In four weeks."

Carson's eyes went wide. "Four weeks?"

"Circuit judge comes through once a month and you just missed him," Rawlings explained. "Bad luck for your friend."

Carson turned back to Tate. He wasn't sure how much he should say in front of the sheriff.

Tate seemed to be thinking the same thing. "You find our English friend?"

Carson did a good job of keeping the surprise off his face. He didn't know how Tate knew he was looking for Nigel Evers, but that could wait for later.

"Haven't found him," Carson said. "Just some business

with that grocery list we've been working on. Thought he might could help with a few items."

Tate nodded, seeming to understand.

"Times up," Rawlings said. "Let's go."

"You need anything?" Carson asked.

"A rare steak," Tate said. "And a bottle of good whisky."

"Fat chance," Rawlings said.

"My pipe and some tobacco?"

Carson looked at the sheriff. "That okay?"

"That's fine, I guess," Rawlings conceded. "Bring it tomorrow. Right now, it's time to go."

Carson promised to return in the morning with the pipe and tobacco and then left. He needed to think what he was going to do next and figured thinking was easier with a plate of food and a cold beer.

CHAPTER 21

Cartwright hadn't been there when Kat Payne arrived to collect her money, but Doyle, who served as his right-hand man, was there to handle the transaction. He opened a strongbox and primly counted out the cash in crisp new bills.

"You'll tell Mr. Cartwright I was here," Kat said. Not a question.

Doyle's smile was tight, as if the gesture pained him. "Of course. Mr. Cartwright always wants to be kept apprised of all the doings of his . . . employees. I shall report to him immediately upon his return."

He doesn't like me and he isn't trying very hard to hide it.

"See that you do." She spun on her heel and left without another word.

Outside, she climbed atop her horse and headed south, veering east. Her destination was about a day and a half ride from Cartwright's sprawling ranch. There was a trading post about halfway to her destination, where she purchased a meal and a bed, and she set out again early the next morning after coffee.

Kat rode into town about midday.

Promontory, Utah, was a town on hold. Not everyone living there realized it. Predictably, the place had risen up around the railroad station, the point where the Union Pacific and the Central Pacific met. Optimism had been high over the last decade. Some construction crews worked feverishly to erect buildings along Main Street, while other projects seemed stalled. The excited talk of expansion and branch lines was beginning to ebb, and only some were just beginning to realize it.

Kat passed the office for the Central Pacific and kept walking. The place she wanted was at the other end of town. She dismounted in front of a single-story building, a sign over the front doors reading "Union Pacific Railroad." The shades in the big front windows on either side of the door had been pulled low. Kat hesitated only a moment before going in without knocking and then closing the door behind her with a soft click.

The outer office was dimly lit by sunlight filtering through the cracks between the shades. There were four desks, two on the left and two on the right. Sheets had been thrown over the desks to keep the dust off. Four months ago the Union Pacific Railroad decided they didn't need to spend money on an office in Promontory anymore, so they'd quietly pulled up stakes and left town. There'd been rumors that Central Pacific would follow suit, but so far they'd only been rumors.

Kat walked between the desks to the back hall, past a few offices, and paused to look at a hand-drawn map on the wall, showing all the railroad lines coast to coast. Existing routes were represented by solid lines, proposed routes as dashes. Two dashed lines originated from Promontory, one going almost due north through Idaho and Montana into Canada. The other angled toward Nugget City and beyond to the Pacific Northwest.

She continued to the end of the hall and knocked on the door. The door jerked open abruptly. Edward Vance stood there wearing a hard grimace on his face. He held a

Colt Army revolver and looked ready to use it. He no longer looked the proper businessman Kat had last seen in Cartwright's office. No tie, collar open, his vest unbuttoned, his hair slightly disheveled.

A sly smile from Kat. "You going to shoot me, Eddy?"

Vance's expression softened and he lowered the revolver. "Hadn't expected to see you so soon."

Kat raised an eyebrow. "You object?"

"Never, baby. Never." Vance snaked an arm around her waist and pulled her against him.

They kissed deep and long before finally pulling free of each other. Vance ushered her into the small room and closed the door. It had once been an office, Kat supposed, but Vance had thrown together a makeshift apartment and had been living there since the Union Pacific's departure. A bunk against the wall under the window. A small table and a single chair. A potbelly stove on the other side of the room with a coffeepot on top of it.

Vance gestured to a whisky bottle on the table. "Drink?"

"Always."

Vance filled a shot glass and held it out to her.

She reached past the glass and took the bottle out of his other hand. She shot him a quick grin, then tilted the bottle back, gulped, and gulped again. She smacked her lips. "Puts hair on your chest."

Vance laughed. "If I believed that, I'd never let you near the stuff." He emptied the shot glass down his throat.

Kat gestured around the room. "I love what you've done with the place."

Vance took back the bottle and refilled his glass. "Since I haven't bothered selling the building yet, I figured it was a good place to lay low. Nobody comes here anymore. Anyway, we need it for our plan."

Kat frowned. "Selling the place?"

"I didn't mention it? My final duty as Union Pacific's last remaining employee in Promontory. Did I tell you I'm still getting a paycheck from the railroad? I think they've forgotten I'm here. Anyway, I'm supposed to sell the place."

Kat had met Edward Vance at a Promontory saloon called the Golden Spike. Vance had been drinking hard, half celebrating and half lamenting the end of his employment with the railroad. She got to know him better, and the more she heard about Union Pacific's abandoned plans, the more she thought she'd found a juicy opportunity. A scheme developed. They needed an idiot and Cartwright had fit the bill perfectly. If he hadn't taken the bait, there were other millionaires on the list they could try, but Cartwright had swallowed the bait, hook, line, and sinker.

In every person's heart there's at least a little larceny, her father had been fond of saying. He'd meant it as a warning that his daughter should be slow to trust strangers, but instead, Kat has used the knowledge to prey on the greedy.

Cartwright had the foresight and the means to turn the information on the new railroad route into millions of dollars. The proposed new routes were known to few, and even fewer knew that both routes had been canceled, at least for the foreseeable future. To Cartwright, it would all seem so ludicrously simple. As one of the few to know of the proposed routes, he could simply buy up the land the railroad needed for its tracks and stations, then turn around and sell or lease it to the railroad for an enormous profit. Additionally, towns that grew up around important railroad stations often became important trade hubs. More shrewd real estate transactions would assure that Cartwright owned that land. In Cartwright's mind, he only had to play his cards right to become the richest man in the West.

There was only one problem. Buying up the land along both proposed railroad routes was prohibitive. There were limits to even Cartwright's wealth. The solution? Cartwright had to know with absolute certainty which route would be chosen, and the best way to achieve that was not to leave it to chance, but to take steps to make sure the route chosen— the Nugget City line—was the one.

That was where Edward Vance came in. Vance presented himself as the railroad executive in charge of recommending to the Union Pacific which route was more viable, and Cartwright's bribe to Vance would assure it was the Nugget City line that was picked.

That was the real prize, the fifty-thousand-dollar bribe. By the time Cartwright realized he'd been duped, that his contract with the Union Pacific was worthless and all of his real estate purchases for naught, Kat and Vance would be well out of the territory.

To add a sense of urgency, Kat and Vance had concocted a deadline. As far as Cartwright knew, the Union Pacific Railroad would be making their decision soon, so Cartwright would have to acquire the land quickly. Thus had the millionaire hired his posse of killers to eliminate anyone not eager to sell. Some miners had been run off their claims and others intimidated. One way or another, Cartwright would have his way. He'd make the deadline . . . but barely. Kat had made sure to get herself hired as one of Cartwright's killers to get close to the man, and she'd succeeded even beyond her own expectations. Getting intimate with Cartwright had put her in a position to manipulate the man. Cartwright wasn't an idiot and she'd needed to be subtle. But she'd been able to nudge things in the right direction.

"Have you hired the fake workers yet?" Kat asked.

"Not yet," Vance said. "I was going to wait until the last minute. No sense telling people who might blab."

Their plan had been to hire people to pose as Union Pacific

employees, sitting at the desks in the outer office, pretending to work. It was all part of the ruse for when Cartwright arrived to sign the final papers. Vance and Kat would need it to look like the Union Pacific was still alive and well in Promontory. The contracts and even the check Vance planned to use were all authentic, letterhead and other paperwork left when the company closed the office. There would be no need to forge anything.

"Don't bother," Kat said. "We're not doing it here."

Vance looked surprised. "No?"

"Cartwright's going to be working to acquire the land right up to the deadline," Kat explained. "Much of it's up around Nugget City. So when the time comes, you're going up there to sign the contracts and deliver the Union Pacific check."

"Cartwright agreed to that?"

Kat grinned. "Of course. Because I told him it was to his advantage. He liked the notion of your coming up alone without a gaggle of railroad lawyers. Also, if he's going to hand over a bribe, he'll feel safer in a place he controls rather than in an official railroad office where a nosey Union Pacific employee might suspect something. He's all for it."

"I suppose that makes sense."

"It actually helps us," Kat assured him. "Pretending this railroad office was still open always struck me as a bit iffy. All we need is one person in Promontory to open his mouth and say the wrong thing, and then we've got trouble."

Vance nodded. "Seems like you've got this figured pretty good. I guess Cartwright trusts your judgment."

Kat snorted. "I've got him right where I want him."

Vance's eyes narrowed. "I'm not thrilled that you've gotten so close to him."

Kat smiled and shrugged out of the shoulder holster with her .32 revolver and hung the rig on a peg on the back of the door. "Now, Eddy, come on. You're not getting squeamish on me, are you?" She began to unbutton her blouse. "Wouldn't you rather talk about more pleasant things?"

Vance grinned as the blouse fell to the floor. It turned out he didn't want to talk at all.

CHAPTER 22

Carson arrived the next morning at the sheriff's office with Tate's pipe and tobacco. The sheriff escorted Carson back to the cell, where Tate sat sipping coffee from a tin cup. He set it aside upon seeing Carson and rose from his bunk, gratefully accepting the pipe and tobacco.

"Sleep okay?" Carson asked.

"Of course," Tate said. "Between the five-star service and the plush feather bed, I'm actually having quite a luxurious little vacation."

"Now I'm jealous," Carson said. "Maybe I should shoot some fellas, too, and get in on this vacation."

Rawlings scowled. "I wouldn't recommend it."

Carson held up a placating hand. "Just a joke, Sheriff. I'm not looking for any more trouble."

Rawlings grunted like maybe he believed that or maybe not.

They heard the outer door open, and somebody shouted, "Sheriff! Old Luke Price is drunk down at Furley's and busting up the place!"

"I'll be right back." Rawlings headed back for the front office. "Drunk this time of the damn morning? Now just calm down and tell me what's going on."

Tate pitched his voice low. "We need to talk fast. No

telling how long Rawlings will be distracted. Sheriff Bedford is dead."

Carson gasped.

"We both know he was on that list," Tate said. "What's more, a mutual friend of ours was spotted in the vicinity. Katherine Payne."

"Kat?" Everything that had happened so far was already confusing enough. That Lady Pain herself was somehow involved made Carson's head spin. "Are you sure it was her?"

"She cut her hair and dyed it black in an obvious attempt to go incognito," Tate said. "But if you think I'll ever forget the face of the woman who shot me, you're crazy. Now, what's all this about an Englishman?"

"His name's Nigel Evers," Carson said. "There's no time to get into detail about it, but he's connected to two men on the list. Men who are dead now."

"Listen, Carson, we're tangled up in things that are going to get us killed," Tate said. "You need to come up with some way to get me out of here."

Carson tsked. "I hate to say it, but you might just have to wait the four weeks. Any fair judge is going to clear you."

Tate frowned, worry creasing his face. "It's not the judge I'm worried about. I asked about Evers when I was looking for you. Anyone could have heard me asking about him in the saloon or written the note that lured me out. And Rawlings appeared on the scene rather too promptly for my liking. I'd prefer not to be in the man's custody any longer than necessary."

Rawlings came back around the corner. "Okay, boys, gonna need to cut this short. Got to go do some sheriffing."

"It might be a couple of days while I check things out," Carson told Tate. "Don't wander off."

Tate rolled his eyes. "Oh, I'll be right here."

Carson checked out of his room at the Golden Duchess,

saddled Jet, and headed south. He still needed to track down McNeil and figure out the man's involvement, but he felt compelled to find out more about Bedford's death. Something big was happening. Tate was behind bars and Carson wasn't sure he could handle everything alone.

And he wanted to see Mary. He didn't see how she could help with his current predicament, but perhaps being with her could steady his nerves. He needed to shake off this feeling he was in over his head.

Except I am in over my head. Damn, I wish Colby hadn't got himself locked up.

He camped at the halfway point, woke the next morning before dawn and went through his morning routine. Coffee and a quick bite of jerky for breakfast. Oats for Jet. He made Boise by midafternoon.

Carson's first stop was the sheriff's office. He dismounted, looped Jet's reins around the hitching post, and went inside.

A man sat at Bedford's desk, a tin star on his vest, hat off and hair mussed. There was a half-empty bottle of whisky on the desk and a shot glass in his hand.

He looked at Carson with tired eyes. "Mister, if you've come in here to report a crime, I'm gonna shoot myself."

"No, sir," Carson said. "I heard about Bedford and thought I might need to come talk to the new man in charge."

"Why? You know something about what happened to him?"

Carson thought about how he wanted to answer that. "It's just that my partner and I were doing a favor for Bedford— sort of unofficial-like—and I thought I'd better check in with someone. My name's Carson Stone."

"The bounty hunter?"

Carson shrugged. "Sort of."

"Yeah, Bedford mentioned you before he . . . He mentioned

you." The man ran his fingers through his hair roughly and made some noise deep in his throat, not quite a grunt but more than a sigh.

"Rough day?"

The man at the desk nodded. "You could say that. I never knew how tough Bedford's job was. I been his deputy for two years, so I *thought* I knew. I didn't. I just had two other deputies quit on me and we were already shorthanded. They said it just seemed like a good time to move on and no offense to me, but I know better. Bedford inspired confidence. I guess I don't. Mayor asked if I wanted to be sheriff, so I said okay. Maybe I should have thought it over first." He refilled his shot glass. "You want a drink?"

"Not just yet."

"Well, have a seat anyway."

Carson eased himself into the chair opposite the new sheriff.

"Hell, I haven't even introduced myself, have I?"

"You'll get there."

"Paul Jessup." He leaned across the desk and they shook hands.

Jessup drained his shot glass, then leaned back in his chair. "I'll be frank with you, Stone. I'm swamped. Partly because I'm shorthanded, like I said, but also because I'm new to being the boss. Here's the point. I know Bedford was worried about all these things he told you about, but I don't have time to look into claim-jumpers fifty miles away when I got problems right under my nose. That's just how it is for the time being. I've passed along everything we know to the mayor. Maybe somebody else can do something, but I can't. Not right now."

Carson nodded and let that sink in. He was starting to warm up to Colby Tate's point of view. There were bad things going on in this part of Idaho, and maybe Colby was right. They had nothing to do with Carson. If Boise's new sheriff couldn't be troubled, then why should Carson bother?

Except Mary's here. What if I settled down, made this place my home? Then Idaho's problems are mine, aren't they?

Carson stood. "I'm not here to put more weight on your shoulders, Sheriff. I wish you luck. Can I ask one favor?"

Jessup spread his hands. "Well . . . you can ask."

"There's a map tacked up inside the door of that gun cabinet behind you. I could make use of it."

Jessup frowned, then stood and went to the cabinet. He opened it, squinted at the map. Clearly, he'd never seen it before. He made his decision quickly, took the map and handed it to Carson. "Take it."

"Obliged." Carson stopped at the door on his way out, turned back to Jessup. "Did the doc look at Bedford after he was killed?"

Jessup nodded. "As a matter of routine."

"Was it a rifle shot that done it?"

"You know something, I need to hear?" the sheriff said.

Carson shuffled from one foot to the other. "Just a notion."

Jessup sighed. "I should probably be more curious. If your notion becomes a fact, come see me again."

Carson nodded and touched the brim of his hat, then left.

He took Jet by the reins and walked him toward the Three Kings. He didn't walk fast. Thoughts crowded his head, and Carson tried to line them up in a way that made sense. Tate had told him he'd seen Kat Payne during the bank robbery that took Sheriff Bedford's life. All he'd seen her do was ride away on a horse, but all of Carson's instincts screamed she was involved. The woman was a killer who cared only about enriching herself. Bedford had been on the death list, so if there was a payday to be had killing the man, Carson had no doubt Lady Pain would look to collect.

And the setup was exactly like something she'd done before. When Carson, Colby, and Kat had all been partners, they'd tried to catch an outlaw during a bank robbery. Before the holdup, Kat had positioned herself on the roof of a building with a good view of the bank. From there, she could shoot down with her rifle.

Carson paused, looked back at the hotel where Tate had stayed, then let his gaze wander to the bank. No doubt about it. Kat would have had a good shot from the hotel roof. Carson was convinced he had it figured. Somehow, Kat had known about the bank holdup—might even have arranged it herself—and had used it as cover to take a shot at Sheriff Bedford and collect the kill list reward money. He couldn't prove it in a million years, but he knew he was right.

He arrived at the Three Kings and tied up Jet near the water trough.

Carson entered the saloon and looked around after his eyes adjusted to the dim interior. There were no other customers and the bartender busied himself wiping glasses with a rag. He considered asking for Mary, but the girls might still be sleeping even this late into the afternoon. If the saloon was having a good night and the whisky was flowing, the revelry could sometimes go until dawn. He couldn't quite picture himself sitting in the saloon and drinking all alone, so he went back out again and stood on the sidewalk, hands in pockets, wondering what to do next.

He left Jet to drink at the trough and ambled back down Main Street. He wandered into a general store, often a town's central hub of local news and gossip. He told the man behind the counter he was looking for someone and was pleasantly surprised when the man cheerfully provided an address. The shopkeeper seemed to know Carson and why he was asking.

Carson found the house on a quiet street two blocks over, a tidy cottage with a well-kept yard. He knocked on the door, immediately wished he hadn't, then figured it was too late.

A woman answered, maybe a year or two older than Carson, with yellow hair and bland eyes, a ruddy complexion, pleasant-looking without quite being pretty. "May I help you with something?"

Carson took off his hat. "Hope I'm not disturbing you, ma'am. I'm looking for Sally Anne Grainger."

"Yes, I'm Sally Anne."

"You don't know me, ma'am, but my name is Carson Stone. Recently—"

"Oh, Mr. Stone! Yes, I've heard all about you," Sally Anne said with enthusiasm. "I can't tell you how grateful I am that you were there to help Cousin Claire when those terrible men attacked. Such a dreadful and horrible episode. Please, won't you come in for some tea or something?"

"No, ma'am, but I appreciate it," Carson said. "Honestly, I just wanted to stop by for a second and ask her how she's doing. I've been out of town a few days or I would have paid a visit sooner."

"That's very kind of you," Sally Anne said. "I'm sorry to say you've missed her. She's gone back out to the farm."

"Oh? All on her own?'

"She's headstrong that way," Sally Anne said. "She hitched up the buckboard, made a stop at the feedstore, and then headed out. I think she means to poke through the ashes and see if she can salvage anything. It's all been such an awful tragedy."

"If you can please let her know I looked in on her," Carson asked.

"My cousin's made of surprisingly stern stuff, Mr. Stone, but obviously she's had quite a blow. It was kind of you to visit. I'll certainly tell her you came around."

"Thank you again, ma'am."

He nodded and left, snugged his hat back on his head, and went back the way he'd come. Possibly, he'd made a mistake coming back to Boise when he could have been in Nugget City hunting down McNeil or trying to figure a way to get Tate out of jail. Yesterday, he felt in over his head. Today, he felt useless.

Not exactly an improvement.

He ended up back at the Three Kings without consciously meaning to. Jet seemed content, so Carson continued into the saloon.

It was indeed a slow day at the Three Kings. Not only were there still no customers but the bartender was nowhere in sight. Maybe he was fetching something from the back room. Carson crossed the saloon and started up the stairs to the second floor. The establishment generally frowned upon men wandering upstairs unescorted, but there was nobody to stop him, so he kept going.

He approached Mary's room quietly and knocked with a single knuckle. He waited, then waited some more, and was starting to think she might be out when the door slowly creaked open.

She rubbed one eye, hair down over most of her face. She wore a loose robe that threatened to slip off one shoulder and give him the whole show. She was a wonderful, gorgeous mess.

"Carson?" she whispered.

Mary put a cool hand on the back of his neck and pulled him down to her. A long, lingering kiss.

"Come in before somebody sees you."

Carson entered her room and she closed the door with a soft click.

Mary jumped back into bed and pulled the covers up to her chin. "It's chilly."

Carson sat on the edge of her bed. "It's not. You just ain't dressed."

"Where have you been?"

"Up north. Business. Just got back to Boise today."

She smiled. "And you came to see me first thing."

"Tried to," Carson said. "I was here earlier, but the place was dead. When I came back, the bartender was gone, so I snuck up here."

"Jake takes the newspaper with him to the outhouse." Mary giggled. "He'd stay in there all day if he could. I think he eats too much cheese."

Carson laughed, then said, "I tried to look in on Claire Grainger. Just to see if she's getting along."

Mary sat up, her back against the headboard, and pulled her legs up to her body, hugging her knees. "Oh?"

"She wasn't there. I talked to her cousin. Anyway, I just wanted to see if she was okay after what happened."

"I know."

"You knew?"

She shook her head. A wan smile. "I mean I know you. Good men are the most predictable."

Carson laughed. "How's that?"

Mary thought about it. "Every kind of man comes through a saloon. Mean ones, sad ones, lonely ones. Men who have no idea what they want but only know they don't have it. When a man comes into the Three Kings looking for a woman like me, you'd think it would be pretty obvious what he wants, but half the time they don't even know. I hate it when they cry. You'd be surprised how often a man comes up here and sits on the side of the bed right where you are now and cries."

Carson wasn't sure he wanted to hear this, but Mary seemed to need to say it, so he kept quiet and let her talk.

"But a good man is dependable," she said. "You can count on him to do the right thing every single time, and there's men you think're good at first, might even believe it themselves, but then, when they're up against the wall and cornered by a tough decision, they show they were never really as good as they thought. A good man does right . . . every single time. And that's you, Carson Stone. And that's why when you said you went around to look in on Claire Grainger, I just knew it. Because Carson Stone would never save no damsel halfway."

"You almost make it sound like it's not a compliment."

Mary shrugged. "Doing the right thing ain't always best sometimes. Being good's no guarantee of being happy."

And Carson didn't know what to say to that either.

Mary slid back down under the covers. "I need just a little more sleep, I think. I don't know if it'll be busy tonight. Maybe not. You can come by and see."

"Okay."

Mary closed her eyes and Carson left, shutting the door quietly behind him. He went downstairs. Jake the bartender was back, and Carson gave him a curt nod. Jake frowned but didn't say anything. Outside, Carson climbed onto Jet and headed out of town.

Claire Grainger's farm wasn't far. There'd never been any doubt he'd ride out to see her.

Carson didn't know if he was a good man, but he reckoned he was exactly as predictable as Mary thought.

CHAPTER 23

Colby Tate paced his cell and smoked. He was glad Carson had brought him the pipe, but he'd need to exercise some discipline. With nothing to do all day, he could smoke through his limited supply of tobacco in a day if he wasn't careful.

He took short, small puffs and let his mind wander.

Tate flexed the hand of his wounded arm. Getting better, but he wouldn't be shooting with it for a while.

He wished he'd had more time with Carson. They needed to figure a way to get him out of jail before Rawlings decided it was safer to simply make Tate disappear. Rawlings didn't seem the most intelligent sort, but he struck Tate as the sort of man who'd survived on animal instinct. Rawlings's sense of self-preservation might suddenly kick in, and then that would be the end of Tate.

I suppose it's possible I have this all wrong. Someone tipped off Gunter and set me up for that ambush, but there's no proof it's Rawlings. I don't really know anything for sure.

But Tate's gut told him otherwise.

But why?

Rawlings was an ornery, unpleasant bastard and bad at his job. But that wasn't enough motivation to kill a man, was it? The sheriff had some connection to all the other happenings, the claim jumpers, the death of Old Dutch Casper, and now this Englishman. Nigel Evers. It was the only answer.

But Tate wasn't going to figure it out sitting in jail.

He considered a number of plans to break out of his cell, but that sort of thing might play right into Rawlings's hands. "Shot while trying to escape" were not the words Tate wanted on his tombstone.

There was nothing for it but to sit and wait. All Tate could do was puff his pipe and hope Carson knew what he was doing.

Nigel Evers considered himself an intelligent man. The stupid, the idiots, and the fools of the world were seldom self-aware, but the truly intelligent paused occasionally to look inward. Self-examination had led him long ago to an understanding that he possessed a modicum of intelligence, not necessarily one of the great philosophers or scholars of the Western world, but a man who possessed an above-average ability to think and reason. Evers was reasonable like that. He believed in self-awareness, not in self-aggrandizement.

He nudged his horse through the sparse woods at a brisk walk. Probably he should have stuck to the road, but he could save a few hours cutting through, and he generally had confidence in his sense of direction.

What had he been thinking about? Oh, yes. Intelligence.

And the intelligent, Evers had observed, were also curious. Intelligence and curiosity went hand in hand. And why Bill Cartwright wanted these people dead had aroused Evers's curiosity.

So Evers bent his brain power toward what the people on the death list had in common. Something political? Not that

Evers could detect. Cartwright's personal enemies? Unlikely. The people on the list seemed too varied, and it seemed improbable that many of them would even have heard of Cartwright.

No, quite obviously—to Evers, at least—the people on the list were in the way of something Cartwright wanted. Mining claims? This area of Idaho was mostly played out as far as Evers knew. Something political? The people on the list seemed too random for that. Some personal grudge? Again, too many people from too many places and backgrounds for that to seem a likely answer.

Then it hit him, something so simple. With a few exceptions, all of the people on the list owned land, in many cases very large tracts.

Take Nora Dell as an example. Her tract of land lay ahead of him, and while it wasn't as large as other parcels, it was arguably an important area. It contained an area in which a road crossed a river at the shallows, the best place to ford the river for many miles. A valuable piece of property? Yes, in a certain context. But what did this one chunk of land have in common with the others?

Cartwright knows something. He's buying up land because he knows it's about to increase in value. And those not willing to sell are being eliminated. But why? What was going to happen?

Ultimately, Evers took comfort in the following thought: He didn't give a damn.

His curiosity about Cartwright's ambitions was just that. Curiosity. An abstract, intellectual endeavor. Getting in the way of the machinations of a man like Cartwright was not only unprofitable, it was hazardous to one's health. Evers had no desire to cross Cartwright. He was simply passing the time with an intellectual exercise.

He emerged from the woods into an open area where a

road crossed a bend in the river, a wide, shallow stretch suitable for fording. On a rise beyond, nestled in a copse of trees, Evers spied the cottage. It looked neat and well-cared-for. Evers nudged the horse into the river, the babbling water not quite reaching the animal's knees. He headed up the rise. Fishing nets hung to dry to one side of the cottage.

Before Evers had a chance to dismount, an old woman emerged from the cottage. She wore men's trousers and a heavy plaid shirt, gray hair pulled back into a tight bun. Deeply lined face, but alert blue eyes. There was a sturdiness about her despite her age. In one hand she carried a thin fishing pole, a small wicker basket in the other.

She squinted up at Evers. "Lost?"

Evers smiled warmly. "No, madam, indeed not. You're Nora Dell?"

"I surely am."

"A pleasure to make your acquaintance. Is there a Mr. Dell?"

"Why? You come a-courtin'?" She cackled loudly.

Evers laughed along with her. "That I should be so lucky."

"Mr. Dell passed on near twenty years ago."

"This is your land, then?"

Nora's eyes narrowed. "Oh, the land again, is it? You're here about that."

"In a manner of speaking."

"Well, I'll tell you what I told the other fella," Nora said. "I'll think on it."

"Sorry. Other fellow?"

"Name of McNeil. I thought the offer low . . . although what he wants with the land I couldn't say. Walter—that's Mr. Dell—said we should build a bridge and charge folks. Never made no sense to me. Anyone can ride across easy enough just like you did."

Evers climbed down from his horse. "I'm not acquainted with Mr. McNeil."

"Well, I suppose you could put in an offer if you've a mind. Like I said, McNeil wasn't looking to spend much. My parcel goes twenty acres in every direction. Walter tried panning for gold but didn't get much. Then he was going to start a farm, but all we ever had was our own little garden. Walter had a lot of ideas but usually didn't get around to trying them out. I'm content to tend the garden and fish and sew in the evening."

"Good fishing here?" He moved toward her as he spoke, an easy, nonthreatening amble.

"More fish in the river than gold. Good trout."

"What kind of fly do you use?"

"I make 'em out of house finch feathers mostly."

"That works?" Evers let his hand drop into his coat pocket and ran a thumb over the smooth surface of the folding blade.

"I'll show you." Nora set the pole aside and dug into the basket.

Evers edged closer, preparing to take the knife from his pocket.

Nora's hand came out of the basket holding an enormous Colt Walker. She cocked back the hammer with a bony thumb. "Step back, boy. I know you're up to no good."

Evers didn't hesitate. He dove under the pistol, making a grab for Nora's legs. The Walker discharged harmlessly over his head but close enough that he felt the vibration of the blast in his skull. He slammed into her legs, and as she went down, Nora slammed the Walker into the side of his head.

Pain exploded in his ear, spots blinking in front of his eyes. The old woman had plenty of strength left in her. They hit the ground, and Evers heard the air go out of her. The Walker flew away back toward the cottage.

Evers struggled to one knee, blinking spots out of his eyes. He saw the old woman staggering up, heading for the Walker on the ground a few feet away.

He drew his six-shooter and fired. Nora screamed, clutched the bloody wound low on her side, and staggered into the side of the cottage. Blood seeped red and thick between her fingers. "You . . . rat bastard . . . son of a—"

Evers fired again. Nora twitched and died.

He stood, legs feeling weak. His nerves were all atwitter. Evers hadn't expected the woman to put up such a fight, and the altercation had left him shaken. Had there been something in his demeanor that had aroused the woman's suspicions? Maybe she was a witch. The thought would normally make him laugh, but he felt off.

He realized there had been a big buildup to the kill, the anticipation of blood, the smooth feeling of his knife blade across her throat. Evers had felt the buildup but not the payoff, not the completion. He'd been cheated of his release.

Evers understood keenly that there was something wrong with him. Again, that self-awareness that came with intelligence. There was something wrong inside his head, but it didn't feel wrong when he was able to reach completion. But fate had thwarted him. The sudden, thunderous crack of gunfire and the stink of gunpowder had rattled him.

Nigel Evers was upset.

His horse had run at the sound of gunfire, but it hadn't gone far. He walked back down to the river, where it stood placidly drinking. Evers took the death list and pencil from his coat pocket. He started to cross through Nora Dell's name when he saw his hand shaking.

This is ridiculous. Get a hold of yourself, old chap. You're not some big girl's blouse.

Evers took a deep breath and let it out slowly. He crossed through the old woman's name with a steadier hand, folded up the list, and put it away. And just like that, he was a hundred dollars richer.

At the moment, however, he felt little satisfaction.

He knelt at the edge of the river, splashed cold water into his face and on the back of his neck. The calming effect was slight but noticeable.

Evers climbed back into the saddle. He'd regained control of himself. But something nagged, an itch still unscratched.

He turned toward Boise and spurred the horse. Perhaps Evers would find something at the Three Kings to satiate him.

Bill Cartwright leaned against the porch railing, looking across his many acres of land at the cloud of dust in the distance. That would be the hands bringing in the herd. Cartwright hated cattle. They stunk and they were noisy. He could tolerate a cow if it was on a plate, medium rare, with roasted potatoes next to it.

So why bother, then? He'd needed a place to conduct his business while in the region, so he'd purchased the ranch. He'd wanted space, not a house in a crowded town with hundreds of eyes and ears. So he'd bought the ranch house and the land for miles around. But he didn't need the damn cows, not if he just wanted space and privacy, so why bother?

Because it's a cattle ranch, and the business of a cattle ranch is cattle. I won't own anything that doesn't earn.

He saw another rider coming ahead of the dust cloud. Maybe they'd sent a man ahead to announce they were coming, tell the cooks to get dinner going.

Cartwright watched the rider come until he saw it was a woman and then, soon after that, he saw it was Kat. He waited.

She arrived a few minutes later. The porch was raised high enough that he was eye to eye with her on horseback.

He looked her over. Dusty from a long ride, pink in the cheeks, sweaty.

"Well?"

"I told him," Kat said. "He'll be in Nugget City on Monday. Is that too soon?"

Cartwright turned, paced the length of the porch and back, thinking. His people were even now arranging the last of the land deals. The holdouts had been . . . dealt with. Mostly. Yes, he was close enough. He could make it work.

"We'll leave Friday," he told her. "I'll pick twenty of my best hands to go with us."

"Why do we need them?" Kat asked.

"Because you killed two of my killers and I have no idea where that damn Englishman has got off to," Cartwright said. "I don't go anywhere without security."

Kat shrugged. "Fair enough."

"Come in, then," Cartwright said. "I'll have Eloise run you a bath. You smell like horse."

CHAPTER 24

The remains of the Grainger farmhouse looked sad and stark from a distance against the gray sky. The chimney still stood straight and tall, a defiant stack of bricks refusing to believe defeat. The next big windstorm would knock it over. Blackened beams crisscrossed each other in a pile.

As Carson rode closer, he realized the rig parked in front of the barn wasn't Claire's buckboard but rather a little surrey, a tall chestnut hitched to it. Carson hadn't remembered seeing it in the barn when he'd been here before. He reined in Jet in front of the open barn doors but didn't see anyone inside.

Raised voices.

Carson clicked his tongue and Jet took him around to the backside of the barn.

Claire and a man stood there facing each other, and the conversation cut off when they saw Carson. Claire looked disheveled, hands dirty with ash, a black streak down one cheek. The man wore a black suit, a string tie. He held a black hat in one hand. Scarred face, sparse beard and mustache, hair thinning on top. Tall but stooped. Their body language was stiff and tense.

"Hope I'm not interrupting," Carson said.

Claire brightened, but the smile seemed forced. "Mr. Stone—Carson! So glad you made it. Thanks for coming."

Carson kept his face neutral. If Claire wanted to pretend he'd been invited, he was willing to play along. No reason to spoil her story until he found out what was going on. "My pleasure, ma'am."

The man in the black suit shifted from one foot to another, his eyes shifting between Carson and Claire. He seemed unsure of himself, and Carson could guess the situation. It was one thing to have strong words with a slip of a girl. It was a different matter altogether having Carson Stone sitting astride Jet, a six-gun on his hip, glaring down at you.

The man scowled at Claire and said, "Just think about what I said."

She lifted her chin. "I will. Good day to you."

The man shot Carson a dirty look, snugged his hat back on his head, and left. A few moments later Carson heard the snap of a buggy whip and the rattle of the surrey heading away.

Claire stood there a moment, staring out across the land, face blank. Carson sat on Jet and waited her out.

Finally she sighed and turned her tired eyes on Carson. "Well, you must have ridden out here for something, Mr. Stone." Not "Carson" anymore.

"If you tell me what that was all about, maybe I can help—"

"It's personal business, Mr. Stone," Claire snapped. "I don't need anyone's help." She wiped at one eye, leaving another black streak across her face.

A pregnant pause.

"Well, you sure as hell need a washrag," Carson said.

She coughed out a laugh, then regained control of herself. "I must look a sight. I've been digging around in the house rubble, trying to see what there is to salvage. Do you really want to help?"

"If you need it."

"I'll keep sifting through the ash," she said. "But the hogs and chickens need fed. I stopped at the feedstore before coming out. It's all still in the back of the buckboard."

Carson climbed down from the saddle. "Simple enough. I can do that."

"Thank you." She headed back toward the remains of the farmhouse.

Carson led Jet into the barn and took off his saddle. He gave the horse a quick brush down and fed him some oats. He fed the chickens after cleaning out the coop. He collected nearly two dozen eggs, gathering them in his hat, and took them into the barn. He slopped the hogs and then took care of Claire's horse, the one she used for pulling the buckboard.

In a way, it felt good. Honest, normal farmwork. Colby Tate was a good friend, and his way of life offered good money. But it took something normal like feeding chickens to remind him that running around playing bounty hunter wasn't something he could do forever.

He glanced up at the sky. The storm hadn't rolled in as fast as he thought it would, but it was still coming. He found Claire looking at the ruined house, a small pile of salvaged items next to her—a blackened coffeepot, a small silver picture frame, a washboard and clothes iron, three forks and a spoon. It was a pitiful collection, and Carson's heart broke a little.

"It's going to rain soon," he said. "Might want to think about getting back."

She didn't turn, kept staring at the rubble. "I'm not going back."

"But—"

He stopped himself. Claire Grainger had already made it clear she wasn't a woman who wanted to be told what to do.

"The animals will need to be fed again tomorrow," she said. "And then the day after that, and then . . . I don't know what. But this is my home. Even if there's nobody left to make it a home. Even if it's just because I have nowhere else to go."

Carson waited. Saying nothing was usually better than saying something wrong.

"I'm sorry," she said.

"What for?"

"For snapping at you. For saying I didn't need your help. I was angry. Because I do need help. Because I have no idea what I'm going to do, and I hate feeling like that. So you have my apologies, Mr. Stone."

"I liked it better when you called me Carson."

And now she finally turned to look at him, her smile weak but natural and sweet. "Carson, then."

She looked back at the rubble and blackened beams that used to be a farmhouse. "Maybe Mr. McNeil was right. Maybe I should just sell."

Carson's eyes shot wide. "McNeil?"

His urgency startled her.

Carson turned toward the barn, then stopped himself. And if he ran in there and saddled Jet and rode after the man, then what? McNeil had too much of a head start, and anyway, Carson didn't even know where he was going. He'd assumed at first that McNeil was headed back to Nugget City, but he might have more business in Boise or a dozen other places.

Carson turned back to Claire. "He wanted to buy your farm?"

"He'd been around before, a few months ago," Claire said. "Grandfather didn't want to sell. He said the price was too low, and we weren't looking to go anywhere else anyway. My grandfather and great-uncle had built the house themselves. I thought that was the end of it, but then McNeil showed up again today. Said I should sell before some other bad thing happened. He never came right out and threatened me, but his tone worried me. I was glad you came along."

"Listen, I've actually been looking for McNeil. He's mixed up in some bad stuff to do with buying up land. There's people been killed over it," Carson said. "If he comes back, get away from him. Or lie and tell him you'll sell just to make him go away."

She shook her head. "It doesn't get easier, does it?"

A crack of thunder. Carson squinted up at the black clouds. "When it rains, it pours."

The sky opened up just as they dashed into the barn. The rain fell hard and stayed that way. Carson estimated it wouldn't let up anytime soon.

Claire looked down at herself, covered with ash, smeared black and matted with sweat. Then she looked at Carson and wrinkled her nose. "We're disgusting. And we stink."

"Slopping hogs will do that."

Claire opened a leather satchel in back of the buckboard and came back with a thick, white bar of soap. She handed it to Carson. "Cut that in half."

Carson drew his bowie knife and sawed halfway through the bar, then sheathed the knife. He took the bar of soap in two hands and broke it in half.

Claire took one of the halves. "No sense letting a good, hard rain shower go to waste."

Carson looked out at the rain, then back at her and raised an eyebrow.

A sly smile quirked to her lips. "Don't worry. I won't peek."

There was a smaller door at the back of the barn. Claire strung a line across that corner of the barn and threw a horse blanket over it to make a curtain. "I'll wash up on this side of the barn. You go out front." She disappeared behind the blanket.

Carson hesitated, looking back over his shoulder at the curtain. The fact was, he did stink. He stripped off his soiled clothes and hung them on a peg with a coil of rope.

He stepped out into the rain and gasped. It was *cold*. He lathered every part of himself, then spread his arms and made a slow turn in the downpour. A crack of thunder sent him scurrying back into the barn.

Carson shook himself off like a dog. He was still wet but couldn't just stand there in nothing but his skin. He took clean clothes from his saddlebags and dressed quickly. His shirt stuck to him, but he felt human again.

"You decent?" Claire called from behind the horse blanket.

Carson indicated he was.

Claire pulled down the blanket. She wore a loose pair of man's work pants cinched tight with a wide leather belt and a heavy blue shirt. Like Carson's, it stuck to her. She shivered visibly and wrapped the horse blanket around her shoulders. "Well, I'm c-clean . . . but I'm f-freezing."

Carson went to his saddlebags and came back with a half-full bottle of whisky. "I've found this to have a warming effect."

"I don't drink."

"Oh." Carson felt embarrassed. "Of course not. Sorry, I just thought—"

"Give it here."

Claire took the bottle in both hands and tilted it back, taking a large gulp. She coughed and sputtered, her eyes watering. "Warm? That feels like drinking fire. My throat's scorched."

"I should have warned you."

She took another, smaller swig. "I can feel the warmth spreading, but I'm still cold."

"I'll start a fire in the smithy forge," Carson said. "Just give me a minute."

He went through the side door to the attached blacksmith setup. It wasn't big. A small hearth and an even smaller anvil and a cooling tub. Probably the old man had done his own horseshoes and nails and such. It wasn't big enough for much more.

He started the fire, and Claire came out behind him, holding the whisky bottle in one hand and the blanket closed in front of her with the other. "Thank you. I always get cold. Even in the summer, at night when the sun goes down."

"We'll get you warm soon."

Carson pulled a bench up close to the hearth and Claire sat. He stoked the fire until it was hot—not hot enough to do any blacksmithing, but enough for warmth.

Claire patted the space on the bench next to her. "There's room for two."

Carson sat, held his hands out to the fire.

Claire took another swig from the bottle, then handed it to Carson. "Better take this. I'll make myself sick."

He took the bottle and set it on the floor next to his side of the bench.

It was close to sunset and dark anyway because of the clouds. He wasn't keen on riding back to town at night in the rain and wondered if he could presume upon Claire to sleep in her hayloft without seeming forward. A moment later she put her head on his shoulder.

"I'm sorry," she said. "Just for a minute, okay? I can barely hold my head up. I just feel dead tired all of a sudden."

Carson wasn't surprised. She'd been through a lot. And she'd worked all day sifting through the ruined farmhouse, and then McNeil had come along and probably frightened her to death. Toss in a couple of shots of whisky, and anyone was bound to feel like they might want to close their eyes and call it a day.

"That's no probably at all. Actually, I was just about to

ask if I could sack out in your hayloft," Carson said. "That okay?"

No response.

"Claire?"

But she was fast asleep.

CHAPTER 25

Carson lined up the bottles on the fence posts of the empty corral.

He'd risen with the dawn, stoked the coals in the smithy hearth, and made coffee. He drank two cups, but Claire still slept in the nest he's made for her in the hay with horse blankets and a bag of flour for a pillow. Carson didn't blame her for sleeping in. The last few days hadn't been good for her, and emotional exhaustion had a way of leaking into the body. She had no idea what her future was going to be, and that would put a strain on anyone.

Carson had slept in the loft, the patter of rain on the roof deep into the night lulling him to sleep.

He heard a yawn and turned to see her emerge from the barn, blanket around her shoulders, hay in her hair.

A shy smile. "I slept too long."

"You needed it."

She watched him place the final bottle on the post and asked, "What are you doing?"

"I'll need to leave soon."

Claire's smile wilted. "Oh?"

"I got to thinking about you out here on your own," Carson said. "You have a gun?"

She looked back at the farmhouse. The rain had turned

the ash into gray mud. "Grandfather had a shotgun. But if it's in there . . ."

"Hold on." Carson went into the barn and came back a few seconds later with a gun belt and a six-shooter. He drew the pistol and let the belt drop to the ground for a moment. "You know how to use one of these?"

"No."

He showed her how to load and unload it and listed the various parts of the gun. Then he handed it to her. "Keep it pointed away from anyone you don't want to kill. Right now, that's you and me."

She took it carefully. "This belonged to . . . him?"

"Yeah." Carson didn't need her to explain she meant the bandit who'd killed her grandfather. "I don't need it, and if it belongs to anyone, I reckon it's you."

"It's heavy."

"You don't want the first time to shoot one to be the time you really need it," Carson said. "They're loud. It might startle you. You need to know what it's like."

She nodded. "Okay."

"Aim it at one of the bottles," Carson said. "Look down the barrel and use the sight. Cock the hammer back with your thumb."

She pointed the six-shooter at one of the bottles. She fired and yelped, taking two steps back. The shot went high, probably landed in the next territory.

"You're right," Claire said. "That was loud. I felt it all the way up my arm."

"You'll get used to it."

"Was I close?"

"You were not."

She muttered something under her breath and lifted the six-shooter again. She fired. The bottle didn't go anywhere.

"You're still high."

She fired three more times and missed three more times. Her face was going red with frustration and Carson worked hard not to laugh.

Claire fired the last round. It splintered the wood beneath the bottle.

"That was closer." She turned to Carson, eyes wide. "That was closer, wasn't it?"

"A lot closer."

"Load it again."

"You do it." He handed her a box of cartridges. "You need to know how."

She emptied the spent shells and thumbed in new ones. Carson had expected her to be awkward about it, but she wasn't. She lifted the pistol, thumbed back the hammer, and fired. She missed and then missed again with the next shot, but she was no longer flinching at the harsh crack of the pistol. She fired a third time and the bottle shattered.

Claire jumped and whooped, her face bright. "Did you see that?"

Carson smiled. "I surely did."

She emptied the gun, loaded it again, and by the time she was done, all the bottles were dead.

"I reckon that's fine for now," Carson said. "Keep that gun close."

Claire took the gun belt from the ground and belted it around her waist. Its former owner had more girth, so she took a moment to adjust it. "Show me how to draw."

"That might be a bit advanced for now," Carson said.

"One day you'll learn I don't do anything halfway, Carson Stone."

He held up his hands in surrender. "Okay. You win. But there's many a man who thought he was a quick-draw artist and ended up shooting off some of his own toes. If you can just get it out of the holster and aim and hit something, let's call it good enough."

She agreed. They spent another hour practicing, and by the end she could draw and fire. She was slow, but she didn't look clumsy. She at least had a chance now to defend herself.

Carson saddled Jet and brought him out of the barn. Claire waited for him, hip cocked and one hand resting on the hilt of her new pistol like a veteran campaigner.

"I don't know about anyone else, but I'd think twice before messing with you," Carson said.

"They call me Deadeye Claire Grainger," she joked.

They stood looking at each other a moment.

"Well." Carson put his hat on. "I have to go."

"You didn't have to help me," Claire said. "Not that day, when those men came. Not yesterday, riding all the way out here to slop hogs and feed chickens."

Carson shrugged. "I never even stopped to think about it. Maybe I'm just slow-witted."

"A lot of men done what you did would want something," she said. "Expect something."

An embarrassed smile. "Well . . . not sure what to say to that. I hope you don't think I'm the sort to—"

She threw her slender arms around his neck and kissed him so hard, he thought he might fall over. The kiss might have lasted for two seconds or a year. Carson lost all track of the world, his head going light. Finally, she pulled away, still looking up at him with huge blue eyes. She kept hold of his neck and his hands went around her back.

Carson cleared his throat. "Why'd you do that?"

A slow smile. "I never stopped to think about it. Maybe I'm just slow-witted."

Carson laughed.

"I know you have things to do, but then I want you to

come back." She put a cool hand on his cheek, rough with stubble. "I thought this would convince you. I don't know what's happened to me. You show up and suddenly I'm drinking whisky and shooting six-guns and throwing myself at you like some kind of—"

He leaned down and kissed her, hugging her tight.

Carson pulled away and quickly climbed onto Jet before he let himself get carried away. "I'm coming back, Claire. Count on it."

He spurred Jet into a run and headed out across the flat landscape. Carson didn't look back. If he saw her standing there, watching him go, he might never have the strength to leave, but he'd meant what he'd told her. He'd be back.

He'd be back or he'd be dead.

Carson camped along a babbling brook that night. The trip back and forth between Boise and Nugget City would probably have gotten tedious by now except that Carson didn't care. Thoughts of Claire filled him. He felt a twinge of guilt that it had taken him so long to remember Mary. He'd have to break it to her when he returned to Boise.

He lay awake a long time, staring at the moon and seeing Claire's face.

Upon arriving in Nugget City, his first obligation was to pay Colby Tate a visit. Rawlings ushered him back to Tate's cell with his usual sour demeanor.

"How's the arm?" Carson asked.

"Getting better," Tate said. "Slowly."

Carson told Tate about visiting Claire. He made a point of *not* mentioning the kiss, but Tate wasn't stupid.

"There's a certain twinkle in your eye when you say Claire's name, old boy," Tate said. "Let's not get distracted from the very important task of getting your good pal Colby out of jail."

An embarrassed smile from Carson. "Don't worry. I can walk and whistle at the same time. You need anything?"

"If you can lay your hands on some pipe tobacco, I'd be grateful," Tate said. "I'm running low."

"You smoke too much."

"Time's up, ladies." Rawlings gestured toward the exit.

"I'll see you tomorrow." Carson turned and left the sheriff's office.

Outside, he spotted an unlikely duo. Major Grady of the US Cavalry conversed with Doris Beckinridge, boardinghouse owner and member of the town council. Grady looked his usual smart, military self in a freshly cleaned uniform. Beckinridge looked prim and severe in a dress of such a dark green as to be almost black. A matching hat with a feather. High-buttoned collar. Gloves. They both looked up as Carson approached.

"Good morning, Stone," Grady said. "Allow me to introduce Doris Beckinridge. She practically runs this town."

Carson tipped his hat. "We've met."

"Should have known," Grady said. "You do get around."

Beckinridge nodded greetings to Carson. "Did you manage to locate our elusive Benson Cassidy, Mr. Stone?"

"I did indeed."

"And did you conclude your business with him to your satisfaction?" she asked.

Carson considered. "It's a work in progress."

Beckinridge smiled. Carson suspected she knew a nonanswer when she heard one.

"What's going on here?" Carson looked up and down the street. Grady's entire command was in motion, troopers saddling horses and checking weapons.

"Got word a band of Bannock is holed up in the hills to

the west," Grady said. "My boys and I are obligated to go up there and dig 'em out."

Carson thought about what Laughing Otter had told him. If the Indians were on schedule, they'd likely moved on by now. All Carson said was, "Good luck, Major. That's some raw country in that direction."

"Don't I know it," Grady said. "The terrain's too rocky in places to drag Bessie along with us, I'm sorry to say."

Grady looked down the street, and Carson followed his gaze.

Across the street and a block down, a detail of troopers backed Bessie—Major Grady's lethal Gatling gun—past the huge double doors of a wide building. A sign over the doors read "Nugget City Firehouse."

"We appreciate having somewhere to store Bessie out of the way," Grady said. "I hope we're not putting anyone out."

Beckinridge tsked. "Sadly, the building has been empty for years. Two years after the founding of the town, it almost all burned in a huge fire. When we rebuilt, we erected the firehouse. The council even voted to allocate funds for a rotary steam fire engine from Silsby Manufacturing Company in Seneca Falls, New York. The stupid thing was never delivered, of course. That's what we get, ordering from a place back East. Everyone there thinks the Idaho Territory might as well be the moon. Anyway, the firehouse is empty, so if we can assist in this small way, we're happy to do so."

"And as I said before, we're most grateful," Grady assured her.

"Miss Beckinridge, I was wondering if I could ask another favor," Carson said.

"I suppose you can ask."

"I appreciated you help looking for Cassidy," Carson said. "As a member of the town council, I reckon you know most folks around here. This time I'm looking for a man named Foster McNeil."

Beckinridge's eyes narrowed. "First Cassidy and now McNeil. You have a talent for ferreting out Nugget City's seediest characters, Mr. Stone."

Carson chuckled. "Not a talent, ma'am. Just my bad luck. And I guess I'm not as good at ferreting as you think, because I don't know where to find him."

"I infer you mean to cause him some mischief," Beckinridge said. "In which case I'd be delighted to tell you."

CHAPTER 26

Claire dropped the bag of chicken feed into the back of the buckboard and wiped the sweat from her brow with the back of her hand. Mr. Reiner at the feedstore had been generous in letting her run up a tab. Like most in town, he knew she'd had trouble, but his generosity didn't extend to loading the wagon for her.

She paused a moment to check her items—the chicken feed, lamp oil, nails, another box of .45 cartridges for her new six-shooter, a heavy blanket, dried pinto beans, cornmeal, a basket of apples, two pounds of coffee, a coffeepot, a deep skillet, oats for her horse, salt, a good knife, thread and needles, a bolt of simple cloth, and a pair of work boots. It was bewildering how much she'd lost in the fire. A woman spent her whole life gathering things, and then they could all be taken away in an eye blink. But they were just things. They could be replaced.

It would have been easy to feel down, overwhelmed. Claire had felt pretty low the last couple of days to say the least. Who could blame her? But she didn't like it. Didn't like feeling whipped.

There's a time to mourn, but there's a time to move on, too, to wipe the tears from your eyes and stiffen your spine and let the world know you're not licked.

Claire didn't kid herself that she'd found courage all on her own. She still felt the flutter in her stomach when she thought of Carson, still tasted him on her lips. She'd never felt this way about anyone before. It was sudden and strange and a little frightening, but she didn't want the feeling to go away.

Satisfied she had everything stowed in the back of the buckboard, she made to climb into the seat and ride away when she heard a voice behind her.

"Claire, how have you been?"

Mary stood in front of her in a pink dress, too many frills, her blond hair in tight curls down over her shoulders. Lace gloves. High-buttoned shoes. A parasol that matched her dress kept the sun off her fair skin, with not a freckle or blemish of any kind. She looked like a bird showing off fancy feathers, and from the corner of Claire's eye, she saw men turning their heads to get a look at her.

Don't be unkind, Claire thought. *She was helpful to you on that terrible day*. She forced herself to smile. There was no reason to be unfriendly.

"I know it's been a hard time for you," Mary continued. "Did my Carson make it out to see you? He said he wanted to check on you. He's just so thoughtful like that, you know?"

Claire felt the smile wilt from her face. *My Carson*, Mary had said. But of course, she'd been riding with him that day Carson had saved her. *Stupid, stupid, stupid*. How could Claire have been so foolish?

"Yes," Claire said. "He's been very kind."

"Isn't he?" Mary glanced into the back of the buckboard. "Some necessities?"

"I've been living in the barn," Claire said. "It's not so bad, really. I have a roof over my head, but there are some gaps in the walls. The wind howls through at night. I have scrap wood to block the holes, but I didn't have nails, so . . ." She gestured at her supplies. "I'm getting along okay."

"You're very brave. I'll need to send Carson out to visit you again and lend a hand," Mary said. "When I can spare him."

"That's . . . thoughtful." Claire shifted from one foot to the other and cleared her throat. "I should go. There's the animals and so much to do."

"Take care of yourself, Claire." A syrupy sweet smile spread across Mary's face.

Claire tried to return the smile but couldn't quite pull it off. She climbed onto the buckboard and situated herself on the bench. She flicked the reins and headed out of town, feeling the other woman's eyes on her but refusing to look back.

Mary stood on the sidewalk and watched until the buckboard turned at the end of the street and clattered out of sight. She smiled to herself with a bitter sort of satisfaction. She'd seen Claire coming out of the feedstore and had seized her opportunity.

Working as a saloon girl had taught Mary to read people, men mostly—which ones could be approached and which ones wanted to be left alone. Which men were ready to spend money and who would try to get by for cheap. Being able to tell the docile ones from the men with meanness in their hearts had been an important survival skill.

But she'd learned to read women, too. She felt the dirty looks of good, churchgoing women who had nothing but contempt for a woman like Mary.

Claire Grainger had been a wide-open book.

Mary had mentioned Carson, and Claire's expression had changed, as if she'd been struck. It had been almost too easy. A sweet, innocent thing like Claire didn't have the same armor that Mary had built up over the years. The world was a hard place, and it would squash a girl like Claire.

And then Mary felt bad.

And feeling bad made her angry.

Why shouldn't I fight for what's mine? I'm not the weak one. I'm allowed to want what I want.

That thought surprised her. It didn't pay to get close to men or let them get close to her. It always ended bad. Why did she give a damn about Carson Stone? He was just another man.

Except he wasn't.

The smug feeling of her petty triumph over Claire had evaporated. Now Mary was annoyed.

Forget it. You have work to do.

Mary headed back to the Three Kings. It was still early; most of the patrons wouldn't show until after sundown, but she was expecting one of her regulars tonight. She wanted to get ready, and she hated being rushed.

First, she took a long bath as hot as she could stand it. The heat loosened her limbs and eased her tensions. Claire was well forgotten by the time she climbed out of the tub and toweled herself off. Her white skin was bright pink. She waited until she was completely dry, then powdered herself all over.

Mary sat on a stool near the tub and painted her toenails the color of a ripe apple. She painted her fingernails to match. Most men didn't care about such details or even notice. That was what she liked about tonight's regular, a very grateful man who appreciated her efforts. He was older, well-heeled, and prominent, a vice president in the territory's largest bank. His wife's passions had cooled in the autumn years of their marriage, and according to him, his weekly trysts with Mary were the only thing keeping him sane.

She dabbed perfume, not a lot but in strategic locations—behind each ear, her throat, belly button, the small of her back, and behind each knee.

Time to get dressed. The Three Kings' parade of women down the stairs to the saloon would be happening soon. The men loved the ritual, and Mary had to admit she sort of enjoyed the ceremony herself, making a grand entrance. She pointed her toes into one stocking, then the other, rolling them halfway up her thighs. A sheer skirt with a generous slit to show leg. A striped bustier that bunched and pushed up her assets for all to notice. A thin silk shawl around her shoulders. Many of the girls wore heels. Mary would have liked to also, to show off her calves, but she was already on the tall side for a woman, and her height often put off shorter men. She stepped into a soft pair of pink slippers instead.

It wasn't an outfit for walking down Main Street in the middle of the day. Proper, churchgoing ladies would faint at such a scandalous display. For the Three Kings, it was relatively modest.

The door to her room cracked open and Louise stuck her head inside. She was a tiny girl with wild brown hair pulled back into a barely controlled ponytail. Her face was pretty, the star feature being her stunning cheekbones. Most of the other girls thought she had some Indian blood. "It's time."

"Okay." Mary stood, glanced one last time at herself in the mirror. She was ready. "Let's go."

They started down the stairs, the applause and hoots rising. Mary scanned the room below as she descended, a big smile plastered on her face. An above-average crowd. Men would spend money tonight. By the time she reached the bottom of the stairs, she still hadn't spotted her regular. Maybe he was running late.

Mary eased through the crowd, and a lanky cowboy latched onto her wrist.

"Hey there, darlin'. Where you off to so fast?"

She smiled up at him. Mary had learned early not to jerk away when a man grabbed her. The more rough around the edges, the more likely he was to take offense at the least little stupid thing. Brutes didn't think. They reacted.

"Hey there, handsome. I'm expected somewhere else, but don't worry, I'll get around to you soon enough. You can count on that." She gave his shoulder an affectionate squeeze with one hand as she casually extracted her other hand from his grip, her smile intact the whole time.

She made her way to the bar and leaned into an empty space. From that spot, she could keep an eye on the front door.

The man beside her offered a polite nod. Then he turned back to his whisky and wiped a light sheen of sweat off his forehead. There seemed like there might be something wrong with him.

"You doing okay tonight, honey?" Mary asked.

He smiled weakly. "Just fatigued. It's been a stressful few days."

"Oh, I like that accent," Mary said. "You're from England?"

"London, yes," he said. "I suppose it sticks out."

"In a good way. You sound so sophisticated."

"You're very kind to say so. I'm Nigel."

"Mary." She offered her hand and they shook.

"May I offer you a drink, Mary?"

Normally Mary would have liked that. Nigel was clean and polite and dressed well enough to make her think he probably had money. Not as much as a bank vice president maybe, but more than half these dusty cowhands. "Honey, I have to be honest. A drink would be wasted on me. I'm waiting for someone."

"I didn't intend to obligate you," Nigel said. "A friendly gesture."

"Well, you, sir, are a real gentleman." She leaned in and lowered her voice. "We don't get a lot of that in here."

Nigel laughed. "I try my best."

Mary saw her vice president walk in the front door. He took off his hat and looked around the room, obviously searching for her.

"I need to go," Mary told the Englishman. "But I hope you come back soon, when I'm free."

"I look forward to it."

Mary waved at her banker, and he smiled and nodded. She paused as she maneuvered through the crowd and pulled Louise aside. "I've got a live one for you."

"Oh?"

"The Englishman at the bar. Not bad-looking. Polite. Seems clean."

"Thank God," Louise said. "I always get the fat, smelly ones."

Mary winked. "Hey, now. We girls got to stick together."

Mary had been nice, had smelled lovely, and her pure, white skin had been so inviting that Nigel Evers had begun to feel that fluttering of anticipation. Oh, yes, she would be more than adequate to satisfy his needs.

But fate had whisked her away. She'd suggested Nigel return another night. He fully intended to do just that.

Louise was a different sort of creature.

She seemed far too eager to please, but after sharing half a bottle of whisky, Evers thought he could turn that to his advantage.

"Perhaps we should go elsewhere," Evers suggested.

Her face brightened, brilliant smile wide and genuine. "I thought you'd never ask. My room's upstairs."

They pushed away from the table and stood, even as Evers knew the girl's room wouldn't serve his purposes. They passed a hall on the way to the stairs and he asked, "Where does that go?"

"Out back," Louise said. "Outhouses."

The hallway was empty and Evers said. "Let's go outside."

Louise hesitated. "I can wait for you upstairs. I mean, if you need to use the . . . uh . . ."

Evers laughed. "I just want some air. It's a lovely night. The storm came through and cleared the sky. The stars are beautiful." He cupped one of her cheeks in his hand. "I would love to see the stars reflected in those lovely eyes."

"Oh." Her smile was so radiant and genuine. "Oh my."

Louise held on to his arm as they walked. Nobody saw them leave and they passed no one in the hall. Evers recognized an opportunity unfolding, and he felt the thrill of anticipation building inside him. This was the medicine he needed. Nothing else was as intoxicating, no whisky or wine. Not even anything offered in the traveling Chinese opium dens that followed the railroad camps.

They left through the back door, and it was like stepping into another world.

Okay, that was an exaggeration, Evers admitted to himself. But they'd left the smoky din of the saloon behind. The night was cold but pleasantly so, crisp and quiet. The stench of the outhouses somewhat spoiled the effect.

"This way." Louise pulled him along. "It's better over here."

They turned at the end of the alley and crossed the street, passing darkened buildings and then coming to a large, empty lot with high grass. Louise took him by the hand, leading him to the center of the lot. "This is a good, open space. We can see the stars better here." She took a slug of whisky from the bottle.

Evers looked up. By a happy accident, the sky really was beautiful, the stars glittering and bright. The moon hung low off to one side.

Louise shivered. "Cold out here." She worked one hand under Evers's jacket, rubbing his back and leaning into him. "Can you warm me up?"

Evers accepted her familiarity but didn't return the embrace. The feeling was strong in him now. It was almost time, and the anticipation was exquisitely agonizing. He wondered how long he could hold on to the feeling before indulging in sweet release. His hand fell into his jacket pocket, closed around the knife.

"You know, you could do anything you wanted out here. Nobody's around." She guzzled more whisky and giggled. "Or maybe somebody could see. I never did nothing like that before, knowing somebody might just happen along and see us."

"Oh, that wouldn't do at all, my dear." Evers pulled the knife from his pocket and slowly unfolded the blade. "Being seen wouldn't be convenient. Definitely not."

She sipped whisky, moonlight glinting on Evers's blade catching her attention. "Cute little knife. What's it for?"

CHAPTER 27

Beckinridge had not spoken fondly of Foster McNeil. Ostensibly a legitimate businessman, he worked as a flunky for a powerful millionaire named Bill Cartwright, and while Cartwright wielded a good deal of economic power in the region, McNeil, according to Beckinridge, had grown far too big for his britches. He liked to throw his weight around, but if he didn't have Cartwright behind him, there wouldn't be much to the man except hot air—again, Beckinridge's opinion.

But to Carson, Beckinridge seemed a no-nonsense sort of woman, and he didn't doubt her opinion was close enough to fact to make no nevermind. Additionally, Cartwright's name had come up too often for Carson's liking. McNeil might be the lackey doing the grunt work, but Carson figured it was Cartwright cracking the whip.

Why is a millionaire having people killed all across the territory?

Carson had his suspicions.

Benson Cassidy had already informed Carson that Bill Cartwright owned at least one building in Nugget City, and Beckinridge had been more than happy to pinpoint the building's exact whereabouts. It was near the other side of town, a block off Main Street. The bottom floor had been a mining equipment outfitter before the bust but was empty now. McNeil's office was on the second floor, a stairway on the side of the building leading up to the outside entrance.

Carson had offered Beckinridge his sincere thanks.

"You're a polite young man, Mr. Stone," Beckinridge had said. "We don't see enough of that in this day and age."

Carson rode Jet at an easy walk, following Beckinridge's directions.

He reached the building, dismounted, and looped Jet's reins around a hitching post, taking a slow and casual look up and down the street. The storefront across the street was empty, too, and no pedestrians roamed the sidewalks. The area seemed like the most deserted part of a town on its way to becoming a ghost, but at least that meant nobody would see him.

He went to the front window of the defunct mining company and cupped his hands against the glass, looking inside. Empty.

Carson hooked his thumbs into his belt and ambled around to the other side of the building, where there was a narrow alley. A set of wooden steps went up to the second story, and Carson climbed them, looking over his shoulder to see he was still unobserved.

The door at the top of the stairs had a sign with gold lettering that read CARTWRIGHT ENTERPRISES and then, in smaller letters, *Foster McNeil, Acquisitions*.

Carson tried the doorknob. Locked.

Carson stood a moment, scratching his head. He hastily assembled a simple plan. There was plenty about it he didn't like, but he didn't have the luxury of waiting around for his luck to change. His pal Colby Tate was currently gathering dust in a jail cell, but if Tate was right about Rawlings being a bad apple, his days might be numbered. All Rawlings had to do was suddenly decide it would be more convenient for Tate to disappear.

Furthermore, every day that passed might produce another dead body like Rollo Kramer, or make another woman a widow like Sally White Dove.

And what's that to you? This isn't your town. This isn't your problem.

Mary's words rang in his ears. *There's nothing more predictable than a good man.*

Carson shook his head. "I'm an idiot."

He went back down the stairs, got on Jet, and headed back. He wanted his room back at the Golden Duchess, but he stopped at the mercantile along the way and bought a small crowbar, a candle, and a fresh book of matches. He didn't kid himself. Carson's plan included breaking the law, and if he got caught, it wouldn't go well. At best, he'd find himself in a cell right next to Colby Tate.

Carson checked into his room, ate a meal, and killed some time reading a newspaper. Night fell. He tried to sleep, but he was too anxious. About two in the morning, he slipped unseen out the back exit of the hotel, the crowbar poorly hidden under his jacket. He reckoned he'd draw less attention on foot, so he left Jet in the stable.

It took about two minutes of Carson skulking from shadow to shadow, but trying not to *look* like he was skulking, for him to realize he'd make a rotten sneak thief. He gave up on stealth and simply walked quietly, hat pulled down low, and made his way to McNeil's office.

If the neighborhood around Cartwright Enterprises seemed deserted by day, it was downright dead at night. Not a single light glimmered in any window of the nearby buildings. For a brief moment Carson felt strange, like some specter haunting abandoned streets. He should be in bed, not planning something stupid.

He shook off the feeling. He knew his task. Time to get to it.

Carson made a slow circle around the building, making sure no one was around. Then he started checking first-floor windows. The first one he tried was unlocked, and he opened it and slipped inside. The mining equipment office was empty, so Carson had suspected it might be easier to break into than the office above, but this was even easier than he suspected. He left the window open in case he needed to make a hasty exit.

Moonlight filtered in through the windows. Carson stood a moment and let his eyes adjust. The stairway leading up to the second floor was across the room. Floorboards creaked as he walked toward it. Everything sounded louder in the middle of the night.

He climbed the stairs and tried the door at the top, hoping he'd get lucky again, like with the unlocked window. No such luck.

He slipped the crowbar around to jam the straight end into the crack between door and frame right where the lock was. He worked it in and then gave it some muscle. It cracked and splintered so loudly, Carson was sure the whole town must have heard it. He froze.

Dead silence. Carson waited another few moments, but apparently nobody had heard the break-in. He pushed the door open, stepped inside, and closed it behind him.

Now, he was completely swallowed by darkness. When he'd inspected the second-floor windows from the outside, he'd observed all the shades had been drawn. Trying to move around without light was asking for a broken neck. He set the crowbar aside and fished the candle and matches out of his jacket pocket.

Carson struck a match and held it aloft. Desks. Chairs. An ordinary place of business.

He made his way to the first desk before the match burned down too far. Then he struck another and used it to light the candle. Of the three desks in the room, only one looked like it was being used, a scattering of papers across the top. Carson spotted an ashtray and tilted the candle sideways over it, dripping wax until he had a little puddle. He set the candle in the wax and it stuck. When he'd purchased the crowbar, he'd almost bought a lantern, too, but he wanted only enough light to see what he was doing. The last thing he wanted was to attract attention from anyone passing by.

Carson sifted through the papers, not really sure what he was looking at. Rows of numbers. He wished Tate were here. A Harvard-educated man might be able to make sense of all this business stuff. He opened the top drawer and took out a stack of papers.

Contracts. At least a dozen of them. Not that Carson knew a damn thing about real estate but reading made it clear what he was looking at—a buyer, a seller, a price. Sally White Dove had signed her name with an X. Foster McNeil was grabbing up a bunch of land on Cartwright Enterprises' behalf.

He searched the rest of the desk but found nothing else of interest.

Well, what the hell did you think you'd find? A signed confession?

He made a slow turn, scanning the rest of the room, wondering where else he might search.

His eyes landed on a large map pinned to the far wall. He went to it for a closer look. It was a map of railroad lines across the western part of the United States and territories. Two dotted lines came up from a place called Promontory, Utah. The map's legend told him a dotted line meant a proposed route and two dotted lines crossed into the Idaho Territory, one going more or less due north into Montana and the other angling more westward past . . .

Nugget City.

This was the first Carson had heard the railroad might be coming through, not that he made such news his business. Still, why *hadn't* he heard? The railroad was big news. A major railroad route could make or break a town. And if ever a town needed a break, it was Nugget City. Hell, all these empty buildings around him could soon be . . .

It was like a bell went off inside his head.

Carson, you ignorant peckerwood, that's the entire point.

The dotted lines were *proposed* routes. Nobody had laid an inch of track, not yet. If a man knew ahead of time where a railroad line was going through, if he had information not available to the general public and the money to do something about it . . .

Bill Cartwright had plenty of money. And even though Carson had never met this fellow, his experience of rich men was that enough was never enough.

Realization struck him like a lightning bolt, and he took Sheriff Bedford's map of claim jumpers and other crimes out of his pocket. He held it up against the railroad map on the wall. Bedford had been meticulous, keeping track and marking the map carefully.

The trail of crimes almost exactly matched the proposed rail route past Nugget City.

Bill Cartwright—or more likely his lackeys—had murdered and intimidated people to get their land, knowing it would be worth a hundred times as much once the railroad came through. Men like McNeil would come around with a low offer. If the landowner didn't like it, too bad.

That's what happened to Claire's grandfather. McNeil made him a low offer and the old man said no. It cost him his life. With the old man out of the way, McNeil thought he could return and intimidate a young girl.

How many times had McNeil done the same thing to others up and down the territory?

Not McNeil, Carson thought. He's just some mangy lapdog. *It's Cartwright who's calling the shots.*

Carson would need to make a point of meeting this Bill Cartwright just as soon as it could be arranged. He had some hard questions for the man.

He sighed and glanced around the office. It probably wasn't wise to linger, and anyway, he doubted he could learn any more useful—

The front door rattled, a key turned in a lock, and a split second later the door pushed inward.

Carson dropped behind the nearest desk, hand going to his Peacemaker as a matter of reflex. The candle still flickered on the desk across the room.

Carson cursed inwardly and drew his pistol.

McNeil walked in and shut the door behind him. "Hey, you here already? Come on now, I don't have time to mess about."

Staying hidden wasn't going to do him much good for much longer, so Carson decided he might as well take the initiative. He stood and said, "Somebody's here. Maybe not the somebody you thought."

McNeil squinted at him. "Who the hell are—hey, you're that sidewinder from the Grainger farm."

His hand went for his gun.

Carson raised his Peacemaker and thumbed back the hammer. "Don't."

McNeil froze, eyes locked with Carson's. Then he slowly raised his hands. "You're making a big mistake."

"You wouldn't believe how often I hear that."

"I'm serious," McNeil said. "If you knew who I worked for, you'd be a little more careful about where you point that gun."

"You work for Bill Cartwright," Carson said. "And you've been having people killed so you can pick up their land for a song. It'll be worth a lot more when the railroad comes through."

A slow frown twisted McNeil's face. "Think you know a lot, don't you, smart guy?"

"Tell me where I got it wrong."

"You're a regular hero type, aren't you?" McNeil said. "First, you save Claire Grainger from the bad man trying to buy her farm, and now here you are, trying to right all the wrongs in Idaho. For your information, I ain't killed nobody. So here's the big question, Mr. Hero. Now what?"

Carson's eyes narrowed. "What do you mean, 'now what'?"

"I mean you're pointing a gun at me," McNeil said. "Going to shoot me? You're holding all the cards, Mr. Hero. Now what?"

That's a pretty good question, actually.

Normally Carson would just turn him over to the sheriff. But that wasn't really an option. If Tate's suspicions about Sheriff Rawlings were correct, taking McNeil to the jailhouse might not do any good. Carson wished yet again that his pal Tate were here to think his way out of Carson's mess.

Maybe I should just shoot him.

Carson took a step back and motioned toward a chair with his six-shooter. "Sit there."

A smirk from McNeil. "What if I don't feel like sitting?"

"Then I'll weigh you down with some lead and put you in any damn chair I feel like."

"Okay, okay." McNeil sat in the chair. "Satisfied?"

"Now just stay there and keep shut a minute." Carson looked around the room again for anything he might use to tie up McNeil.

Carson's plan was pretty feeble, but it went something

like this: He wasn't about to take McNeil to Rawlings, not until he could verify one way or another if the sheriff was trustworthy. Oddly, there was one person in town Carson did trust. Doris Beckinridge. The woman was prim and proper and as stiff as a dead squirrel, but maybe those were the exact reasons Carson *did* trust her. She was on the town council, which meant she had some authority in Nugget City. He'd go to her and spill the whole story. Maybe she knew a fast way to reach a federal marshal.

Carson saw McNeil look past him at something, and nearly at the same time he heard the telltale clack-click-click of a hammer being pulled back on a six-shooter. Carson started to turn.

"Don't you move a muscle." Rawlings's voice.

Carson froze.

"About damn time you got here," McNeil said.

"Don't give me none of your lip, McNeil," the sheriff said. "You want me to save your ass, then shut up and let me save it."

Carson's mind raced, but he couldn't think of anything to say that would help.

"Scoot over to that desk," the sheriff said. "Nice and easy. Then set that gun on top. Do anything stupid and I'll fill you full of holes."

Carson wasn't sure which desk the sheriff meant, so he chose the one with the candle. He moved slowly and set the gun on the surface.

"Now turn around. Don't do nothin' sudden."

Carson turned to face the sheriff, his hands in the air. Rawlings's shadowed face looked sinister in the flickering candlelight, or maybe that was just something Carson imagined. He'd never liked the sheriff and had always suspected he was rotten.

Rawlings kept his gun trained on Carson, but his eyes slid to McNeil. "How much does he know?"

"He knows I've been buying up land and why," McNeil said. "He was in here snooping around."

"Then that's bad luck for him," Rawlings said. "I can't throw you in a cell next to your pal, Stone. You know too much."

At that moment Carson reckoned he was about two seconds away from getting shot.

He bumped his butt back into the desk behind him. The candle toppled over and winked out, plunging the room into total darkness. The sheriff fired just as Carson dove to the floor, the pistol shot shaking the room, the flash like a jagged burst of lightning.

Carson crawled around to the other side of the desk as another shot went over his head. He got to his feet and scampered in the darkness, ducking his head low. He tried to remember where the back stairs were and bumped into another desk with a grunt.

Rawlings fired at the sound but missed again.

Carson desperately tried to find the stairs down, blinking his eyes, trying to adjust. It was no use. He couldn't see a thing. He stepped through—

And there was nothing under his boot.

He pitched forward, hitting the stairs hard, rolling and sliding and bruising until he found himself in a heap at the bottom. He picked himself up and limped toward the open window as fast as he could make himself move, expecting any second to feel a hot chunk of lead in his back.

He crawled through the window, dropped to the ground on the other side, and ran, wincing from a pain in his knee. He picked a random street and kept going.

Rawlings would be after him. No doubt. Carson Stone was now a wanted man in Nugget City.

CHAPTER 28

A thin mist blanketed the rocky hill country west of Nugget City.

Major Grady's command had made camp the night before in a flat area at about a thousand feet of elevation. Men in groups of four and five huddled around campfires, sipping coffee and finishing breakfast. Men attended the horses tied to a picket line. There was no hurry. Grady and his sergeant smoked, sipping coffee and waiting for the scouts.

Ten minutes later the two scouts returned and presented themselves to the major.

"Report, Corporal Alan."

The man with the corporal stripes on his sleeve stepped forward and saluted smartly. He was a veteran in his thirties, a little gray just beginning to show in his beard. "Bannock, sir. Straight up into the hills maybe two miles."

Major Grady upended his tin cup, ridding himself of the coffee that had gone cold. "A war party?"

"It was too risky to get closer without being seen, sir," Alan reported. "So I don't have exact numbers. But it just seems like they're sitting there. My guess is not a war party. But I can't say one hundred percent for certain."

"Two squads?"

The corporal nodded. "I reckon that would do it."

"Pick two squads, sergeant," Grady ordered. "We go in five."

The sergeant stood and flipped a tired salute before moving off to make ready. Grady checked his pistol while he waited. Four minutes later the sergeant had the squads assembled so Grady could address them.

"Okay, listen up, troopers," Grady said matter-of-factly. "You know how to do this. Sergeant, you take one squad up the right, I'll take the other up the left. Keep quiet and spread out. Don't do a damn thing until you get the order. Questions?"

There were no questions.

"Move out!"

They eased through the mist and up into the hills, taking it slow. When they got close, Corporal Alan nudged Grady and pointed. He saw the camp through the trees, a few Bannock moving around. It didn't look like much. He watched for a few minutes but didn't see anything of interest. No sign of weapons.

Grady leaned in close to the corporal and whispered, "Take over the other squad and send Sarge back this way."

"Yessir."

A minute later the sergeant appeared and knelt next to Grady behind a large boulder. "Sir?"

"Tell me what you think, Sergeant."

"A pretty shabby-looking bunch, sir. At least, that's how it looks from here."

"Agreed. How's your Bannock?"

"Lousy," the sergeant said. "But better than yours."

Grady couldn't disagree. He hadn't picked up much of the language and had mostly let Bessie do the talking for him.

"Okay, pick two men," Grady told the sergeant. "Go in with guns low. Make sure they see you're there to talk. Find out what you can. If we've got this all wrong and they start fighting, get low and I'll bring up the squads."

The sergeant saluted. "Yessir."

A minute later the sergeant and two troopers headed for the camp, standing tall and making it clear they weren't trying to hide. Grady braced himself for gunfire and war cries, but they never came.

Grady waited, then waited some more. He lit his pipe and smoked.

The sergeant and the other troopers returned. The sergeant told the other troopers to return to their places, and then he reported to Grady.

"There ain't no fight in any of them," he said. "About twenty in all, old people and the sick, and a few squaws to take care of 'em. There was a whole bunch that took off two days ago, but these here would have slowed them down, so they were left behind. A pretty sorry lot, if you ask me."

Grady sighed and looked at the camp. His orders were to round up any stray Bannock, but he couldn't imagine what would be accomplished putting old men and women in chains and dragging them back to the fort. Surely the US Cavalry had better things to do.

Grady made an about-face and pointed back down the way they'd come. "Sergeant, what do you see down there?"

The sergeant turned and looked. "Sir?"

"Look straight ahead, Sergeant. Do you see any Bannock?"

"Down there?"

"Yes, Sergeant, I'm asking you a very specific question. Do you see any Bannock?"

"Not . . . not down there, no."

"Then what will your report be?"

The sergeant seemed to catch on. He pulled his pocket watch from his vest and squinted at it. "I'll report that at approximately seven forty-two a.m. my commanding officer asked if I'd spotted any Bannock Indians in the . . . uh . . . designated search area. After a careful look, I reported that no such indigenous personnel were spotted."

"Then that concludes our business, Sergeant," Grady said. "Pass the word to the men, reminding them exactly what they've seen and haven't seen."

"Yessir."

"And Sergeant, form up the men and take charge of them. You might as well head back to Fort Hall," Grady said. "I'll take Corporal Alan and a detail to fetch Bessie from Nugget City."

And if Grady had himself a steak and a few drinks at the saloon and a night in a comfy bed before heading back to the fort, then well, why not? What was the point of being an officer if he couldn't enjoy it now and then?

Kat rode next to Bill Cartwright at the head of a column of twenty men, all hard-looking characters with six-shooters on their hips. Cartwright wasn't the type to take no for an answer, and in New York or Chicago that meant one thing, but this far west, it meant men with guns. It meant brute force.

In another time Cartwright would have been some feudal lord, Kat mused. Might and strength would have been all the law that was needed in a time of barons and knights. He wouldn't have needed a bill of sale to show he owned some piece of land. Conquest would have been enough. Now there needed to be contracts, signatures in ink. The law was a thing written down for all men to follow.

And yet at the same time, the law could be a fragile thing if there weren't men ready to back it up with lead. Cartwright understood the law.

And he understood lead.

That was why twenty armed men were going with him to Nugget City.

Back in the chuckwagon, that four-eyed pencil-neck Doyle rode along with the cook. Cartwright would conquer. Doyle would make sure the paperwork was in order.

Kat shook her head, laughing inwardly, but not letting it show on her face. *That fool marches at the head of his little army, playacting at being a general. I'll slip away with his money and he'll be left with nothing but acres and acres of worthless land.*

Vance had already told Kat the Union Pacific had given up on both lines through the Idaho Territory. They didn't think the effort was worth it.

I just wish I could be around to see the look on his stupid face when the news goes public and he realizes he's been had.

But Kat was too smart for that. She'd be long gone with the money by the time Cartwright understood the time, money, and effort he'd wasted. If she knew Cartwright— and she did—he'd be doubly furious knowing he'd been taken in by a pretty face. *You always think you're on top, that you're one step ahead, don't you, sweetie?*

But those were always the men easiest to fool, in Kat's opinion. So confident. So arrogant.

They made camp that night, the cowhands erecting a huge tent for Cartwright, as if he were a Persian prince. They set up a table for him, with a linen tablecloth, fine crystal for his wine, cloth napkins. The cook served prime rib, while the cowhands gathered around campfires, scooping beans from tin plates.

Kat, of course, joined him for dinner.

"The wine is quite good," she said.

"The best this side of the Mississippi . . . which isn't saying much," Cartwright said. "Oh, I know a few well-off families in Frisco who might do better. It's a port town, after all. I'm thinking of buying some land in California. I'm told it's good for vineyards. There's a man there who says the soil is perfect and that one day, California might produce a red wine that rivals that of France. It's nonsense, obviously, but I sort of admire a man who is so ambitious he can't be put off just because something is outlandish." Cartwright laughed. "Anyway, I like the idea of my name on a label, that years after I'm dead, people will talk about me."

"Won't your name be on railroad stations?" Kat asked.

"You know, I actually hadn't thought of that," Cartwright admitted. "The William Cartwright Railroad Station has a rather grand sound to it."

"Willy's Whistle Stop." A playful gleam in Kat's eye.

Cartwright chuckled. "Not quite as grand."

"Cartwright Crossing has a nice ring to it," Kat said sincerely.

Cartwright refilled both wineglasses. "Cartwright Crossing. I like the way those words come out of my mouth. Simple but memorable."

They finished dinner and opened another bottle of wine.

"Kat, you're like no other woman I've ever met," Cartwright said.

She grinned. "I'll bet you say that to all the girls who gun sheriffs for you."

"I'm not kidding," Cartwright said. "You're tough, but you're feminine. Hard and soft at the same time, so to speak. And you're smart, not just knowledgeable but cunning. We make a formidable team."

"Not that I'm opposed to compliments, but are you leading up to something?"

"I'm a rich man, and powerful," Cartwright said. "And if this deal with the railroad unfolds the way I think it will . . ." A shrug.

"You'll be even *more* rich and *more* powerful," Kat finished for him.

"Richer certainly," he said. "But what does that mean? I mean, isn't there a point when a man is so rich, it no longer matters? Is there finer wine than the finest? How much bigger can a house get? A man can only occupy one room at a time. What can I buy that I can't already own? Fast horses, fine art, the best clothing. I can have these things already."

Kat thought about it. "But you can't buy power. Money helps. A lot. But there's something more."

"Exactly so," Cartwright agreed. "And power is exactly what I'm interested in. With control of the railroad towns, I will control—in part—what moves on those railroads. I'll be in a position to grant favors. Big favors for important people. And at the right time, I'll expect those favors to be returned."

"And what will you be asking for when it's time to call in these favors?"

"The one inevitable thing is change," Cartwright said. "Right now there are opportunities in the territory, opportunities I'm currently taking advantage of. But this won't be a territory forever. Idaho will eventually be a state. A blind man can see it coming. The railroads will make Idaho the gateway to the northwest. Washington and Oregon will be the next big thing. I can smell it."

Kat thought about it for a moment. A slow smile crept across her face. "You're going to run for governor."

"Yes. That's step one."

"Step one?"

Cartwright grinned.

Kat blinked. "President?"

He sipped wine. A slight shrug. "As I've said, I admire someone who is so ambitious he won't be put off just because something is outlandish. There's no challenge in doing something easy."

"And I fit into this . . . how?"

"A man can't do something so outlandish without the right person by his side," Cartwright explained. "Bodyguards and lawyers and accountants aren't enough. I'm talking about a person who's an equal partner in the outlandishness. A confidante and a companion. Not just a person. A woman. A special woman."

Kat leaned back in her chair, eyes narrowing as she appraised the man.

Cartwright hadn't actually used the words. *Wife. Marriage.* But his meaning was clear. Kat had to admit to herself that she was flattered. Cartwright wasn't looking for a wife. like a pretty piece of fluff he could wear on his arm like an accessory. He wanted a partner, someone who'd have his back.

That he'd put that kind of trust in her only confirmed she'd duped him completely.

And yet . . .

Her scheme with Vance was about to come to fruition, and that would mean a pile of cash. She could do what she wanted, go wherever she pleased. Kat liked the simplicity of it. Get paid and then disappear.

But Cartwright was worth millions, and he was offering to take her down the craziest path of her life. Kat might just find out she liked the taste of power. And if it didn't work out to her satisfaction . . . well, accidents happened all the time, didn't they? If something happened to a husband, it was the wife who inherited.

So . . . possibilities.

"I can tell by that very pregnant pause that you're thinking it through." Cartwright smiled. "Good. Keep thinking. There's no hurry, after all. I need to conclude this railroad business first, and make sure it's on track . . . so to speak.

So no decisions. Not yet. But I realize my suggestion could be taking you by surprise. Maybe you can share your first impressions."

Kat tossed back her wine and slid the glass across the table toward him. "I'm exactly one more glass of wine away from being in a sharing mood."

Nigel Evers had a good dinner at a quiet café. He took the long way back to his hotel. A good walk, in his opinion, aided in the digestion.

His mood remained good, tranquil and content. Evers's encounter with Louise had produced the desired effect, offering the release he'd needed, quieting his mind. There had been an effervescent quality about her, an energetic way of embracing life, and taking that—everything that had made her Louise—had been red meat for his soul.

Now he would go back to the hotel and look again at the death list and contemplate his next target. Just the idea of it initiated again that tingle of anticipation. This was how it started, just an idea that he would be taking another life, that some stranger was out there walking around, doing normal things, completely unaware that the universe had set Nigel Evers into motion, and the end result would be another light snuffed into darkness.

His pace quickened, and a minute later he found himself crossing the lobby of his hotel, eager to get to his room and check the death list. A woman would be ideal, but there was also proximity to consider. Now that the process had started, he didn't want to pick someone who was a three- or four-day ride away.

The man at the front desk chased him down. "Sir! Sir! A telegram came for you."

Evers took the telegram and gave the man a coin. "Thank you kindly."

Evers read the telegram twice to make sure he understood. He frowned and read it once more. It was from Cartwright's assistant, Doyle, and essentially brought Evers's services to an end. Apparently, enough of the men and women on the list had been eliminated to accomplish Cartwright's goals.

Nigel Evers, for the moment, was unemployed.

Not that the money was really the issue. The telegram had assured that payments would be made for all efforts prior to the news Evers's services would no longer be needed. He'd be able to live comfortably for a while.

No, the real issue was that Evers was already looking forward to his next encounter. The expected release would need to come in a timely fashion. Otherwise, Evers would begin to . . . itch.

He went to his room and took off his jacket. He hung it on the hook on the back of the door. He kicked off his shoes.

Then he paced the room.

He paused at the sideboard where there was a nearly full bottle of whisky. He poured himself three fingers and drank, his mind turning over his options. Finding a new employer who required Nigel Evers's very specific skills would take time. He'd need to take steps in the meantime.

The girl at the Three Kings, the one with the white, flawless skin. Evers searched his memory for her name.

Mary.

As soon as he thought of her name, something inside him clicked, and he realized he had the answer. Tonight?

No. Too soon.

He filled his glass with whisky again and emptied it.

He'd need to take his time and do it right, but already

he felt happy to have made the decision. The warmth began to build, a pleasant anticipation that would eventually build to a blinding, agonizing need.

Nigel Evers smiled at the thought of a bright-red splash across a clean, white throat.

CHAPTER 29

Carson Stone realized he'd made a mistake.

He'd limped as fast as he could away from the Cartwright Enterprises office, taking random left and right turns to throw off any pursuit. He'd found a nook under a set of outside stairs up the side of an abandoned building and scooted into it. He was worried he'd hurt his knee badly taking a tumble while escaping, and he sat a good ten minutes, prodding and massaging it to see how bad the injury might be. He stretched the leg out in front of him and finally decided he'd be okay.

The mistake had been not going straight back to his hotel. Carson had been so worried about his leg that he'd wasted time. If he'd gone straight back, he could have fetched Jet from the stable and gotten clear of Nugget City.

It would be a bad move trying to get to Jet now. Rawlings might have somebody there waiting for him. Did the crooked sheriff have a bunch of crooked sidekicks on the payroll? Carson wished he'd taken the time to find out. He should have known better than to get into other people's business without considering the consequences.

He stood and tested the knee. Not bad. He skulked from shadow to shadow. While Carson had sat there massaging his knee, he'd come up with a plan. He wasn't going to fix this mess on his own, and Colby Tate couldn't help him from inside a jail cell. Carson headed for the one person in town he thought he might trust.

Dawn was still a few hours off when Carson found himself standing in front of Doris Beckinridge's boardinghouse. He looked around to make sure he wasn't observed before approaching the front door, but the streets were as silent as a graveyard. He knocked and waited.

If it was one of the girls who answered—if anyone answered at all—he'd have to convince her to wake Doris. He waited another moment, then knocked again, constantly glancing over his shoulder. He felt exposed just standing there, sure that Rawlings or one of his lackeys would happen along any moment.

He raised his hand to knock again, but a voice on the other side of the door said, "Announce yourself. What legitimate business could anyone have at such an obscene hour?"

Carson smiled and shook his head. That was Doris Beckinridge sure enough. "Carson Stone, ma'am. I apologize for waking you."

A long pause. "I'm assuming this isn't a social call. Can I assume further that this is a life-or-death situation?"

"You assume correctly, ma'am."

Another pause. Then the clatter of a chain and the click-clack of a lock. The door creaked open enough for Carson to see she wore a heavy, flannel gown, her hair tamed by a net. She cradled a double-barrel shotgun under one arm.

Beckinridge scowled. "Talk fast, Mr. Stone."

"Sheriff Rawlings is in the pocket of a millionaire named Bill Cartwright who's been buying up land and having people killed if they won't sell," Carson said. "I broke into Foster McNeil's office to dig up whatever dirt I could, but

Rawlings caught me. Now he's looking to put a bullet in me his first opportunity."

Beckinridge sighed and opened the door wider. "You'd better come in and start over from the beginning. I'll put on some coffee."

There was a small table in the corner of a large kitchen, and Carson sat there explaining himself while Beckinridge went about the business of making the coffee. He spilled the whole story in an orderly fashion, providing as many details as possible. He started with the sheriff in Boise asking him and Tate to look into some claim jumpers and then went into Sally White Dove, her husband, the dead ferry operator, and then selling her land. Others had sold, too, often next of kin after the murder of a relative. He told her about Claire Grainger and her murdered grandfather and the later encounter with McNeil.

Thousands of acres of land had traded hands, and all that land had two things in common. First, the buyer was always someone acting on behalf of Bill Cartwright. Second, the tracts of land matched one of the Union Pacific's proposed routes almost exactly. Carson shared his opinion: Anyone who had advance knowledge of the route could buy up the land cheap and make one hell of a profit. Bill Cartwright was a rich man about to get a lot richer.

Beckinridge absorbed Carson's story, her stoic expression never wavering. She set two cups of coffee on the table. Carson declined cream and sugar. She sat opposite him, cradling her cup with two hands.

She sighed and asked, "Why me?"

Carson raised an eyebrow. "Ma'am?"

"You're in a tight spot, Mr. Stone. That much is obvious, and you need help," she said. "Why especially do you think I'm your best choice?"

"To be frank, there's not a lot of choices," Carson explained. "My partner's in the slammer. Normally I'd go to the sheriff, but he's the one trying to kill me. You're on the town council, and you strike me as a no-nonsense woman. You seem the sort who always insists things be done the proper way, and if there's something improper going on in your town, I'm guessing you won't stand for it. And I doubt you frighten easily."

Beckinridge nodded. "I appreciate those words and happen to agree with all of them. Very well, I'll help you. Please understand that I'll need proof. I've never been fond of Sheriff Rawlings, and it's no surprise to me that he might be mixed up in something untoward. But he keeps the peace in his own heavy-handed way. I won't turn against him just because I dislike the look of his face. Having said that, you could have run. Instead, you came to me looking to set things right. I consider myself a good judge of character, so I'll give you the benefit of the doubt. How do you propose we proceed?"

"First thing's first," Carson said. "I'm slightly embarrassed to admit it, but I've misplaced my Peacemaker. I'm a bit anxious walking around naked, if you'll pardon the expression. I'm wondering if I could borrow your shotgun."

"I think we can do better for you than that." She rose from the table. "Wait just a moment."

Beckinridge left the kitchen and returned quickly, carrying something wrapped in cloth. She set the bundle on the table in front of Carson. "See if that will do the trick."

Carson unfolded the cloth, revealing a revolver.

"My brother bought that brand-new three years ago," Beckinridge said. "To fend off Indians and bandits, I suppose. He was determined to make his fortune panning for gold, but, of course, he never had any luck. When he died last year, he left me a flea-bitten mule and that garish firearm."

Carson examined the pistol. He supposed "garish" was the word for it, nickel-plated with ivory on the hilt. A lot prettier than a gun needed to be just to put a hole in a man. But the Remington was a solid gun. "Obliged, ma'am. This'll do just fine."

She took her seat again and sipped coffee. "Now, I assume you've some sort of plan."

Searching the dark and silent streets of Nugget City with that idiot McNeil reminded Sheriff Rawlings that he didn't always have it figured exactly right. Normally the sheriff was glad he hadn't put on any men full-time as deputies. More men meant more people Rawlings would have to let in on his secret. That or work extra hard to keep them in the dark.

At it had always been Rawlings's intent to work smart, not hard, and it had always seemed smart to him that the fewer people who knew he was working for Bill Cartwright, the better.

Rawlings had always enjoyed being sheriff. Not because he had some love affair with law and order. More like he enjoyed the power a tin star gave him. When Rawlings talked, men listened. When he strutted down the sidewalk, people stepped aside. He was well aware that not everyone respected Tad Rawlings.

But they all respected the tin star.

And as much as Rawlings liked being sheriff, he liked money even more. Bill Cartwright secretly paid Rawlings a nice chunk of change each and every month to make sure things in Nugget City went the way Cartwright wanted them to go.

But now was one of those times it sure would have been helpful to have half a dozen deputies on the payroll so he could make a proper search. After Carson Stone had escaped his clutches, Rawlings and McNeil had spent a half hour running around like chickens with their heads cut off, peering into every shadow and dark alley, trying to find the little rat.

Rawlings had finally decided they were getting nowhere, He ordered McNeil to keep watch on the stables behind the Golden Duchess. Stone might have already skipped town, obviously, but on foot without horse or weapons or any supplies at all? Rawlings doubted it. There was a good chance Stone would try to fetch his mount first.

"Stay hidden," Rawlings told McNeil. "Shoot first if you see him. We'll make up a story later."

"I don't like this," McNeil said. "I'm here to buy property for the boss. I'm not some hired gun."

"Nobody's asking you to be a gunslinger," Rawlings said with impatience. "Shoot him in the back for all I care. I'm the sheriff, remember. I'll make sure nobody asks questions. Now stop wasting time and get over there."

McNeil reluctantly agreed, still muttering to himself as he left in the direction of the stables.

Rawlings checked a few abandoned places he figured a fugitive might want to hole up, but there was no sign of Stone.

Stop running around without a plan, you damn fool.

The sheriff tried to get into Stone's head. What would a man in his predicament do? A man on the run needed help. He needed a friend, and Stone's only friend in Nugget City . . .

No, Stone wouldn't really . . . did he have the guts to . . . ?

Rawlings couldn't think of anything more embarrassing than having Carson Stone bust his partner, Colby Tate, out of jail while Rawlings was running all over town looking for him. It would be a bold move—maybe even stupid—but Rawlings could imagine it was just the sort of thing that uppity Stone fellow would try.

Big stinker thinks he's going to make a fool out of me in my own town? We'll just see about that.

Rawlings hurried it back to the jailhouse. He was about to rush in and make sure the jail's only prisoner was still there when he spotted the folded-up piece of paper stuck in the crack of the door. He snatched it, unfolded it, and began reading.

Sheriff Rawlings,
    I know when I'm licked. I'm offering a trade. Let me get my horse and other possessions without any trouble and I'll leave town and keep my mouth shut. Otherwise, I'll make my way to a federal marshal and spill all I know. Maybe he won't believe me, or maybe he will. Let's both avoid trouble. Meet me at dawn inside the old Territory Bank building. Nobody will see us there, and we can settle this hash.
                    Carson Stone

Rawlings read the note a second time. Either Stone was a fool or he thought Rawlings was. Maybe he thought to lie in wait and ambush Rawlings when he arrived. Or maybe while Rawlings was wasting his time at the old bank building, Carson would circle back to fetch his horse. That would suit Rawlings just fine because then McNeil could shoot him in the back.

The sheriff considered how he'd handle it, and in a few moments he had a plan. If it was a distraction so Stone could get his horse, McNeil would get him. If not, Rawlings would get to the bank building ahead of Stone and turn the tables.

Either way, Carson Stone wouldn't be causing him any more trouble.

McNeil crouched in the empty stall across from the one with Carson Stone's horse. He had a good view of the other stall and would be able to gun Stone down easily if he showed to collect his animal. The idea of shooting the man in the back didn't sit well, but McNeil was no duelist. The idea of a fair fight was laughable to him. Just sounded like a fast way to get killed as far as McNeil was concerned.

And if the choice was Stone getting killed or himself . . . well, then he'd shoot the man in the back. Rawlings had given him a short, twelve-gauge coachman's gun to do the job.

No choice, really. It had to be done. McNeil was in too deep and had orchestrated too many crooked deals for Cartwright. He hadn't known about the killing at first. But when people ended up dead—the very same people who owned the land Cartwright wanted—well, he put two and two together. He'd never been involved in any of the killing personally.

On the other hand, McNeil hadn't done anything to prevent it either.

So, yeah. Carson Stone had to go.

McNeil stretched one leg out in front of him and then the other. He'd been waiting there for hours and had almost dozed off twice.

This is a messed-up situation and that's for sure. Why didn't that moron Rawlings just shoot Stone when he had the chance?

Cartwright was on his way to town to finalize the last few purchases before the railroad man showed up to do the deal. McNeil had invited the sheriff to his office to go over the final details, but he'd almost wet himself to find Stone there instead, pointing a gun at him. If Rawlings had just shot the man one second sooner . . .

No sense crying over spilled milk now. I just want to get this over with.

He slapped his own face lightly when he caught himself dozing off again. McNeil wondered how long he was supposed to wait. What if Stone never showed up at all?

This is just damn stupid. If he doesn't show soon, I'm getting the hell out of here. If that dumb bag of rocks Rawlings can't clean up his own mess, then to hell with—

A shuffling noise caught McNeil's attention. Lantern light spread through the stable. McNeil crouched lower, clutching the shotgun, and waited for Stone to come into view.

But nobody did.

More sounds came from the other side of the stable, metal and wood. Somebody was sure enough doing something. McNeil rose slowly, peeked over the edge of the stall. Through the hanging tack and harness, he saw a figure, a man with his back to McNeil, bent over a workbench and attending to some chore.

McNeil shifted his position to get a better look. The man wore a leather apron and a battered sombrero.

Of course. The old hunchback who tends the horses. There's at least four or five animals in here to feed and water. It must be getting near breakfast time for the early risers. He's got some kind of odd name. What was it?

Jackrabbit.

Whatever the old man's given name might be, McNeil had never heard it. Now that he knew who it was, he could squint through the dim light and see the hump on Jackrabbit's left side. He moved closer and saw Jackrabbit scoop oats from a barrel into feed bags. As suspected, the old man was simply about his business of caring for the animals.

McNeil considered what to do now. He couldn't very well murder Stone with Jackrabbit watching. Maybe he could simply ask the old man how long he was going to be. If he was just going to take fifteen minutes to feed and water the horses, McNeil could wait him out, but if Jackrabbit was going to muck out stables the rest of the morning, there was no point waiting around.

"Jackrabbit!" McNeil called. "You're making an early start this morning."

The old man didn't turn around.

McNeil frowned. *What's the matter with the dumb codger?*

Then he remembered Jackrabbit was deaf. He could shout at the man until kingdom come and it wouldn't make no difference. McNeil tucked his shotgun under one arm, aimed at the ground. No sense scaring the life out of the old man. He walked toward him, Jackrabbit still scooping oats. Maybe he'd make up some errand for the old man to send him away.

McNeil tapped Jackrabbit on the shoulder. "Hey there, old-timer. I'm wondering how long you'll be—"

Jackrabbit spun around, and suddenly McNeil saw a flash of nickel plating and felt the barrel of a pistol tucked up under his chin, the metal a cold shock against his skin. The sound of a hammer cocking back turned his bowels watery.

Carson Stone grinned at him from beneath the sombrero. "You can play this smart, McNeil, or you can play it dead. What's it going to be?"

CHAPTER 30

Tad Rawlings went home, splashed water on his face, and fixed a pot of coffee. It had already been a long night and there was still work left to do. He checked his pistol and grabbed a Henry rifle from over the fireplace.

Still nearly two hours until dawn, and the sheriff wanted to make sure he got to the Territory Bank building ahead of Stone. He headed out at a brisk walk, taking the long way around. Nugget City slept. Not even a stray cat meowed in the distance.

Rawlings arrived at the back entrance of an empty building across the street from the Territory Bank. It was a small building, two stories. The bottom floor had been a shop that had sold and repaired shoes. It had been owned by a dour Czech who lived over the shop in a small apartment. Like so many, he'd packed up and moved on after the bust.

Rawlings climbed the back stairs up to the little apartment. The door was open and the interior was empty except for the dust that covered the floor. Nobody had been here for a long time, maybe years. Moonlight came in through the front windows, but it was still fairly dark, and Rawlings was glad there was no furniture to bump into.

He knelt at the front window and opened it quietly. From this spot he had a good view of the bank's front door.

The Territory Bank had been Nugget City's second banking institution and catered more toward the mining industry. Both individual miners and large companies did business there. When the boom went bust, so did the Territory Bank.

Rawlings stuck a cigar in his mouth but didn't light it. He didn't want either the glowing end or the distinct odor to give him away.

Let's keep it simple, Rawlings had told himself. *The bank has no back door. That means when Stone arrives, all I have to do is put a bullet in him with this Henry rifle and done is done.*

Unless McNeil gets him first.

So Rawlings waited.

As dawn crept closer, Rawlings began to wonder if he'd been outfoxed. If he could think to arrive early to bushwhack Stone, obviously Stone could think of the same thing. Maybe Stone was in there right now, waiting to put a bullet into Rawlings as soon as he walked through the front door.

In which case Rawlings could wait him out and then plug Stone when he left the bank.

But how long do I wait? Patience was never one of my virtues.

The first hint of dawn began to glow in the distance. The longer Rawlings waited, the more likely someone would see if anything happened. It was a dead part of town, but the sheriff wasn't keen to do anything in daylight.

Damn it, I'm going to have to see if he's in there. If he ain't, I'll check with McNeil.

He went back down the back stairs and circled around to the front of the building, looking both ways up and down the street to make sure nobody saw him. He studied the windows of the bank across the street, trying to catch any hint of movement in the shadow. No luck. If Stone was in there, he was keeping himself hid.

Rawlings took a deep breath, let it out slowly . . .

And dashed across the street.

He was briefly out in the open and braced himself for a blaze of gunfire.

None came. He made it across the street and put his back up against the front of the bank between a window and the front door. Rawlings stood there a moment, panting, his palms sweaty on the Henry. He took slow breaths until his heart settled. Rawlings was no longer the skinny kid of his twenties. He was middle-aged and felt it.

I need to lay off the biscuits.

Rawlings listened for a moment but didn't hear anything. He reached over to the front doorknob and twisted slowly, trying not to make noise. It was unlocked. He pushed it open abruptly, the heavy wooden door swinging inward, and stepped back quickly, again expecting hot lead to come flying at him. Nothing happened.

Rawlings cleared his throat. "You in there, Stone?"

A pause. Then, "I'm here."

Rawlings tried to estimate where the voice came from, but it was no use. Stone was somewhere in the dark depths of the bank. It had been a while since the sheriff had been inside, but he tried to remember the layout. Long benches flanked the door just inside, where people could sit and wait. Rawlings seemed to recall a door somewhere off to the left, a manager's office maybe. Desks in the middle, where folks could sit and talk to bank officers, apply for loans and such. Rawlings hadn't done much banking himself, but he had a general notion of what went on. In the back, a row of teller windows, three in all. No, four now that he thought about it.

Plenty of places for Stone to hide and squeeze off a shot at Rawlings if he went inside.

"Your note said some kind of trade," Rawlings said. "Come out and let's talk about it."

"Come out and get shot, more like," Stone called back. "I saw you coming from the shoe store. A man doesn't need a rifle to talk a deal."

"I suppose you think I should thank you for not taking a shot at me, then," Rawlings said.

"Maybe if I had a Henry rifle, I would have."

Rawlings chuckled. "So, how do you want to do this?"

"Come in here and we'll talk," Carson said. "For all I know, you got a dozen men out there waiting to gun me down."

"I feel a bit insulted you think so little of my intelligence, Stone," Rawlings shouted. "You won't come out here and get shot. I'm not going in there for the same reason."

"I'm the one that wanted to talk, remember? What does ambushing you get me except maybe a quick laugh? I need you to give me safe passage. I want my horse and then I'll go. I want your word that when I leave town, that's the end of it. You won't chase me down later."

"And what do I get in return?" Rawlings asked.

"I'll keep my mouth shut about certain things."

"Certain things like what?"

"Like I'm all done shouting about this through a doorway. I need to look you in the eye when we make this deal and know you don't have deputies ready to gun me down."

This was getting nowhere, Rawlings thought. Stone obviously wasn't coming out. And the gray light of dawn was starting to brighten. The sheriff didn't have the time or the patience for a prolonged standoff. Furthermore, he actually believed Stone. The man found himself in over his head and now just wanted to get out with his skin. Rawlings had always heard that trustworthy men trusted too easily. Maybe Rawlings could turn that to his advantage.

"Okay, Stone, let's work this out," Rawlings called. "No need for any more trouble for either of us. Toss out your gun so I'll know you're serious about cleaning up this mess without violence."

"I don't have a gun and you know it," Carson said. "I left it on a desk in McNeil's office."

True enough, thought the sheriff. Rawlings had ordered Stone to put it there himself.

Still . . .

"There's more than one pistol in the world," Rawlings called. "And I just don't believe you'd show up for a chat like this without iron on your hip. You're not as smart as you think you are, Stone, but you're not a damn fool."

A long pause.

"You still with us, Stone?"

"What about your guns?"

"What the hell about them?" Rawlings said heatedly. "I'm the sheriff of this damn town, so hell yeah, I'm armed. You're the one wants to talk, now throw your damn gun out and prove it."

"Take your rifle across the street and leave it leaning against the front door of the shoe shop," Carson said.

"What the hell will that prove? I'll still have my six-gun."

"A holstered six-gun is different from having a Henry pointed at my nose," Carson said. "Then at least it'll seem like you're coming in to talk and not to shoot. Take the rifle across the street and I'll toss out my pistol. Call it a gesture."

Rawlings cursed to himself and tried to figure what trick Stone was trying to pull, but the sun was coming up. He couldn't stand there all day trying to figure every angle. He went across the street and left the Henry, as instructed. He returned, making sure not to step in front of the open door. There was still the chance Stone might take a shot at him.

"I left the rifle," Rawlings said. "Now, you toss out your pistol and we can get on with it."

"Okay, here it comes."

Rawlings caught a flash of nickel in the moonlight, and then the pistol landed in the dirt street.

"Just remember to keep your hand away from your six-gun when you come in," Carson called.

"Or what? You just tossed out your pistol." Rawlings thought about it for a moment. "How do I know you don't have another weapon?"

"You *don't* know," Carson said.

Rawlings sighed. "Then what in the hell are we accomplishing here?"

"We both need to feel a little bit safe, so we can talk," Carson explained. "But we also need to feel a bit nervous, so nobody tries anything."

It made an odd sort of sense, Rawlings had to admit. *And there's no time to think of anything else. I need to get in there and have my chance at him.*

The sheriff didn't call out—he didn't want Stone to have any warning. He rushed inside the bank and immediately moved to one side. He didn't want to stand in the doorway and offer Stone a silhouette. He knelt in the darkness, waiting for his eyes to adjust.

Rawlings was tempted to draw his gun, but Stone had been right. He was just a little bit nervous. Could Stone see him? Would he whip out a second pistol and open fire if Rawlings went for his shooter? For now, best to talk.

"Okay, Stone, I'm in here," Rawlings said. "All my armies waiting to bushwhack you outside can't help me now. So talk."

"I want you to fetch my horse," Carson said. "Tie his

reins to a tree limb at the edge of the forest south of town. Somewhere along the road so I can see him. And I expect to find all my belongings still in my saddlebags. And I better not see anyone waiting for me for a mile in any direction. In return, I'll keep my mouth shut."

"Keep your mouth shut about what exactly?" Rawlings asked. "All you have are guesses."

Rawlings played for time. Every time Stone spoke, the sheriff got a better fix on him. All Rawlings needed was one good shot.

"Bill Cartwright's been buying up land," Carson said. "And you killed anyone who wouldn't sell."

"Watch who you're calling a murderer," Rawlings barked. "I never killed nobody. Cartwright had hired guns for that. My job was to make sure nobody in Nugget City poked into Cartwright's business. He paid me a pretty penny for it, too."

"But you lured my partner, Colby Tate, into a trap," Carson said. "You knew that big Bavarian was gunning for both of us and you wrote that note to set him up."

Rawlings chuckled. "I was sort of hoping that dumb Kraut would do my work for me. But when I had a chance to kill Tate, I didn't. I slammed him in a cell. So I ain't no damn murderer. But you cross me and I'll kill you, Carson Stone. Count on it."

A pause, and then Stone said, "Heard enough?"

Rawlings frowned. "Heard enough of what?"

But Stone hadn't been talking to the sheriff.

A yellow-orange glow brightened from behind the teller cages. Figures rose up from behind the counter, some holding lanterns.

"Yeah, we heard enough," one of them said.

Rawlings fought off a wave of confusion and squinted into the lantern light. "That you, Jacob Prescott?"

"It's me. And most of the town council. Enough for a quorum. I didn't believe it until I heard it out of your own mouth, Tad."

"On conspiracy, I'd imagine," said a woman. "And attempted murder. Probably a number of other things once we sort through the details."

Doris Beckinridge's voice.

Rawlings blinked. "Damn it, I'm the sheriff!"

"A mistake that will be rectified as soon as the council votes," Beckinridge said.

"Give it up, Rawlings," Carson said. "You're caught."

Rawlings turned toward the voice. In the lantern light he could dimly see him now, Stone off to the right, standing next to one of the desks.

Anger, frustration, and hatred rose up hard in Rawlings. *Carson Stone, you rat bastard, son of a bitch.*

The sheriff went for his gun.

He'd been ready for it, had suspected all along that Sheriff Rawlings was too stupid and too ornery to come quietly.

Rawlings went for his gun and Carson dove behind the desk next to him.

Shots fired. Shouts and panic from the men and women of the town council as they ducked for cover. Rawlings shot at them, too. Two seconds of confused chaos as the sheriff fired wildly, shots ricocheting around the interior of the Territory Bank.

Carson crawled to the edge of the desk, his hand closing around the gun he'd stashed there earlier, the twelve gauge he'd taken off Foster McNeil.

Rawlings fired at Carson, wood chips kicking up from the side of the desk six inches from Carson's face.

Carson turned the shotgun one-handed toward Rawlings,

aiming along the floor. He squeezed both triggers, and the 12-gauge bucked and belched fire and thunder from both barrels.

A storm of double-aught buckshot tore through Rawlings's lower leg from ankle to knee, blood spraying, flesh scorched from the bone. Rawlings went down hard, screaming and screaming and screaming.

Carson scrambled to his feet and headed toward the sheriff, the members of the town council emerging from their hiding places, crowding in behind him. Rawlings cursed a blue streak, face red as a tomato. His pistol lay two inches from his open, twitching hand, and Carson kicked it across the room.

The council crowded around to look down at the sheriff, some holding up lanterns.

"Good God," said a woman. She was the only other female member of the town council in attendance, a stout woman with a concerned expression. "We should call the doctor."

Carson looked down at Rawlings's ruined leg. Shattered ankle barely attached to the rest of the leg by sinew and tendon and a thin shard of bone. Blood pumped freely from the wound, a syrupy, red puddle spreading rapidly from beneath the sheriff.

"I don't think the doc would get here in time to do any good," Carson said.

Rawlings's red face was already going gray. The rage had drained from him, and he looked up at each face in turn, eyes going glassy. "You . . . damn people. So high . . . and mighty. I'm the sheriff, damn you. I'm the . . ."

His eyes rolled back white. A long, final sigh leaked out of him.

The man Rawlings had identified as Jacob Prescott tsked and shook his head. "Poor Tad. He never did seem like the type what could stomach prison. I could've told you he wouldn't come along peaceful."

"Well, you *didn't* tell us," Doris Beckinridge said crisply. "Never mind. The situation has resolved itself."

The council fell into a heated discussion about what to do next, and Carson took the opportunity to step outside. He took in a deep lungful of fresh air to wash out the stench of blood and gunpowder. He spotted the nickel-plated Remington in the street, plucked it from the dirt, and wiped it on his shirt.

It sure was a pretty shooting iron.

He squinted at the horizon. Daylight had arrived. He suddenly felt very tired.

Carson sensed someone behind him and turned. Beckinridge approached, hands clasped primly in front of her. "Well. That was all rather loud and unpleasant."

"I thought if we had him dead to rights, maybe he'd come quietly. I was wrong," Carson said. "Sorry about that."

"Don't be sorry," she said. "We had a disease in our town. Sometimes the only cure is for the surgeon to cut it out with the sharpest of scalpels, and that can get messy."

"There's more disease coming, I'm sorry to say. Cartwright's still out there. Rawlings was just his lapdog."

"Yes." Beckinridge frowned. "The rest of the council and I have been discussing that."

Carson held out the fancy Remington butt-first toward Beckinridge. "Obliged for the loan, ma'am."

"Keep it. You'll need it. The council just took a vote, and the result was unanimous," Beckinridge said. "Congratulations, Mr. Stone. You're Nugget City's new sheriff."

CHAPTER 31

The pleasant hum of anticipation buzzed through each of Nigel Evers's extremities, reaching every toe and fingertip.

Mary. Tonight.

Evers had been thinking about her nonstop, while eating or lying awake in bed. Her clear, white skin so perfect, her red lips. She seemed almost like some painting rather than a real woman, an ideal, something abstract. But then, at exactly the right moment, Evers would prove her to be real, oh yes, flesh and blood, warm and human.

He finished a late breakfast, then took a leisurely stroll through downtown Boise. It was too soon to go to the Three Kings. The working girls didn't start so early. It struck him that he'd been too late last time. Mary had already been spoken for by the time Evers had seen her. He didn't like the idea that some other man might have her attention when he needed her for his own purposes.

Evers changed directions and headed toward the Three Kings.

It was early, but not too early for the saloon to be open. A pair of old men sat at a table off to one side, slowly making a bottle of whisky disappear while they played checkers.

The bartender leaned against the corner of the bar, reading a newspaper.

He looked up as Evers approached. "Set you up with something, friend?"

"In a manner of speaking," Evers replied. "I was wondering if I might . . . uh . . . inquire about the ladies."

"Go right on and inquire. Plenty of gents do," the bartender said. "Ladies usually come downstairs after sunset. No particular time. Not an exact science. They make a parade out of it sometimes. Most folks think it's fun."

"I've seen," Evers said. "A grand spectacle indeed. There's a particular girl I'm interested in. When I was in the other night, she was already taken. I'd hate to miss my chance again, if there's possibly some way to . . ." He spread his hands, as if open to ideas.

The bartender scratched his chin. "Make a reservation?"

"If that's not putting it too crassly."

"Not at all, sir, not at all. I suppose if you put down . . . some kind of deposit?"

Evers had no doubt a portion of such a deposit would find its way into the bartender's own pocket.

"Which of the ladies should I tell to expect your company tonight?" the bartender asked.

"Mary."

"A fine choice." The bartender frowned. "Sadly, Mary ain't available."

"Oh?" A tightness in Evers's chest.

"She took off a little while ago," the bartender told him. "The girls take off on personal business every now and then. I got the notion Mary wouldn't be back tonight."

Creeping anxiety spread through Evers. This was very bad news indeed. He'd been expecting . . . counting on . . .

reaching a certain point by tonight, the slow build that had already begun, culminating in sweet release.

The bartender said something and Evers snapped out of his daze. "Beg pardon?"

"I was just saying there's always one of the other girls," the bartender suggested.

Evers blinked. The bartender's voice echoed strangely, as if the man spoke from the bottom of some deep hole. Evers shook off the feeling, gathered himself. "Other girls?"

September was potato harvesting month in Idaho, and Claire was already behind. She'd been up since dawn, digging potatoes one row at a time with a hoe, then coming back along the row and filling burlap sacks. She intended to fill the barn with her own personal supply to last her through the winter. Some would be set aside for seed potatoes.

Her grandfather the last decade or so had made an excellent arrangement with a score of Bannock women who'd help bring in the harvest in exchange for a quarter of the potatoes they dug up.

But the Bannock had been driven off and her grandfather was dead. Claire was alone.

She looked down at herself. Filthy. Her hands and forearms were completely caked with dirt to the elbows. Claire knew that by tonight her back and shoulders would ache. She looked across the wide field.

How am I going to do this?

One potato at a time.

Stop stalling and get back to work.

But she paused, spotted a wagon coming down the rise toward the farm. It was a big freight wagon with high wooden sides. It was too far to get a good look at the man driving the wagon. *Moving pretty slow. I think it's a pair of mules pulling it, not horses.*

Claire stood and watched it come, not eager to get back to the potatoes.

The wagon got closer, and Claire saw it wasn't a man driving the wagon but a woman in a man's clothing, and then a minute later she saw it was Mary.

What in the world is she doing here?

Mary reined in the mules along the edge of the field. She circled behind the wagon and came back with a digging fork and a shovel, one resting on each shoulder as she headed along the potato row toward Claire. She stopped five feet away and waited.

Claire didn't say anything. She could wait as long as anyone.

"I guess maybe I was rude to you yesterday," Mary said.

A pause, and then Claire said, "It's possible I gave you reason."

Mary looked back at the wagon and then at Claire again. "Biggest one I could find. Figure you can get a lot of potatoes to market."

"Where'd you get it?"

A shrug. "Men like to do me favors."

Claire had nothing to say to that.

"I never dug up potatoes before," Mary said. "Show me."

"Just thought this would be a fun change of pace?"

Mary sighed and looked across the field. "Doesn't look like fun. Looks like a lot of hard, backbreaking work, and I'm already thinking I probably made a big mistake. But a long time ago I was alone and needed help and didn't get it. And now I work at the Three Kings."

Claire raised an eyebrow. "You saying if I don't get this harvest in, I'll end up at the Three Kings?"

"I'm saying it looks like you could use a hand, and it's better to have help than not."

"Take that fork and start at the other end of this row," Claire said. "We'll work toward each other, then bag the potatoes after they're all dug up. After that we can start filling the wagon."

"Okay."

The women got to work, starting with unhitching the mules from the wagon and watering them.

Then back to the field.

Mary was soon as dirty as Claire. They bagged potatoes and stacked the bags in the barn. Then they started to fill the big wagon one wheelbarrow full at a time. They both worked hard, each woman refusing to allow the other to see how miserable she was.

Mary had been right, of course. It was backbreaking work.

Claire paused about an hour before sundown. "You'd better go if you want to get back."

Mary stood, hands on hips. "You sleep in the barn?"

"Yes."

"Room in there for me?"

"I guess."

Mary nodded. "Okay, then. Let's use up the daylight."

They worked with redoubled effort even though their bodies screamed exhaustion. The sun went down and the women dragged themselves into the barn. Claire lit a lantern and Mary collapsed into a pile of hay.

"I'm going to die," Mary said. "I'm not even kidding. I'm going to lie here and die."

"I'm going to heat some water," Claire said. "Do you want to wash?"

"I don't think I have the energy."

"Hey."

Mary lifted her head from the hay and looked at Claire. "Thanks."

"Don't thank me yet," Mary said. "How much of the wagon did we fill?"

"Maybe twenty percent."

Mary let her head drop back into the hay. "Good God. Is that all?"

"Even if we fill the wagon, we'll only have put a dent in it. I sure miss those Bannock women." Claire explained the arrangement from previous harvests.

"I guess I'll need to stay tomorrow and help again," Mary said.

Claire shook her head. "I can't let you do that."

"There's no point taking the wagon back if it's not even half full," Mary said.

"Don't you need to get back to the Three Kings?"

"Yes. Ray will grumble, but I'm his best girl and he'll get over it." Mary heaved herself to her feet, groaning all the way. "Be right back."

Mary returned a moment later with a cloth bag. She plopped down into the hay again, opened the bag, and pulled out a bottle of whisky. "This'll ease the sore muscles."

Claire hesitated.

Mary uncorked the bottle and took a stout swig. "Forget being ladylike. It's just us girls."

Claire sat next to her and took the bottle in both hands. She remembered how it burned going down when Carson had offered her a drink, so she took a small sip at first and then a slightly larger drink. The warmth was pleasant this time. She wiped her mouth with the back of her hand.

Mary looked at her and laughed.

Claire frowned. "What?"

"You wiped dirt under your nose." Mary laughed again. "It looks like you have a big mustache."

A hesitation, and then Claire laughed, too, and took another drink.

Mary took the bottle back and drank. The two women laughed and joked and drank.

A little while later the jokes were all used up and everything went quiet. There was only the shifting of the animals and a stiff breeze outside.

"I kissed him," Claire said.

She didn't have to explain who she was talking about.

"Why tell me?" Mary asked.

Claire lay back in the hay and blew out a long sigh. "So you'd know it was me that done it, that I kissed him and not the other way around. So that when you see him again . . . I don't know. So you won't hold it against him."

"He kiss you back?"

Claire didn't reply.

"Never mind," Mary said. "Men will do as they please. I've learned that from experience. There's no sense putting a claim on Carson. He's a good man but still a man. It would be like laying a claim on the sky. The sooner you learn that, the sooner you protect yourself from getting hurt. I forgot that the other day when I was rude to you." She paused to drink whisky. "That was just me trying to hang on to what I thought was mine."

Mary waited, but the other woman didn't say anything.

"Claire?"

Claire snored softly, the gentle sound of a purring cat.

CHAPTER 32

Carson Stone stood in his hotel room at the Golden Duchess and splashed cold water in his face. It had been less than two hours since his confrontation with Rawlings at the old Territory Bank building.

A man needs sleep, doesn't he? But there was no time for sleep.

Bill Cartwright was coming.

He still couldn't believe what he'd gotten himself into. He'd protested, yelled, sulked, and listed a half-dozen reasons it was a terrible, terrible idea. But Doris Beckinridge was a formidable woman and didn't take no for an answer.

Like it or not, Carson Stone was Nugget City's new sheriff.

Temporarily, he'd insisted. It wasn't his nature to turn his back on people in need, but he couldn't picture himself retiring in Nugget City after a long life of law enforcement.

Clean trousers and a fresh shirt. He strapped on his gun belt, Doris Beckinridge's garish Remington in the holster.

Okay, Sheriff, get to work.

He went downstairs to the lobby, where Beckinridge and Jacob Prescott waited.

Beckinridge handed Carson a mug. "Coffee."

He took the mug gratefully. "You read my mind."

Beckinridge cleared her throat, obviously about to deliver a prepared statement. "The council has authorized me and Mr. Prescott—"

"Mostly her," Prescott interjected.

Ahem. "The council has authorized *the both of us* to liaison with the acting sheriff—that's you, Mr. Stone—on all matters concerning Bill Cartwright," Beckinridge said. "The town's resources are at your disposal . . . within reason, obviously."

"I appreciate that, ma'am," Carson said. "I still think you folks are making a big mistake, but I'll do my best."

"The Nugget City town council is not in the business of making mistakes, Mr. Stone," Beckinridge said. "You've proven resourceful, trustworthy, and brave. Certainly, you're an improvement over our previous sheriff, so the bar's been set quite low. My primary question is, how do we proceed from here?"

"Why don't we just arrest Cartwright the moment he arrives?" Prescott asked. "We know he had people killed so he could buy the land."

"Maybe we'll do just that," Carson said. "But a powerful man like Cartwright might decide he'd prefer not to be arrested. From what I hear, he's not short of henchmen. There's places in this world where the law is the law. And other places where the law is only what you can enforce. There's another concern. Yes, he's had men killed . . . if you believe that. Personally, I do. But none of us witnessed him do it. Hell, I never even met the man. There's two men sitting in the jailhouse right now and I need to talk to both of them. After that I might have a better handle on what to do next."

"That sounds prudent to me," Beckinridge said. "Let's meet again later this afternoon."

"One more thing." Prescott held out his hand. "This is for you."

Carson looked down at the tin star in the palm of Prescott's hand. He tried to imagine the thing pinned on his vest and couldn't. He took it and stashed it in his shirt pocket. "I'll put it on later."

"Good luck, Sheriff Stone," Beckinridge said. "Until we meet again."

Carson gave them a nod and left the hotel. He was glad to be away from them, if only because he didn't think he could take one of them calling him "sheriff" again.

A little over a year ago I was an outlaw on the run and now I'm a sheriff? The world's gone crazy.

He entered the jailhouse, his new office. He circled back to the cells.

"Stone!" called McNeil. "How much longer am I going to be in here? I told you everything I know. You said it would help if I cooperated, and I'm cooperating."

"And you'd better keep cooperating if you know what's good for you," Carson said. "Don't worry, you and I are going to have a nice, long talk real soon."

McNeil made an irritated noise and plopped back down on his bunk.

Colby Tate stood waiting in the next cell. "I was wondering if I'd see you today. Please tell me you've brought more tobacco."

"I got something you'll like even better." Carson jangled a set of keys in front of Tate and then unlocked the cell.

Tate's eyes popped wide. "How did you get Rawlings to agree to this?"

"I shot him."

"I . . . don't know if you're joking or not."

"It's a long story. Come with me."

They went back to the front office of the jailhouse. Carson took the seat behind the desk and motioned for Tate to take the opposite chair.

"I hope you really did shoot Rawlings," Tate said. "Otherwise, you're going to be in a peck of trouble when he sees you sitting in his chair. Don't they usually put you in jail if you kill the local sheriff?"

"Something much worse," Carson said.

"Do tell."

Carson fished the tin star out of his shirt and pinned it to his vest.

Tate blinked. "Please tell me this is some sort of ghastly prank."

Carson told him the whole story: breaking into McNeil's office, getting caught, fleeing into the night without his gun, and going to Doris Beckinridge for help. Carson had honestly thought Rawlings would give himself up after a quorum of the town council heard him confess his corruption. Carson had taken no pleasure in blasting the sheriff's foot almost completely off his leg. On the other hand, he couldn't honestly say he felt bad about the man bleeding to death.

"Shrewd going to Beckinridge," Tate said. "Points for that."

Carson knew there was more. "But?"

"But have you lost your mind? Bedford was a good man and good at his job," Tate reminded him. "Rawlings was a corrupt bully. These men had only two things in common. They were sheriffs and now they're dead. That star on your chest might as well be a bull's-eye. As bounty hunters, we bring in bad men, but unlike sheriffs, we get well-paid, make our own hours, and turn our backs on anything that seems too risky. Sheriffs are paid garbage. The very people you're sworn to help will praise you one day and complain about every little thing the next. And I don't know if you've noticed, Carson, but Nugget City is not exactly the garden spot of Idaho."

"It's temporary, Colby."

"I know you, Carson, and—"

"It's *temporary*," Carson insisted. "I didn't create this mess with Cartwright, but I went snooping in McNeil's office and had a hand in stirring things up. I clean up my own messes. And these people need help." Carson locked eyes with Tate. "And I need a deputy."

Tate sighed, looked down at his arm in a sling, flexed the hand.

"How is it?" Carson asked.

"A little better each day," Tate told him. "But I won't be able to shoot with it. Not for a while."

"I remember some bounty hunter telling me he could shoot better with his left hand than most men could shoot with their right," Carson said.

"Flatterer."

"Colby, this is serious. I need you."

Tate sighed and stood. "I don't like it, but I need a hot bath and something to eat besides cold beans. Maybe I'll be in a better frame of mind after that."

Carson dug into his pocket and slapped his room key from the Golden Duchess onto the desk. "I moved all your stuff into my room. Take your time. Get cleaned up. Get a meal. And think about what I'm asking you."

"I will." Tate took the key. "But you think about what you're getting into."

Tate walked out the front door.

Carson sat at Rawlings's desk—*his* desk—for a few minutes, thinking.

Colby will come around. He has to.

He took a chair to the back part of the jailhouse and set it in front of McNeil's cell, straddling it backward. "Let's talk."

McNeil came to the front of the cell, grabbing the bars.

"I've already told you all I know. Look, Cartwright paid me well, so I did what he asked. But he's no friend of mine. We're not brothers. If I can help you get him, I will. I just don't know what you want."

"I reckon that's what we need to figure out," Carson said. "But first, I want to make sure you understand your position. Everyone in Nugget City knows Doris Beckinridge. I take it you're familiar with her also?"

"That sour witch? Yeah, of course I know her."

"Keep a civil togue in your head," Carson warned. "But if you mean she's stern, yeah, I agree. Sort of what I was getting at, actually. Rules are important to a woman like her. If you've murdered a man, you'll hang. She'll see to it. But if there's a nickel fine for spitting on the sidewalk, she'll chase you just as hard for that nickel. There's no *looking the other way* with her. Are we agreed?"

McNeil nodded. "Sounds about right."

"I'm not a lawyer," Carson said. "So technically I don't know what you're guilty of, but I damn well know you're guilty of *something*. Doris Beckinridge will take a train back to Boston and return with a lawyer even if she has to carry the man on her back if that is what it takes to sort out what you're guilty of. Conspiracy to defraud or something, maybe. She won't let it go." Carson thumbed the star pinned to his vest. "But *I'm* the sheriff now. And maybe under certain circumstances I could bring myself to look the other way. Like if I thought I could catch a bigger fish by throwing back a smaller one."

"I'm a small fish," McNeil said. "Hell, I'm a damn minnow."

"I've got a witness that knows you gave whisky to Bannock Indians to burn down a trading post." Never mind that the witness was a Bannock himself probably halfway to Oregon by now. All McNeil needed to know was that Carson knew what he'd done.

McNeil suddenly looked like he might be sick.

Carson scowled, his words taking on a serious tone. "However, if I thought you were guilty of murder, we wouldn't even be talking. Nobody was killed when the trading post burned."

"I *swear* to you, I had nothing to do with killing anyone," McNeil said. "I'll admit I got a little loud with folks sometimes, trying to convince them to sell, but I never harmed a soul."

"Okay, then. Let's go over again what you told me last night." When Carson had taken McNeil prisoner the previous night at the stable, his interrogation of the man had been rushed. Now, in the light of day, he wanted to be a little more methodical.

"He's supposed to be here tomorrow," McNeil explained. "He'll have men with him."

"Is he expecting trouble?" Carson asked. "Or expecting to cause some?"

"Not necessarily," McNeil said. "It's just his way. He likes to be in control of things, and muscle helps him do that. If he was a businessman in New York or Philadelphia, he'd be surrounded by lawyers and accountants and yesmen. But this is the West, so he surrounds himself with guns."

"And you say he's on his way here to sign the final deal with the railroad?"

"That's right."

"Why here?" Carson asked. "Seems out of the way."

"A fair point. Never occurred to me to ask," McNeil admitted. "Maybe because he has to finalize one last deal and the seller is here."

"One last deal?"

"The last chunk of land he needs to link everything up," McNeil explained. "Then Cartwright will own uninterrupted real estate the entire length of the proposed railroad line. Cartwright couldn't do the deal without it. The Union Pacific needs to know they can complete the route. It all happens tomorrow afternoon. First the real-estate purchase and then the deal with the railroad."

"And who owns this final tract of land?" Carson asked.

"Ben Kramer," McNeil said. "He inherited the land after his cousin Rollo was murdered."

Carson needed to run his plan past Colby Tate. Maybe someone with Harvard book learning could tell him how to make it better.

More likely he'll try to talk me out of it. Maybe I should listen.

Carson knocked on the door to his own room. No answer. He knocked again, then tried the knob. Unlocked. He entered. It took Carson a second to realize what was different. All of Tate's possessions were gone.

He left the room and was back down the hall at a quick pace, down the stairs to the lobby.

"Sheriff Stone!" the front desk clerk called to him.

Carson paused. It was strange to be called "Sheriff Stone."

The clerk held up a room key. "Your friend Mr. Tate left this for you."

"I'll be back for it!"

Carson headed out back, where he found Tate leading his horse out of the stable, saddled and ready to go. The bounty hunter looked his normal, dapper self again, freshly bathed, a clean shave and a fresh gray suit, only his arm in a sling any hint of recent trouble.

Carson flushed with anger. "You're just running out without a word?"

"Adieu!" Tate mounted his horse. "I have too grieved a heart to take a tedious leave."

"Don't give me that Shakespeare crap," Carson snapped. "You're running out on me."

"Who's running out on who?" Tate shot back. "You didn't consult with me before pinning that star on your chest. You didn't ask me if I was eager to play hero because let me tell you, brother, I'm not." His demeanor softened, and he looked down at the arm in the sling, flexing the fingers again. "I'm not whole, Carson. It's . . . just not a good bet."

Carson blew out a sigh, took off his hat, and slapped it against his thigh. Pure frustration. He couldn't do this without Tate.

At the same time, he realized he wasn't being fair. Colby was hurt, and his confidence wasn't there. Maybe Carson was being selfish. He stepped back from Tate's horse.

"It's okay," Carson said. "I'll figure something out."

"If anyone can, it's you," Tate said. "Look, I'm heading south. I'll ride slow. In case you change your mind."

Colby Tate clicked his tongue, and his horse took him away at a trot.

Carson watched him go. He rubbed his eyes. Tired.

Now what?

He still had a plan. It might stink, but it was a plan. Time to find Doris Beckinridge.

CHAPTER 33

Mary had been right.

The mules were a pain in the ass.

Claire jerked on the reins and then jerked harder, and the huge, creaking wagon full of potatoes clattered to a halt. She noticed that Mary was holding on to her shoulder.

Both women smiled at each other, nervous relief.

"I thought we might tip over coming around that one corner," Claire said.

"I told you." Mary shook her head and rolled her eyes. "Rotten mules."

"I can handle them."

After sleeping like the dead in the barn all night, Claire and Mary had risen with the sun and filled the wagon with potatoes. They both looked a mess, and Claire was pretty sure it would take three bars of soap to get clean again.

And there's still plenty of potatoes left to harvest. How am I going to do this?

Claire told herself not to dwell on it. One day at a time. For now, that was all she could handle.

Mary stood up suddenly, waving at a man crossing the street. "Patrick! Over here!"

A man in a brown suit looked up, startled to hear his name. He was in his midfifties, going gray, a healthy paunch in front of him. He changed course, walking toward the potato wagon. "Beg pardon, ma'am, but do I know—Mary?"

Mary climbed down from the wagon. "I know, I know. I've looked better."

"What happened?" Patrick asked.

"I've been digging potatoes." Mary turned to gesture to Claire. "Patrick, please meet Claire Grainger. She's the one who's benefiting from your generous loan of the freight wagon."

"Oh, uh . . . yes. Good to meet you." Patrick tipped his hat. "I never met your grandfather, but I'm sorry for your loss."

"Claire's going to need the wagon a few more days," Mary told him.

Patrick shifted awkwardly. "Now, Mary, I have a freight company to run and—"

"You know you have a dozen more wagons bigger and better than this old thing," Mary said. "It's practically falling apart."

"Them mules alone cost—"

"Patrick Ezekiel Sweeney!" Mary had raised her voice and stomped her foot. "Is a successful man like you really worried about a couple of half-witted, flea-bitten old mules?"

Patrick looked up and down the street with alarm, and Claire could guess what he was thinking. The man was standing in the middle of the street talking to a woman who worked at the Three Kings. Anyone might see, maybe even someone from church.

"Okay, okay, lower your voice, Mary." Patrick took off his hat and placed it over his chest. "Miss Claire, of course you can use the wagon and mules a couple more days. I know it's a hard time for you."

Claire barely managed to keep the grin off her face. "I'm

obliged. Trust me when I say everyone's going to know what a kind and generous man you are, Mr. Sweeney."

"Well, don't tell too many people," Patrick said. "Too much kindness and generosity can put a man out of business."

Mary ran a finger along Patrick's jacket collar. "I knew there was a good man inside you. I think you've earned a little something extra this Saturday night."

Patrick put his hat back on, turning abruptly to walk away. "Okay, okay. Lower your voice."

Mary looked at Claire, a twinkle in her eye. Both women giggled.

Claire grew serious, cleared her throat. "You're the only one who helped me. Lots of people looked sad and offered condolences and said, 'isn't it a shame,' but you're the only one who helped."

"No. Carson helped, too."

Claire looked embarrassed.

"I wish I could do more." Mary's eyes drifted to the Three Kings. "I've already been gone too long."

"I know."

Mary reached up and gave Claire's hand a squeeze. "I'll see you again when I can."

Claire smiled, suddenly too choked up to talk.

Mary gave her a last encouraging nod, then turned and lifted her skirt, trotting across the street to the saloon.

Claire took a deep breath. She was on her own again, but there was a vague comfort knowing she had a friend, even if it was the most unlikely friend she could have imagined. Her thoughts drifted to Carson—*no. Keep your mind on the task at hand*.

She had to yell at the mules and flick the reins three times to get them moving, but at last Claire had the wagon headed toward Wilson's Market. Wilson was the biggest produce man in Boise and had done business with her grandfather for years. He'd take the potatoes. That, at least, was one thing she could count on.

Then what?

Back to the field, girl. There's still a bunch more spuds out there.

Mary walked into the Three Kings. The place was crowded this time of day, but nobody seemed to be having a good time, nobody drinking or playing cards.

Something's happened.

Jake was behind the bar. "You can't come in here right now, miss. The sheriff is upstairs and—Mary?"

Mary scowled. She knew what she looked like, but people didn't need to keep reminding her. "What's going on, Jake?"

"Girl was killed." Jake shook his head. "It's a damn mess up there."

Mary gasped. "Who?"

"Connie Shepard."

Mary barely knew her. Connie was new, a leggy girl with freckles and sandy hair.

"But why? Who did it?"

"No idea," Jake said. "We were crazy busy last night. Nobody saw her leave with anyone. It's damn scary, if you ask me. I wonder what she might have said to set him off. I remember a girl getting her arm broke once because she laughed at a fella's . . . well . . . you know." Jake motioned vaguely below his belt. "But this?"

Two cowboys entered the saloon, and one waved to Jake. "Couple beers over here, Jake!"

Jake held up his hands in a hold-on-there gesture. "Sorry, boys. We're closed for an emergency."

"Now don't give us no grief, Jake," the cowboy said. "We come a long way and we're powerful thirsty."

Jake engaged the cowboys in a friendly argument and Mary slipped away. She circumvented the small crowd of men at the foot of the stairs and headed upward. Nobody stopped her. A smaller group of men stood outside Connie's open door, looking into the room. They didn't notice Mary coming up behind them.

She looked past them into the room.

Paul Jessup was there. She'd forgotten he'd taken over as sheriff. The look on his face made it clear he wasn't enjoying his job, not today. Ray stood next to him, white as a ghost, eyes haunted. There was a doctor, too, holding his telltale leather bag, bent over to examine the nude figure sprawled on the bed.

Connie's eyes were open wide, glassy and unreal. Blood across her throat and soaked into the sheet next to her, such a bright red it seemed obscene.

Mary turned away, hand going over her mouth to stifle a cry. She fast-walked down the hall to her own room. She didn't want to see anymore.

Who could have done such a thing?

Nigel Evers ate a hearty, late breakfast. Three fried eggs and biscuits. Link sausages. Hot, strong, black coffee—it was bloody difficult to get a proper cup of tea in this place.

He felt good, physically and mentally.

There were a few reasons for this. First, he was well-rested. He'd had a late night at the Three Kings, and when the sun had risen, the early rays streaming through his hotel window, he'd rolled over and caught another couple of hours. He had nowhere to be, no master to obey, and he found he was enjoying himself. All good things must come to an end.

But not yet. Not today.

His evening with—what was her name again? Ah, yes. Connie. His evening with Connie had been a tonic to his damaged soul, the release as keen and as exquisite as ever. He'd been concerned that switching his focus from Mary to another woman might undermine the experience, but in the moment, the bliss had been a bright and sharp explosion of satisfaction.

And yet, at the same time, it had whetted his appetite for the next encounter. The real prize still dangled in front of him. Mary was still out there, and the delay had only made Evers more eager for her.

Evers had played it smart. When the bartender had offered to reserve a girl for him, he'd almost accepted. The notion had appealed to Evers's sense of efficiency, but that would have given the law something to go on. Evers didn't want to leave a trail.

So he'd waited until late, easing into the Three Kings, not drawing attention to himself. Men were well into their cups. They hadn't bothered to notice Evers as he moved through the crowd. He'd enjoyed it, the feeling of being a jungle cat on the prowl for prey.

And then he'd spotted her. She'd tried her smile on some cowboy who'd shook his head and walked away. Evers had slipped in effortlessly to take the cowboy's place. Some polite chat. It still amazed him how impressed these girls were with good manners.

No one had given them a second look as they'd headed upstairs.

The look in her eyes, the startled betrayal as the blade cut across her throat . . . so perfect.

Evers reached for his mug and drank.

Good coffee.

CHAPTER 34

"You don't fool me." Cartwright laughed. "You just don't want to spend another night in a tent."

Kat laughed along with him. Let the poor fool think whatever he liked as long as he didn't suspect what she was really up to. "It's just smart. If I ride ahead, I can scout out the situation. You don't want any surprise when you reach Nugget City, do you?"

"I don't know what surprise you think there will be," Cartwright said. "I'm going to buy a piece of property, then sign a contract with the Union Pacific. And then if there's a decent bottle of champagne in that raggedy little town, we'll celebrate. What could go wrong?"

"That's why they're called 'surprises,'" Kat said. "You don't know they're going to happen."

Cartwright laughed again. "Suit yourself. I'm glad I have a tigress looking out for me."

On her own, Kat could ride a lot faster than Cartwright, all of his men, and their support wagons. She could get there by sundown. And while, yes, she did plan to spend the night in a comfortable hotel bed, she had other reasons for wanting to get there ahead of Cartwright and his band of cutthroats.

Vance would be there waiting for her.

He would be expecting a romantic interlude. Fine with Kat if that was what it took to keep him wrapped around her little finger. But if all went according to plan, Vance would meet with Cartwright tomorrow. Papers would be signed. And then Vance would leave with fifty thousand dollars. Kat had no intention of letting Vance get too far with all that money. Trusting people was a dangerous habit. She felt confident she had the man under her spell.

That wasn't quite the same as trust.

So her intention was to go over the plan and then go over it again, and anything she could change to her advantage, she would.

Cartwright kept the money in an iron box with a huge padlock in one of the wagons, a man with a shotgun guarding it. Kat had briefly considered contriving some plan to break into the iron box, or even make off with it somehow, but she discarded the notion. Cartwright would immediately notice and raise the alarm. If she stuck to her plan with Vance, it might be days or even weeks before Cartwright realized he'd been duped.

And by then, Kat would be far, far away.

It had been dark over an hour by the time she rode wearily into Nugget City. She checked into the Golden Duchess, bathed, and set aside her dusty travel clothes and changed into a long, green dress, bodice tight, neckline cut low. A matching clutch just big enough to conceal the derringer.

She ate at a table alone in Nugget City's best restaurant, which wasn't even good enough to be the third-best restaurant in Boise. A nearly undrinkable bottle of wine.

Never mind. She wasn't on vacation. But she did need an opportunity to observe the town and its folk. Nothing seemed askew. She glanced out the window. Few pedestrians, men and women on their way home after a hard day's work or perhaps to one of the local saloons to unwind.

A man came down the sidewalk near the restaurant, thumbs hooked into his gun belt. He came into the light of the window, and the star pinned to his vest. This must be the local sheriff. What had Cartwright said his name was? Ah, yes, Rawlings. Cartwright had the man on the payroll, so—

Kat turned away abruptly, heart thumping wildly in her chest. It wasn't Rawlings.

Carson Stone? What in the hell is he doing here . . . and sporting a tin star?

Madness.

Maybe she was mistaken. She thought about it. No, that face, the ruined earlobe. It was Carson all right.

Kat's mind raced. If his being in Nugget City was a coincidence, she'd eat her hat. She'd have to find out what was going on before Cartwright arrived. For all she knew, they'd all be riding right into a trap.

The waiter came to her table. "Can I bring you anything else, ma'am?"

"I'm fine for the moment," she said absently, then, "wait!"

The waiter turned back to her. "Ma'am?"

"I've only just arrived in town, but I heard there was some . . . uh . . . excitement recently? Something to do with the sheriff." She was fishing. Hopefully it wasn't too obvious.

"Yes, ma'am. Crazy stuff," the waiter said. "Looks like our sheriff was up to this or that—I don't know the details, but something crooked, I suppose. Town council appointed a new sheriff. Don't think I caught his name. I wish I could tell you more."

"Thank you so much."

The waiter nodded and left.

Kat quickly gulped down half a glass of the terrible wine. Something crooked indeed. How much did they know? All of her careful planning could go up in smoke. It might all be for nothing.

Calm down, girl. Panic won't help. I need to find out how bad this is and see what can be salvaged.

Damn, damn, damn. Once upon a time she'd emptied a rifle at Carson Stone and missed. *I wish I'd drilled the son of a bitch right between the eyes.*

Kat forced herself to calm down. It would do her no good to draw unwanted attention to herself. She paid her bill, not rushing and remembering to smile. Everything was fine. Nothing to see here. No reason to be suspicious.

She left the restaurant, forcing herself to walk slowly, just a lady out for a pleasant after-dinner stroll to aid in her digestion.

But Kat's eyes darted in every direction. She couldn't let Carson spot her. That would spoil everything. She entered the hotel, crossed the lobby without making eye contact with the desk clerk, and went straight up to her room.

Kat entered her room and shut the door quickly behind her.

"There you are, baby." Vance lay sprawled on her bed, boots kicked off, his jacket thrown over the bedpost. There was an open bottle of whisky on the nightstand, and he held a glass of the stuff in one hand. "I thought you'd never get here."

"Shut up." Kat put her ear to the door but didn't hear anything in the hallway. She was certain she hadn't been followed, but paranoia was the virtue of the survivor.

Vance rolled out of bed and approached her. "You okay?"

She snatched the glass from his hand and downed the whisky in one go. It was a welcome change from the bad wine. "We've got trouble."

"Tell me."

"Carson Stone is Nugget City's new sheriff."

"So what? I never heard of him."

Kat explained rapidly and as well as she could with the limited information she had. Rawlings had been Cartwright's man. He was out. Carson Stone was an old adversary. He was in. And if someone in Nugget City knew Rawlings was crooked, maybe they knew about Cartwright too. If the new, so-called sheriff arrested Cartwright, or if Cartwright got wind there was trouble and aborted the whole thing, Kat and Vance could kiss that fifty-thousand dollars goodbye.

Kat crossed the room, grabbed the bottle, and refilled the glass. "A fine mess." She shot back the whisky.

Vance sat on the bed and pulled on his boots. He stood, grabbed his jacket.

Kat narrowed her eyes. "Where are you going?"

"To see if I can get more information," Vance said. "He knows what you look like. He doesn't know me. Stay in the room."

He kissed her on the cheek and left.

Kat refilled the whisky glass and sipped. There was no point getting nervous about it until they had more information and could decide what to do.

She was nervous anyway.

Kat paced the room, drinking whisky, methodically thinking through how all this might go. The original plan had been simple. Vance would sign the papers on behalf of the railroad and Cartwright would think he'd just made the deal of the century. Then Vance would take his bribe money and leave. There was an abandoned mining camp about six miles west of town where Kat planned to meet him as soon as she could slip away without arousing suspicion. And then . . .

Well, that was a work in progress.

She waited an hour and then waited some more, and she was just considering going out to look for him when Vance returned.

He smelled like tobacco smoke and beer.

"You've been to a saloon," she said.

"Of course I have. That's where men drink and like to talk."

"What did you find out?"

"Everyone seems to know Rawlings was crooked, but nobody seems to know exactly how," Vance said.

"Then maybe they don't know about Cartwright."

"Or those who know aren't spreading it around," Vance said.

"What do we do?"

Vance grabbed the whisky bottle, started to pour some, then put it back, blowing out a sigh and running nervous fingers through his hair. "I don't know."

Kat thought a moment. "We go through with it."

"That's your plan? Do what we were already going to do?"

"That's the plan for you," she said. "There's no reason anyone should suspect you of anything. Only the two of us know we were planning to swindle Cartwright. If something happens, look surprised and outraged. You're a representative of the Union Pacific Railroad."

"What about you?" Vance asked. "If this Stone fellow recognizes you, it could spoil everything."

Kat poured herself a fresh whisky. "I'm still working on that part."

Doris Beckinridge hadn't been impressed by Carson's plan, but she'd admitted she didn't have any better ideas. They needed the cooperation of one other person for the plan to work, and Beckinridge said she'd attend to it. They'd made plans to meet again later.

Now, it was later that same evening and Carson walked the quiet streets of Nugget City to meet her. Most businesses were closed this time of night, shades pulled low, and only a restaurant and the saloon down the street still open.

Carson headed for the town hall.

As promised, the door had been left unlocked. Carson stepped inside, shutting the door behind him. Ahead was the big meeting hall for town business when the public was invited to participate. The space also doubled as a courtroom when the circuit judge made his routine appearances.

Carson turned left to the little office down the hall and knocked.

He recognized Prescott's voice say, "Come in."

Carson pushed the door inward and entered. "How did it go?"

Prescott sat behind a small desk and Beckinridge sat in the chair next to it. Both looked worn out.

"He's not keen on it," Beckinridge said.

Carson frowned. "What do you mean? Did you explain?"

"I appealed to his sense of civic duty," Beckinridge said. "Kramer said he'd rather have the money."

Carson pushed his hat back on his head and spit a curse. His eyes came up to Beckinridge. "Sorry, ma'am."

"Understandable under the circumstances."

After Rollo Kramer's murder, his nephew, Ben Kramer had inherited the final tract of land Bill Cartwright needed for his deal with the railroad, and Ben was scheduled to meet with Cartwright tomorrow.

Carson's plan had been inspired by his encounter with Sheriff Rawlings. They'd gotten Rawlings talking and he'd incriminated himself in front of witnesses. Carson wanted to try the same thing with Bill Cartwright. Carson had intended to impersonate Ben Kramer and meet Cartwright and . . .

Well, he wasn't quite sure. Get him to talk somehow. It had never occurred to Carson that Ben Kramer would want nothing to do with the scheme and apparently didn't consider law and order its own reward.

"Ben Kramer agreed not to mention that we'd approached him with this scheme," Beckinridge said. "In exchange, we won't interfere with his business transaction. Evidently, Ben has debts. Selling his uncle's land will get him clear."

"Well, maybe I'll just arrest Cartwright as soon as I see the son of a bitch," Carson said, frustrated. "That would throw some cold water on Ben Kramer's business transaction right quick, wouldn't it? McNeil already said he'll testify to save his own neck."

Beckinridge sighed. "Carson."

"And while Cartwright's sitting in jail, we can gather more evidence," Carson went on. "We can get people to talk."

"Carson!" she said more firmly.

He looked at her with fire in his eyes. "What?"

Beckinridge shook her head. "It was never a good plan."

"It worked on Rawlings," Carson insisted.

"But it won't work on Cartwright," Beckinridge said. "I'll admit that Rawlings had a sort of low cunning, the same as any chicken-stealing weasel. But at his core, Rawlings was a mouth-breathing imbecile who was more than willing to shoot his mouth off because he thought he was talking to a man he was about to kill anyway. You and I have never met Bill Cartwright, but we both know he's cut from different cloth than a brute like Rawlings. You don't get to be a rich and powerful businessman without thinking two moves ahead of your enemies."

Carson groaned out a sigh and slumped into the small office's remaining chair. "I reckon the plan did have some . . . weak spots."

"Cartwright won't spill his guts in a room full of witnesses. He'll let his lawyers poke holes in McNeil's testimony. Have you ever seen a slick, back East lawyer at work?

McNeil will end up in jail and the judge will apologize to Cartwright for the inconvenience," Beckinridge said. "But that's if—*if* Cartwright deigns to let you arrest him. You told me he'd have men with him. Cartwright might simply decide he's not in the mood to be arrested."

Carson's eyes shifted from Beckinridge to Prescott.

An apologetic shrug from Prescott. "She's not wrong. This town made a mistake trusting all of our law and order to one man. He had no permanent deputies. That's why we turned to you in our hour of need. There's no gunslingers in this town, no hard men to help you. We're just regular folks. Hell, the last time I shot a gun was in the war, and even then, I did most of my work with a shovel, digging graves at Andersonville. You try to arrest a man like Bill Cartwright like some ordinary criminal and good people could get hurt."

A long, uncomfortable silence.

Then Carson said, "So that's it? We let Cartwright do his real-estate deal as if he's just doing his business like usual and pretend he hasn't intimidated people and had them murdered?"

Beckinridge sat back in her chair, hands folded in her lap, head down. A moment later, her head came up again slowly, her tired eyes going to Prescott. "Jacob, there should still be a fire going in the stove in the back room. Brew us some coffee, won't you? We might be here a while."

Prescott stood with a groan, rubbing his back. "Probably a good idea. I reckon I could use a cup myself."

Beckinridge waited until Prescott had left and shut the door before saying, "I didn't want to say anything in front of him."

Carson raised an eyebrow. "Oh? You have an idea what to do about Cartwright?"

"I do. I've thought about it quite a bit, and I don't see any other way," she said. "We're going to have to kill him."

CHAPTER 35

Kat pulled on her boots, squinted at the bright line of daylight slicing through the narrow gap where the curtains met. She'd overslept, but no damage done. Cartwright wasn't due until sometime after lunch.

She poked the lump under the covers. "I'm going."

Vance snorted awake, rolled over, and rubbed his eyes.

"I'm leaving a note at the front desk for Cartwright," Kat said. "I'll make up some reason I can't be there. But *you* will be there. Just like we discussed."

"I remember."

"Just do the deal as if everything is fine," Kat said. "There's no reason for you to act as if anything's wrong."

"I *remember*."

"I'll be at the abandoned mining camp," she reminded him. "Meet me as quickly as you can get away without drawing attention to yourself. I've planned our route to Frisco. Tell you all about it when you get there."

"I'll be there," Vance said. "I'll wear out a horse getting there."

Kat put her hands on either side of his face and pulled him in for a long kiss. She let him go and then grabbed the half-empty whisky bottle from the nightstand. "I'll need this to pass the time while I'm waiting for you."

* * *

Carson wiped his sweaty palms on his pants.

This is a bad idea. Something's gonna go wrong.

He knelt next to the low parapet encircling the roof of one of the buildings toward the south end of town. Newcomers to town coming north would ride right past it on their way into Nugget City. A three-story building, storefronts below, and apartments where the proprietors lived above.

Cartwright and his people would pass by right below him. Carson lifted the gold-plated Winchester and sighted along the street. It would be an easy shot.

A bad, bad, bad idea.

He told himself to shut up. He'd already been around and around with Beckinridge about this, and in the end he'd seen it her way.

Or maybe she just wore me down.

It had been a shock to Carson when she'd suggested assassinating the man. And that's what it was. No sense sugarcoating it. Assassination.

"It's not fair," Beckinridge had said. "That the laws meant to protect common folks could be twisted and abused so a man like Cartwright could get off without so much as a slap on the wrist."

Carson had pointed out that they couldn't predict what would happen. Who knew what a judge might say, or a jury?

"I don't believe it," Beckinridge had said. "I don't trust it. There is a higher law than man's law. There is a justice beyond what is written on paper and what lawyers say. Our dead deserve such justice. Bill Cartwright deserves the wrath of such justice."

Carson couldn't dispute her. Hadn't he said basically

the same thing, that it wasn't fair Cartwright would get away with it?

But now he was on a roof, waiting to bushwhack a man like some lowlife back-shooter.

It didn't sit well.

Okay, so I shoot a man off his horse? Then what? He's got a small army of gunslingers with him.

"And when the man they're paid to protect no longer needs protection?" Beckinridge had asked. "They will be in disarray. Cut the head off the snake, Mr. Stone, and watch it flail."

Carson shook his head. *Here's hoping for disarray.*

When Prescott had returned with a pot of coffee and three mugs, he'd poured it around, and they drank in awkward silence.

Finally, Prescott had set his mug on the desk and said, "Okay, what am I missing?"

Carson had gestured to Beckinridge. Be damned if he'd say it.

She'd hemmed and hawed but had finally explained, back straight, chin up, daring her fellow councilman to find fault.

He'd looked deep into his coffee mug as if hoping to find answers there. A long pause to put all previous long pauses to shame.

"Jesus." Prescott looked up from his coffee mug. "Well, we sure as hell can't tell anybody."

And that had settled it.

But Carson hadn't slept worth a damn. He racked his brain to think of another solution. There were no options without risk, no course of action that guaranteed justice would be served.

So here he was on the roof. Waiting to shoot a man who'd never see it coming.

Did Rollo Kramer see it coming, or Old Dutch Casper Jansen, or Claire's grandfather?

Carson Stone never wanted to be a bounty hunter. He twice as much didn't want to be sheriff.

He swung the Winchester south, looking down the barrel toward the wilderness beyond the city limits. No sign of them yet.

Carson had let Foster McNeil out of his cell and given him very strict instructions. Act normal. Go through the motions of the land sale. All McNeil had to do to earn his freedom was to keep his mouth shut and let whatever was going to happen play out. But if McNeil tried to warn Cartwright, did anything to double-cross Carson, he'd go to jail for a long time.

"And don't take him to your office. Make up some excuse," Carson had told McNeil. "We want him where people can see him. Take him to the saloon. Tell him you're buying drinks to celebrate the deal."

Not that Cartwright would make it that far. Anyway, Carson wanted to make sure he came down the main street, not some back way to McNeil's office.

Figures in the distance, coming down the road toward Nugget City, at least twenty on horseback and a couple of wagons bringing up the rear. Too far to see faces, but it had to be Cartwright and his retinue. Carson leaned low against the parapet and watched them come.

Slowly, details came into focus, faces taking shape as they came into town. Hard-looking men. Riding among them was an arrogant-looking dandy in a fine gray suit and a red vest and a string tie, back straight in the saddle, head turning casually from side to side as if surveying a kingdom he'd just conquered. McNeil's description had been right on the money. The man couldn't be anyone but Bill Cartwright. He held a buffalo-hide briefcase on the saddle in front of him, straps with big brass buckles. The man held on to it like it was important.

Carson sighted along the Winchester's barrel. They'd all be surprised when he fired and Cartwright fell off his horse, all wondering what to do next, looking for where the shot had come from. Carson had already planned his escape down the back way. He'd be well away from the scene by the time they got their ducks in a row.

Carson set his sight on the middle of Cartwright's chest, but one of his hired guns rode in between them. For the next few seconds Carson had trouble getting a clear shot, Cartwright riding in and out among his men.

In all the bounties he'd ever hunted with Colby Tate, he'd never killed a man in cold blood. He'd given each and every one a chance to give up and come quietly. Some had. Many hadn't. But if they hadn't, it was on them. They'd been given a chance. But now . . .

Assassin.

They came up the street, and Cartwright rode clear of the other men. Carson aimed the Winchester.

Assassin.

He took dead aim at the center of Cartwright's chest. An easy shot. The man would never know what had hit him. Carson put his finger on the trigger.

Assassin.

It was odd that the empty storefronts would make him happy, but Cartwright often saw opportunity where others saw only ruin and defeat. Once he'd concluded the deal with the Union Pacific Railroad, he'd try to keep it quiet for as long as possible and buy up many of these buildings for pennies on the dollar.

Whipsaw reined in his horse next to him. Cartwright had no idea why the man went by that name, and frankly, he didn't give a damn. Too many of these cowhands thought they had to advertise how hard they were, sporting flashy shooting irons or going by tough nicknames. Stupid. When it came time to be tough, let it be a surprise.

Still, there was a good chance this Whipsaw fellow lived up to his tough name, Cartwright supposed. He looked the part, that was for sure, black hat and black vest, five days' stubble on his jaw, hard, mean eyes, and an ugly scar over his left eye and down along a nose that had been flattened by frequent fisticuffs. He kept the other cowhands in line, and that was what mattered to Cartwright.

"Boys could do with something to clear the dust out of their throats, Mr. Cartwright," Whipsaw said. "Looks like a saloon yonder."

"Let's get our bearings first," Cartwright said. "I'm supposed to meet—ah. There he is."

Foster McNeil waved from the sidewalk, and when Cartwright returned the wave, McNeil came across the street to greet him.

"Welcome to Nugget City, Mr. Cartwright," McNeil said. "Not much to look at, I'm afraid."

"It'll be the garden spot of Idaho by the time I'm finished with it, McNeil," Cartwright said. "I am very serious. Let's get to your office and buy a piece of land."

"Oh, about that." McNeil's eyes darted up and down the street, dabbed at the sweat on his forehead with a handkerchief. "Might be better if we conducted our business elsewhere."

Cartwright looked down at the man from his horse, eyes narrowing. "Everything okay with you, McNeil? You seem a bit jumpy."

"Do I?" McNeil put the handkerchief in his trouser pocket. "I suppose I'm nervous. We were buying up land pretty fast there at the end, trying to beat the clock. I'll be honest, there was a time I didn't think we'd make it."

Cartwright laughed. "Well, we've got one last transaction, and then you can put your feet up. You were saying something about your office?"

McNeil composed himself. "It's small and stuffy, and I figure you've come too far not to sit somewhere comfortable and have a drink. I see you've got your troops with you. Let's set up at the saloon and get a few bottles for these men."

"That would suit me right down to the ground." Whipsaw grinned at Cartwright.

"Looks like you'll get your way after all, Whipsaw," Cartwright said. "But don't we need some privacy?" he asked McNeil.

"The Lucky Strike doesn't do a lot of business this time of day," McNeil said. "And I've got a nice, quiet corner table picked out. We'll be okay."

"Pass the word," Cartwright told Whipsaw. "We're setting up shop at the saloon."

The men were overjoyed to hear it.

Cartwright dismounted in front of the Lucky Strike and hitched his horse to the post along with the others, keeping a tight grip on the buffalo-skin briefcase the whole time. Fifty thousand dollars was a lot of money to carry around. It wouldn't do to drag around a big iron box, so he'd transferred it to the briefcase that morning.

He walked into the saloon with McNeil, who gestured to a corner table. "Nobody will bother us there."

Cartwright looked around the interior of the saloon. McNeil had been right. The place wasn't busy at all. One man leaning against the bar, nursing a beer. A couple of old gents at a table near the window.

The cowhands all crowded in next, spreading out and taking over a half-dozen tables.

McNeil waved at the bartender and raised his voice. "Let's get some bottles for these boys!"

A whoop of appreciation rose from the cowhands.

"Right away!" replied the bartender.

Cartwright nudged Whipsaw. "Stay close." He tapped the briefcase under his arm. "Important papers in here."

Whipsaw nodded. "Right."

Cartwright trusted his men, but there were limits. Best he didn't advertise he was carrying so much money. But Vance had been clear. A check wouldn't do it. Cash only. Not that Cartwright blamed the man. One didn't usually take a check for a bribe.

They sat at the corner table and McNeil filled shot glasses with whisky.

Cartwright took another look around, this time searching for someone in particular. He'd expected to see Kat long before now, but instead he saw his assistant, Doyle, entering the saloon. Cartwright waved him over.

"We need to buy our property first," Cartwright reminded McNeil. "And then we'll see the railroad man."

"They're both at the Golden Duchess," McNeil said. "It's the only decent place in town. The other hotel's a fleabag."

"Doyle, head over to the Duchess and tell Kramer we're ready for him," Cartwright said.

Doyle left, and by the time he returned, Cartwright had made two shots of whisky disappear down his gullet. He was feeling good about life. Cartwright had plans—big ones—and it was all finally coming together.

"Mr. Kramer is on his way," Doyle reported. "Also, the front desk clerk had a message for you." He handed Cartwright an envelope.

Cartwright opened it and saw it was from Kat. It read:

I'll meet you later. I've gone to see the local doctor to get a tonic for my cramps as I'm having my monthly—

Cartwright abruptly folded the paper and put it away. That was enough of *that*. He didn't need the gory details. The important thing was that Kat would be along later. Fine.

Ben Kramer arrived. He was nervous and fidgety. Cartwright put it down to the fact that he was about to get a nice chunk of money. Not as much as the land was actually worth, but more than Kramer had seen before in his life. That was how it was with some people. Good luck was something so foreign to them that they didn't trust it.

Papers were signed. Cartwright gave the man a check. Kramer couldn't leave fast enough. The whole transaction took less than ten minutes.

"One down and one to go." Cartwright downed another shot of whisky and rubbed his hands together. "Bring me the railroad man."

CHAPTER 36

He just couldn't bring himself to do it.

Carson took his finger off the trigger and let Cartwright go by.

I've killed men . . . but I'm no assassin.

He climbed down the back staircase, and by the time he circled to the front of the building, Cartwright and his men had gone down to the saloon. Carson stood and watched them for a moment, knowing what he'd do next but wishing he could think of something better.

He looked back the other way toward the wilderness south. The urge to bolt was strong. Carson could be with Claire by tomorrow if he rode fast. He realized he hadn't thought of Mary first and felt bad about it. If he lived through the day, he'd need to figure out how to tell—

Carson blinked, focused on the figures in the distance. Three riders . . . no, four. More of Cartwright's men? Stragglers? He didn't think so. Carson watched them come, shapes congealing, bluecoats now plainly visible.

Major Grady and three of his men rode up a few moments later, reining in their horses next to Carson. "Carson Stone. Didn't expect to find you still hanging around Nugget City."

"I see you only have a fraction of your command with

you," Carson observed. "You didn't run into an extra-vicious band of Bannock, did you?"

Grady shot his men a quick look before answering. "We didn't see any Bannock. I sent the rest of the men to the fort, and the four of us—wait a minute. Are you sporting a tin star? Did you get on Rawlings's good side by some miracle and wrangle a job as deputy?"

Carson sighed. "That's a story, and there's no time for it. To be frank, Major Grady, I could use your help."

Carson explained briefly.

Grady shook his head. "You're in a pickle, Stone, and that's for sure. I'll be honest, I'm not sure what the rules are for putting myself and my men under civilian command, or using US troops for local law enforcement, but I'm not about to let a sheriff get murdered in his own town. We'll help all we can and let the rules sort themselves out later. But you're buying the drinks afterward."

"Fair enough."

They talked for another minute, Carson explaining what he had in mind and what he wanted Grady and his men to do. The major had a few helpful suggestions. The odds were still against them, but the time for talk was over.

"I reckon I better get to it," Carson said.

"Good luck," the major said. "See you when it starts."

Carson flicked him a two-fingered salute and headed up the street toward the Lucky Strike Saloon. Nerves tightened his gut.

"Mr. Stone!"

Carson turned to see Doris Beckinridge stalking toward him, face flushed, posture rigid.

"What *happened*?" she demanded. "He was supposed to be . . . you were supposed to . . ."

"I changed the plan."

"*You* changed—on what authority did you—?"

"*My* authority," Carson said. "I'm the sheriff. Not anyone

else. You and your council made that happen, and I reckon you can undo it with a vote tomorrow. Nobody said the law would be easy. What you asked me to do might have been expedient, but it was wrong. I think you know that."

Beckinridge looked outraged. Then ashamed. And then resigned. "What can I do to help?"

"Get Prescott and whatever other trustworthy help you can find," Carson told her. "Clear the streets, but do it quietly. Tell folks along Main Street to close up shop. But it's got to be quiet and orderly. We can't tip our hand. And you've got about three minutes to do it."

"Oh, for the love of—" Beckinridge turned abruptly and headed off at a fast walk.

Carson took a deep breath and headed toward the saloon, slow, deliberate steps. His heartbeat clicked up a notch.

He paused at the swinging doors at the entrance to the Lucky Strike. It sounded like any other busy saloon, men talking and laughing, the clink of glasses.

Foster McNeil emerged from the saloon and stopped short when he saw Carson. "I did it just like you said. Kept my cool. The railroad man's sitting at the table with him, along with one of Cartwright's yes-men. There's a rough-looking fellow, too. Some kind of bodyguard, I take it. The whole saloon is filled with Cartwright's guns. You sure you want to walk in there?"

Carson nodded. "Go on home and wait. You've done your part for now."

McNeil didn't need to be told twice and skedaddled quick.

Carson blew out a breath he didn't know he'd been holding. *Well . . . I guess I'm about to interrupt everyone's good time.*

Edward Vance made a pretty good show of looking through all the contracts. He didn't care. None of it was real, but he had to go through the motions. As far as that blowhard Cartwright knew, this was the biggest land deal in the history of the Idaho Territory. Vance had to look like he was taking it seriously.

Cartwright's sidekick, Doyle, handled most of the paperwork, pointing out where each man should sign and initial and so on. There were multiple copies of everything.

Cartwright sat back the whole time, grinning like an idiot and sucking back whisky. He had some kind of tough-looking bodyguard with him called . . . what was it? Hacksaw? No, it was Whipsaw.

Whipsaw had been tossing back whisky nonstop and looked to be gearing up for a grand old time. He lit a cigar for Cartwright. Puff, puff. The air filled with gray smoke. The Lucky Strike would soon be full of drunk cowhands all drinking on Cartwright's tab, celebrating his new deal, but Vance planned to be gone long before then.

His eyes went to the buffalo-skin briefcase on the table next to Cartwright.

Cartwright caught him looking, put a hand on the briefcase. "Some additional paperwork to take back with you. For your records." Cartwright winked.

A polite nod from Vance. "Obliged."

"But of course, you can't just rush off," Cartwright said. "You'll have to celebrate with us. This is a big day."

"That's generous," Vance said. "But it's a long ride back to—"

"Nonsense!" Cartwright insisted. "One drink surely."

Vance had to be careful not to raise suspicions. He couldn't seem too much in a hurry. He smiled big. "Well, hell, it would be rude not to have at least one drink."

Cartwright laughed and puffed his cigar. "That's the spirit."

They finished signing papers, and Doyle shuffled them into two stacks, copies for Cartwright and copies for the Union Pacific Railroad. Vance took ownership of the copies on behalf of the railroad, trying not to be obvious about looking at the buffalo-skin briefcase.

Cartwright poured everyone at his table a fresh shot of whisky. He raised his glass and indicated others should do likewise. "A toast. Today we plant the seeds of greatness. Soon this territory will—"

"Bill Cartwright!" shouted a voice with authority.

Conversations hushed. All heads turned to the man standing just inside the saloon doorway, thumbs hooked into his gun belt and a gleaming star on his vest.

"Bill Cartwright," repeated the man with the star. "You're under arrest for fraud and conspiracy to commit murder."

Carson was acquainted with the saying "you could have heard a pin drop," but this was the first time he understood it so completely. All eyes were on him. As soon as the words had come out of his mouth that he was there to arrest Cartwright, he realized how foolish they sounded.

He'd thought that the authority that came with the tin star would mean something because it meant something to him. It wasn't Carson Stone who'd come for Cartwright. It was the law. Who could refuse? But Cartwright had already proven the law meant very little to him.

It was why Carson couldn't just shoot the man off his horse when he rode into town. Even if the law meant little to Cartwright, it *did* mean something to Carson, and if those who upheld the law didn't respect it, why should anyone else?

None of that meant it was a smart move to strut into a saloon full of men who'd likely try to shoot the star right off him.

It was only a moment, but it seemed to stretch forever, everyone gawking at him like he was some idiot child who'd just announced he was going to jump to the moon.

"You don't have to be dramatic," Cartwright said finally. "If you wanted a drink, you could have just said so."

Half-hearted laughter rippled through the saloon.

Carson let it pass, then said, "With respect, Mr. Cartwright, I need you to come with me."

"Where's Rawlings?" Cartwright demanded. "He was Nugget City's sheriff last I heard."

"He retired," Carson said. "I'm the one that retired him."

"And who the hell are you?"

"Carson Stone."

Recognition crept into Cartwright's expression. "I know that name. You and I have a mutual acquaintance."

Instinct told Carson he knew exactly who Cartwright meant. "We can discuss that later."

"Now, listen, Stone. I'm here on legitimate business. If there's been some misunderstanding, I'll give you the names of my lawyers and they can answer any question you might—"

"You know that's not how it works, Mr. Cartwright," Carson said. "If there's been a misunderstanding, you can tell it to the judge."

Cartwright's face went hard. "I don't like being interrupted. Do you have evidence I've done something wrong? A witness, maybe, or—"

"Save it for the judge," Carson said. "You'll hear everything the witnesses have to say then."

Cartwright's face went red. The man was ready to chew nails.

A tough-looking customer with scars on his face sat next to Cartwright. He sucked back a shot of whisky, then slammed the glass down hard on the table. He stood slowly. "Man said he don't like to be interrupted. Might be you need a lesson in listening."

Everyone in the saloon went tense. Carson could feel it, like the whole world holding its breath. Even the air in the room seemed like it didn't dare move.

"Easy, Whipsaw," Cartwright said. "I'm sure the sheriff doesn't want anyone hurt. That's why he's going to walk out of here. Stone, if you have concerns, there's a more sensible way to go about this."

"You're getting arrested today, Mr. Cartwright," Carson said. "Get your mind around it."

"And who's going to arrest him?" Whipsaw asked with a sneer on his face. "You, all by your lonesome?"

The sound of US Army carbines being cocked made half the men in the room flinch.

Heads turned to see the three men in blue who'd slipped in the back door while everyone had been watching Carson and Whipsaw face off. Only the one with the corporal stripes— Alan?—was missing. One trooper covered half the room with his carbine, the other trooper covering the other half. Major Grady stood with his hand on his holstered revolver.

You sure as hell cut it close enough, Grady.

Carson forced a casual coolness into his voice. "Glad you could make it, Major. I take it the rest of your men are in position?"

"The company is arrayed outside and undercover," Grady said. "I figured crowding them all in here might only instigate something."

Half the heads in the room turned again to look out the front window, hoping to catch a glimpse of the cavalry troops.

Of course, none were out there. Carson was betting big on this bluff and, again, it had seemed a decent ploy before he'd walked into the saloon and put himself in harm's way. He hoped being "undercover" was enough to explain why there were no troops in sight.

Whipsaw, at least, wasn't convinced. "I don't see any bluecoats out there. If you like the odds, just go ahead and arrest us. Try it. That's twenty of us against four of you."

"Five." A man at the bar turned around, a smug look on his face despite the fact that his right arm was in a sling.

Carson couldn't stop himself grinning. *Colby Tate, you crafty son of a weasel, I knew you wouldn't let me down.*

"Four or five. So what?" Whipsaw's eyes bounced between Carson, the cavalrymen, and the fellow at the bar. "You're still outgunned by a mile. And if there's a whole company of troopers out there, I'll eat my hat."

Carson could see the man was tensing, ready to try something. Whipsaw's hand slowly hovered out over his six-shooter.

"Touch that pistol and it's the last thing you'll ever do," Carson warned.

Cartwright could see it, too. "Let's all take a breath here."

"Listen to your boss," Carson said.

But Whipsaw's eyes were still going back and forth, measuring, guessing, liking his chances. From the corner of Carson's eye, he could see the rest of the men in the room bracing for something to happen.

Whipsaw's fingers twitched.

Carson's eyes narrowed. "Don't."

Whipsaw went for his gun.

And a hundred things happened at once.

Tables overturned, and men reached for six-guns, bottles and shot glasses flying and smashing on the floor. Whipsaw's gun hadn't even cleared the holster when Carson fired, the slug slamming into Whipsaw's chest. He spun around and away, blood trailing.

Cartwright and the other two men at the table dove for the floor.

Carson didn't have time to admire his marksmanship. He crouched low, shifting sideways as lead flew every which way inside the saloon. Colby Tate drew left-handed and gunned down the two men at the table nearest him as they rose from their chairs and reached for their pistols. The cavalry carbines spit fire, and a cowhand's head was knocked back as the shot ripped through his skull in a splatter of bone and blood.

Major Grady drew his army pistol, shooting a lot but not hitting anything. At least he was keeping their heads down.

Cartwright drew his pistol and backed away, a handful of his cowhands covering him. Carson advanced, overturning Cartwright's table for cover, shooting twice, splinters kicking up from the table that Cartwright and his men had likewise overturned for cover.

Tate fired again, then leaped up and slid across the bar, ducking down on the other side. A storm of lead ripped into the bottles behind the bar, glass and booze raining.

One of the men on the floor began crawling past Carson. Toward the buffalo-skin briefcase.

The cavalrymen fired again, and two more of Cartwright's cowhands bit the dust.

The man next to Carson put his hand on the buffalo briefcase. Carson spun and pointed the Remington at the man's face. "Leave it." If it was full of contracts or other potentially incriminating papers, it might be evidence he'd need.

The man froze.

"Clear out." Carson waved toward the door with his gun.

The man hesitated, eyes going to the briefcase, but then he staggered to his feet and ran for the door, bullets flying over his head.

One of the cowhands stood to get a better shot at Carson, but Carson fired first, catching the man in the throat. He went down gurgling blood.

One of Grady's cavalrymen took a bullet to the shoulder and grunted in pain. The other trooper caught him before he fell.

"Stone!" Major Grady shot Carson a look.

Carson understood. Time to go.

He grabbed the buffalo-skin briefcase with one hand and emptied the Remington at the cowhands with the other. He ran for the front door as Major Grady took his men out the back. Carson had hoped Cartwright would cooperate. He'd hoped they'd fall for Grady's bluff that an entire company of troopers were outside. It hadn't worked out.

Time for plan B.

Carson ran out the front door of the Lucky Strike, hot lead chasing after him.

Cartwright cursed a blue streak as he crouched behind the overturned table.

They had their opponents badly outnumbered, but they were being shot at from three different directions. Cartwright's men were confused and disorganized.

The cowhand next to him finally got off a good shot and wounded one of the cavalry troopers.

And then Stone bolted for the front door.

Taking Cartwright's buffalo-skin briefcase with him.

Cartwright fired, but the shot went wide, and the man wearing the tin star was out the door.

Suddenly, all was quiet in the saloon, gunsmoke hanging heavy in the air. Cartwright stood and looked around. Six of his men lay dead. Two others were too wounded to carry on. "Where'd that fellow behind the bar go?"

"I saw him clear out with the cavalrymen," one of the cowhands said.

"Never mind them." Not only did Stone have fifty thousand of Cartwright's dollars but who could say what evidence he had? Must be something big if Stone thought it enough to arrest Cartwright, and that wasn't good. "Get after that so-called sheriff. Find him and kill him!"

His men rushed from the saloon, pistols drawn.

Cartwright walked over to where Doyle still cowered on the floor, arms over his head. Cartwright reached down and took Doyle under one arm, pulling him to his feet. A wet spot covered the front of Doyle's pants.

"Good God, Doyle," Cartwright said. "You've pissed yourself."

CHAPTER 37

Carson took a quick right turn after leaving the saloon, then a left down the alley out back, and ran flat-out until he reached the Golden Duchess and ducked into the hotel's back door. He cut through the lobby, where he found Carlton at the front desk.

"Hello, Sheriff," Carlton said. "I thought I heard gunshots. Is there anything I should—"

"Hide this!" Carson shoved the briefcase at the man.

He was out the front door, not even waiting for Carlton to reply. Carson paused in the shadow of the hotel's front porch overhang. He emptied the spent shells from the Remington, and they bounced around his boots, rolling across the floorboards of the porch. He quickly reloaded.

Carson saw and heard Cartwright's cowhands spill out of the saloon down the street. He counted a dozen of them.

He crossed his fingers for plan B because there sure as hell wasn't a plan C.

Carson started across the street, not moving too fast. He needed to give them a chance to spot him, but he couldn't be too obvious. No jumping up and down, waving his arms, or shouting, "Hey, over here!"

He was almost all the way across the street when he finally heard one of them shout, "There he is!"

Carson turned up the street and ran.

Shots flew past his head on both sides.

Beckinridge had done her job clearing the street. No townsfolk in sight. If Carson got himself killed with his own foolish plan, then so be it, but the last thing he wanted was for a stray bullet to kill an innocent bystander.

Carson ran to one side of the road, ducking around the corner of a building, giving Cartwright's men a chance to catch up. He caught his breath, then took off running again. He slowed slightly, letting them get closer, and veered toward the building with the big, barn-size doors. If he didn't time this right, he'd only succeed in getting himself shot full of holes.

He stopped in front of the doors. Looked over his shoulder at his pursuers. They were almost right on top of him. Carson slammed the big door with his fist five times hard.

Then threw himself on the ground.

The big doors of the firehouse swung outward, revealing Corporal Alan and the gleaming barrels of Bessie.

Alan cranked the weapon. The barrels of the Gatling gun spun, spitting fire and lead. The storm of death tore through the cowhands. They screamed and twitched and died. A few on the edges of the killing ground tried to run, but the corporal swung Bessie, cranking for all he was worth, shredding flesh, a red mist filling the air.

In a few seconds it was all over. A dozen men sprawled in the dirt, blood leaking from their bodies, making thick, red mud. A few moaned, calling out with their final breaths before dying.

Grady stepped out of the firehouse, raising a hand. "Hold fire, Corporal."

Carson stood, dusted himself off, and walked toward the slaughter. He looked at the face of each dead man. None were Cartwright.

Colby Tate appeared behind him. "What a mess."

"I tried to take him in," Carson said. "Just arrest him like any sheriff might do." He gestured at the dead men. "I didn't want this."

Tate said nothing.

Carson walked to the saloon. All the horses were still tied out front. He went inside. Nobody there. With no men to back him up, Cartwright would be looking to escape, wouldn't he? But the horses were out front. If he needed to find another, he'd have to go to . . .

The stables.

Carson ran out the saloon's back door and down the alley again. The Golden Duchess's stable was the closest if Cartwright wanted to steal a horse. He arrived and stopped himself from rushing inside. It wasn't so long ago that Foster McNeil was in here waiting to ambush him. Best to go cautiously.

He went into the stable, the Remington cocked and ready.

Jet was there, as were a couple of other horses. There were a few empty stalls. Had other horses been there before? Carson couldn't remember. There was no sign of Cartwright, but obviously he could have taken a horse and made his escape while his men were getting slaughtered by Bessie. Carson sighed and uncocked the revolver, slipped it back into the holster.

He left the stables and went back inside the Golden Duchess. Someone would need to chase down Cartwright wherever he went. The man would be a wanted fugitive now.

But somebody else will have to do it. I'm finished.

Carson's only plan now was to pack his things and go. There was a lady waiting for him, and he wanted nothing more than to see her. He would pause on his way out of town to track down Doris Beckinridge and return the tin star. They'd find a better man to be sheriff.

He went upstairs to his room and entered.

A man waited for him, standing awkwardly on the other side of the room, a big wet spot across the front of his trousers. Carson recognized him as one of the men who'd been sitting with Cartwright in the Lucky Strike.

Carson's hand fell to his six-shooter. "What are you doing in—"

Something struck him cold and hard at the base of his skull. Lights went off in front of his eyes, a spinning feeling, and suddenly he was on the floor, blinking his vision back. He felt someone behind him take his pistol, then heard the door close.

"You took something that doesn't belong to you, Stone." Cartwright's voice.

Carson took deep breaths, collected himself. He looked up at Cartwright.

"My man Doyle here is an astute fellow." Cartwright handed Doyle the Remington he'd taken from Carson. "He was here in the hotel earlier to fetch a couple of my business associates, and he happened to notice your name on the register at the front desk. When you told us your name in the Lucky Strike, he remembered."

Carson laughed.

"Let me in on the joke, why don't you?" Cartwright said.

"If you kill me, I'll still have the last laugh," Carson told him. "One day you'll turn your back on Lady Pain and she'll stick a knife in it. She's the mutual acquaintance you mentioned, isn't she?"

"Perhaps you weren't man enough to handle Kat, but I am," Cartwright said. "We're to be married, if you must know."

That only made Carson laugh harder.

"You'll be laughing out the other side of your face if you don't cooperate," Cartwright said. "We've searched this room with no luck. Now, you're going to tell me where my briefcase is."

"Why should I?" Carson asked. "You're going to shoot me anyway."

"Maybe and maybe not," Cartwright said. "Get on my good side and maybe you've got a chance."

"You guarantee not to shoot me?"

"I guarantee I absolutely *will* shoot you unless you start talking," Cartwright said.

Carson used the bed to push himself to his feet. "I'll show you where it is."

"Let's move slowly, shall we?" Cartwright kept his revolver trained on Carson.

Doyle pointed Carson's own Remington at him, too. He held the gun awkwardly, as if he was not accustomed to firearms.

"Just take it easy, the both of you," Carson said. "Nobody needs to get shot here."

"Just tell me where the briefcase is," Cartwright said. "I'll send Doyle to see if you're lying or not."

"No deal," Carson told him. "I was on the run and stashed it in a tricky place. Easier to show you."

"You're stalling."

"Of course I am," Carson admitted. "If we're outside where people can see, maybe you'll be less likely to shoot me. You want your briefcase. I want to live."

Cartwright laughed, sinister and mirthless. "You want to live an extra two minutes? Fine. But do anything stupid and I'll shoot you down and find the briefcase myself."

Cartwright wasn't a fool. Carson absolutely intended to try something stupid. He just had no idea what that might be, but the first step was to keep from getting shot for as long as possible. He'd need to stay alert for his chance.

He didn't have to wait long.

They stepped out of the hotel room, and he heard someone yell, "Carson!"

Colby Tate stood at the end of the hall, lifting a pistol left-handed.

Cartwright grabbed Carson by the arm and pulled him in front to use as a shield. Tate hesitated.

Take the shot, Carson thought. *You can do it. Even left-handed*.

That was when Doyle erupted from the room, Carson's gleaming Remington in his hand. This must have been Doyle's idea of heroics, leaping recklessly into the fray. He fired the Remington, a wild shot that dug into the ceiling.

Tate returned fire, hitting Doyle square in the chest. Doyle was knocked back into the room, only his boots sticking out into the hallway.

Cartwright aimed his pistol at Tate.

Carson grabbed Cartwright's arm and yanked it up just as it discharged, ceiling plaster snowing down on them. They pushed and pulled, fighting over the pistol. Cartwright was a sturdy man with some muscle. In the corner of his eye, Carson saw Tate trying to find a clean shot but hesitating. Carson knew his friend well and could almost read his mind. Tate wasn't as sure with his left hand and didn't want to accidentally shoot his friend.

Cartwright understood the situation, too. He threw his other arm around Carson in a half bear hug, keeping him close, so Tate couldn't shoot. Cartwright's revolver was sandwiched between them. They continued their tug-of-war battle, shoving and pulling, each trying to gain leverage. Carson took a big step back . . .

. . . into nothing.

The floor went out from under him, and he tumbled down the stairs, pulling Cartwright with him. Both men grappled as they bounced down the stairs, each still trying to take control of Cartwright's gun. *Bounce*. Carson felt a sharp pain in his ribs. *Bounce*. His head struck a banister support.

They hit the bottom of the stairs and rolled into the lobby.

"Good Lord!" Carlton shouted from his spot behind the front desk.

They rolled to a stop, Carson ending up on top. He tried to wrench the gun away from Cartwright, but the man yanked it back.

"I'm not letting you spoil everything I planned," Cartwright said through clenched teeth. "I'm not going to let—"

Bang.

Carson heard and felt the gun go off between them, the heat of it scorching his chest.

I've been shot. Good God, I'm dead.

He rolled off Cartwright, backing away into a sitting position, hand automatically going to his chest.

No blood.

Carson looked at Cartwright.

He lay on his back, coughing blood. A red stain spread on his shirt in the middle of his chest. He tried to speak, coughed blood again. It dripped down his chin. He tried to roll one way, then the other, trying to get up, but he couldn't. Like a turtle flipped on its back.

Carson stood slowly, unable to rip his gaze away from the dying man.

"I was . . . I was building . . . a legacy," Cartwright sputtered. "Something . . . that would last."

This wasn't what Carson thought being a sheriff would be like. Nothing like the stories of two men facing off in the street at high noon, one man fast on the draw, the other one slow and dead. All Carson could do was watch the life fade from Cartwright's eyes.

His money and power won't save him now.

A long, last breath leaked out of Cartwright, his eyelids lowering slowly, slowly, and closed.

Tate came up behind him, held out the Remington to Carson.

Carson took it and slid it into the holster. "Thanks."

"You've done a man's work, sir."

Carson looked up to see that Doris Beckinridge had entered the lobby, Jacob Prescott lurking behind her. Townsfolk crowded the hotel's big front windows outside to get a look at the bloody scene.

Carson approached Beckinridge, stepping around the corpse on the floor. He took the tin star off his vest and handed it to Beckinridge. "The job's done, ma'am. I'll let you and the rest of the town council take it from here."

CHAPTER 38

Carson saddled Jet and led him out of the stable, where Tate was already waiting for him astride his own horse.

"I take it you're heading back to Boise."

Carson nodded. "Reckon so."

"Seems as good a direction as any," Tate said. "Need some company?"

A shrug. "Couldn't hurt."

"Carson, please. Stop begging. I'll be happy to ride with you."

Carson grinned and mounted Jet.

Carlton came out the back door in a rush, puffing, checks red. "Mr. Stone, don't forget this!" He held up the buffalo-skin briefcase.

"Thanks." Carson took the briefcase and hung it on his saddle horn. He supposed it didn't matter anymore what evidence might be contained within. Cartwright didn't need a trial. He needed an undertaker. But the buffalo skin looked sharp. Maybe Carson would keep it for himself.

"Safe travels, gentlemen," Carlton said.

"You run a quality establishment," Tate said. "I look forward to staying again should fate ever bring me back to Nugget City."

"And of course you're always welcome," Carlton replied. "Provided your next visit is a bit less . . . uh . . . exciting."

"A reasonable request," Tate said. "No promises."

Carson laughed. "Take care, Carlton." He clicked his tongue and Jet was off.

There was one shack in the abandoned mining camp that wasn't completely falling apart. Kat sat in the shack's one rickety chair, her bare feet propped up on a stool toward the blaze in the tiny stone fireplace. She was glad it wasn't raining because she could see sky through the half dozen holes in the roof.

Doesn't matter. I'm not on holiday.

And the whisky helped pass the time.

Kat poured herself another shot and wriggled her toes in front of the fire. She was just starting to doze off when the sound of a horse snorting caught her attention. She jumped to her feet and went to the front of the shack, peeking through the shredded remains of the thin curtains.

Edward Vance climbed down from his horse and tied it to a post.

About damn time.

She watched Vance unstrap a carpetbag from his saddle. He carried it toward the shack.

Kat backed away from the front door, hands behind her back, waiting. This was it. Her heart hammered in her chest like a nervous rabbit's.

The door opened and Vance entered. He saw her and smiled. "Damn. I'm glad to see you."

Kat's eyes went to the carpetbag, then back up to Vance. "Glad you finally made it."

She brought her hands around front, leveled the derringer at Vance's chest and fired. The pop of the little gun startled

Vance. He flinched and dropped the carpetbag. Then he looked down at his chest in disbelief.

Blood.

Vance's eyes went wide. "You've got to be kidding me."

He collapsed to the floor, muttering a string of bewildered obscenities.

Kat ignored him and rushed to the carpetbag. "Finally. All the work and planning. Finally!"

She opened the carpetbag, blinked at the contents. She reached in, pulled out the dirty shirts and socks. "What?" She upended the bag. Dirty underwear. "Where's the money? Damn it, Eddy, where the hell is the money?"

Vance made a fluttering, wheezing sound, and Kat realized he was laughing.

"What's so funny?"

"That . . . new sheriff," Vance said. "Carson Stone."

Kat went cold. "What?"

"I was . . . so close. Almost . . . had the money." Vance clutched his chest, blood oozing thick between his fingers like raspberry jam. "Stone stopped me. He . . . took it. It was in a . . . buffalo-skin . . . bag. Almost had it."

He started laughing again, and it became a hacking cough.

"I still don't see what's so funny."

"You m-murdered me . . . for . . . my dirty laundry. Damn, I love you, but . . . I always knew . . . I should never have . . . trusted you . . ."

"I don't think I want to listen to your jabber anymore," Kat said.

She aimed the derringer at his forehead and pulled the trigger.

Nigel Evers walked into the Three Kings Saloon and immediately spotted the object of his desire. Mary flirted with a lanky cowboy at the bar, laughing at some unheard joke. He watched her a moment through the crowd.

The saloon's clientele was subdued this evening, no rowdy songs or laughter. Evers knew the reason for it. When Louise had disappeared, there'd been curiosity, but it wasn't unheard of for a girl to get fed up with the life and vanish overnight. The talk was Louise had always been a bit of a free spirit, and many said they hadn't been surprised.

But the girl found bloody in her bed . . .

Well, that was another kettle of fish. They all now thought there was a vicious murderer among them.

And they are correct.

But others thought it must have been some demented stranger passing through. Many were warming up to the notion. And why not? There'd never been that sort of trouble before in the Three Kings.

Evers bellied up to the bar near Mary and the cowboy, not intruding on their conversation. He ordered a beer, drank it slowly. Eventually the cowboy drifted away, and Mary turned to Evers.

"I'd hoped to see you in here again," she told him.

"How could I stay away from someone as lovely and pleasant as you?" Evers said.

She beamed, smile wide. "You don't have to flatter me, you know." She lowered her voice. "I'm sort of a sure thing."

He laughed gently.

Evers felt it stirring, building. The release he craved dangling in front of him for the taking.

They talked for a few minutes about small things, where he'd lived in England, her childhood. There was a way about her Evers appreciated. No pressure, Nothing pushy. She knew her value completely, knew that Evers found her captivating.

"I'm so sorry. Where are my manners?" Evers said. "Can I offer you a drink?"

She put one of her slender, graceful hands on his arm. "There's a bottle of whisky in my room."

And then Evers said something that surprised even him. "I'm sorry. I can't."

The look on Mary's face was almost comical. She'd obviously thought she'd had matters well in hand.

One more night. Let me prolong this just one more night.

Evers knew he'd have to leave town after another killing. Nobody would believe anymore it had just been a stranger passing through. So he'd wait, push the sweet agony to its limits before seeking the longed-for release.

It was delicious. The terrible need inside him.

"Please don't misunderstand, Mary," Evers said. "I do want to go to your room. Very much. But I need to meet someone. I just stopped in for a quick beer. However . . ."

Mary arched an eyebrow. "Yes?"

"If I were to come back tomorrow night. At the same time," Evers suggested. "Would you meet me right here at our spot at the bar?"

A smile warmed her face. "I'd like that."

CHAPTER 39

Carson and Tate spent the night around a campfire, not talking much. Carson especially wanted nothing more than to put Nugget City behind him.

They started early the next morning, and just outside of Boise Carson reined in his horse.

"What is it?" Tate asked.

"I'm going to make a side trip," Carson said.

Tate turned his head toward the Grainger potato farm. "You've made your choice, then?"

"There was never a choice," Carson said. "Not really."

"Well, I'm going to find a soft hotel bed and a good bottle of brandy and read a book until I go to sleep," Tate said. "Good luck, Carson." He spurred his horse and waved as he rode off toward Boise.

A little less than an hour and Jet topped the bluff just before the farm. Carson looked down and saw a figure walking out of the barn, carrying a bucket. She stopped and looked at the rider. From this distance she wouldn't be able to see who it was, only that she had a visitor.

Carson clicked his tongue and Jet galloped toward her.

When he got closer, she dropped the bucket, ran toward him.

Twenty feet away, he reined in Jet and leaped from his horse.

"Carson!" Claire ran toward him.

She threw herself into his arms so hard, she almost knocked him over. They kissed hard and long, as if it were the only thing they ever intended to do.

Finally Claire broke away from him, grinning ear to ear, searching Carson's face. "What are you doing here?"

"There's nowhere else I should be," he said. "Nowhere else I want to be."

He told her about everything that had happened in Nugget City. All of the blood and killing.

"I don't want to be a sheriff or a bounty hunter either," he said. "Not anything where my job is to shoot another man. The only good thing that kept me going was thinking about you. Doing what I needed to and finishing it so I could be done and see you again."

"I love you, Carson," Claire said. "I'm so afraid to say that out loud, but I'll just bust if I don't."

They kissed again.

He pulled away and suddenly looked troubled. "I have to go into town. I have to tell someone something. Something that can't wait."

"I'll hitch up the buckboard," Claire said. "We can go into town together."

"You don't need to do that."

"Yes, I do," Claire said. "Because Mary's my friend and I should be there."

"Your friend?"

"That probably surprises you, doesn't it?" Claire laughed nervously. "I think she felt sorry for me. She's been helping. Mary's smart, Carson. She knows that I . . . that you and me . . . well, let's just say she won't be so surprised when you tell her what you want to tell her."

Carson nodded. He owed Mary an explanation face-to-face. Maybe Claire being there would make it easier. "I'll help you hitch the buckboard."

They went into the barn and Carson put the harness on the horse.

"You okay?" Claire asked. "You got a worried look on your face."

"Nervous, I guess," he told her. "I don't want to hurt Mary's feelings."

Claire laughed. "She's tough enough to recover from you, Carson Stone. I don't know if this helps, or if you even want to hear it, but I think she's got her eye on a new fella now."

Carson frowned. Claire was right. Carson didn't want to hear it.

"Some Englishman," Claire said. "Oh, I don't know if she actually fancies him, but she's always going on about his accent and his good manners and—"

"Englishman?" A twist of panic in his gut.

"That's what they call men from England, isn't it?"

"I've got to go," Carson said urgently. "I've got to get to the Three Kings as fast as I can."

He turned and bolted from the barn.

Claire followed. "What are you—Carson!"

But Carson had already leaped into Jet's saddle, riding hell for leather toward town.

Mary joined the routine parade of girls down the Three Kings' stairway, meeting a subdued cheer. The place hadn't been the same since the murder. People would forget eventually . . . but not yet.

She searched the saloon with her eyes, but Evers hadn't arrived yet. Never mind—she was sure he'd be along.

Mary maneuvered through the room, nodding and smiling and exchanging brief salutations but avoiding prolonged conversation. She knew Nigel was coming and she intended to be available for him.

He was a gentleman, and Mary appreciated that. He would probably not want anything weird or disturbing in the bedroom. Furthermore, she found him charming. There was no rule that said her job must eternally be a chore.

And then Nigel walked through the door, looking as dapper as ever, a bounce in his step. He was eager to see her, which made Mary a little giddy.

Nigel took her hands, gently kissing the fingers of each. He smiled at her, eyes twinkling. "Do you still have that bottle of whisky in your room?"

Mary giggled.

Jet tore through the streets of Boise, Carson leaning low in the saddle. Pedestrians scattered before him. He'd apologize later.

He dismounted in front of the Three Kings and rushed inside without pausing to tie up Jet. He stood just inside the door, scanning the interior. No sign of Mary. He stalked across the saloon to the bar and waved down the bartender, a man he'd seen a number of times before, although his name didn't immediately come to mind.

"How do there, Stone?" the bartender said. "Haven't seen you in a while."

"I need to see Mary."

"Hold your horses," the bartender said. "She not available."

"What does that mean?"

The bartender frowned. "You *know* what that means. She's entertaining. If you want to leave a message, I can make sure—hey!"

Carson ran for the stairs.

"Now, damn it, you can't go up there!" the bartender called after him.

Carson took the stairs up two at a time, ran down the hall, and pounded on Mary's door. "Mary!" He tried it. Locked.

He slammed his shoulder into the door, heard the wood splinter. He slammed again and it flew open. Carson rushed inside.

The Englishman—what was his name—Evers!

Evers was on top of her in the bed, jacket off and the rest of his clothes rumpled, shirt collar unbuttoned, hair mussed. He held a knife to Mary's throat. His other hand covered her mouth. Her head turned to Carson, eyes wide and terrified. She wore only a flimsy shift and white stockings.

Carson's hand dropped to the Remington. "Get off her!"

Evers grabbed her by the arm, hauling her up and twisting her to face Carson. He stood behind her, his other hand still holding the knife to her throat.

"I'll kill her," Evers said calmly and quietly. "I will draw a red line right across her soft throat. Get rid of that gun. Put it on the sideboard. Slowly."

Carson froze, his eyes meeting Mary's. She trembled, and a tear leaked from the corner of one eye.

"That wasn't a suggestion." Evers gave Mary's throat a little nick with the knife. She gasped. A thin trickle of blood, a vivid red against her smooth, white throat. "The gun."

Carson leaned to the left and set the Remington on the sideboard.

"There. That wasn't so difficult," Evers said.

Carson took a step forward, hands spread in a no-problem-here gesture. "Let's just all calm down and—"

"Stop! I'll slice her."

Carson stopped. There was only the bed between him and them. "Now what?"

"That's what we're going to discuss," Evers said. "I intend to walk out of here and you're going to—"

Carson leaped across the bed.

Evers cut into Mary's throat. She screamed.

Carson latched onto Evers's arm, his weight carrying him across the bed and pulling the knife away from Mary. Carson held on to Evers with a death grip, dragging the other man down on top of him.

"Mary, run!" Carson shouted. He was vaguely aware of her scrambling across the bed toward the door.

Evers kneed him in the gut and Carson sucked for air.

The Englishman raised the knife and then brought it down fast.

Carson swept his arm across to block him, connecting with Evers's wrist. Instead of plunging the blade straight into Carson's face, it bit deeply into his shoulder. Carson grunted rage and pain.

"Like that, do you? Does it tickle?" Evers twisted the knife.

Carson yelled, tried to buck the man off. He remembered one of his father's fighting tricks, one he'd used more than once. Just the right spot on a man's wrist. Sensitive. Carson didn't know why. He was no surgeon, but it was a spot that hurt like holy hell.

He reached across with his other hand, grabbed Evers's wrist and dug his thumb into the spot just as hard as he could.

Evers flinched back in surprise and pain, letting go of the knife and rolling off Carson.

Carson staggered to his knees. The knife was still stuck in his shoulder. He yanked it out.

Just as Evers kicked him in the side of the head.

The knife flew out of Carson's hand and he heard it clatter across the floor. He flopped backward, blinking stars out of his eyes, hands up to ward off whatever blow was coming next. He managed to get to his feet and clear his vision just in time to see Evers coming at him. He'd retrieved the knife and intended to stick it in Carson's belly.

A clap of thunder shook the room.

Bone and flesh flew from the top of Evers's head, blood spraying. Evers's eyes shot wide and he staggered back, dropping the knife. He stumbled a confused circle before falling back into the window, an elbow shattering the glass.

He turned his unblinking eyes on Carson. "What . . . what . . . what?" And then he worked his mouth a few more times, no words coming out until he finally fell into a heap and never moved again.

Carson looked at his shoulder. Blood soaked the sleeve.

He turned to see Mary standing in the doorway, a two-handed grip on the Remington, smoke oozing from the end of the barrel. Eyes big as dinner plates.

"Are you all right?" Carson asked.

She said nothing.

"Mary?"

"Jesus," Mary whispered. "I shot him."

Claire finished hitching the horse to the buckboard in a hurry and chased after Carson. She'd never driven it so fast, and it rattled and clattered and hit every bump like it was going to fly apart.

She didn't care. Carson had left in a panic. Something was wrong.

There was the fleeting notion that Carson had heard about Mary's interest in the Englishman and had become jealous. She discarded the thought as fast as she'd thunk it. He hadn't cared that Mary might have moved on. It was only when Claire had mentioned it was an *Englishman* that he became alarmed.

She reined in her horse in front of the Three Kings. People crowded the front door, trying to see inside. Whatever Carson had been worried would happen must have happened already.

Claire left the buckboard and pushed her way through the crowd.

A middle-aged man took her by the elbow. "You don't want to go in there, miss. No place for a young lady."

She yanked her arm away and went inside.

Claire had never been inside the Three Kings before, nor any saloon actually, but she wasn't some naïve fool. Instinct told her to go upstairs. Her heart threatened to beat straight out of her chest.

If something's happened to Carson . . .

She put it out of her mind until she reached the top of the stairs and followed the crowd to the open door of a bedroom. She pushed her way inside.

And gasped when she saw Carson on the bed, shirt off, a doctor bent over his bloody shoulder. "Carson!"

"Get her out of here," the doctor said. "I need to finish these stitches."

A sheriff's deputy put a hand on her shoulder. "Come on."

"Wait! It's okay." Mary came out of the room, took Claire's hand. "I'll take her."

Mary held a thick shawl closed around her shoulders with her other hand. There was white gauze tied around her throat with a bandage, red seeping through. She led Claire down the hall, away from all the activity. Some of the other girls stood in their doorways, watching events unfold with open curiosity.

Claire gawked at the bandage around Mary's throat. "What happened?"

"It looks worse than it is," Mary said. "Two stitches."

Claire shook her head, a hundred questions trying to come out at once. "But what . . . what *happened*?"

"Well, you know that Englishman?" Mary said. "Turns out he . . . he was . . ."

Mary burst into tears, sobs racking her body, thick tears rolling down her cheeks. Claire threw her arms around her, and the two women held on to each other as Mary cried it out. She gathered herself and told Claire the tale—Carson arriving just in time, getting stabbed, and Mary shooting the man.

Mary wiped her eyes. "I thought I knew men. God almighty, he had me fooled, didn't he?"

Carson emerged from Mary's room, the doctor walking next to him. Carson wore his shirt unbuttoned over a heavily bandaged shoulder. He looked ashen and unsteady.

"You've lost a good bit of blood," the doctor said. "You'll need to take it easy."

Mary leaned in, whispered into Claire's ear. "Go on. Take care of him. He's yours now."

Claire looked at Mary. "But . . . are you okay?"

"I've got my girls," Mary said. "Go on."

Claire gave Mary's hand a final squeeze, then went to Carson.

Her arm went around his waist and he leaned on her.

"Thanks," he said.

They went down the stairs carefully. The doctor helped Carson onto the buckboard bench, where he sat with his shoulders slumped.

"I feel dead tired," Carson said.

"He's coming down from it all," the doctor said. "He needs rest."

"Hold on," Claire said.

She fetched Jet and tied him to the back of the buckboard. There was some kind of briefcase strapped to his saddle. The leather—buffalo hide?—was soft. She put it in the back of the buckboard.

"Get him into the bed of the buckboard," Claire told the doctor. "He can lie down."

"That's not a bad idea," the doctor admitted.

They helped Carson into the back. He stretched out and Claire put the briefcase under his head for a pillow.

The deputy, who'd been upstairs, came out of the saloon, holding up a six-gun and a gun belt. "Don't forget this, mister."

"I'll take it," Claire said. "Obliged." To Carson, she said, "I'll hold on to this for you while you rest." She took the gun from the holster, admiring the gleaming nickel and ivory hilt. "Well, now, isn't that a pretty thing."

Carson laughed weakly. "Too pretty, if you ask me."

Claire holstered the gun and strapped the belt around her waist. "It'll be here when you want it . . . although you might have to fight me for it. I like shiny things."

Carson snorted. "Keep it."

The doctor cautioned Claire not to let Carson exert himself. She assured him she'd watch the patient like a hawk and fill him with soup.

Claire climbed onto the buckboard's bench, flicked the reins, and was off.

Claire had no idea she was being observed. The woman in the shadows across the street had watched the whole scene unfold. She untied her horse from the hitching post, mounted, and followed the buckboard at a safe distance.

CHAPTER 40

Carson lay in the back of the buckboard, the gentle jostling like being rocked to sleep. He would have slept all the way back except the occasional rut or stone jarred him awake again. He looked up at the night sky, a million stars brilliant against a velvet backdrop.

His shoulder throbbed with a dull pain, but mostly he was just tired. It didn't matter. It was all finally over. He could sleep for a week if he wanted. Claire would take care of him. The thought made him smile.

Carson was suddenly aware the buckboard had stopped. Claire's face appeared above his. "We're home."

Home. The word sounded right. Yes, this was home.

Claire helped him down from the buckboard and into the barn. They passed through to the little smithy, where Claire stoked the coals in the forge and got a fire going. He sat on the bench and warmed himself. It was the same bench where he'd sat with Claire and she'd fallen asleep, her head on his shoulder.

God, that seems like a hundred years ago.

Claire peeled him out of his bloodstained shirt. "I'll wash this later, but I'm not sure it's worth the trouble."

She took the shirt away and returned with a horse blanket and draped it around Carson's shoulders. "Hungry? Thirsty?"

Carson shook his head.

"Stay here by the fire," Claire told him. "I'm going to unhitch the buckboard and put it away. Don't worry. I'll take care of Jet. When I come back, I'll set you up in the loft. I'll make you comfortable."

"Thank you."

She turned to go.

"Claire."

She paused, looked back.

Carson summoned the energy for a smile. "Maybe we should . . . I don't know . . . get married or something."

She stared blankly at him for a moment, blinked once, then laughed. "Carson Stone, that is, hands down, the worst proposal I ever heard. I'll let it go because you've had a rough time. After a good night's sleep, you can try again tomorrow."

"Good idea," Carson said. "I'll practice a few times in the mirror."

Claire walked away, shaking her head and laughing.

Carson sat and stared into the fire.

Claire was right, of course. She deserved better. But Carson couldn't let another night go by without telling her how he felt. It hadn't been right with Mary, but he hadn't been able to see it until he felt how right it was with Claire. Like finally slipping your foot into a shoe that fit perfectly.

Holy smoke, I can't say that when I propose. A shoe? I really am bad at this.

Carson had just started to doze when he heard Claire come back. He looked up and saw her across the fire, approaching the forge from the other direction, a silhouette in the darkness. She came into the smithy, stepping into the light and—

It wasn't Claire.

Kat lifted the derringer and pointed it right at his face.

She always did favor that little gun.

And why not? She'd killed enough men with it. Except

for the short hair, she looked pretty much the same. A man's tan trousers and a blue shirt. The .32 revolver in the shoulder holster not quite hidden by the brown doeskin vest. A dangerously pretty woman.

Carson opened his mouth to speak, but Kat put a finger to her lips in a shush gesture.

"Quietly please," Kat said in a low voice. "What's her name? Claire? I've been out there listening in the dark. Such a pretty little thing. Would be a shame for her to come back and interrupt before we finished our business." She waved the derringer at him to make sure he understood.

Carson felt himself go cold. He was almost too tired to care if she shot him, but Claire . . .

"What business is it you think we have?" Carson asked in a voice barely above a whisper.

"Don't play stupid," Kat said. "You've got something that doesn't belong to you. Where is it?"

Carson frowned. Hadn't Bill Cartwright said basically those exact words to Carson just yesterday? *She must be after that damn briefcase. What the hell's in it?* He felt foolish for not bothering to look.

"I don't know what you're talking about," he said.

"You always were a bad liar, Carson," Kat said. "Now stop messing around or I'll shoot you and ask your girl-friend the same question."

"Carson?" Claire's voice. Sounded like she was calling to him from the other side of the barn.

Kat's head turned at the sound of the voice.

Carson sprang up from the bench and ran back toward the barn. He heard the little pop of the derringer but kept running, vaguely aware Kat followed.

Another pop, and Carson felt something bite deep into the back of his thigh. He went down, turned to see Kat still coming. He couldn't stand, tried to scoot away.

"Oh stop it," Kat said. "You're not going anywhere."

Carson tried to stand but went down again immediately. He reached back to touch the wound and his hand came away bloody.

Kat stood over him, casting a long shadow in the lantern light. She smiled, wicked and predatory. "Our conversations aren't as fun as they used to be, Carson." She broke the derringer's breach, then fished into her pocket for shells to reload. "So I think I'm just going to shoot you and your girlfriend and then have a look around and find what I want on my own. To be honest, I've been wanting to shoot you for a long time. You cost me a lot of money. Maybe you forgot all about that, but I haven't. I'm going to shoot you up close and look you in the eye when I do it."

Kat started to thumb the first shell into the derringer but paused, sensing something. She looked around.

Claire stood in the barn's open doorway, her eyes locked on Kat, one hand out to her side. She still wore Carson's Remington.

"Step away from him." There was an edge to Claire's voice, maybe fear or maybe anger.

Or both.

The two women stood frozen for a moment, eyes locked.

Kat dropped the derringer and the shells, fumbled into her vest for the .32.

Claire's hand fell to the Remington, drew it from the holster in one smooth motion, and cocked the hammer back with her thumb.

Kat barely had the .32 out of the shoulder holster when Claire fired, the sound of it filling the barn.

The slug slammed into Kat's chest, lifting her off her feet. She fell flat on her back with a thud, the .32 revolver flying away. Nobody said anything for a few seconds.

Slowly, Claire approached the other woman, looked down

at her, nudged her with a boot. Kat didn't move. Claire slowly lowered the gleaming Remington back into the holster, sighed, and turned to Carson.

"I gunned down a woman for you," she said. "Now you've *got* to marry me."

EPILOGUE

One month later . . .

Carson still limped.

It wasn't bad, but it was noticeable. The doc had told him to keep taking walks and stretching the muscles and the leg would be back to normal sooner or later. The doc had also told him to try not to get shot or stabbed for a while.

So far, so good.

He stood a few minutes and watched the house being built. The frame had gone up quickly. The rest was coming along.

Hank Baily walked up and stood next to Carson, both watching the house together.

"She's going to be a beauty," Baily said. "I've got one of my men bringing in the river rocks for the fireplace, and once we get that wraparound porch in place, you'll really see something, I can tell you."

"I believe it," Cason said.

The house would be larger than the one Cartwright's hired killers had burned down. When Carson had finally gotten around to looking in the buffalo-skin briefcase, he was surprised to find fifty thousand dollars. It was a fortune.

The money wasn't Carson's, not really. On the other

hand, Bill Cartwright had no use for it anymore. At the very least, Cartwright owed Claire a house. What Carson would do with the rest of the money . . . well, that remained to be seen.

Claire put a thousand dollars of her own in the bank. The bounty for Katherine Payne. Claire had never shot anyone before but dealt with it with surprising aplomb. He let her keep the Remington. It was too pretty a gun for his liking.

"Carson, thanks so much for hiring me and my crew," Baily said. "After our last job went south . . ."

"Stop thanking me," Carson said. "Just get a roof over our heads before the first big snow."

"Not a problem," Baily said. "Say, would it be okay . . . I mean, would you mind if . . ."

"Yes, you can knock off early today," Carson said.

"It's just that I've got to get these boys some booze and female company at least once a week."

"Go on, then," Carson said. "You've earned it."

Baily slapped Carson on the back, then ran off to tell his crew the good news.

A few minutes later Carson saw a rider coming who turned out to be Colby Tate. He no longer had his right arm in a sling but complained it still didn't feel exactly right. Carson reckoned he was still a faster draw than most.

"The house is going up fast," Tate commented.

"I guess Baily knows his stuff."

"You sound surprised."

Carson chuckled. "I guess I am a little."

"Here's something that might amuse you," Tate said. "Guess who I saw in the Three Kings last night?"

"Mary."

"No. I mean, well, yes, and she seems to be doing well if you're curious, but that's not who I mean," Tate said. "I mean someone who's not usually there."

"President Hayes."

"And suddenly the game has grown tiresome, so I'll just tell you," Tate said. "That oily scalawag Benson Cassidy."

"The slicker!" Until that moment Carson had forgotten the man existed.

"The same. Seems his luck has changed. The pearl is back in his tiepin and his suit is clean and pressed. I infer he took the money you paid him and tripled it with some lucky cards. Anyway, he's on his way to greener pastures and passed through Boise. He bought me a whisky and told me some interesting things about our recent adventures."

"Do tell."

"Apparently there is no new railroad line at all," Tate said. "It was all part of some elaborate confidence trick on Bill Cartwright, cooked up by a former employee of the Union Pacific and our former associate, the late Lady Pain."

"Wait. What?"

"They took a bribe from Cartwright for advance knowledge so he could buy up all the land. Then, when the railroad came through, the land would be worth ten times as much, but as I've already said, the railroad wasn't coming," Tate explained. "The Union Pacific did have plans at one time, but they were abandoned quite a while ago."

Anger rose in Carson. People killed and swindled. All for a lie.

Then Claire came out of the barn, carrying a bucket to slop the hogs. She saw Carson talking to Tate and waved. Her smile flew all the way across the yard and hit Carson like a lightning bolt. He felt the anger drain out of him like water.

There's no help for the past. I'm only thinking of the future now.

"Anyway, I'm heading south before winter gets here for real," Tate said. "I just wanted to say goodbye."

"Let me guess what you're going to say next," Carson said. "Sooner or later, I'll get bored or restless or something and want to come bounty hunting with you again."

Tate looked at the girl slopping the hogs, then back at Carson. "No, old sport, not this time. I think this time you'll make it stick."

They shook hands, and Tate rode away.

Carson hobbled to the pigpen just as Claire was finishing.

"Hello, Mrs. Stone," he said.

She smiled, blush blooming in her cheeks. "Hello, Mr. Stone."

Carson had felt bad not telling Colby, but Claire and Carson had agreed. A preacher and just the two of them, an exchange of vows. It was their secret, not forever but for a while, so it could just be the two of them. They wanted to keep the world out for a while. They didn't want to answer questions. They didn't want congratulations.

They just wanted each other.

He scooped her up suddenly. Claire yelped and dropped the bucket. "Carson!"

"Come on, woman. There's something I want to show you in the barn."

Her blush deepened.

Carson took two steps, grunted, and almost stumbled.

"Carson, your leg. The doctor told you to rest."

"Fine, then," he said. "Let's go lie down."

Look for the next Carson Stone western,

SHORT ROPE FOR A TALL MAN,

coming Spring 2023!

Visit our website at
KensingtonBooks.com
to sign up for our newsletters, read
more from your favorite authors, see
books by series, view reading group
guides, and more!

BOOK | CLUB
BETWEEN THE CHAPTERS

Become a Part of Our
Between the Chapters Book Club
Community and Join the Conversation

Betweenthechapters.net